DARKNESS
IN
THE BLOOD

More Warhammer 40,000 from Black Library

DANTE
A Blood Angels novel by Guy Haley

• MEPHISTON •
by Darius Hinks

Book 1 – BLOOD OF SANGUINIUS
Book 2 – REVENANT CRUSADE
Book 3 – CITY OF LIGHT

SONS OF SANGUINIUS
A Blood Angels omnibus by various authors

INDOMITUS
A novel by Gav Thorpe

• DAWN OF FIRE •
Book 1 – AVENGING SON
by Guy Haley

Book 2 – THE GATE OF BONES
by Andy Clark

• DARK IMPERIUM •
by Guy Haley

Book 1 – DARK IMPERIUM
Book 2 – PLAGUE WAR

BELISARIUS CAWL: THE GREAT WORK
A novel by Guy Haley

SPACE MARINE CONQUESTS

THE DEVASTATION OF BAAL
A Blood Angels novel by Guy Haley

ASHES OF PROSPERO
A Space Wolves novel by Gav Thorpe

WAR OF SECRETS
A Dark Angels novel by Phil Kelly

OF HONOUR AND IRON
An Ultramarines novel by Ian St. Martin

APOCALYPSE
An Imperial Fists, White Scars and Raven Guard novel by Josh Reynolds

FIST OF THE IMPERIUM
An Imperial Fists novel by Andy Clark

DARKNESS IN THE BLOOD

GUY HALEY

BLACK LIBRARY

A BLACK LIBRARY PUBLICATION

First published in 2019.
This edition published in Great Britain in 2021 by
Black Library,
Games Workshop Ltd.,
Willow Road,
Nottingham, NG7 2WS, UK.

10 9 8 7 6 5 4 3 2 1

Produced by Games Workshop in Nottingham.
Cover illustration by Johan Grenier.
Chapter icon by Wayne England.

Darkness in the Blood © Copyright Games Workshop Limited 2021. Darkness in the Blood, GW, Games Workshop, Black Library, The Horus Heresy, The Horus Heresy Eye logo, Space Marine, 40K, Warhammer, Warhammer 40,000, the 'Aquila' Double-headed Eagle logo, and all associated logos, illustrations, images, names, creatures, races, vehicles, locations, weapons, characters, and the distinctive likenesses thereof, are either ® or TM, and/or © Games Workshop Limited, variably registered around the world.
All Rights Reserved.

A CIP record for this book is available from the British Library.

ISBN 13: 978 1-78999-302-8

No part of this publication may be reproduced, stored in a retrieval system, or transmitted in any form or by any means, electronic, mechanical, photocopying, recording or otherwise, without the prior permission of the publishers.

This is a work of fiction. All the characters and events portrayed in this book are fictional, and any resemblance to real people or incidents is purely coincidental.

See Black Library on the internet at

blacklibrary.com

Find out more about Games Workshop
and the world of Warhammer 40,000 at

games-workshop.com

Printed and bound by CPI Group (UK) Ltd, Croydon, CR0 4YY

For more than a hundred centuries the Emperor has sat immobile on the Golden Throne of Earth. He is the Master of Mankind. By the might of His inexhaustible armies a million worlds stand against the dark.

Yet, He is a rotting carcass, the Carrion Lord of the Imperium held in life by marvels from the Dark Age of Technology and the thousand souls sacrificed each day so that His may continue to burn.

To be a man in such times is to be one amongst untold billions. It is to live in the cruellest and most bloody regime imaginable. It is to suffer an eternity of carnage and slaughter. It is to have cries of anguish and sorrow drowned by the thirsting laughter of dark gods.

This is a dark and terrible era where you will find little comfort or hope. Forget the power of technology and science. Forget the promise of progress and advancement. Forget any notion of common humanity or compassion.

There is no peace amongst the stars, for in the grim darkness of the far future,
there is only war.

CHAPTER ONE

STORM CALLED

Bloodcaller was an ancient ship. Its keel was laid down in ages so distant there were none alive who remembered them, at least none with noble hearts. A battle-barge of the Adeptus Astartes, masterfully built and furnished with technologies now forgotten, it stood the test of voyage and battle with indomitable strength. It had fought the length and breadth of the galaxy. It had caused the end of worlds. It had witnessed the death of suns. It had defied warp storms that saw lesser ships founder. It had pierced psychic tempests to bring the deliverance of angels to planets thought doomed. It had sailed true through daemonic attack and the dread shadow of the hive mind. Such glory it had won, such renown for its Chapter, there was little its vigilant machine-spirit had not witnessed.

But this storm was something new. *Bloodcaller* had never seen the warp so disturbed.

Hurricanes of souls roared through the empyrean. Where

one died away, fury spent, another was already rising. Vortices of raw emotion drew to themselves coalescences of energy so intense they verged on attaining consciousness, before melting to nothing, stillborn gods.

Only a ship so indomitable as *Bloodcaller* could pass unharmed through the warp. Currents raced between storm fronts, tearing ships from their courses. Daemonic beasts assailed everything that dared their realm, breaking Geller fields open to feast on the souls inside where before they had been confounded.

To brave the warp in those times was to leap knowingly into insanity. So many vessels were lost without trace, or emerged light years and centuries away from their destination, or they came out void of the living, their halls crowded with ghosts and their machine-spirits supplanted by diabolical beings.

Many did not come out at all.

This was the legacy of the Warmaster Abaddon; the Cicatrix Maledictum, the Great Rift that tore across the galaxy's middle and gutted the stars and threw the Sea of Souls into bedlam.

Few dared to travel in the aftermath of the Great Rift's opening.

Bloodcaller dared. The Blood Angels dared. War was everywhere. The Adeptus Astartes would not shirk from their calling.

Through towering waves of raw pain and eddies of loss, *Bloodcaller* forged a path for other ships, leading an armada of vessels gathered from far-flung stars. Alone, the ships were lost, isolated, impotent. Together, they would be strong, the basis of a fleet to save an empire.

In *Bloodcaller*'s wake the flotilla plunged and rolled. The ships yawed hard in countercurrents. Whirlpools of screaming faces threatened to pull them into the depths of agony. *Bloodcaller*'s metal moaned in pain. Its reactors howled. Its

Geller generators spat smoke and sparks, but on it went, on for the sake of mortal men, its steely soul undaunted.

Each moment in the warp risked disaster, but the Imperium was beset on all sides. The ships had to get through. At a time when every gun in every pair of hands counted, a warship was a precious thing indeed.

In the time of the Cicatrix Maledictum, ancient traitors strode the cosmos. Planets burned across the realm of man.

Commander Dante, lord of the Blood Angels, had sworn to put an end to that.

High up on *Bloodcaller*'s command spires there was a chamber as richly decorated as any king's. In that chamber, there was a sarcophagus.

The chamber was black in all aspects. The floors, walls and ceilings were clad in black marble veined with darker blacks. All its numerous carvings and statues were worked from the same black stone. The artworks depicted noble heroes bearing the arms and armour of the Blood Angels Chapter. They were protectors of humanity, but in the light of the firebowls the sculptures appeared entirely sinister. Flickering flames lent their features a semblance of movement that would have disquieted the sturdiest of hearts. There was but one occupant in the room, and he was deep in slumber within the sarcophagus. He was Dante, the greatest-hearted of all mankind's heroes, and in that moment he saw nothing.

His sarcophagus stood upright. A sculpted face covered the upper portion. Through its eyes of red crystal murkier red could be perceived. Though made principally of ivory, the sarcophagus was covered in ornamentation and inlaid gemstones that made it glitter. All were hues of red: rubies, carnelian, red sapphires, blood diamonds, topaz, garnet and jasper. About the flat, broad head was a coronet of the rarest of all: bloodstone from Baal. It was an idol garlanded in crystallised blood.

Blood was everything to Dante. The blood of his gene-father shaped him. The blood of humanity called to him for defence. The blood of the alien, heretic and traitor demanded to be spilled.

The pounding of twin hearts filled his hearing with a river's torrent, torrents of red, torrents of black, twined forever inseparably. Hot and sweet, the darkness in the blood spreading through his veins was enough to poison, but never enough to kill. Blood brought him torment and joy. It damned him. It renewed him. Blood was his saviour and his damnation.

Dante floated in vitae. The stolen life of innocents filled his mouth, his nose, his stomach and his lungs. It bathed his unseeing eyes, it stoppered up his ears. The temperature of the liquid and his body were precisely matched, so he could not tell where his body ended and the blood began. He was deep in the renewal phase of the Long Sleep, but all was not as it should be. The machines embedded in the sarcophagus exterior blinked uncertainly. There was an admixture of Dante's own blood in the suspension mix, and most dilute, a touch of the divine: Sanguinius' own essence mixed into Dante's.

Dante's body was covered in cuts, many deep, some not healed. Huge, crescent wounds overlaid the scars of ancient wars. He was a Space Marine. The wounds were inflicted months before. They too should be pale marks now, healed shut by his enhanced physiology and become only memories of pain. It was not so.

Dante bled.

Shifts in the voidship as it ploughed on through the storm pushed his slumbering body about. The feeds plugged into his brachial and femoral arteries tugged. He did not feel their sting. Dante was absent from his body, lost in the healing coma, and his soul wandered the halls of recollection, remembering a battle fought long ago.

Another time, another war, and *Bloodcaller* suffered. Atmosphere bled from a thousand cuts. Its armour was shattered. Its weapons broken. Systems wept power from ruptured conduits. Yet it persisted, and its great reactor heart laboured to keep the few who remained living alive.

The battle was over, but a new struggle had begun.

'He is not worthy!' Chaplain Keshiel rose from his seat in the Great Basilica and slammed the head of his crozius onto the ground. The power field was active, and the crack of it contacting the paving reverberated around the hall in electric thunders. The four-sided head buried itself in the deck.

Dante stood silently as the rump of the council deliberated. There were twenty-five thrones; all but four were empty, sixteen were draped in funeral black. The rubble of the chamber's facings lay piled in the coign of floor and wall, exposing the naked plasteel beneath. Generations' worth of art was so much powder and grit. The fine dust of destruction filled the ship. It contaminated the seals of the Space Marines' power armour. Motors ground unpleasantly. Machine-spirits complained into their wearers' helms.

The last members of the council looked down on Dante. The High Chaplain Bephael survived, as did two Sanguinary Priests of middling rank, and Keshiel. Upon them rested the future of the Chapter.

'He is the last of our captains,' said Sanguinary Priest Gallion. 'There is no other. He must take this office. There is no other choice.'

'He is not worthy!' Keshiel roared again. He released the haft of his weapon, leaving it embedded; the energies cloaking its head arced into the floor and frittered it away atom by atom. 'That he is the last is no reason to choose him.'

'It is the precise reason we should,' said Estius, the second priest. His white armour had been battered back to the gunmetal grey of bare ceramite. One salvaged arm was the vibrant red of a battleline brother.

'And what of his deeds?'

'There have been greater men elevated to the office, I admit,' said Gallion. 'But although his story is yet short, he has the capacity for glory.'

'There have never been lesser than he,' Keshiel said. The bones sculpted into his armour shone white against their black background. 'One day, he may be a worthy candidate, but now?' Keshiel spoke as if Dante were not there. 'The Eighth Captain? It is not his moment.'

'Then what do you propose?' Estius said.

'The Council of Blood and Bone should rule the Chapter, as is our custom. We should return to Baal, and rebuild our numbers. Let the centuries run and time present us with a new candidate. It may even be that Dante will rise to the role. But I say again that he is not worthy, not now, not like this.'

Bephael remained silent throughout. Helmed, both hands gripping the armrests of his throne, and with the great axe of his office propped against his seat, he resembled a statue. It was not right that the Executioner's Axe should be so placed, but the blood thralls were all dead, and the stand it occupied broken. Dante felt the axe's presence keenly. It was the instrument of judgement, and he was being judged.

'He could refuse,' said Bephael eventually. His voice was deep and dark, a growl from a cave.

'My lord?' said Estius.

'He could refuse. If he does or does not, the problem remains the same. A Chapter must have a Chapter Master.' Bephael leaned forward in his throne. The black wings that framed it seemed to flex and spread. 'What do you say, Dante – if this burden is placed upon you, will you bear it? Will you lead us?'

Dante stood in silence. He was drained by battle. His limbs were weak from hewing the foe. Without his armour to support him, he felt he might not be able to stand. The Emperor had made him strong, but no warrior in existence could have undergone what he had without effect.

'He does not answer,' said Keshiel with satisfaction. 'See, my lords? What aspirant to this highest of roles would remain silent when questioned about his suitability to lead?'

'Why do you not answer, Captain Dante?' asked Bephael. He spoke quietly in all circumstances, yet his words carried far more power than the hectoring of Keshiel.

'I do not speak, for what can I say?' said Dante. 'So many heroes are dead. So many better than I. I stand before you not by merit but by happenstance. Chaplain Keshiel is right.'

'You are a hero yourself, as all Blood Angels must be,' said Bephael. 'You are a captain of the Adeptus Astartes. You are a lord of men. You, who have witnessed the Sanguinor more than any other. Surely it is a sign you have been chosen.'

'That is so,' said Dante. 'Still, I am not ready.'

In the present, in his sarcophagus, Dante let out a silent moan. Machines chimed alarms as the level of Dante's own blood in the fluid rose. They went unheard.

Bloodcaller shook hard in the storm.

CHAPTER TWO

VOYAGE

In another chamber not far from Dante's slumber, Mephiston, Lord of Death, struggled against the warp. The Chief Librarian knelt, fully armoured, at the centre of a ritual circle carved directly into a single slab of porphyry that made up the room's floor. The skulls of the damned burned in bronze bowls, their flames an unnatural crimson. Six of Mephiston's acolytes stood around him, their blue armour near black in the bloody glow, their right arms bare of plate, and their veins opened, allowing their vitae to run into the channels of the circle and moat Mephiston with the stuff of life.

A Space Marine's blood clots quickly, so each of the Librarians was attended by a mute librarium serf, all tongueless so they could not speak of their master's deeds, and all blindfolded in case what they saw drove them mad. They held razor-edged knives of bone at the ready to reopen their masters' wounds, their fingers resting lightly on the forearms of the Librarians to judge the flow. The Space Marines could not do this for themselves; they were lost in the inner spaces of the mind, all of them chanting, their bass voices shaking the walls with hymns of protection.

Mephiston's eyes were rolled back into his head, presenting only the whites to the world. He saw nothing. Only Epistolary Rhacelus, reckoned by many to be among the most mighty of the Blood Angels' Librarius after Mephiston, kept watch with eyes that glowed an unsettling blue. He stood above the others upon a podium raised by a curl of stairs decorated with images of death. The stink of blood teased the Red Thirst out from under Rhacelus' iron control. The light was awful, profane, where it should have been pure.

'Tainted blood for tainted rituals,' he growled.

In his witch-sight he saw the shadows of the things outside the Geller field move across his brothers, talons caressing, mouths gaping with insatiable hunger. They had no power to harm, not yet, but one slip in the ritual guarding Mephiston's being and the floodgates would open, and the horrors outside would come pouring into the ship to devour their souls.

It was Rhacelus' duty to guard against that happening. The shadow-things clustered about the Lord of Death most densely, though they were equally as repelled by him as attracted, darting close and then racing away in fear. Hollow eyes stared longingly at the spirit tethers linking Mephiston's body to his soul. The tethers showed themselves as ribbons of red that shifted like blood in the water. Like blood in the water, they drew predators. The tethers rose from the Chief Librarian and went out through the walls of the ship as if they were not there. In some sense, they were not, and Rhacelus struggled to stop the reality of plasteel and stone from melting away from his witch-sight, exposing his soul to the full regard of the warp itself. Rhacelus had no desire to experience that, not in a storm of such fury. He could not do what Mephiston did. The Lord of Death's soul was outside the ship, in the warp itself, riding the waves of damnation.

Bloodcaller shuddered. It bounced three times, following steps down to uncharted hells. The blood in the channels of the circle rippled. The serfs and Librarians swayed. Rhacelus gripped the railing of his podium until the tremors passed. Metal moaned. Outside the heavy doors of the sanctum a bell tolled.

'Come, Mephiston, be swift,' Rhacelus said. 'The ship will not take much more of this.'

Lord Admiral Danakan was thinking about the fighting at Teleope again. There was a fixed point halfway between the command throne and the main hololithic display. He found if he stared at it for long enough with unfocused eyes he could see the faces of his crew burning in the fires. He didn't want to do it, but he felt compelled to stare without blinking until his vision blurred and his lenses twitched, and the plasteel and bronze swam away into flame.

'They say there is an angel leading us through the storm.'

Danakan blinked. The fires vanished. Ornate plasteel and bronze, dimly lit by the operating lights of multiple stations, took their place. He looked up sharply at the man standing beside his command throne. 'Flag-lieutenant? Did you speak?'

'An angel, my lord,' said Juvenel. He stared at the shuttered oculus like it were open and he could see the way ahead. His feet were planted far apart against the plunging and shuddering of the *Dominance*, which he bore with a seasoned voidsman's confidence. 'I heard tell that an angel guides Lord Dante through the warp. That is how the Blood Angels can find their way without the light of the Astronomican.' His hands were clasped behind his back, nestled against the pure white silk of his cummerbund. Juvenel's high-collared jacket was spotless navy blue, his breastplate polished to perfection. Danakan had once been like that, the very image of a dashing officer. His own uniform was as clean, as well cared for, but it felt grubby, too tight, and nothing he did could rid him of those feelings.

The ship rumbled and yawed to port. A minor commotion broke out in a command pit near the helm as a team of officers battled to right the ship.

'Steady as she goes there!' Juvenel barked.

'The Emperor looks on us kindly,' said Danakan distractedly.

There was an angel on the bridge, though this one was merely a decoration leaping from the wall. It was usually obscured by the tri-d display, but with the hololith off, Danakan saw it looking down upon the crew with a sad expression, its hands outstretched. Many ships had representations of the Emperor's mercy like that. They were supposed to remind a man of his mortality, and his duty, and that the Emperor watched over them while they fought and died in His name.

Dominance trembled and ceased its listing.

'Damn storm,' said Danakan.

'Dante has a better angel than ours,' said Juvenel, following Danakan's gaze.

'Indeed, flag-lieutenant,' said Danakan.

Juvenel checked the chronograph mounted in his vambrace. 'Time for reports?' he asked.

'Proceed, flag-lieutenant.' Danakan kept his voice level. He needed only a moment. If he could banish the memories, focus on the present, his crew would never know what tormented him. He would be his old self again.

Juvenel walked to the railing surrounding the command

dais. He obscured Danakan's view of the angel, and Danakan craned his neck to keep its comforting face in sight, before catching himself and resuming his pose of studied authority. Nevertheless, he was relieved when Juvenel paced on.

'Ladies and gentlemen of the *Dominance*,' Juvenel said, raising his voice. 'I know you're all pretending not to listen to our conversation, but you hang on every word we say up here. You heard us, watch end reports! Give them now. Helm, if you please, begin.'

'This is a rough day, sir,' reported the senior sub-lieutenant at the helm block. 'Nothing the *Dominance* can't handle.'

'I'm sure the ship can handle anything. I am more interested in your performance, Sub-Lieutenant Crendor.'

'Pardon my below-average abilities, sir, but with a ship like this, how can we fail?'

Laughter came from all over the command deck.

Danakan glanced from the angel's face. He envied Juvenel's light touch with the men. Such was Juvenel's skill at command, the Masters of Discipline spent most of their time bored in their niches.

'Navigatorial liaison, your turn, if you please,' Juvenel said. 'What do our seers have to say?'

'Nothing that causes us harm, sir,' came the response.

'Give me status on the Geller bubble.'

'Maintaining at seventy-four per cent efficacy. We have a minor drop in speed relative to the other ships, but our escorts are maintaining formation,' said another.

Juvenel frowned. 'That is not permissible. Do you have a cause?'

'Cause unknown. Efficiency of warp drive is falling. The decline is slow, but it is marked.'

'Upgrade records for this watch to delta level. Inform the

Magos Majoris Fong-493-Cho-Hai to encourage his transmechanics to greater effort,' Juvenel said. 'I wish to see the operational parameters of the drive and fields raised before the next watch is done. Someone must answer.'

Dominance grumbled through a rough tangle of currents. Juvenel paced on steady legs up and down the edge of the dais.

'All of you, here, you serve this ship, you serve the Emperor, and you are lucky to do so under the auspices of Admiral Danakan, hero of the Gleaming Reach, master of a hundred ships.' Juvenel raised his hand in the direction of the admiral. 'This man is one of the Imperium's greatest living voidsmen. If you fail, I will condemn you, and that might make you afraid. But fear more disappointing our lord and master – he is a true hero of the Imperium. Do not measure yourself by your shipmates' standards, but by his.'

Danakan saw them glance at him. He saw their adulation. He no longer felt worthy of it.

Juvenel leaned on the rail of the dais, and called down to the captain's platform at the foot of the steps. It was hardly less ornate or imposing than the admiral's.

'Shipmaster, record in the log at zero three-three all well in the warp. Geller field unsatisfactory. Return it to proper function. Ship's ministry, submit detailed reports to the shipmaster. If we slow further we'll fall behind and attract attention. Be vigilant for warp entity ingress. Sound the watch change. Admiral, any additional orders?'

The watch bell rang, monstrously loud. Danakan shrank inside. The noise was repeated all through the ship. A subtle stirring added itself to the vibrations of the vessel as tens of thousands of people moved.

'Admiral?' Juvenel prompted.

'No further orders,' Danakan said.

'As you command.' Juvenel bowed. 'I shall take refreshment. If you wish to join me, my lord, I would be honoured by your company.'

'I think I shall stay here a while longer.' The angel's bronze eyes stared accusingly into his. The fire was creeping back into his vision.

A hushed bustle took the command deck as the watch changed. Men and women filed in. Priests from the ship's ministry blessed them as they waited to take their places. Crew exchange took place sequentially, from the least important systems to the most crucial, so that the vessel would not be disadvantaged should it be attacked. All over the vessel a similar procedure was under way.

'Thank you, Juvenel. Maybe I will see you later.'

Fragrant smoke from the priests' censers reminded him of fire.

Danakan had no wish to spend time with Juvenel. He did not want to reveal himself a coward.

Juvenel bowed and departed. The last of the officers took their places. The bell for the watch change rang again. The priests gave their last benedictions and quiet descended.

Danakan stared into flames only he could see.

As men had once stood upon the prows of wooden ships in the teeth of earthly storms, blasted by rain and wind so hard they could barely see the rocks they feared to founder on, so Mephiston flew ahead of the *Bloodcaller* in the warp tempest. The similarities ended there, for this storm had real teeth that rasped and snapped at his spirit.

Giant red wings extended either side of Mephiston's spirit form. A glittering shield of bloody droplets surrounded him.

Trails of energy tethered him to his body. All were red, the blood of the living warding him in the land of the dead.

Minor, half-formed creatures rushed at him. They gnawed upon his soul tethers. Though the tethers broke under their fangs, they re-formed quickly, and he only diverted his will to drive the pests off when their attentions became irritating.

Few could risk exposure to the warp in that way. To look at it was to go insane, or worse. To swim its otherworldly waters was nigh impossible. But he was Mephiston, the twice born, the Lord of Death, and the warp held no fear for him.

Sometimes the warp was a swirl of colours. Sometimes it was nothing at all. Impossible landscapes unfurled themselves before him. Other worlds, other times, and the whimsies of mad gods. Half-formed dreams shimmered into and out of view. Howling beasts tore at themselves. Shoals of souls sped screaming by. Every thought he had took form and with vicious faces mocked him before dissipating like smoke on the wind. He ignored it all, and kept his mind clear, focusing on the safe deliverance of the fleet.

A glint of gold far ahead led him onwards. The heaving landscapes of the warp obscured it often, but always he found it again. Sometimes, the ships got nearer to the guide in the storm, and Mephiston saw white wings beating tirelessly. An angel showed them the way.

There was no other beacon to follow. The Astronomican, the great guiding soul light of the Emperor, was invisible, obscured by the Rift slashing time and space in two. Without the Astronomican, the Navigators of the *Bloodcaller* had nothing to chart a course by. Their warp eyes were fixed therefore upon Mephiston, while those in the rest of the ships in the fleet followed the *Bloodcaller*.

Mephiston had performed this duty several times. His

efforts enabled the fleets to make longer journeys than the short, perilous hops travel was generally restricted to in Imperium Nihilus. According to the old tomes, entering the warp carried the risk of spiritual annihilation. Mephiston had read many dire warnings concerning this, and of the dangers of corruption. Warp-walking was the province of the misguided sorcerer. It was a trick of the damned.

Yet Mephiston felt no shadow on his soul. Instead he found himself returning to the mortal universe with the powers of his mind stronger than before. That was a matter of concern.

His misgivings took form around him, showing him twisted versions of what he feared, and what he hoped.

Do not be distracted, he told himself. Every one is a lie.

Mephiston snuffed out the half-things with a thought.

Ahead, the gold of the Sanguinor's armour winked, drawing him further into the storm.

CHAPTER THREE

ESCAPE FROM RONENTI

'For the love of the Emperor, keep firing!' Chattay Ebasso led by example, loosing a couple of shots from his lascarbine at the fanatics pouring up the stairs towards them. He blew a fan of feathers from his eyes. The uprising had come so quick they'd been caught wearing their ceremonial uniforms. But they were safe, more or less. The steps swept down a knife-edge ridge towards the palace. There was no way up to the landing circle but those stairs. There was room for a firing line five wide on the top step. It was a good position to hold. The fanatics had few real weapons, only repurposed tools. A rivet gun would put a hole in a man's head, but they lacked range and accuracy. The rebels got little further than lascarbine maximum range before they fell down dead, holes burned through them by the Shieldguard Gubernatorial. They wavered a bit, then came on again, pushed by the men and women behind, obligingly presenting the next line to be gunned down.

'Ten men! That's what I said I'd need to hold these stairs to General Than. Do me proud, boys, drive them back, make me right and not a liar!' Ebasso's voice was deep and musical. Women liked his voice. He liked women. If they asked, he'd sing for them. That was usually enough to get what *he* wanted. Looking at the ragtag army of masked insurgents climbing towards the landing platform, he thought it likely he'd never sing again. The landing was used for show and official occasions, so the populace could see their lord ascend to the stars when he must leave Ronenti. It wasn't in the best of places to achieve orbit, but all things considered, Ebasso was glad it was there.

The rebels had set fire to the palace. Thin blue smoke was coming from the windows. Little licks of flame followed quickly. The fire was a surprise and spread fast, like the uprising.

'Vox-man, give me status on aerial clearance!' He had to shout loudly – the screaming of the worker horde drowned out even the snap of lasguns going off inches from his face.

His vox-operator was crouched back from the stair top, face screwed up in concentration. The whites of his eyes were slits in the dark skin of his face. Sele was a good soldier. Ebasso fervently hoped he'd live, and not solely because if he did, Ebasso himself would probably survive. He liked his men, and they liked him. He knew all their names, not like some officers, and they did what he said because they wanted to. Damn it if he hadn't had a good career ahead of him, before the uprising surged out of nowhere and threatened to bring the war with the south to a shock conclusion.

'Fourteen fliers inbound,' Sele said. 'Notification from Bandan Port air control. They can't tell if they're friendlies or not. Maybe a mix.' He twisted the dial on the backpack set that he'd placed on the landing-pad decking. 'They're saying we should retreat, regroup there. Elements of the Third Army hold the perimeter. They say they're safe.'

'Fine words for people hiding behind high walls!' Ebasso fired as he spoke. He kept the gun tight in to his cheek, even though the heat from repeated discharge was starting to burn his skin. 'They haven't seen this, and they're sure to be the next target for the Djesseli dogs. We're getting our lord off the planet. We've lost this war, I won't lose him.'

He jerked his head back over his shoulder at the youth cowering behind the platform's retractable shielding.

'Aha! They are coming!' Sele said. '*Radiant Day* is in contact. Estimated time until shuttle arrives, fifteen minutes or less.'

'Thank the Emperor the enemy have no voidships. Your excellency!' Ebasso shouted at the boy king. 'Good news, eh?'

The governor's response was drowned out by the howl of engines as the fourteen fliers roared down at them. Ebasso recognised the markings of the turncoat Sixth Tier squadrons. Not the best the Djesseli Combine had, but not the worst.

'Incoming!' screamed Rusto Divani. Another good man, one made dead in the next second.

The Sixth Tier squadron opened up, strafing up the stairs and catching many of their allies as they zeroed in on the Shieldguard's position. Ebasso's men dove in all directions to avoid the bullets. The lucky ones got behind the pad shields. The pieces of the unlucky ones were spread liberally about. The Sixth Tier roared overhead, close enough that he could count the teeth in the swamp tiger emblems on the wings. There were eight aircraft, a number that became unexpectedly seven as one of the Swamp Tigers came apart delicately in the air, like a paper lantern catching fire.

'The others! The others, they're ours!' Sele said. 'Ident codes confirm.' A less experienced man would have smiled, but Sele was focused on his job. Ebasso took only the best for his command.

Five fighters loyal to the governor howled on the Swamp Tigers' tails, lancing the air behind them with lascannon fire and lines of tracer bullets. Another of the rebels' craft took a hit with a bang like a hammer striking a metal crate, and it peeled away trailing smoke and fire. The rest split and fled in all directions. Their pursuers divided up to chase them down.

The roar of the jets rumbled off over the hills to the north. There was still snow up there, undisturbed, pristine, untouched by the summer or by the war. Ebasso stared at it, momentarily lost in the gleam of white on dark rock, when renewed shouting from the horde drew his attention back to the earth.

Blood ran down the steps. Two of his warriors had been obliterated. Lucky, really, so few had died. But it made a lot of mess. Further down the blood flowed in a sticky river. The Swamp Tigers had carved a line of red into the horde, and many had died, more trampled by their fellows as they panicked and fled.

Ebasso wrinkled his nose at the stink of opened guts. It was shocking what an autocannon hit would do to a man. That was all he thought. He'd become inured to death a long time ago.

'Sixth Tier aren't any match for First Tier pilots,' said Kole Nanda, as the aircraft vanished over the horizon, still duelling.

'That's true, but are we going to be any match for them?' said Demeni Tarassi drily.

'Sele! See if you can get them back, I don't want to live this out only to get shot down before we make the *Radiant Day*.'

'The rebels are picking themselves up. They're coming

again,' said Huntu Ha. He knelt, unbothered by the bloody mess soaking into the feathers of his court uniform.

The horde were coming again; they were slow, they were unsure now, but it wouldn't take them long to get their enthusiasm back. There were over a thousand of them against the seven Shieldguard Gubernatorial left. Ebasso's men faced death with a lack of concern. They would go to the Emperor. This was a worthy end.

'Fifteen minutes is all we need,' Ebasso said.

While the horde wavered, his men cleaned off the focusing arrays of their guns and swapped out power packs. Their conversation was punctuated by hard snaps and businesslike clicks.

'Can we kill that many, to hold them off for that long?'

'I can, but you don't shoot as fast as me, Demeni,' said Nanda.

'I hit more than you do.'

Fele Retass took up a lascarbine from one of the dead, made a half-hearted attempt to wipe the gore from it, and whistled sharply. 'Hsst! Your excellency!' he said.

Governor Jemmeni uncurled enough for Retass to toss him the gun. The governor caught it awkwardly.

'Best use this, every shot is going to count.' Retass said, with a dazzling smile. They were a handsome band, chosen for their looks as well as their ability.

'I don't know how!' said the governor. He looked appalled by the blood getting onto his hands from the gun.

'It's easy, your excellency. Point it, squeeze the trigger. Light your target. Think of it like a stablight,' said Retass.

'Only a lot more stabby,' said Nanda.

They grinned, all except Sele, who was pressing the earpiece of the vox-set so tightly against his ear it looked like he wanted to push it into his head, and the governor, who was too scared to do anything other than blink.

'Twelve minutes,' said Sele. 'They've got a clear run. No other craft in the sky.'

'Twelve minutes?' Huntu Ha sucked air through his teeth. 'It's only three minutes since you told us fifteen?'

'Excitement like this stretches time,' said Ebasso. 'Now still your tongues and look to your guns. They're coming in again, and this time they mean it.'

Huntu Ha was the first to fire. Then they were all at it, silent with concentration, aware that each missed shot was another step closer for the enemy.

The twelve minutes were the longest of Ebasso's life. The enemy rediscovered their fighting spirit. Slipping in the blood of their own and clambering over their corpses on the steep steps did not dishearten them, but seemed to give them strength, so that by the time they were a few hundred feet away, they were frothing with battle lust. His men fired and fired, but the weight of the horde pushed the rebels closer, until their makeshift weaponry was in range, and rivets and nails began to zing off the stone of the stairs. Huntu Ha swore colourfully as a nail buried itself in his thigh. Nanda fell with a soft moan as a rivet punched through his eye and into his brain. The horde came closer and closer. Ebasso measured time in charge count. The gun's pack swiftly drained. He ejected it, and slapped in another, keeping the carbine aimed as he did, and firing the moment the gun's simple spirit sang out acceptance of the battery. The horde tumbled down, their bodies bouncing off both sides of the ridge. The Shieldguard prioritised those wielding ranged weapons. A few of them had actual guns. These died first.

The thin scream of aircraft engines came as the horde were within striking distance.

'They're here!' Sele shouted.

A burst of heavy bolter fire followed his announcement, driving back the horde. Bodies exploded into nothing. Jetwash buffeted them all. Retass was furthest forward. He was the first to fight hand to hand, fending off a length of spiked pipe with the butt of his gun and bayoneting the bearer in the throat.

The lighter's engines roared. Heat curled the feathers of Ebasso's cloak. Voices shouted through the engine howl. The horde pushed forward. Huntu Ha fell. Chiki Natassa was suddenly fending off three at once. The steps were narrow, but the crowd had weight, and they pushed the Shieldguard back.

Behind him, Ebasso heard landing claws connect with rockcrete.

'Now,' he shouted. He loosed a final shot, burning off a man's face, mask and all, grabbed one of Governor Jemmeni's arms and hauled him up. It didn't look like he'd fired his gun.

Aircrew reached for the governor and yanked him through the open slide door of the lighter. Rivets and nails clattered off the side of the ship. Ebasso followed. He stood on the deck and looked out. He didn't feel much safer there.

'Men! Men! Get aboard! Now, now!'

Sele made sure to grab his vox-set and shove it into the transit bay before he got on himself. The rest were swamped by an enemy who had recently been friends. Ebasso wondered if his neighbours, even his family, were out there in the seething crowd. He could not see. Hidden by masks and bloody robes they all looked the same, and they all shouted the same thing:

'The Emperor protects!'

'We've got to go! We've got to go now!' the flight officer shouted, his voice grinding out of a vox amplifier.

Only two of the Shieldguard were left outside the lighter. One turned back to look at Ebasso, and there was resignation on his face as he vanished under a swarm of flashing knives. Hands reached for the ship. Men tried to pull themselves in. Ebasso shot people that were so close he could have embraced them. They fell shrieking. He stamped on hands. He bludgeoned with his gun butt.

'Up! Up! Up!' called the flight officer.

The heavy door slammed, taking fingers off. The engines roared. The crowd's voices were cut dead by plasteel walls.

None too gently, the ship jerked up into the air, nails, rivets and bullets rattling from its sides like rain.

'You're hit,' said Jemmeni. He had to shout. The lighter crew were wearing vox-sets against the engine noise. The ship was a utilitarian model, without even the comfort of acoustic baffling.

Ebasso looked at his shoulder. A nail head pinned his feather cloak to his flesh. He pulled it out. After that it began to hurt. Ebasso threw the nail on the floor. He glimpsed the governor's gun. Full charge lights, full shot count.

He looked away, out of the small door portal. Thick, scratched glassite afforded a poor view, but it was enough to see they'd done the right thing in fleeing. The lighter tilted, showing him the blazing palace and the city. More fires had been set in the streets. The horizon glowed with greater conflagrations. The rumours said the Djesseli were burning all the cities they captured. Ebasso had seen the intelligence reports. The rumours were wrong; what was happening was far worse.

They passed the cloud layer. The ground vanished. They

were going up rapidly. Acceleration weight crushed at him. He slid down the door into a sit before the black of space showed itself at the edge of Ronenti's sky.

'What do we do now?' Jemmeni said.

'We do what your father would have done,' said Ebasso. Jemmeni shrank back from his glower. Ebasso regretted his anger. Jemmeni was a boy still, not yet grown into power.

'I don't know what he would do!' said Jemmeni. 'Please tell me!'

Engine roar diminished. The ship vaulted out of Ronenti's gravity well into the heavens.

'We go to Baal,' said Ebasso, more gently. 'We shall seek out Commander Dante. If we can survive the trip, we shall ask his counsel.'

Jemmeni nodded, still terrified. 'Baal. Dante,' he said. 'Yes, yes, the Blood Angels.'

CHAPTER FOUR

WARPFALL

Juvenel waited by the shipmaster's quarters where the admiral resided. Four iron skulls stared at him with sapphire eyes. Two armsmen stood at attention either side of the doors. Their energy pikes glimmered with active power fields. The pistol grips of their shotguns protruded from the holsters upon their backs. Reflective void visors hid their faces. He could have snuck in the back way, up through the maintenance shafts and past the admiral's private salvator pod bay. That wasn't the done thing.

'Did the admiral receive announcement of my arrival?' he asked of the machine lurking behind the blue eyes of the skulls.

<Arrival of first officer Juvenel announced,> the machine said.

'I have waited for four minutes.'

<Arrival of first officer Juvenel announced,> the machine repeated. <Four minutes ago,> it added, unhelpfully.

'He is in there, isn't he?' Juvenel asked one of the guards.

'I have not seen the admiral leave his quarters since his arrival shortly after watch change, sir,' the man said.

'Did he say anything to you?'

'Nothing, flag-lieutenant,' said the man.

'How did he look?'

The sentry didn't reply immediately. 'Preoccupied, sir.'

'Then he didn't ask not to be disturbed.'

'No, sir.'

'In that case...' Juvenel cleared his throat. 'Override code number three-three-nine, Flag-Lieutenant Juvenel, Arran, ident number 78899021-12, first officer Imperial battleship *Dominance*.'

<Override code accepted.>

'Then open the way,' said Juvenel.

Locks disengaged within the doors. They slid back, revealing an unlit hall.

'Stay alert, men,' Juvenel said sarcastically. 'The admiral may need you to protect him from my concern.'

He passed inside. His boots thumped on rugs whose patterns were meaningless in the gloom. The high chandeliers were unlit. A few electro-flambeaux showed the way. Juvenel strode on.

Soft footsteps padded out of a side door hidden behind a statue.

'First officer?' The admiral's steward hurried after him. 'What are you doing here? How may I assist you?'

Juvenel turned briskly on the spot. 'I've come to pay respects to the admiral.' He smiled at the man pleasantly. Steward Fresne was a small, gentle-looking fellow in feminine robes, but he was anything but soft. He had a network of spies throughout the fleet, and an uncompromising attitude to business. 'I am sure you already knew that.'

Fresne neither denied nor confirmed, but left Juvenel to guess. 'You are concerned about our lord?'

'I am,' said Juvenel.

Fresne nodded. 'Come with me,' said the steward. The pair of them continued on together. 'If I was not also worried for him, there is no way I would let you in here without his permission. I did not see you, is that clear?'

'Understood.'

They stopped before a tall door. A pair of giants stood on plinths either side, weighed down by voidships carried on their backs. A huge brass aquila hung from chains between them.

'"Carried on the backs of mortal men," that's how the fleet motto goes.' Juvenel frowned. 'A ship's keel may break, so might a man's spirit. Then who carries the burden?'

'I have come to find the motto ironic,' said Fresne. 'Lord Danakan has not been himself for some months. The combat at Teleope took its toll. Were it not for your support, flag-lieutenant, I fear the mask would crack.'

'It is not my role to protect the admiral, but I will help him. The man's a hero. There are few men I admire. I admire him. Or I did.' Juvenel looked up at the door. 'I will do what I can.'

'He is inside. Please, if you can, help him. If news of his condition reaches the wrong ears...'

'I might be the wrong ears, Fresne,' said Juvenel. 'I have a lot to gain if he loses his nerve. Lord Dante risked much to bring us out of the Tardin Sector. We would have been stranded forever if the Blood Angels hadn't received our astropathic distress call. It's a miracle they came at all. Dante needs these ships for his new fleet. He'll need a competent commander. The admiral's losing his mind. I'd say I was fairly high up the list for Danakan's replacement.'

'You do not see yourself in that role,' said Fresne.

'How do you know I do not?' Juvenel asked, although what the steward said was true; he had no desire to usurp the admiral.

Fresne shrugged.

'Knowing of my habits is not the same as knowing me. I might covet his position. How do you know I'm not moving against him right now? Your whisperers might be everywhere, Fresne, but you can't know what's in my mind.'

Fresne raised his eyebrows.

'Throne damn it, Fresne, I'd know if you had some sump-witch psyker poking in my brain. I take precautions.'

'You don't like me very much, Juvenel. I understand. We both have the best interests of our admiral in mind, but also the best interests of this fleet. If the admiral is declared unfit, then the blow to morale will be immense. The fleet might fragment. What use would that be to the Imperium?'

'Liking you doesn't come into it. As it happens, I've no time for those who skulk behind the scenes pulling ropes to make us all dance. I prefer an honest fight.'

'Honest in the way your family secured your commission? They paid rather a lot of money, so I hear.'

Juvenel sucked air through his teeth. 'Look, I'm trying to warn you. Don't trust anyone with what's going on with him. You're taking a risk here. We are both on the same side, but we might not always be.'

'I know I am taking a risk, so please prove me right. Help him.'

'You must be desperate, to agree with me.'

'I calculate everything, Flag-Lieutenant Juvenel.'

Fresne bowed and disappeared into the dark.

Juvenel waited for Fresne's footsteps to recede before he pushed the door open.

* * *

The empyrean was Guondrin's birthright. All his life was dedicated to its understanding. All his being was turned to its exploitation. His people knew the warp like few others. They did not fear it.

But Guondrin was afraid.

He sat rigid upon the throne of seeing. His black, pupilless warp eye stared through terrors he would rather not see, fixed upon the oily writhing of *Bloodcaller*'s Geller shields.

Four others stared with him. Nine thrones were installed in a chamber meant for only one. Four of those were empty. The throne room was rank with sweat. Guondrin had ridden other vessels, in better times, and remembered the days when he felt godlike in the warp. Since the Rift, every voyage was a ride upon a bolting steed, every passage wracked with storm. One Navigator would no longer suffice. Where Navigators' lives had been measured in centuries, they were now measured in voyages.

There were Navigators in every Great House who refused to sail while the Rift yawned wide. He had not been one of them. He had thirsted for adventure, convinced every trip would bring him more power, more glory.

He had more than his fill of all that.

He missed his silks and wine. He missed his courtesans.

The warp screamed into his face. Terrible visions battered his soul. Every conceivable horror and more was his to suffer. His warp eye ached from staring into the storm.

There was no blazing light of the Astronomican to sail by. In Imperium Nihilus, he must rely on more esoteric means of navigation, following streams of thoughts and fears. The direction of etheric winds and their eddying revealed mass concentrations on the other side of the veil dividing materium from immaterium. At least, that was the theory. Guondrin and his fellows were skilled in the arts of their ancestors, ways preserved since before the ignition of the soul beacon. These skills were little use in the raging chaos the immaterium had become. Were it not for *Bloodcaller*, *Dominance* would have been lost.

Guondrin lost sight of the nearest ship, a destroyer of Battlefleet Ultima that raced on with the determination of a hound on the hunt. One moment it was there, a surging, dark shape wrapped in a writhing psychic shield, then it was gone, swallowed up by garish veils of colour thicker than driven rain.

'Where is it, where it?' Kaskaskay, to his right, shouted in panic.

'Keep your eye on the *Bloodcaller*, forward quadrant, follow the path of the second sign,' Guondrin said. He panted the words. He tasted blood in his mouth.

'The Emperor, oh the Emperor, they can see me!' Kaskaskay said.

'Emotive wavefront approaching in the vector of the eleventh sign. Increase scry range, thrones two and six,' Guondrin ordered. 'We're losing velocity. We're going to lose sight of the fleet. Fix position, and find them as soon as the wavefront is past.'

A giant swell of longing washed towards the fleet. *Bloodcaller* hit it head on, rising up and rushing down the other side, followed by dozens of ships. The *Dominance* laboured behind. For a moment, Guondrin found himself alone.

Kaskaskay, to his right, began to moan.

'Notice of import,' Guondrin said, the words summoning down a servo-skull with the wide horn of a vox protruding from its jaws. 'Shipmaster, this is Navigator Praecipus Guondrin. We have lost sight of the fleet.'

The servo-skull took his report and sent it to the command

deck. So great was the peril to a man's soul in that room that the skull's eye sockets were covered over by sanctified cloth. Seeing through the naked oculus endangered the residual spirit said to cling to such devices.

'Prepare for directional shift on my command.'

Viscid energies streamed from the armourglass, aping water with sinister intent, hiding the play of insanity from the Navigators. Hexagrams inscribed into the surface glowed with brilliant power. All that divided the sorcery within from that without was the imposition of form. Man forced order onto chaos. Chaos would force itself upon order. In the depths of the warp the price of losing the struggle was plain to see.

Guondrin's mundane eyes blinked under the blindfold tied about his face, daring him to look with mortal sight upon things no human should ever see. His senses were so heightened he felt every thread of the silk weave brush his eyelashes with painful intensity.

'Attempting to re-establish visual contact,' he said. His throat was drying. His lips were cracked. 'Request reduction in speed of ten per cent, begin slow arc port.' Words of quantity and position meant nothing in the no-places of the warp, but they must be said, and they must be acted upon as if they were real. Acknowledgement of the unreality surrounding them would imperil the ship.

'Inform astropaths to prepare teleprayers requesting empyrical positioning. Hold before sending. Await my request.'

A heavy surge of terror lifted the ship. Guondrin's teeth clamped tight. He whispered the first of the twelve orientations to drive the fear from him. Guondrin was a slight being. His warp eye aside, he resembled a baseline human of delicate build, but his bones were voidborn weak. His jaw creaked.

TuMar Ikuo in throne four shrieked.

'Thone four, maintain emotional balance.' Guondrin's words left his mouth barely comprehensible and drenched in spit.

'Praecipus, I have sight of the *Bloodcaller*.'

'Confirm identity of the speaker. I disavow falsehood, and will deny the machinations of the warp. Tell me true, did you speak, throne six?'

'It is I, Hethen of House Umarri. I vouch for myself, by the Emperor's grace and mercy.'

Guondrin struggled to perceive a way through a reef of screaming eyes that turned into mouths vomiting multi-coloured lightning. Swirls of colour wrapped themselves about his perception, blunting his vision. Fond memories were twisted into the vilest perversions and flung into his soul like darts. He saw everyone he had ever met die a thousand terrible deaths.

'I see nothing. I do not see the ship.'

'Predicted position of *Bloodcaller* in the ninth house of the fourth sign,' Hethen said.

'We are turned about!' Kaskaskay shouted.

'Maintain calm,' Guondrin demanded.

The machine-spirit of the *Dominance* steadied Guondrin. It was single-minded and pure. The four other Navigators were joined in series to Guondrin's mind via manifold link, and together they worked to triangulate the position of the *Bloodcaller*. The *Dominance* sliced through a wall of fear as tall as a galaxy. Warp engines shrieked through the structure of the hull. Scaled hands raked the Geller fields. Nameless beasts led the prow. Still Guondrin peered ahead, risking his sanity for the safe passage of his ship, searching for the *Bloodcaller*. He saw nothing in the turmoil of the storm, only certain doom.

He felt Kaskaskay losing himself. They were all of different houses, an unusual arrangement, but useful for the spread of differing gifts they brought. Kaskaskay was a tall, spindly creature, born to a strain far removed from the human norm, and they had exchanged few words. Yet through the link Guondrin knew him better than he knew himself. They had shared minds; now he felt Kaskaskay's mind fail.

Black madness crawled along the neural shunts, threatening to destroy them all. Insanity offered a way for what was out there to get inside. Immediate action was required.

Mercy protocol, throne three, immediate effect. Guondrin's thoughts were carried away by the hardlines linking him to the vessel. *Dominance* was an unsentimental ship, and obeyed without demur. The craft trembled. Guondrin felt a panicked thought from his fellow, then it was gone. Kaskaskay slumped forward, his brain smashed. A retractable bolt set at neck height rasped back into its housing. Kaskaskay's soul was cast into the ocean of being and there devoured. Guondrin saw it happen.

Dominance sailed on. The things swimming in its wake snapped at each other with half-formed jaws. Guondrin could not see them, but he felt them, and their presence sent ice down his spine.

There was a flash of pure light in the unnatural hues of the warp. A vision of a golden angel and a winged shadow in black engaged in vicious battle. They were tiny, too far to see as anything but motes, and yet simultaneously so huge they filled everything. A golden sword connected with a black sword, sending shockwaves through the warp that buffeted the *Dominance*. Another blow brought a cascade of light of every colour that blew away in unfurling flags. Guondrin gasped with relief.

Against the lightning of the angels' struggle, he saw *Bloodcaller*.

'Bring the ship around, one hundred and twenty degrees to portside. I have the fleet in sight! Ninth house, fourth sign, as you said, Hethen.'

'My thanks, Praecipus.'

Dominance flew forward, cutting across a notional diagonal to rejoin the flotilla.

'Thank me when we are out of this storm,' said Guondrin.

Danakan was sitting in the dark staring into the fireplace when Juvenel came in. He clutched a goblet of wine without drinking from it. He did not look up.

'Admiral?' Juvenel said.

Danakan frowned woozily at his first officer. 'What are you doing here, Juvenel? I thought I politely declined your invitation to dinner. I didn't expect you to come here to drag me out.'

'I'm not dragging you anywhere, my lord,' said Juvenel. He looked about the room for a seat, found one, and pulled it in front of the fire. Parts of the admiral's outer uniform were draped on the furniture. His meal sat untouched on the long banqueting table. Without servants, Juvenel thought Danakan might quickly slip into slovenly habits. That wasn't like him at all.

The admiral slouched further into his chair. 'You know what I mean, Juvenel.'

'I do.' He sat down.

'If you're going to be impertinent enough to sit without my offering, I suppose I ought to offer you some wine.'

'Thank you.' Juvenel picked up a goblet. Thanks to Fresne's efforts, it was spotless. He held it out to Danakan. When the admiral poured, the metal jug rattled on the lip of the goblet. Wine slopped over the edge.

'Throne save us all,' Danakan said.

'From a little spilled wine, sir?' said Juvenel.

'You really are too much, Juvenel.'

Juvenel sipped the wine and stared into the fire. The dance of the flames was hypnotic.

'This is good wine,' he said.

'I am the bloody admiral, Arran. I should have good wine.'

'You are.' Juvenel took another sip. 'Sir, I am not going to ask permission to speak freely, because I do not think you will allow me to.'

'It never stopped you before.' Danakan took a long pull at his drink. He spilled it into his beard, and wiped it away with a shaking hand.

'Sir, you're not yourself.'

Danakan sighed. 'I had hoped you had not noticed.'

'I noticed. Fresne has too.'

'Yes, well, what does that little eavesdropper not see? He's probably outside the doors with his ears pressed to the metal.' He raised his voice and turned around in his chair. 'Listening right now!'

'He probably is,' Juvenel said.

'You have the manner of a man who is choosing his next words carefully, Juvenel,' said Danakan.

'I am,' he replied. 'I am concerned. We are concerned, Fresne and I.'

'I am touched. I would have thought that you might be eager for an opening, an ambitious young man like you.'

'Sir, please. You are a hero of the Imperium. You are a hero to everyone in this fleet. The Iron Master, that's what they call you. We need you. What with everything that has happened, the losses, the Rift, the state of the warp. Without you, I fear the fleet will fall apart.'

'I am touched,' said Danakan sarcastically. The *Dominance*

shuddered. Danakan blanched.

'Damn your misery, sir. I need you. What use is this fleet to Lord Dante if its master loses his mind?'

'So I'm losing my mind now?'

'Sir, please!'

Danakan rubbed at the bridge of his nose, hard. When he took his hand away he looked at Juvenel properly for the first time. His eyes were red. 'I hear you. These people, they need me. Once, I wanted to be needed.' He shuddered. 'There are screams that pass you by and leave no impression. You survive in service long enough, you see people die.' He smiled bitterly. 'I have seen a lot of people die. On my first mission of my first command – it was a little torpedo boat, crew of hundreds, that's all, very fast, beautiful little thing – but on my first mission, my command deck took a glancing hit. Just shrapnel, but she was a fragile ship. Took out half the ceiling, and all the way down the wall. The oculus popped out like a lens from a dropped monocle. I barely survived. I saw most of my command crew sucked out to their deaths in the void. All I had to show for it was a bit of void burn. Two weeks in the medicae, I was fine.' He took a shaky drink. 'The deaths didn't bother me. The screams didn't bother me. I was like you, full of the swagger of youth and the desire to serve. They died in service. I lived, and could serve further. All for the Emperor. That was all there was to it. Glorious,' he said heavily. 'I've seen ships die. I've seen worlds die. The death of a world is an abstract to a ship lord. It is a burning orb. You cannot see the inhabitants die. You do not hear them. World death is vectors of attack and bombardment solutions. A ship is more personal, easier to relate to. But the dead, what are they? Floating motes vented into the void. I've seen so many people die, Juvenel. I've been responsible, but for the longest time I did not care. It had to be done, so it was.' He drained his goblet and poured himself more. 'I think it began to change when we burned that aeldari corsair fleet off Desdemona. Such beautiful things, frying in their own fires, and I thought, how like us they are. I'd never thought that before. I think, I think...'

He lapsed into silence, staring into the fire. 'I'll tell you what I think,' he said eventually. 'The screams don't matter at all on their own, but they pile up in your soul, higher and higher, until some balance is reached and it tips, and the screams that do not matter become the screams that do matter very, very much. I saw them burn, Juvenel, all of them on the *Eternal Blade*, before they got me out of there. I was saved. I know I'm the damned admiral and everything, but every night since, I have seen my crew burn again, and I ask myself, why not me? It's going to happen again, sooner or later.'

He drank the cup dry again. It did not stop his hands shaking.

'So, flag-lieutenant, you may well need the Iron Master, but I'm afraid he is not here any more.'

Guondrin's life had become cramped and depressing. As he fought against the storm, his mind returned to comforts lost. A Navigator's career began meanly, but once proven and out of the lower ranks and the vileness of a containment blister, a Navigator could expect his own manse. A small oasis of civilisation in the joylessness of voidships, replete with the luxuries of home. For the fortunate, there were silks, servants, wine, song, and respect. A Navigator of a capital ship like the *Dominance* had a palace of surpassing beauty.

That was no longer the case. So many Navigators were required to find a way through the warp now, Guondrin was forced to share his accommodation. Attrition among his people was high. After the Rift opened, the Paternova issued a bull commanding a reduction in attendants in all manses for fear of warp corruption. No dancers, no singers, no fine chefs or major-domos to ease a Navigator's burden. The *Dominance*'s navigatorial quarters became squalid for lack of servants.

Guondrin was of high birth, used to the very finest of things. Even so, he had not resented the reduction in circumstances, not at first.

Not any more. Now he was tired to the bone. His warp eye ached. Now he would kill for a good amasec and the skills of a well-trained body slave, but he'd settle for ten minutes alone in a quiet room.

TuMar Ikuo was whispering the same thing to himself over and over again.

'Paternova, Emperor, Paternova, Emperor, Paternova, Emperor.'

The stress of navigation pained Guondrin. Visions of such awfulness. Bloody sweat seeped from his pores, gluing his robes to his skin. His mortal eyes ran. He was shouting into the room without realising, thrashing against his input cables. All the Navigators were bound to their thrones. They had to be.

Colours swirled and swam. His warp eye bled freely. There was calm in the warp, and beauty too, if one knew where to look. Like the angel fighting its own shadow in the night. This was the guide of the Blood Angels. There was purity in it.

He saw beauty in the power of the ships and the way they forged on through the tempest. He saw glory in the endless possibilities the warp possessed. There was a gift of power somewhere in the madness.

The storms would pass, and life would return to normal. Guondrin refused to believe the dire pronouncements that they lived at the end of times. The Imperium had persisted for ten thousand years, the Navigators far longer. They would survive, and prosper again.

He held onto these thoughts, and to the sense of wonder the deeps provided.

If only he weren't so tired.

He tried to work up enough spit to swallow. His mouth and throat were dry as desert sands.

If only he could have a cup of wine.

The angel and the shadow turned around in the sky, now the size of men, now the size of gods. Black sword met golden. They pushed against each other, neither strong enough to best his opposite. Between the angles of their straining blades, Guondrin stared into a shimmering that rippled beauteously, and calmed, and he saw a vision of himself years ago, a patch of the past that manifested thousands of miles from the *Dominance*, yet near enough to touch and taste. He saw himself as he was during the time of his first real assignment, in a courtyard where gentle fountains played, and greenery swayed in the ventilation breeze of the ship, and laughing women served him fine wines from a hundred worlds.

The scene changed. It took on a tainted air. Clean light shone a sordid pink. His past self looked back at him, and beckoned. The doppelgänger blinked, and his eyes, all of three of them, were black as oil.

In his throne, Guondrin's bloody sweat ran cold. He dismissed the images.

'We have drawn the attention of entities in the warp,' he gurgled. 'Increase Geller field output. Accelerate. Throw them off. Hurry!'

'My lord, the enginarium reports problems with the field. We are travelling at maximum speed,' said Hethen.

'Tell them to try!' Guondrin shouted.

Hethen relayed the command. A few moments later, the frequency of the ship's vibration shifted, the subtle sign the reactor was pouring more power into the Geller field and drive. This was mortal power, and therefore only supplemental to the dark technologies that pushed the ship through the warp, but it might help. The ship moved more quickly, catching up to the *Bloodcaller* and the rest of the flotilla.

It was too late.

Rameese in throne five began to howl. His cries carried mind to mind. His fists beat against the metal of his throne. Something wicked approached them head on, obscuring the shadow and the angel, then the rest of the fleet. Guondrin tried to look away, but it would not relinquish his vision, and poured vast and shining into his sight wherever he looked. With increasing horror he knew it saw him too. Within its terrible form was all the pleasure of the world. He denied it, he shouted prayers. It had seen him, looked into him, violated his memories, but he would not succumb.

His mouth was so dry. His body hurt.

Life was better then, the shadow said to him. It can be so again.

If only I had a cup of wine, he thought.

A single, simple longing was enough to damn him.

An intelligence slipped down the light reaching his warp eye. A sense of pressure mounted in his nose and throat. Something probed at him, using him as a way through the field.

'We are sighted! We must leave the warp!' Guondrin said. The words were strangled in his throat, and the sense of dread built, crushing down on his will. His hands twitched so sharply his knuckles cracked.

'Prepare for immediate emergency translation!' He told the ship's machine-spirit, not the captain. The ship would sing it wide. All the crew must know. They would come out hard and tumbling from the warp. The ship was ready. It understood. *Dominance*'s iron soul shouted the news across all decks in a rapid stream of binharic. A hundred thousand voxmitters translated it into Naval Gothic.

The pressure in Guondrin's throat grew. He struggled to breathe. Every breath he took brought a choking musk into his lungs. Blackness tinged his warp sight.

As calmly as he could, he sent commands to the enginarium and Geller generatorium. The tone of the ship's sound changed as the warp engines prepared to fire. The teeth-prickling feel of pre-translation crawled all over the ship.

'Now! Now! Get us out of the warp now!' His voice was barely a whisper. His tongue was fat in his mouth and tasted abominably sweet.

Darkness grew in his vision, swamping his mind, filling him with madness. The thing was ahead, unknowable in its monstrosity, trying to get in. Guondrin's soul shrivelled as his mind tried to give it form, finding only horror.

'Warp breach imminent,' he whispered. 'Prepare to offer mercy to Navigator thrones five and one.'

A torrent of colour poured over the prow of *Dominance*. Black lightning flickered around the ship. Geller generators screamed. Warp engines spooled up to slice a path from the insanity of the warp to the stillness of the void. A ragged gash cut down through the madness, revealing the cold, logical blackness of real space. Tendrils of half-formed matter reached for the stars beyond. The thing was in their way, blocking their exit. It had its claws in him. It looked out through his eyes. It hungered at what it saw. The hexagrams in the oculus glared bright enough to blind.

Guondrin moaned.

A cup of wine in gentler days. He could taste it now. He could hear the laughter of his servants.

With a convulsive heave, the ship burst from real space. Power spiked all over the vessel, burning out systems. Guondrin felt his humanity slipping away. His flesh crawled and bulged. Rameese screamed in agony.

'No, no, no,' Guondrin moaned.

Through the eyes opening all over his face, Guondrin saw the thing in the warp slither free, pass into reality and plunge into the ship.

Alarms blared everywhere. The ship wallowed powerless in the void. The rift was slow in closing. Vast arms of energy reached for the *Dominance* to drag it back in.

The thing was in the ship. It was in Guondrin. His fellow Navigators thrashed in their restraints and screamed as it touched their souls.

'Execute mercy!' he said. Scented slobber ran over his chin. Needle teeth burst from his gums. 'Execute mercy! Kill me!'

The spiked bolt slammed out of the throne, shattering his spine and punching up into his brain. His service was done.

And yet he was not dead.

The golden angel battled a monstrous being who wore an angelic shape, but who was comprised entirely of darkness. The pair of them swelled to immense proportions. The fleet sank within them, became part of them.

A sense of terrible dread filled Mephiston, drawing his attention behind him, back the way they had come. He saw the

Dominance plunge out of the warp into a field of stars, pursued by a swarm of shadows. A ripple across the seething energies around him drew his attention to another ship, and he saw its Geller field collapse. The warp bubble went out, came to a dragging stop, and was set upon by horrors beyond counting.

The golden angel and the black angel did not see. They continued their fight. The black parried the blade of the gold, flinging back its foe. Then the black angel turned and stared into Mephiston's soul.

Its being sucked at him, drawing the Lord of Death towards it. Mephiston felt it swell up, threatening to pull him in and consume him, so he threw himself out of the warp, back into the relative safety of the *Bloodcaller*. Such pain there was from so abrupt a shift, gone in an instant as his soul sped back into his body.

Settling back into reality made his soul crawl, as if being free in the warp was his natural condition, and flesh a terrible prison. Mephiston drew a great racking breath into his lungs. With disgust he felt them quiver. Such carnal impermanence was no vehicle for his immortal soul.

The feelings passed. He lived again as a man, though he could not forget his numinous state out there in the wild seas of possibility. The peril of the black angel did not seem so great, and he half desired to face it.

His eyes opened onto a room full of blood scent and the droning of counter-sorcery.

'My Lord Mephiston?' Rhacelus came forward, his horned staff levelled at the kneeling Mephiston's head. 'Why do you return? Is it you?'

'It is I, my brother,' said Mephiston, his voice hoarse. Wearily, he got to his feet. 'No beast but I resides within this body. Stand down. I have ill tidings.'

Rhacelus scrutinised him. His glowing blue eyes were proof against any falsehood.

'I see it is you.' Rhacelus settled his staff's butt upon the floor. 'Cease the ritual!' he commanded.

There was no finale to the chant. It trailed off, reluctantly dying. Each Librarian practised his art according to his own gifts and preference, and so awoke from their trances in their own time. The Librarians returned themselves to their mortal bodies. Ties of brotherhood did not go beyond the realm of matter. Every one of them was forever alone in the face of the powers behind reality.

Tired eyes opened in drawn faces. Only Mephiston seemed unaffected, appearing instead invigorated, a fact that Rhacelus noted with concern. A lesser psyker might have attempted to probe Mephiston's mind, but Rhacelus knew better than to try that.

'What is happening, my lord? We are not yet at Baal,' Rhacelus said.

'The Sanguinor is assailed by a black angel in the empyrean,' said Mephiston. 'Daemons flock to us. The *Dominance* has fallen out of the warp, and several other ships are under attack. Bring the rest of the fleet into real space now. Inform Commander Dante's servants that he should be awoken immediately. We are at war again.'

CHAPTER FIVE

THE DOMINANCE

Dante coughed, spraying his four servants with blood. They did not flinch but continued their ministrations, first wiping his eyes with soft cloths so he might see, then gently grasping him to raise him from his sarcophagus. Their hands slipped on his blood-slick skin. He tried to shake them off but he could not rise alone. He trembled, for though the room was warm he felt intolerably cold. His muscles disobeyed him. He shamed himself with his weakness.

He grasped the sides of the sarcophagus. His fingers were numb and would not grip. His left hand slipped free, slapping against his muscled chest and bringing forth a spike of pain from his wounds.

'Steady, my lord!' said one of his blood thralls. They struggled to lift him. Dante was old beyond imagining, but the Emperor's gifts spared him the infirmities of age. He was still tall, an ogre of a man, heavy with muscle and bones dense as rock.

'Enough,' he croaked. He raised his arms one after the other, forcing his servants to release him. He gripped the sarcophagus sides again and pulled himself upright until he stood on unsteady legs. He wavered, but he did not fall. He hawked blood from his lungs and spat it into the sarcophagus' gurgling drains. The iron taste of it stirred the thirst, and his weakness became a lesser concern.

'I will stand on my own. Get back from me.'

The blood stink was hot in his nostrils. His servants' arteries pulsed invitingly. His fangs twitched in his gums.

'You must get back.'

'My lord,' one said. They bowed and took several steps away.

The sarcophagus lid was held clear on carved levers, but there was a lip as high as Dante's knee at the bottom of the coffin, and he struggled to raise his foot over it. His limbs were rubbery, his skin without feeling, except where his wounds throbbed. Dante was used to hiding discomfort, and managed to step out with dignity. Rivulets of vitae ran off his body and splattered on the floor. His servants took another step backwards. Their fear was rising. He could smell it on them.

'Calm yourselves,' he said. He tugged out the lines plugged into his neural ports. 'I am awake.' He swallowed the vitae lingering in his mouth. He yearned for fresher fare, pumped hot by dying hearts. He held out his hand. One of the servants hurried to collect his robes and give them to him. They bowed with every completed action. Dante took a step forward, and was surprised when his foot failed to support his weight and his leg folded under him.

His men rushed to catch him, grunting with the effort at halting his fall. They were all strong, yet they laboured as if they attempted to hold up a collapsing temple.

'Enough, enough!' Dante said. He shifted his weight, recovered his balance and stood slowly.

'My lord, I am sorry,' said their leader. 'We had to interrupt your healing sleep. Lord Mephiston...' The man paled as he uttered the name, and his words faltered. 'Lord Mephiston sent word that we have been forced to come out of the warp.'

Dante stared at the man until he looked away. Though the thrall was in the prime of his life, and all the harm done him by his early life banished by Imperial technomancy, already Dante could see him aged and feeble. His name was Colma, and he was Dante's equerry. Every one of the sixty-seven equerries before Colma had withered and died before Dante's eyes.

Perhaps Colma would be the last.

'Then we are not at Baal,' said Dante.

'Not yet, my lord. The Lord Librarian Rhacelus spoke of a deadly shadow. We are deep in interstellar space, some light years from our home. I am sorry, I did not fully comprehend.'

'You are young,' Dante said, and that was true, at least for a while. 'You will learn.'

'Captain Antargo is coming to escort you. Battle comes.'

'Then prepare me. I would be ready by the time he arrives.'

Orfeo, another of his servants, hurried to a cupboard hidden within the wall's carvings, and from inside fetched out a ewer of wine, a goblet and a smaller vial. The vial was elegantly blown from smoked glass, with a bloodstone stopper. The servant set all upon a table, filled the goblet from the ewer, then drew out the stopper from the vial. A dripper was attached, and with it he put nine drops of dark liquid into the wine, stirred it, and gave it to Dante with a bow.

Suddenly wracked with thirst, Dante took the vessel and downed the wine. The first flavour to hit was the sweetness of the grapes of the Verdis Elysia. The wine was of an old vintage, and of dwindling stocks. Nothing had grown in the Chapter's fields since the devastation of the Arx Angelicum. The second taste was subtle, but more arousing; the salt iron of blood. It excited Dante's omophagea, bringing a little flash of stolen memory, and a yearning for more. One thirst was slaked by the drink, the other hardly blunted.

Invigorated by the fortified wine, Dante's strength returned, and he became steady. 'More,' he said. Orfeo hurried to obey.

Now Dante was up, his servants set about their allotted tasks, fetching towels and scented water to wipe the blood from Dante's face and hands. One noted his demeanour in the commander's Book of Hours, giving thanks while he wrote that Dante had awoken sane and hale.

Colma cleared his throat. He had a scroll and an autoquill ready. 'My lord? Did you see anything while you slept?'

Dante accepted a second cup of wine and sipped it. 'I dreamt of disaster,' he said.

Colma dutifully noted this down. 'Of what manner, my lord Dante?'

'Nothing worthy for the record. A disaster of long ago, not one to come. I do not have much of Sanguinius' foresight.'

'It could still be a portent,' said Colma. He looked up from the scroll. He had very fine handwriting. Blood thralls were expected to master all things appertaining to their service. They were no different to their lords in their desire for perfection.

Dante shook his head. Blood was drying into the wrinkles of his face, caking his long white hair. He caught sight of himself in the polished walls of stone. A half-reflection, but the bloody wrinkles made his age apparent. He averted his gaze.

'It is not a portent. It was a memory. An unwelcome one.'

Dante placed his goblet upon a tray carried by one of the four.

'I am unclean. I do not have time to purify myself. Prepare my lavatesarium for my return so I may cleanse then. Open my armoury.'

'I shall see that it is done,' said Colma, bowing crisply. He moved quickly. His mind was quick to find ways to serve Dante's every need. These traits would not last. In no time at all, Colma would become as slow as poor Arafeo had been, and then what? The next, and the next, and then another, on and on; a parade of brief youth, infirmity and death hobbling on for Dante to survey, forever.

Colma opened the portals to the armourium with minimal ceremony. Dante's quarters aboard *Bloodcaller* were an exact match for those on the *Blade of Vengeance* – large, sumptuous and for his use alone, though many of the weapons cases lining the armourium hall were empty. There had not been time, when the *Dominance*'s distress call had come, to transfer his relics aboard before the Blood Angels set out on their rescue mission.

His thralls began to sponge the drying blood from his naked body.

'Stop,' he said. 'I shall fight blood-clad. I find myself waging war against time above all other foes. I shall give it no advantage. Garb me.'

The thralls fitted his bodysuit to his filthy body, and began the process of armouring him with the aid of specialised servitors. Many of the prayers of armament they abbreviated or left out. As they worked, anthems began piping through the ship, calling the vessel's complement of Blood Angels to arms.

'My lord, battle approaches,' said Orfeo.

'Faster,' said Dante. 'Speak not. War is on us. Let the sound of arming tools be our prayers.'

His servants obeyed, and abandoned the sanctifications altogether.

Dante was being bolted into the last of his golden armour when the door chime tolled and a brass putto lifted its head from the carvings of the wall and cried out.

'Lord Dante, Antargo comes, the Master of Sacrifice, captain of the Third Company, Lord of the Ironhelms!'

Orfeo moved to the door, depressing a bloodstone button on his vox-badge to speak with Dante's visitor. 'My lord, please wait, Lord Dante is not dressed!' he managed, but too late. The door opened, and Antargo pushed past Orfeo with two Sanguinary Guard.

'We do not have time for ceremony, thrall, out of my way,' he said, only to stop uncertainly when he saw that the Chapter Master's head was bare.

Dante turned from the captain, and held up his hand. Antargo, understanding his error, looked uncomfortably away. Dante did not like others to see his face unless he chose to reveal it. The Sanguinary Guard clashed their vambraces together in salute and turned their backs. From Colma, Dante took the Deathmask of Sanguinius and placed it over his head.

'Listen to my servants next time, Antargo,' said Dante. He stared at the captain through ruby lenses. Antargo was one of Cawl's Gift, and still young.

'Forgive me, my lord,' Antargo said, his eyes fixed on the carpet pattern, his cheeks colouring at the indiscretion. 'I could not wait. Lord Mephiston has commanded the fleet exit from the warp. He sent me here to find you personally.'

'That is no excuse for your unseemly haste,' said Dante.

'There is a problem.' Antargo looked unsurely at the thralls.

'Speak freely in front of them, they are my honoured servants.'

'Daemons, my lord. We have manifestations on seven ships, chief among them the *Dominance*. Lord Mephiston speaks of an attack in the warp.'

'When we leave the hunting grounds of the tyranids, I almost miss the shadow they cast,' said Dante grimly. 'The warp is no place for humanity in these benighted times.'

Dante took his axe and pistol from their stand, then waited while his jump pack was raised up by a monotasked armoury servitor and pushed into place. As soon as the interface between armour and pack kissed he stepped away. Power flooded his battleplate. Information ran up the helm display. Dante deactivated it. He felt stronger behind Sanguinius' holy visage.

'Lead on, Antargo. We must retake the *Dominance*. It would irk me to rescue this fleet only to lose its most powerful vessel.'

Antargo got to his feet, unable to meet his lord's eye, then walked out. Dante followed, and the Sanguinary Guard fell into line with him.

'Mephiston,' said Dante, opening a direct vox-link. 'Tell me what has occurred.'

A flight of Thunderhawks sped towards the *Dominance*. No weapons locked on to them. No challenges were issued. Dante's vessel went at the head of the three, golden where the others were red, always first into action.

'Nothing seems amiss,' said Antargo, examining vid-feed shone onto the back of his eyes. 'The ship is intact. I see no signs of external damage.'

'Daemons are rarely interested in wounding beings of metal,' said Dante. 'Their passions lie in tormenting the soul and the flesh.'

'As you say, Chapter Master. I do not underestimate the peril we fly towards. I merely suggest the *Dominance* might easily be returned to service.'

'Watch your manner, captain,' said Daeanatos, Exalted Herald of Sanguinius, Dante's chief guardian. 'You speak with the greatest hero of the Imperium, and the lord of all this side of the Great Rift. Surliness is an offence to his glory. Commander Dante may not be a primarch, but he is the Lord of Angels.'

'I did not intend to dishonour myself, my lord,' said Antargo. 'I am a straightforward man. I apologise if my manner irritates you.'

'Think nothing of it, Antargo. Your combat record and ability in command make amends for any supposed offence,' said Dante. He was distracted, hardly hearing what Antargo said. The wounds in his chest throbbed.

Daeanatos switched his vox to a private channel. 'You are too gentle on them. They have no manners, these young ones. They need schooling in the graces and the virtues.'

'Do you think your position as my aide gives you the right to speak to me so?' said Dante.

Daeanatos laughed. 'I am a straightforward man too, my lord. But I have a little more polish. I thank the Great Angel himself for his brother Guilliman's intervention, but he could have given these newcomers a little courtesy.'

'The Lord Guilliman's manners are not the same as ours,' said Dante. 'But he is courteous to a fault. It is not the fault of the teacher, but of the warrior. They will learn.'

'This new breed should watch their tongues.'

'New breed, still of our blood,' said Dante.

'Yes, my lord, but soon there will be only them. We must pass on what we are.'

'I daunt him.' Dante looked back through the hold of his ship. So many of the Space Marines in the transit bay were Primaris brethren, most of them Mars-born. Many had never seen Baal before their arrival, and though they bore the colours of the Blood Angels, they knew little of the Chapter's ways.

'So now they have nerves to be daunted too,' said Daeanatos. 'Cawl's get seems more imperfect the longer I look.'

'Any man has nerves when standing in the presence of I, greatest hero of the Imperium and the lord of all this side of the Great Rift,' said Dante, mocking Daeanatos' own words.

'Fair point,' Daeanatos said. 'I would affect greater seriousness, my lord, or you shall destroy the illusion for me completely.'

Dante called up a close-up image of the *Dominance* from the Thunderhawk's augurs. Interstellar void black; so far from any sun, the light of the stars was too feeble to provide more than a darkling twilight. The ships in the fleet were bright as temples, but the *Dominance* was a shadow in space, lit eerily by corposant foxfires crawling in the deeper places of its hull. These faded as Dante watched, and it became forbidding as a tomb.

'We approach, my lord,' said Antargo.

The *Dominance* was a Retribution-class battleship, approaching six miles in length and three abeam. It blotted out the stars. Even so, at the Thunderhawk's speed they would quickly overshoot it.

'Decelerate. Make a visual pass. Let us see the vessel before we look for a suitable landing point,' Dante commanded.

The Thunderhawk slowed and turned to fly parallel to the

Dominance's vast bulk. The blur of the battleship resolved itself into hard lines, buttresses, statues of angels and heroes holding weapons out against the cosmos.

Dante examined the findings of the Thunderhawk's augury. The reactor was out. Shuttle bays and windows were empty as the eyes of the dead. Atmospheric fields were off.

'All shielding is down, my lord,' the pilot reported.

They approached the prow.

'Turn us about, take us in to the primary hangar,' said Dante. 'Best we concentrate our efforts where the bulk of the crew might be found.'

'As you command.'

Accelerative forces tugged at Dante as the pilot brought the Thunderhawk over and down in a wide loop, and spiralled the vessel about to bring it back on the same orientation as the *Dominance*. The wide aft of the ship came at them, the aquila figurehead on the superstructure guarding command decks that were as dark as all the rest.

The hangar was hidden by the aft quarter's armour vanes. The Thunderhawks passed between hull and outrigger. Before they lost sight of the fleet, Dante checked over the progress of actions ongoing aboard the other vessels. Two were purged, the others remained in the hands of the enemy. Casualty counts ticked up slowly in his visor, Adeptus Astartes only. Naval losses would be far higher.

'If Mephiston is correct, and the source of the contamination is here, we must be quick. We can ill afford delays, and I will not lose this ship,' said Dante. 'Take us in. Let us see this done and be on our way. These ships are crucial to our fleet plans.'

The Thunderhawk slowed as it came towards the main hangar. The armoured doors were wide, and the space behind open to the void. The view of inside was obscured by billowing thruster gases. The vid-feed in Dante's helm went dark. His auto-senses worked with the machines of the gunship to compensate, and showed him a cavernous hold full of shadows.

'No sign of any material damage here, either,' said Antargo. 'Where is the crew?'

Tarpaulins covering shuttlecraft flapped back in the violent effusions of the gunship's thrusters.

'Put us down,' Dante said.

The pilot obeyed, choosing a landing pad near the entrance, with good fields of fire towards the ship's core. He brought the gunship into a hover, before pivoting it on the spot and landing, its weapons facing inwards.

Maglocks thumped off through the transit bay.

The ramp descended into the airless hangar. Dante was out first, flanked by half a dozen of his golden guard.

Antargo's two Intercessor squads spread out to form a cordon in front of the gunships. They would go no further until Dante had given his judgement on the situation.

'Gravity plating functional. Life support operational. If we close the blast shields we could reintroduce an atmosphere in here. Someone vented this on purpose.' Brother Techmarine Delphinus stood in front of the gunship, reading information from his wrist cogitator. 'All systems running as normal on back-up power banks and secondary generating facilities. The main reactor is offline. Beyond the hangar airlocks there is an atmosphere. I am receiving no response to my messages to the command deck or command nodes of the ship.'

'Keep trying. Do not attempt to delve too deeply into the vessel noosphere,' said Dante. 'Isolate all systems from the ship's spirit before connection.'

'"Corruption of flesh is expected, for the flesh is weak. Corruption of the machine is all the more invidious, for the machine is strong,"' Delphinus quoted. 'I shall be careful. Give me the word, and the doors shall open.' He found his way to a terminal set between two large cargo doors.

Mephiston descended the ramp of his own transport with four of his Librarians and more of Antargo's men. Mephiston's gorily styled armour stood out against his followers' sober blue.

Dante steeled himself against the air of foreboding that preceded the Lord of Death. Few beings made Dante uncomfortable. Mephiston was one.

'My lord Dante,' Mephiston said. 'My instincts were correct. The *Dominance* is the focus of the evil in the fleet. I can feel it.'

'Fighting continues on five ships,' said Dante. 'The Neverborn find it easier to cling on to existence since the Rift opened. Our exit from the warp should have banished them back whence they came.'

'We live in a new age,' said Mephiston. 'Darkness is all around us, pressing in,' he said. 'This ship is the locus of damnation.'

'Your advice, Chief Librarian Mephiston?' said Dante. 'It will take us hours to sweep the *Dominance*, how might we most quickly achieve victory.'

'The source will be easy to find. There will be one mind here and one alone that has given the warp beasts ingress.'

'A hidden witch among the crew?'

'An untutored mind is the key to the doors of the immaterium,' said Mephiston. 'But the manner of the ship's egress from the warp suggests the problem was known, and the desire was to contain it by severing the links of the Neverborn from the immaterium by emergency translation. As the problem was detected and action taken quickly enough to save the ship from loss in the warp, it is my opinion that the breach occurred within the ship's psychic staff, either the astropaths or the Navigators.'

'There have been many ships lost in similar circumstances,' said Antargo. 'When I was with Lord Guilliman, he took great pains to shield his psykers from the warp, and yet there were many losses, especially on this side of the Rift.'

'Fear not. Lord Guilliman lacked Lord Mephiston,' said Daeanatos.

'I and my Librarians will lead the way,' Mephiston said. 'Incursions of daemons are best dealt with by those with warp ability.'

'Agreed,' said Dante.

'I find they die just as well to a sword,' said Daeanatos. 'But the Lord of Death is our best weapon.'

'Our swords will still be needed, brother. We follow a simple plan, without complication,' said Dante.

'We do not know the enemy's strength,' said Antargo.

'We do not need to,' said Dante. 'If the breach is closed, the incursion will be curtailed. If it is not, the enemy will be functionally infinite. Find the breach, close it, and the day shall be won.'

'I do not like this,' said Antargo. 'I advise destroying the ship.'

'How many Retribution-class war vessels do you think are left in this half of the Imperium, captain? I lack the Lord Guilliman's resources. This ship is worth a great deal to us. Battlefleet Nihilus has need of it.'

'You may leave this task to us, if you wish, lord regent,' said Mephiston. 'You need not jeopardise yourself.'

'No,' said Dante. He ignored the implication that he was weak. Although he hid his pain, whispers travelled far. They knew he was injured. 'It has been too long since I tested my axe. Search this deck, then form a cordon,' Dante commanded. 'Sergeant Amatine, leave a demi-squad here to secure the landing zone. Should the enemy come, retreat to the ships, depart, stand off and await orders. Do not risk the Thunderhawks, we have precious few of those too.'

'Yes, Lord Dante,' Sergeant Amatine responded. His second took command of four Intercessors, and they peeled off from the main force to stand by the gunships as the rest of the Space Marines fanned out across the command deck. Once the three gunships were empty, there was a little more than a demi-company aboard the ship, drawn from Antargo's Third. All were Intercessor and Hellblaster squads.

'We shall begin our divinations,' said Mephiston.

'Lord Mephiston,' Dante said. 'Take a little time. Scry this vessel well. I want it purged and the fleet under way as soon as possible, but I will not strike blindly.'

'It shall be done, my brother,' said Mephiston. He bowed, and signalled his psykers. They drew away and formed a circle, and there began their rituals.

'Search this deck,' Dante commanded. 'Perhaps we shall gain insight into what we face here.' He looked about the space. Darkness lurked in every nook and cranny. 'Something is watching us.'

Ruby light shone from Mephiston's circle. Dante paid their sorcery no heed. Psychic talent ran strongly in the blood of the Sons of Sanguinius, and their use of the warp was commonplace.

Stablights spread out across the deck, flashing off stacks of supplies and inactive ships.

'Lord Dante,' one of the warriors voxed presently. *'Human remains.'* He fed Dante a view of a stack of barrels from his auto-senses. Something glistened on the ground.

Dante and his guardians strode over to the warrior to see more clearly. On the other side of the barrel stack a mash of flesh and blood was spread liberally around.

'Here is something amiss,' Daeanatos said. 'Where are the rest of the crew? This deck should be crawling with servitors and serfs.'

'Most will be dead. Human lives and human misery are the food of the daemon,' said Dante. 'But if we are fortunate, some might yet live.'

Mephiston's sigil flashing in Dante's helm announced vox communication.

'The centre of the disturbance is in the Navigators' tower,' the Lord of Death said.

'More Navigators lost,' said Dante. 'The houses are growing reluctant to risk their members.'

'They must learn to better guard themselves against the warp,' said Mephiston. *'The current conditions in the empyrean are a danger to them, but they do not see it. We lost ships because of their hubris. Doubtless it will not be the last.'*

'The quickest way, my lord,' said Delphinus. He transmitted a cartolith to them all, with the route to the target precisely traced through.

'Then we move,' said Dante. 'Librarius, to the fore. Ward your minds, my brothers. The creatures of the warp have grown strong of late. Prepare for combat.'

The flickering blue of power fields shone off armour as weapons were energised.

Delphinus opened the doors. Atmosphere blasted out in a cone of white. As the Space Marines passed through, their red battleplate rimed with frost. There were no returns on their auspexes, and their sight was limited by the rush of air.

Unseen by Dante's men, a pool of shadows split and slithered across the deck, following after.

CHAPTER SIX

SHADOWPLAY

The strike group went deep into the ship. When they reached its grand, colonnaded spinal ways, Dante divided his force. He would lead the largest contingent with Mephiston, Rhacelus and Antargo towards the source of corruption. The rest were split into small bands, placed under the command of Mephiston's Codiciers and sent out in all directions.

'Search out the crew,' Dante ordered them. 'Kill anything that should not be here.'

To Delphinus, he gave the task of assessing the reactor for reignition.

'Prepare the machine-spirits for reawakening,' he said. 'Once we are done, this vessel must be ready to travel as soon as possible.'

They exchanged oaths to accomplish their allotted tasks, and departed on their separate errands. Dante's group headed upwards and forward, towards one of the ship's great lifter nexuses, hopeful of finding swift passage up into the command spires.

Rhacelus walked with the Lord of Death. His psychic senses prickled with the touch of the warp. The ship bore little sign of damage from its rapid exit from the empyrean, but the unpleasant energies of the warp lingered. This put Rhacelus on his guard, but far more of his attention was absorbed by the presence of his lord, whose soul blazed bonfire-bright in his witch-sight.

They had spoken of this, he and Mephiston. The Lord of Death's powers were growing.

There were few signs of the crew anywhere. Blood was splashed liberally on the walls of one chamber, and the plating gouged by deep claw marks, though no bodies were visible. In another place further on, the severed heads of four servitors rested at the crossroads of a transverse way and a minor walk, staring away down each corridor. They saw no other signs of any soul, living or dead. Bioscanners gave blank returns. Voxes hissed with strange static that hummed and whispered, only to collapse back into electronic noise when hearkened to.

'It is as if the ship was abandoned,' said Daeanatos.

'It is taken,' said Dante. 'The hand of the warp is heavy on the *Dominance*. The only questions are, what manner of foe has manifested here, and when will they attack?'

'We will find them soon enough,' said Daeanatos, 'and the crew.'

'The crew will all be dead,' said Antargo. 'I have walked the deck plates of too many daemon-haunted ships to judge their survival likely.'

As they ventured further, the silence became oppressive. Places that should teem with human life were empty, and yet everywhere there remained signs of people, as if the entire crew had stepped out for a moment, and would imminently return. The paraphernalia of everyday life lay abandoned. Transport vehicles stood unpiloted, engines running. In the refectoria, warm mugs of recaff stood on tables. Dante stepped over a clipboard of store dockets riffling in a ventilation breeze. Self-motivated mechanisms still ran. Where they required human control their ready lights gleamed, awaiting input.

'The machines of this ship are unaffected,' Dante said.

'That is so. I shall tell you something strange, though.' Delphinus paused by a control panel and stabbed a mechadendrite into an input port. 'A ship of this size should have a complement of servitors in the thousands,' he said. 'But I can find no trace of them.'

'Disconnect yourself and move on, Techmarine,' Dante said.

'There is no corruption in the machine world of this vessel,' Delphinus said.

'There appears to be no corruption,' said the Chapter Master. 'You are not as safe as you believe. Disconnect.'

'As you say, my lord.' Delphinus' probe whipped out of the socket and back into its housing.

There was a tranquillity aboard one should not find on a starship. The quiet hum of shipboard systems and the creak of metal shifting soothed the Blood Angels' warrior instincts, and a peculiar soporific effect fell on them that they struggled to combat.

'The influence of the warp is strong,' said Rhacelus. 'I see a presence shifting in the currents of the immaterium. We are being led onwards.'

'Where there is intention from the denizens of the warp, there is greater danger,' said Mephiston. 'I too sense it. I taste it. They call to me.'

'I hear nothing, my lord,' said Rhacelus.

'The words are not meant for you, Gaius,' said Mephiston.

There came a moment when everything seemed to change. Rhacelus and Mephiston were walking ahead of the rest down a secondary way, nearing the lifters to the command decks, when they passed some unseen barrier, and the feeling of the vessel altered.

Mephiston passed through first. Then Rhacelus. Both came to a sudden halt. Mephiston swept his gaze from side to side, and held up his hand.

'What is it?' said Rhacelus.

'Turn around and look behind you.'

Rhacelus did as he was bid. The corridor was empty. 'Where are the others?' he said.

'Watch,' said Mephiston.

A trio of Intercessors crossed an invisible threshold, guns up, ready for combat.

'Lord Mephiston!' one said. 'We thought you taken. You vanished.'

'As did you. This is intentional warpcraft, no anomaly,' Mephiston said. 'Go back. Tell Lord Dante the passage is safe, but that there is a temporal barrier here set by our enemies. If the commander desires to proceed, tell him my advice is to signal the fleet. Warn them that our locators will vanish from their communications web, and that we will not be contactable.'

One of the Intercessors bowed and went back, vanishing a few feet from his brothers.

'You two, range ahead, fifteen yards,' Rhacelus said to the others.

'My lord,' one said. They jogged ahead, red armour blending into the gloom.

Rhacelus took a deep breath. Blue warp light glowed around his skull-headed staff.

'That will not be necessary, Gaius. Not yet.'

'I prefer to be ready, Mephiston,' he said. 'Even if it risks attracting the foe.'

'Employing your powers is a risk.'

'You employing yours is a greater one. Your gift is a torrent to my trickle.'

'It is still getting stronger,' said Mephiston.

'How do you fare?'

Mephiston's helm tilted towards Rhacelus. 'I feel the power in me, Gaius. I feel I could end the galaxy if I chose.'

Rhacelus grunted. 'Best not do that, then.'

Calistarius of old would have shared Gaius' smile. Mephiston had not a whit of humour in his body and stood silent and icy.

A second later Dante appeared with two of his guardians at his side. They emerged as if they came out of deep water, their weapons appearing first, then disembodied hands, then their faces.

'Fascinating,' said Rhacelus.

'Lord Dante,' said Mephiston. 'The servants of the Dark Powers play their tricks.'

'How far are we from our proper timeframe?' said Dante.

'It is impossible to tell, it could be a dislocation of a second. I do not think it more than days. The ship's condition appears the same this side of the time effect as it does on the other. Observe.'

He played a light from his high suit-collar over the wall. Bloodstains there were dry and brown, but not yet black with putrefaction.

Dante put out one golden hand and thrust it through the

space he judged to divide one time from another. It duly disappeared. 'We seem free to move between the two,' said Dante.

'It is a challenge,' said Rhacelus. 'We are being goaded.'

'There is no signal from the fleet,' said Delphinus. 'I assume in this timeframe they have moved on.'

'Is that likely? Surely Captain Gallimimus would not leave the lord commander behind. Have we not only been moved in time, but also been pushed into some other place far from them?' said Antargo.

'It is possible,' said Mephiston. 'It is also possible they were attacked or driven off. Most likely is that we accomplished what we came to do, returned and departed with them. Whatever has occurred, it is of little consequence. Once this is resolved and we return to where we should be, whatever has happened in this time stream will cease to be.'

'Until then we are isolated,' said Antargo. 'There are but seventy of us spread over the ship, twenty here.'

'If we press on, we will be cut off from reinforcement from within the vessel and outside it,' said Rhacelus. 'Whatever is in here wants us alone.'

'We are being challenged, that is all,' said Dante firmly. 'The beings of the warp are tiresome in their predictability.'

'You should think about going back, Lord Dante,' said Mephiston.

'I will not do so,' said Dante. 'This is likely a trap, but it could equally be a ploy to separate us. I could step through that veil and find myself alone and under attack. We shall see this task done together, brother.'

'As you wish, my lord,' said Mephiston.

'The way ahead is clear,' voxed one of the Intercessors ranging ahead.

'Then we proceed,' said Dante. 'The lifter nexus should be half a mile ahead.'

When the rest of the party came through the temporal barrier, Mephiston bade Rhacelus go ahead with the Intercessors. 'Guard them,' he called after his friend. 'Limit the use of your powers. We are in the enemy's territory now. Do not give it strength.'

'As you wish, Lord of Death,' said Rhacelus.

Sergeant-at-Arms Tephis held up his arm to tell the party to halt. Juvenel ducked back into cover.

'Wait,' he said. The rest of them held their ground behind Juvenel. The first officer's palm was damp on the butt of his pistol. His finger cramped with the expectation of pulling the trigger. Seven armsmen protected the admiral a few feet back. There were a gaggle of other crew behind them, ranging from the lowest rating to senior warrant officers.

There had been substantially more of them a few days ago.

With the environmental controls out, heat beat at them. Sweat ran into Juvenel's growing beard. He preferred to be clean shaven. He couldn't stand the itch.

Tephis panned the stablight mounted on his shoulder back and forth across the corridor. It was wide and not too ornate. Not as many places for shadows to hide.

'Is there anything there?' hissed Midshipman Chorkin. She was small and young, but braver than most of the others.

Juvenel shook his head and frowned. 'Shh!' he said. The light ran over the shadows, banishing them instantly. They shrank back into the grille covering the cabling trench running down the corridor centre. They vanished around the stanchions reinforcing the walls. They fled up into the beams, where water ran from stalactites of rust. Drips flashed in the light as they fell and splashed on the ground.

So readily did the shadows vanish that when one did not retreat, but instead screamed and reared high into glistening, wet blackness, they all jumped.

'Emperor's teeth!' someone swore.

Juvenel was already firing by that point.

Las-shot was best against the shadows. Juvenel worked that out early. It made sense that if they did not like light, they would like coherent beams of it even less.

Sergeant-at-Arms Tephis opened fire at the same time. The carbon spray of his shotgun hissed into nothing on contact with the shadow.

The shadow billowed up to the ceiling, like a rush of oil falling upwards, and reared over the sergeant.

Juvenel's first shot burned a smoking hole right through the living black. It shrieked and dropped down, taking on the shape of a scuttling, bent-legged thing. Glossy fangs sprouted from a newly formed maw, and it rushed away from the shocked Tephis towards Juvenel. The other officers stepped out behind Juvenel, laspistols out, rangefinders winking.

They riddled the shadow being with holes before it got to them. It sprang up, and for a moment it writhed, its form re-coalescing into a vaguely humanoid shape sporting a pair of giant crustacean's claws.

Juvenel put a final beam through its forming head, and it split into shreds and vanished.

Laspistol barrels creaked with dissipating heat. Juvenel holstered his gun. The rasp of metal on leather was unpleasantly loud.

'Any more?' he hissed. He couldn't help but whisper. The ship seemed to listen to anything louder.

Tephis gave him a blank look from beneath his visor.

'Are there any more shadows?' Juvenel approached him, grabbed his shoulder and leaned in close. 'Pull yourself together, man!' he whispered. 'I appreciate that shook you up, but we need a little more spirit here. The other armsmen are looking to you.'

Tephis nodded once. 'Yes. Of course. Armsmen! Flood this place with light.' He looked to Juvenel. 'We might as well scare them out. They know we're here now.'

'Now that's a bit more like it,' Juvenel said. He released the sergeant.

Stablights came on in profusion, lancing through the dark, and lighting up whole sections of the corridor at once.

Ensign Elmor came to Juvenel's side. He still had his laspistol out. Its barrel radiated heat.

'Funny old turn of events when the officers have to protect the armsmen,' he said.

'Their shotters are useless,' said Juvenel. 'We should find them lasweapons, if we can.'

'There's an armoury five decks down from here. We should go there next. The hardline you wanted is over there. Get to that first, sir. We should be moving on.'

'The hardline is why we're here.' Juvenel went to a section of the wall where a box was bolted. A red canister was strapped to the wall next to it. He took out a pouch of tools from his belt, selected a handled socket spanner and undid the bolts holding the box shut. There were a number of useful supplies inside.

'Chorkin!' he called over his shoulder. 'Get this stuff out, would you?' He caught sight of Danakan. The admiral gave him a grim nod.

Chorkin squeezed in to take away the items stowed in the

box. Behind them, held closed by straps embossed with the aquila, was an emergency hardline handset.

'How do you know the shadows haven't got into the damn comms system?' said Elmor.

Juvenel shrugged. 'I don't.' He glanced at Elmor. 'Do you have a better idea?' He picked up the vox-horn, listened a moment, then set it back. 'Nothing. No ready signal.'

Elmor looked at him, then jerked his head backwards. 'What are you going to tell the admiral?'

Before he could answer, a crackle of static and a burst of voices came loud over Juvenel's vox-clasp. There'd been nothing on their comms systems for days except the whispers of the shadows, and the party froze.

When nothing came, they relaxed a touch. Juvenel's finger uncurled from the trigger of his pistol. He hadn't even realises he'd drawn his gun again.

'It's the vox, stand down,' said Juvenel. 'Someone's trying to signal us.'

'Who, first officer?' Danakan asked. Juvenel gave a silent prayer to the Emperor that he be the only one to hear the tremor in the admiral's voice.

'I don't know.' Juvenel unhooked his vox-clasp and fiddled with the settings. He called forth only sibilant whispers that came close to forming words, but fell disturbingly short.

'Shut that off,' said Tephis. 'Please, sir,' he added, remembering who he addressed.

'Do as he says,' said Danakan.

'Wait a minute,' said Juvenel. He strained his hearing. 'There is something... There!' Underneath the hissing of the vox was the faint pulse of Imperial signum beacons. 'Friendly forces. They're finally here.' He couldn't hide his own relief.

'How can you know it's not a trick?' Ensign Follin spoke only in terrified whispers. Juvenel frowned at him.

The hissing gabbled on, terrifying yet seductive, full of false promises of salvation. Juvenel sniffed.

'Can anyone smell perfume?' he said.

Two dozen gaunt faces stared back.

'Please, Juvenel, shut it off now,' said Danakan. 'The whispering is upsetting the men.'

Juvenel glanced at the admiral's face and wished he had not. It glowed sickly white in the dark corridor, and his eyes were unnaturally wide.

'I can only agree,' said Juvenel, attempting to project enough calm to cover Danakan's nervousness. If Danakan had his courage, he would have ordered him to silence the vox, not asked. 'I will check every fifteen minutes.'

'Perhaps Lord Dante has come for us,' said Chorkin. Her young face shone with hope beneath the grime and sweat.

'He's taken long enough. It's been a week,' growled Tephis. 'What have they been doing all this time? Sitting in their thrones and sipping wine while we die here?'

'I shall take it that this encounter unnerved you, sergeant. But I warn you, know your place,' said Elmor harshly. 'Even the admiral wouldn't question Lord Dante.'

Elmor stared at Tephis until he looked down.

'My apologies, sir,' the man muttered. 'I've had a fright, that is all. I shall watch what I say.'

'Don't argue, men. We should pray that it is them,' said Danakan. He affected an air of insouciance that just about passed muster, but only just.

Juvenel frowned to himself. Tephis wasn't the only one close to losing his nerve.

'Let's move on,' Juvenel said. 'We shall see if we can find

their signal. If the Blood Angels can help us retake our ship, we'll get out of here with our honour intact as well as our lives. That's something worth fighting for.'

Although Dante's splinter force was in constant communication, no vox warning came when they encountered the foe, nor was there any indication that their signals were being suppressed. The sound of gunfire alone signalled their advance party was under attack.

'We are ambushed. Move up to engage,' Dante said. The Axe Mortalis crackled in the stale air as he upped the output of its disruption field.

The Space Marines ran down the corridor towards the noise of battle. A domed chamber opened up ahead, where several corridors joined. Shrines were set under arches between the corridor mouths.

'A midship temple,' said Dante. 'The kind of place the Neverborn enjoy profaning.'

The two scouting Intercessors had reached the far side of the room before being set upon. The flash of their bolt rifles flickered, periodically driving back the dark. At first it seemed their brothers were shooting at nothing. There were no returns in their helms, and their threat indicators hovered uncertainly at the edges of their displays, awaiting an enemy to lock onto.

A dark shape wrapped itself around one of the Space Marines.

'The shadows. They are under attack by the shadows,' said Dante. 'Illuminate them.'

Stablights fixed on black shapes speeding around the room. When caught in the full beam of the light they keened and attempted to flee. They appeared wet, like oil, until they escaped the light and slipped into the dark places of the chamber, where they became impossible to tell apart from natural shadow.

'They do not like light,' said Dante. 'I shall see how they enjoy my axe.'

He ignited his jump pack and thrust upwards, lofting himself close to the apex of the dome, then came down in a perfectly controlled descent to the aid of one of the battle-brothers. His Sanguinary Guard followed him, slicing into the streams of darkness in the air.

Dante aimed a blow at the thing wrapping itself around his warrior.

The Axe Mortalis cleaved the shadow. There was no resistance to the blade, but the power field reacted as if the mass were solid, and the shadow screamed. It recoiled from the Chapter Master, coming free from the battle-brother as it did so, then lunged for him with whipping pseudopods. Where they lashed Dante's armour, the golden ceramite smoked.

Dante leapt backwards on twin blades of flame. The Perdition Pistol gave a roaring cough. The shadow took the hit, and spread wide, then drew itself back together and flew at Dante.

The rest of the force emerged into the chamber, filling it with their fury. Rhacelus and Mephiston came forth, casting bolts of psychic power at the things attacking them.

Everywhere the shadows dived down onto the Space Marines. Bolt weapons roared, but the micro missiles they fired passed harmlessly through the beings. Shadows wrapped around Space Marines in deadly embraces, lifting them off the ground and smothering them in darkness. Plasma did a little better, the intense light the Hellblaster guns gave out driving back the shadows.

But the might of the Librarius was of a different order, and where the ruby light of their psychic bolts went, shadows died.

'Dante!' Rhacelus shouted. He raised a hand glowing with the power of the warp.

Dante dove out of the way. A lancing red light struck the shadow squarely in its middle. It wailed and fell, hitting the floor with real weight.

Dante landed, his golden boots ringing on the floor. He approached the shadow writhing on the ground. It was taking form, becoming something else.

Black wetness split like a birthing sac. A pale-skinned daemon rose from the steaming mess, black, pupilless eyes full of longing hatred fixed on the Chapter Master, and it screeched through a lamprey-toothed maw, before launching itself at Dante with a serrated claw held out to decapitate him. It was supernaturally fast, beyond the reflexes of even the Adeptus Astartes to follow.

But Dante was the greatest of them, with a millennium and more of combat experience. He fired before the outreached pincers could end his life.

A roaring hit from the Perdition Pistol annihilated the creature's upper half. Backward-jointed legs tumbled to the ground. The remains bubbled, hissing vapours, sinking into the gaps between the deck plating.

'Daemonettes,' he said. 'The creatures of the Dark Prince.'

Polyphonic screaming came from all over the chamber as daemonettes shed their shadowed skin. They moved so fast, running along the walls, vaulting over the heads of their foes. Chitinous claws snapped at blood-red giants, carving furrows into armour and flesh, bringing wet vitae to stain the ceramite and make it glisten. Trails of bolts chased the creatures around the room, blowing holes in the walls and floor.

A daemonette advanced on an Intercessor. It danced through the stream of bolts coming at it, seeming to skip through space in horrible, jerking movements that contrived, somehow, to appear graceful. The Intercessor's gun ran dry, and he cast it aside, simultaneously drawing his combat knife. Few warriors could hope to beat the daemon's speed. It crossed the eight feet separating them in a flash of pale skin, skewering the warrior through his midriff and ripping upwards, opening armour and hardened ribcage. Glistening ropes of viscera spilled out. Still the Space Marine fought as the creature rode him down, its clawed feet in his guts.

Rhacelus was surrounded by the creatures, fending them off with a glittering golden shield conjured around the end of his force staff. His warp-touched eyes blazed through his eye lenses, shining with undeniable power on the creatures. The light caressed smooth curves and soft leathers, highlighting the daemons' savage beauty, and arresting Dante's gaze.

'The beasts of Slaanesh cloud the mind,' Dante said to himself. He shook off their allure, leaping into the air with a burst from his jump pack. The sudden lurch as he took to the air tugged hard at his wounds, but he bit back the pain. 'I fear no daemon glamour,' he shouted. 'I am a son of the Great Angel. Look upon my face and see the wrath of Sanguinius live again!'

The psy-projectors in his mask amplified his voice so that it boomed like that of his demigod father. His shouts struck terror into mortal soldiers, deafening them physically and shocking them psychically. The daemonettes suffered a far greater effect. Dante's righteous rage slammed into them as surely as a blow, sending them reeling and screeching from Rhacelus.

Dante clanged down next to the Epistolary. 'The daemonkin are vulnerable to our weapons, but they are faster and deadlier in this form. We must get out of this chamber,' he said. 'That way.' He pointed his axe towards the far door. 'Masters of the Librarius, clear a path for us.'

Rhacelus nodded. 'Aye, my lord.' He passed his staff from one hand to the other. Ruby flames burned around his hands.

'It shall be done,' said Mephiston. His eye lenses glowed with psychic intensity.

'Company, prepare to advance,' Dante said. 'Engage at distance. Resist the urge to fight with the foe at close quarters. Beware the thirst. Shoot them down where you can. Leave the rest to the Lords Mephiston and Rhacelus.'

The Intercessors formed up on Captain Antargo, his orders and warnings forging them into a fluid firing line even while the daemonettes tried to assail them. Disciplined volleys of fire drove the creatures back, but the Space Marines could not force a way through by martial might alone.

'There are more of the foe incoming,' Antargo voxed. His statement was undercut by evil laughter ringing in the Space Marine's vox-beads.

'Now,' said Dante.

Mephiston and Rhacelus handled the destruction allotted them according to their preference. Rhacelus conjured up a storm of ruby lances that he flung at the daemonettes. Each one thrown looped about to chase its target down. When they hit, the creature impaled let out a dreadful shrieking as it was consumed by crimson fire, and exploded violently, showering the room with gore that evaporated into black smoke.

Mephiston moved into melee range, drawing his great sword, Vitarus. Ruby flames licked up the blade. Psychic power coursed over his limbs, shifting him beyond the run of time and granting him incredible speed. Daemonettes came at him in streaking blurs, but he was faster, evading their blows, channelling power from the warp into Vitarus and cleaving the daemons into nothing.

'Forward!' commanded Dante.

The Space Marines followed their Librarians, cutting a swathe through the creatures in the chamber as they advanced. Hundreds more shadows were pouring out of the tunnels leading into the way temple, and once within, split open, birthing further monsters. Creatures of hideous beauty rose from shadow-sacs, steaming with perfumed fluids.

Mephiston moved with a duellist's grace, his sword never still, his aim never faltering. Every blow sent another daemonette screaming back into the warp, and was ready to be followed by another blow, and another, so that the Chief Librarian was hidden by a wall of crimson flame that flickered with each unlife taken.

Rhacelus followed close to Dante, hurling his spears into the tunnels as he advanced. They pierced dozens of creatures and shadows each before fizzling out. Their light caused the shadows to fly back from their passage, and the daemonettes to wail and cover their soulless eyes. Rhacelus' powers opened up channels in the daemonic host that the Intercessors and Hellblasters were quick to exploit, switching their targets with incredible discipline, widening the lanes carved by the crimson lances, and felling the onrushing creatures.

'They have poor purchase on this realm,' Rhacelus said. 'Their bodies dissipate as soon as they are slain. There is little of the warp to sustain them. The more we kill, the weaker they will become.'

Mephiston spun around, cleaving a dozen of the creatures down, then leapt high, borne aloft by a pair of wings edged with red light. Androgynous figures leapt at him, trying to claw him down, but he held out his sword, and called down a lightning strike of ruby blasts that slew them all.

Dante fought alongside the Third Captain. Antargo's bolt pistol spat death. His sword cleaved limbs from bodies. Dante slew his share, using his armour's weight and his jump pack's thrust to bowl knots of the creatures down, finishing them with his axe and his pistol as they fought to untangle their claws from one another.

The white ceramite wings of the Sanguinary Guard cut though a rising mist of black vapours. The Blood Angels were most of the way across the chamber, but still in danger of being swamped. Mephiston charged on ahead, dragging with him veils of lightning and power, blasting aside the thin cordon of daemons barring their exit.

'Now! Now! Hurry!' Dante shouted, his psychic amplifiers roaring out his commands. He was becoming uneasy. Mephiston's display of power tugged at something deep inside him. He could sense it in the others, the first stirrings of the Thirst, the first calling of the Rage.

The Space Marines ran. The Sanguinary Guard formed a rearguard, protecting the backs of their fellows until, in a tempest of witchfire, plasma streams and bolt explosions, the last of them had crossed the final yards of the chamber, and had begun the descent down the tunnel at the other side. A half-squad of Intercessors turned about, loosed a three-shot burst, then bowed down, allowing the Sanguinary Guard to swoop in over their heads to the centre of the group. The Intercessors then stood and fired backwards as the party moved downwards, obliterating daemons as they attempted to follow them into the tunnel.

Mephiston and Dante slew the last two daemonettes themselves, force sword and power axe sending them screaming back into their master's exquisite hells. Mephiston slowed to human speeds, the lightning crackling from his armour fizzled out, and he extinguished the fire wreathing his sword.

'We are close,' he said.

CHAPTER SEVEN

A GENEROUS OFFER

They moved at a steady pace towards the lifter nexus. The corridor was wide enough only for three men abreast. With the Intercessors standing shoulder to shoulder and putting out a solid wall of shot, it did not matter how fast the daemons were. Their every sortie failed. The corridor echoed with their dying screeches. They became unwilling to attack. The angels of death taught the daemons caution.

'I feel the breach,' said Rhacelus.

'The locus is ahead,' said Mephiston.

A hot wind blew up at the Blood Angels, carrying with it the sickly stench of rot inadequately masked by perfume. The choruses of whispers swelled in crescendo on the vox, dying away into fractured laughter.

'It stinks of death,' Antargo said. The Space Marines closed their breathing grilles in a brief burst of metallic scraping. 'Throne, I can still smell it.'

The shrill hunting cries of daemonettes called after them, but the creatures came no closer and gunfire abated.

The Space Marines slowed. Stablights mounted under their guns played over walls running with mucus. A soft lilac glow crept up the corridor to meet them. The scent of musky perfume intensified. A gentle moaning came to them.

Antargo punched a sequence into the keys of his wrist auspex. 'I do not know what you sense, Brother Epistolary, or you, Lord of Death, but I believe we have discovered the crew,' he said. 'I have a massive bio-sign ahead.'

'What is it?' said Dante. 'Are they all there?'

'It is unclear,' said Antargo. 'One reading gives me thousands of hearts beating. Another suggests none.'

'Go carefully, fire only when sure of your targets. Our ammunition is dwindling,' said Dante. 'Isolated in time like this, we have no chance of resupply.'

The way became slippery with marbled slime. It had no obvious source, emerging from the metal itself. It reeked of heavy, florid perfumes. Music struck up ahead of them, sounding as if at a great distance that rapidly closed. Cymbals and drums played frantic percussion to a tune plucked out of screaming harps. Sighing songs halfway between ecstasy and pain played against them discordantly.

The light, music and perfume grew stronger, making the Blood Angels' senses ache. By the time they emerged into the lifter nexus their auto-senses were struggling to compensate.

The rear third of the *Dominance* was a collection of towers that rose up together like a small city. The lifter nexus was situated on the ship's spine at the base of the foremost tower. A number of converging ways came together there, and the nexus included a major stop for the vessel's aft-to-prow transit lines. There were wide platforms that allowed the raising of stacks of containers from deep in the holds up to distribution hubs, and banks of smaller cars for the transportation of personnel. It was one of the great arteries of the *Dominance*, a place where men and supplies could quickly pass from one place to another, vital to the operation of the ship.

Designed as a large, vaulting space, the nexus was crisscrossed with raised walkways. Its ceilings were ribbed with steel vaults, and ornate buttresses reinforced the inner walls. A large part of this architecture was obscured.

A pillar of living flesh hundreds of feet tall occupied the centre of the shaft. Save where it intersected with bridges carrying roads over the nexus, it stood unsupported, holding itself up with hydraulic pressures that made it throb. Liquid slicked its sides, and the smell of perfume became almost overpowering, even through the Space Marines' void-sealed armour.

Antargo's auspex trilled the tinny hymns of bio-detection. He shut it off.

'The crew,' said Antargo. 'By the Emperor, that thing is the crew!'

Arms and legs hung from the sides of the column like the cilia that crowd the human gut. Thousands of eyes blinked in rippled patterns, so many that when they moved to look upon the Blood Angels, it could be heard as a sticky rustling.

The music grew louder. The screeching and laughing of daemonettes came down at them from above and across the shaft. Hundreds of them appeared, lining every bridge and balcony. They stared at the Space Marines.

'This is a trap,' said Dante.

'It is,' said Mephiston, 'but of what kind?'

The daemons hissed in unison, the noise rising and falling with no reference to the screaming tune. They rattled their claws, clacking them together or rapping them on the metal of the ship. The whispers on the vox merged with their chant.

'Iii-isss. Iiii-issssssss,' they said.

The music grew in volume, agonised cries played as a tune, drums rumbled.

'Kyyy-rrrrissssss, Kyyyy-rissssssssss,' they chanted. They began to dance, circling each other and crashing their claws together in strange courtship.

Mephiston looked up at the tower of flesh. The surface undulated with deep movement.

'What are they saying?' said Daeanatos.

'Kyriss. One of the greater servants of the Dark Prince,' Mephiston said. 'It is coming. I sense it.'

'We should never have come here,' said Antargo. 'Form a circle!'

The Space Marines faced outwards, guns pointing in every direction. Daemonettes emerged from the tunnels leading into the transit nexus. They were thin, insubstantial things, streaming dark vapours.

'Look! We have a chance,' said Rhacelus. 'They are struggling to maintain themselves. Their hold on the materium is weakening further. They will be easy to kill.'

'I am not sure,' said Mephiston. 'Their master feeds off them to manifest. Once it is through, they will become strong again.'

'Kyriss! Kyriss! Kyriss!' The chants of the daemons became louder, more exultant. Whole sections of the unholy congregation were dancing now, hurling themselves around with increasing abandon, leaping and whirling, claws crashing, all the while chanting, 'Kyriss! Kyriss! Kyriss!' They fell upon one another, disported with each other, killing in their ecstasy. 'Kyriss! Kyriss! Kyriss!'

'Let us fight our way out now, while they are enraptured,' said Antargo.

'We stand here. I will send this horror back to its lord in pieces,' said Dante. 'We do not run from daemon, xenos nor man.'

Rhacelus put up his hand to his helm and grunted in discomfort. The crystalline matrix of his psychic hood flared. 'It arrives!'

A new voice crooned softly over the racket of the daemons.

'KYRISSSSSSSSS,' it moaned, soft as a lover, loud as a god.

The pillar of flesh convulsed and spasmed. Thousands of mouths opened in its towering flanks and screamed in perfect harmony. A point of red appeared halfway up the pillar's length. Blood dribbled out, turning into a rivulet of crimson, then a fall. A huge black claw punched outwards and sawed down, opening the stolen, merged flesh of the crew. Blood gushed to the ground. The claw drew back within. Skin tented around its tip as it pushed out, before splitting again along the glossy black of its point. A second claw followed, opening up ragged slits a dozen feet high in the side of the column.

'Kyriss! Kyriss! Kyriss!'

The daemonettes were slaughtering each other, crying with joy as they died upon each other's claws. Their essences streamed upwards as smoke, and were sucked towards the quivering shaft of flesh.

The claws began a frenzied stabbing, ripping chunks out of the column. Long peels of skin and muscle rolled down the side. A pair of enormous hands scrabbled at the sagging lips of the wound, found purchase, and pulled.

A long, bovine head the size of a Space Marine and crowned with sweeping horns forced its way out. Shoulders struggled after, the claws stabbing and rending to make the hole bigger.

The daemon pushed at the gap, its long tongue whipping about its muzzle. It lowed with the effort, until it reached a crucial point, squirmed free, and came out in a rush of blood and gore.

Kyriss turned its tumble into a graceful fall, upper arms held over its head, the lower, more humanoid pair pushed together as if in prayer. In this pose it landed with a resounding boom some way forward of the Space Marines' position, crushing some of its ecstatic worshippers under giant, booted hooves.

'I say we kill this thing, right now,' said Daeanatos.

'Open fire,' said Dante.

At once, the Space Marines blasted at the daemon. It grinned, showing broad, perfect teeth set with patterns of jewels. With clenched fists it walked slowly forward, deliberately setting itself into the storm of bolt-rounds. They exploded inches from its skin, consumed by golden flashes and chimes of haunting beauty. Puffs of scent accompanied every detonation. Flashes of glorious vistas danced in the fires before the Blood Angels' eyes.

Vapours drawn from the daemonettes streamed into the greater daemon. Blood flowing from the column nourished it. It swelled, its muscles filling out, its body gaining mass and solidity, becoming more real with every passing second, all while the fury of the Blood Angels battered against its psychic shields. As it approached, blood sank away into flesh, revealing skin the colour of pale roses. Its filthy loincloth unstuck from its legs and fluttered clean with a waft of lavender scent. Black leather boots drank in their coating of gore and gleamed. The rings piercing the beast's flesh flashed with sudden brilliance. Then it was soft, free of blood, its tattooed skin revealed, its pierced breasts uncovered of gore, its manicured nails perfect. Fresh lacquer gleamed on lobster claws in exquisite, maddening patterns. The music reached a climax and, celebrated by a chorus of screams, Kyriss came to a halt and bowed low in a complicated fashion, pushing one beautiful leg out and dropping low on the other, its four arms spread wide, fingers gyrating to conduct the applause of its servants as it brought its dance to an end. Still the Space Marines fired on, their weapons next to useless.

Kyriss drew itself up. It was huge, heavily muscled, wildly handsome and gorgeously ugly. Its movements were feminine. Its stance was masculine. It was neither male nor female nor a mix of the two, but both at once, and to the utmost degree. Its presence stirred half-forgotten desires in the minds of the Blood Angels. It tugged on the ribbons of the Red Thirst.

'Good day, little angels,' it said, amused and offensive, warm and damning. Its voice was honeyed poison. All who heard it knew it for death, and wanted to hear more because of it.

The daemon surveyed Dante with high amusement as his men's rounds and plasma streams exploded harmlessly around it.

'Flecks of metal and chemical fires. Do you think these things can harm me?' it said. *'I am one of the six handmaidens of She Who Thirsts. Enough!'*

It clashed its hands together. Bolts stopped mid-air. Plasma streams were frozen. Its servants halted in their orgy of violence, made statues delivering killer strokes or licking the life fluids of their fellows off their bodies with serpentine, barbed tongues.

Dante and Mephiston alone were unaffected. Mephiston raised his hand to banish the sorcery, but Dante stopped him.

'Wait,' Dante said.

'That's better,' Kyriss chuckled. The bells hanging from its

horns rang prettily. *'You must be the Great Dante, the aged wretch who became king of half the galaxy. How old you are. How wrinkled and unattractive. Truly time is cruel to mortals. I apologise. I did intend to come to you some time ago, Lord Dante, but mortal years are hard to judge. I quite lost track. But here I am, Kyriss the Perverse, Keeper of Secrets of the six great lusts, king of pleasure, lord of longing, queen of desire, general of the fifth host of Slaanesh.'* The god's name echoed around the hall. The eyes upon the bleeding flesh pillar fluttered.

'All I see is another preening, misbegotten warp spawn,' said Dante.

A flicker of disappointment crossed the beautiful, taurine face of the daemon. It regained its arrogant manner quickly enough, but Dante saw.

'Oh well. Your time in this realm is running out, and so is mine. Aeons ago I brought your gene-father an offer of everlasting power and friendship from the Dark Prince, out of my lord's love and respect. For my pains I was beheaded, and my lady insulted, for my looks were ruined, and I was her favourite, even then.'

'If what you say is true, what was done once can be done again,' said Dante. 'Your posturing does nothing to make me fear you. I have stood against more impressive beings than you and prevailed.'

'My dear child, who will do this deed?' Kyriss chuckled. *'You are nothing. I remember the ages when gods walked the stars. Such days! Your species came so close to apotheosis. For the sake of a moment's hesitation, it was all gone, all lost, and humanity doomed.'* It held up its humanoid hand, and pinched thumb and forefinger together until a small gap remained between them. Through this space it peered

with one jewel-like eye. *'Such a tiny space between success and failure. You are misguided wisps of soul that name yourself as angels, ha! Weak, feeble, thirsty! But you...'* It pointed at the Lord of Death. *'You are Mephiston. You turned aside Ka'Bandha, the servant of the witless Blood God. He and I are old foes. I hope you made him hurt.'*

Mephiston looked to Dante. 'It is dangerous to hear this thing out,' he said.

'By their boasts do our enemies reveal themselves,' replied Dante.

'Do we now?' said Kyriss.

'Are you to fight us or not, daemon?' Dante said.

Kyriss crouched down, so that its snout was level with Dante's golden helm. *'Do you mind? I'm enjoying myself. Have you any idea how tiresome the chatter of these fools is?'* It waved its hand at its servants. *'They are so servile they laugh even when I mock them. If it is battle you desire, then I shall give it to you. My master-mistress is a generous patron. He-she only wants you to be happy. If it is death you crave, I shall give it to you – but first, my offer.'* Kyriss stood tall and spread all its limbs. *'Khorne is not the only god who covets your bloodline. Slaanesh dreams in his fragrant sleep how fine it would be to turn you to her cause. You are a brotherhood beset by temptations, the temptation of blood, the temptation of rage, and what is your artistry if not a tentative fumbling for excess? You are natural warriors for the Dark Prince's cause.'*

Kyriss wove beguiling gestures in the air, stirring the blood stink and perfume together.

'Alas you suffer, denying yourself the pleasures bound into your beings. So po-faced, so miserable. You, Dante, old and straight. Mephiston, the so-called Lord of Death, your soul is

barren of all but pomposity.' Kyriss clapped its humanoid hands together. *'It can be otherwise. Now is the great era of Chaos! This order you deem natural is nearly done. The empyrean floods into the realm from every corner. The boundaries between the warp and the materium fray to nothing. Your cause is lost. Soon you will all be dead, in body and in soul. This reality will sink into the great potentialities of the warp, but you need not die. The warp can be a heaven. Every dream you have ever had, every lust or want, can be sated there. All you must do is reach out and take my prince's patronage. Embrace the rage within yourself, embrace Chaos. I ask for one of you alone to join me in the warp and become Slaanesh's champion. If you do this, I shall free your kind from the Black Rage. Your curse will be lifted, and when the time comes you shall rule perfect principalities in Slaanesh's name. If that doesn't excite, then think of how many people you can save, not that that matters.'*

'Impossible,' said Dante. 'Nothing can cure the Rage.'

'It is impossible, but I can do the impossible as easy as...' It lifted its hand as if about to snap its fingers, then smiled and let it drop. *'As easy as that, anyway.'*

'If Lord Dante is so poor a reflection of our father,' said Mephiston, 'then why do you want him?'

Kyriss pulled an expression of mock confusion. *'Oh, you think I want him?'* The daemon laughed. *'Why would I want him?'* It laughed and laughed. *'Oh, I am sorry, forgive me. Please.'* It calmed. *'Oh my. No, what I want is–'* Kyriss uncurled a forefinger slowly and pointed it at Mephiston– *'you.'*

'No,' said Dante. The field of his axe flared bright.

'Cannot your Lord of Death answer for himself?' said Kyriss. *'Or are you the keeper of his tongue?'*

'I have heard enough. It betrays itself and its master's goals in being here. Answer it now, brother,' said Dante.

'Gladly.' Mephiston's eyes flared. Time snapped back into action. Once more, bolts flew on. Plasma splashed against Kyriss' psychic wards. The daemon winced.

'Very well, battle it is,' sighed Kyriss. *'So we'll start with you, Brother Dimus.'* It smiled at one of the Intercessors.

Kyriss lifted up its perfect, hideous hand, and clenched it tight.

Brother Dimus exploded with a crack of shattered ceramite and a spray of blood.

'It is a cliché, but apt to say – if you will not join me, then I shall destroy you all.'

CHAPTER EIGHT

WORSE ENEMIES

At the Keeper of Secrets' word, the daemonettes surged forward, leaping from the balconies and pouring from the tunnels. Immediately the Space Marines turned a portion of their fire upon them, obliterating those daemonettes nearest. They were so tightly packed it was impossible to miss. Bolts passed through several bodies, slaying them all, before finding a daemon substantial enough to trip the bolt's mass detectors. The daemonettes were weak, and the shrapnel from exploding rounds killed more.

Kyriss reached down to pull a scabbarded sword from nothing. Armour and a bandolier of knives appeared upon its person. It tugged the sword free, releasing a blade of bone scrimshawed with hundreds of wailing faces.

'The Sword of Six Thousand Miseries!' it roared and leapt into the middle of the Space Marines. They parted smoothly, but the beast caught one under its hoof, pinning him to the deck. It swept its sword down towards a scattering squad,

only for the blade to be intercepted by Dante's axe. There was a calamitous bang. Unnatural energy reacted with the pure, machine-given powers of the Axe Mortalis, and a chip of warp-born bone spun away from the impact, making the sword scream. Kyriss pushed down into the contact. Dante was forced to his knees.

'Feeble. So very feeble. I will win.' It raised a giant serrated claw. *'For a start, I have four arms. I shall add your miseries to the rest imprisoned in my sword.'*

Dante brought up the Perdition Pistol to fire. Kyriss' claw lashed down with impossible speed towards his face. Dante shouted out the cry of angels.

'For Sanguinius! For the Emperor!' His psychically amplified words smote the daemon with the pure rage of Sanguinius, making it reel. Dante turned his head just in time. The claw flashed past his face, shearing off his jump pack's right jet. Warnings rang in his helm. Kyriss' weapon slipped along the Axe Mortalis.

Dante hooked the axe's head over the Sword of Six Thousand Miseries and yanked back. His transhuman might was nothing compared to the strength of the daemon, and he was wrenched clean off his feet. He managed to thrust with his back foot enough to turn his tumble into a roll, flipping hard over his broken pack. Kyriss was on him in an instant, claws stabbing down. Dante fended one off, spun around and sank the head of his axe deep into the other. Chitin cracked. Pale fluids spattered him, making his head spin with their musky stench. He barely avoided a return blow from the sword. Kyriss would have finished him had not Rhacelus appeared at his side, staff upheld, and the daemon's blow slammed into a glittering shield of psychic force.

'Oh that's very tricky, very tricky indeed,' said the daemon

in annoyance. It swept its free hand across the air above the shield, which gave out in a shower of sparks. Rhacelus cried out and staggered back.

'Now. I am going to kill you. After that, I'll hunt you down in the warp and eat your souls. I've not got much to do this century.'

Dante slammed into Rhacelus' side, knocking him away. The daemon's sword sliced down between them, cutting into Dante's greave. The blow shook him, but the ceramite held.

'You are beginning to annoy me,' said Kyriss.

It raised its claws to strike again.

There was a flash of red light. A detonation Dante felt in his flesh rather than heard. Kyriss shrieked, a mixture of pain, surprise and perverse pleasure. Its claw fell to the ground. Kyriss held up the stump and stared at it in fascination. The cut was clean. Slowly its ichor rose and poured over the top like wine from an overfilled glass.

Mephiston flew over the daemon on wings of red light. His eye lenses blazed. Vitarus roared with crimson fire. Lightning stabbed out from him, and where it hit the daemonkind they screamed and burned.

'Ah!' sighed Kyriss contentedly. It licked fluid from its stump. *'An actual challenge.'*

'Leave the daemon to Mephiston, my lord,' Rhacelus said.

'He cannot defeat such a being on his own,' said Dante.

'He can,' said Rhacelus. The power pouring from the Lord of Death reflected off their armour. 'We need to get back.'

Mephiston dived at the daemon, his sword poised to strike. Kyriss brought its bone blade up to meet it. A flash of crimson sheet lightning blazed, dazzling them all. Dante expected Mephiston to be thrown back by the parry, but the swords remained locked, and Mephiston leaned in hard, energies arcing around him.

'What is happening to him?' shouted Dante over the crackling of psychic force. 'How long has he had such power?'

'There are matters we must discuss, my lord,' said Rhacelus. 'Perhaps not now?'

They staggered away from the thunderous fury of Mephiston's battle with Kyriss. Elsewhere, Space Marines fought with the daemonettes. Several of Antargo's company had fallen, but they held their lines. The enemy's numbers, seemingly endless before, were thinning rapidly. Some of them evaporated into nothing before they struck. Those furthest from the fighting were vanishing into the dark, never to return.

The circle of Space Marines opened to let Dante and Rhacelus within. The Epistolary staggered, and leaned hard on his horned staff, spent by his psychic exertions.

'The column. The damage to the column is weakening the daemons' hold,' Rhacelus panted. 'The power of the empyrean flows most strongly there. It is from there that the corruption comes.'

'Then we shall bring it down. Destroy the column!' Dante ordered. 'Fire support squad, target the column of flesh! Maximum power!'

The order spread through the force. Intercessors wheeled around to allow the Hellblasters to take up position. Their plasma guns flared with building energy, charge coils glowing electric blue.

Kyriss saw and lunged for the warriors, but Mephiston swooped down, interposing himself between them, Vitarus breaking more chips form the warp blade of the daemon.

'Fire!' shouted Dante.

Streams of incandescent gas roared from the Hellblasters. Their weapons' machine-spirits chimed loud alarms as their systems overloaded. One gun overheated, blasting out coolant that wreathed the bearer. He grunted in pain and cast the gun down, but enough fired on to do the work. The plasma streams sliced through the column, turning the melded crew into steam and purging their corrupted flesh with the blessed white heat of technology. Near the impact site, flesh cooked black, blistering red and raw further out. The beams snapped off. A huge gash had been burned into the flesh column, and it listed, the mouths in its side screaming with all-too-human voices, viscous fluids flooding into the lifter nexus.

'Again!' Dante fired.

The Hellblasters fired a second time. Guns vomited streams of burning plasma into the column, setting it ablaze. Oily black smoke billowed upwards, hiding the heights of the lifter nexus behind reeking clouds. Then the streams sliced through the column, and it fell amid a whooshing rain of burning fat.

A peal of awful thunder shook the ship from stem to stern. A tremendous wailing battered at their ears. Where the column had stood, a vortex opened. Black lightning fringed it. Colours of no mortal hue bled from the edges.

'Shield your eyes!' Rhacelus shouted. 'We stare directly into the warp.'

A great rushing gale of air raced from every quarter as the warp devoured the ship's atmosphere. The daemonettes exploded into writhing clots of black vapours that were sucked towards the vortex. Claws turned to wisps of nothing on armour plates.

'Back! Back! Everyone back!' Dante shouted. 'Back from the breach!'

The ship shook, tormented by the warp rift taking shape at its heart.

'We have moments before the ship is torn to pieces!' Rhacelus shouted.

Kyriss and Mephiston battled on, even as Kyriss was pulled towards the warp, hooves screeching on the deck as it fought to maintain its grip on reality.

'This has to end now, or we will lose the *Dominance* at the last stroke.' Dante glanced at his broken jump pack.

Rhacelus sensed what he intended.

'No, my lord!'

But Dante was already running for the daemon.

When Rhacelus tried to follow, a bolt of energy blasted him backwards.

Dante and Mephiston faced the daemon alone.

Mephiston flew about the daemon's head. Vitarus darted in to slash and cut. Red fire pulsed from his hands. The Lord of Death's aura of psychic power engulfed Dante's soul, pushing down his mind and tearing at the mental chains with which the commander had bound the Red Thirst. Blackness burned in Dante's blood, sending his hearts into a thundering gallop. Blood sang in his ears.

With the daemonettes vanishing, the others switched their fire to the greater daemon. Again they were foiled. Beams of plasma seared the air, splashing against the daemon's unholy protection. Bolts veered off course or exploded short of Kyriss' milky skin. But Vitarus could not be stopped, and cut through the glittering energies. The empowered edge of the sword rang off Kyriss' armour as often as not, but Mephiston was a cunning warrior, and when he could he avoided the scintillating plates, and cut deep wounds into the daemon's body. Kyriss' reach was long, and Mephiston was forced to close in. Kyriss plucked daggers from its bandolier and flung them with deadly accuracy. Mephiston swept Vitarus at them, smashing them into skeins of smoke that whipped away towards the yawning vortex. Kyriss leapt into the air, spinning with all its arms extended, and the Sword of Six Thousand Miseries skimmed Mephiston's face by a hand's breadth.

'Finish it!' Dante shouted. 'The ship will be destroyed if it is not banished.' The thirst had him. The words were poorly formed.

Kyriss leant gracefully aside and executed three quick parries of Mephiston's sword.

'Ah! The aged prince, come to fight me, tilting at windmills he cannot defeat.'

Dante accelerated, drawing back the Axe Mortalis to swing at Kyriss' ankle. The power field boomed as it encountered daemonic flesh. Kyriss howled. Milky fire burned around its empty fist, and it cast it at Dante. The commander stood his ground.

'I deny you and all your temptations!' he roared.

The arcane machineries of Dante's mask turned his wrath into a bolt of psychic force. The flames burst apart, and the shout hit Kyriss, staggering it back towards the gaping portal.

Dante ducked a piece of debris the size of a Dreadnought. Mephiston dived. Vitarus flared.

'For the Emperor! For Sanguinius!' Mephiston cried, and drove the point of his force sword deep into Kyriss' lower left shoulder.

Kyriss grunted. It punched at Mephiston, sending him spinning head over heels through the hurricane. His psychic wings vanished, Vitarus fell point first and stabbed into the metal, and Mephiston crashed down to the deck, where he was blown along by the wind. He righted himself and stood, boots locked to the metal. He clenched his fists, drew them back, and bright flames ignited around them. Light burned in his eyes. The vortex howled as Mephiston drew upon the raw power of the warp. A spiral of energy twisted out of the hole in reality and funnelled down into the Librarian.

An explosion of pure energy knocked Dante back. Kyriss wheeled its arms, its grace momentarily lost as it fought to regain its balance and stop itself falling into the rift. The psychic blow sent a wash of fury racing through the hurricane, hitting Dante after it impacted Kyriss.

Dante howled. The present receded. He was in another ship, another time, his body that of a demigod, knowledge of certain destruction foremost in his mind as he marched to confront his brother. Dante had glimpsed this before, the death visions of his blood. He saw through the eyes of Sanguinius. He teetered on the edge of madness, but his will was strong and he forced it back, refusing to give in to the pull of the past.

Dante blinked the sights away. He saw Mephiston before him. A giant, winged shadow, a black angel, stood behind him, its movements a perfect match for the Lord of Death's.

Mephiston and his shadow punched forward.

From his hands leapt the apparition of a gargantuan spear. Kyriss made a pass with its hands, forming a wheel of blasphemous letters before it, but the spear burst it asunder and pierced the monster's chest. The spear carried on until its full length had buried itself in the daemon, Kyriss' body swallowing it up to leave a smoking black wound.

Kyriss roared. It stood on the brink of the shaft, the vortex pulling at it.

'There is a darkness in your blood that cannot be denied!' Kyriss shouted. *'Today or tomorrow, you shall pledge yourselves to the gods in the warp.'*

Mephiston was glowing too brightly to look upon. The shadow was a towering shape behind him. The Lord of Death was losing control; his powers arced around him in wild bursts.

'This ends now,' Dante said.

He ran hard, and jumped high, swinging the Axe Mortalis around in a brutal stroke.

Kyriss raised its sword to block it, but Dante was not aiming for the weapon.

The axe chopped into Kyriss' wrist, severing it with the cracking boom of annihilated atoms. The daemon shrieked and recoiled, teetering towards the roaring portal leading to the immaterium. The sword, the daemon's hand still clamped about its hilt, wheeled end over end into the maelstrom.

Heedless of his own safety, and biting hard against the pain of the wounds in his chest, Dante leapt upon a guard rail and pushed off, bending metal with his armoured weight. He fired his remaining jump jet, leaning into the unbalanced thrust to keep his course true. He fired the Perdition Pistol into Kyriss' shoulder as he ascended, then used the momentum of his fall to bury his axe head in the monster's chest. The shock of the blow shook him, and he cried out. Scabs cracked. Blood trickled from his injuries.

His weight pulled him down. The axe slit open the monster from collarbone to crotch. Purple guts rained from its opened midriff, spilling all over the commander. Dante gagged on their obscene scent, and fell badly, landing on the deck in a shower of daemonic fluids. Decompression wind pushed him towards the vortex.

The mortally wounded Kyriss fell upwards. Dante clamped his feet to the ground and leaned into the roaring hurricane. He crouched down, letting the wind blast over him. Then Kyriss hit the indefinable barrier between the materium and immaterium. There was a cacophony of howls, and a single final boom.

The vortex shut with a deafening shriek. The hurricane stopped. But the storm was not over.

Mephiston was on his knees, bent double, his form shrouded in intolerable light.

Energy poured into him. His body glowed with uncontainable power. Sparks arced over the ground and skittered away.

'Mephiston! Mephiston! Lord of Death!' Dante pushed himself up from the ground with the head of his axe. 'Cease your sorcery!'

A building sense of danger emanated from the Chief Librarian. A barely visible skin of energy raced out from Mephiston. It passed over Dante. Immediately the twin curses of his bloodline devilled him again. A quenchless need for blood hit him. Flashes of a brother's face twisted by hatred rose in his mind. The plunging, final thrust of a clawed fist came to take his life.

'Mephiston!' Dante shouted. He staggered forward. The bubble exploded ever outwards, passing over Antargo's company. From his warriors came howls and cries Dante knew only too well. He pushed on through Mephiston's uncontrolled power. Sparks crackled over his armour's surfaces. Its machine-spirits wailed. Systems gave out. The need for blood nagged at him.

From the left came a figure in blue battleplate.

'Mephiston!' Rhacelus was marching forward, his staff glowing with counterspells, pushing through the storm of power around the Chief Librarian. Mephiston turned to look upon his friend, and a bolt of ruby lightning passed between them, blasting Rhacelus from his feet and slamming him into the wall.

The Lord of Death shook. He looked up at Dante. His helm lenses glared too brightly to look into. The psychic hood built into his collar failed, crystals shattered, and smoke streamed from his back. His helmet's lenses burst. Dante heard the ring of weapons in a battle ten thousand years done. Dark flames kindled in Mephiston's eyes, licking at his helm and turning it black.

'Help me,' Mephiston said. 'Help me.'

Dante was beset by sadness. Visions of ancient horrors threatened to drown him. His men howled with the agony of betrayal as their minds crumbled, but nothing was as terrible as the helplessness he saw in Mephiston's eyes.

'You... must... kill me!' Mephiston snarled.

'No,' said Dante. He spun the Axe Mortalis around in his hand, and with the poll of the axe shattered Mephiston's psychic collar, then with a second blow broke open his helm. The power field scorched Mephiston's face down to the raw muscle, but the psychic tumult ceased. The black fires went out.

Mephiston collapsed to the deck, unconscious.

From behind came shouting.

Dante's ears rang. He turned and saw his warriors wrestling with those whose minds were gone, screaming of betrayal and primarchs dead since the dawn of the Imperium. Rhacelus lay at the base of the wall. Antargo was struggling to control the afflicted warriors. Dante watched in horror as the Third Captain was forced to ram his power sword through the chest of one who could not be subdued.

The Chapter Master looked down at Mephiston's smoking body. Where unburnt, his skin had stretched and turned crimson. His fangs protruded so far from their sockets they dragged bleeding furrows in his chin. As Dante watched, they retracted, and the rubescence of Mephiston's flesh faded. But he was alarmed: Mephiston's appearance reminded him of the beasts that once dwelled in the Tower of Amareo.

'A darkness in the blood,' he said. He was tired. His blood still ran, lubricating his bodyglove and pooling in his boot.

He opened his vox-channel to the *Bloodcaller*, half expecting it to be silent, but the vox came clear and true, and Gallimimus responded himself.

'*My lord! We thought you lost.*'

'We were. Perhaps we still are.'

'*My lord?*'

'The ship is retaken. Lords Mephiston and Rhacelus have suffered injuries. Clear the embarkation deck of *Bloodcaller*. I want no brothers present when the Librarians are brought aboard.'

'*What manner of danger caused this?*' asked Gallimimus.

'A grave one. Inform the Librarius to prepare Mephiston's sarcophagus for his immediate internment. Send word to Baal to gather all members of the Council of Bone and Blood and the Red Council that can be recalled,' said Dante. 'Inform the ship logisters to formulate a plan to recrew the *Dominance* and get it under way. As soon as it is done, we shall depart. There is no time to waste.'

CHAPTER NINE

A PROBLEM OF FAILURE

There was the odour of roasting flesh. Danakan was never free of it. He smelled it every time he drew a breath. It clung to him no matter how often he had his uniform laundered or how often he washed himself. The smell followed him about, condemning him. He knew it was all in his mind, that nobody else could smell it, yet part of him feared it was apparent, and the others *could* smell it, and that somebody someday would turn around and point the finger of accusation.

You let them die.

That happened in his nightmares, right after he relived the event. It happened every night without fail; he saw the crew alight like candles, fat running from screaming faces in the plasma storm. Eyes cooking in their heads. He told himself they were quick deaths, and they were, but it didn't help.

He saw them in the day. Every time he blinked. Sometimes when his eyes were wide open. He saw them in the *Dominance*. He smelled the crisping flesh. He heard the screams.

They drowned out Juvenel's voice when he asked him for direction. They made him slow. Even when the pale-skinned warp things came bursting out of the shadows and attacked his men, he found it hard to pull the trigger, he found it hard to aim. Even when bladed forearms punched through human bodies and tore them in half, spraying red into the black, lightless ways of his ship, the smell, the sights and the sounds of the firestorm overwrote the horror of the present, blending with it. Terror should lend urgency to a man's actions. In the past fear had given him the edge he needed. It had toughened him. Now it paralysed him. Old screams blended with new screams, and there was nothing he could do.

The things came out of the dark, shrieking and singing and stabbing. Their scent made him dizzy, and that was when the burning faces started dancing in the dark. His dead crew were laughing as they melted. Something came at him through the accusing throng of the dead. A ruby beam of light took its head off, and it fell at Danakan's feet.

Then Juvenel was shouting at him. There were shots going off everywhere, men dragging at him, trying to pull him back. The group Juvenel had so carefully shepherded was being torn apart. They were all going to die.

But they didn't.

Booming guns opened up, obliterating the warp xenos. Rocket flare from bolts lit up the way they were trapped in. Pale bodies detonated with ecstatic shrieks. A warrior in blue marched forward between his brothers, pale flames around his head and hands. The xenos things could not stand before him, and then, and then...

'Lord Admiral Danakan?'

There was a pulse of something awful radiating out from deep in the ship. A shadow that curdled his very blood. The flames around the warrior's hands burned with unbearable intensity. He fell, red fire burning from every armour joint, just like his crew, ablaze and dying.

The dead warrior's name scroll stuck in his mind. Peloris.

'Lord admiral?'

A hand touched his shoulder. Inside, Danakan recoiled, but his body remained passive, pliant and dull as clay.

He looked up. He blinked heavy eyelids. An earnest Blood Angels thrall looked down on him.

'My lord, are you unwell?'

Danakan managed a smile. It felt slippery on his face, as if it were made of ice and balanced unsurely upon his skin.

'Trials of battle, I'm afraid. I'm a little tired, that is all,' he lied.

'Very good.' The thrall stood back. 'I apologise for the wait, my lord.'

The thrall's voice was distant and indistinct, like the murmur of a river out of sight. Danakan's vision swam and refocused, taking in the ornate antechamber he waited in. He had been there for twenty minutes at least, but he felt like he were seeing the gilded angels and triumphal paintings for the first time. The way into Dante's state room was open. The thrall indicated he should stand.

He got up and hitched his sword back onto to his belt and adjusted his pistol. The thrall bowed.

'This way, my lord,' the thrall said.

The smell of roast meat wafted out, accompanied by the sound of agonised screams. Sweat sprang up on Danakan's face. His stomach contracted into a tight, heavy ball. He had little taste for meat any more.

'Dinner is served,' said the thrall.

The tinkling thrum of harps played him in.

'Lord Admiral Danakan, I thank you for coming.'

Dante was out of his armour. Danakan realised straight away how ridiculous it was to be surprised by that. He was much older looking than Danakan expected. Huge muscles moved beneath his simple robes of red and black, and his hands were smooth, but his hair was long and snow white, and his face had a weather-beaten look. Lined and careworn, as if sculpted by the wind. If he were a normal man, it would have been the face of a farmer or a sea captain in the last years of life. But Dante was not a normal man.

'I thank you for inviting me, my lord.' He essayed a stiff bow. The tall brocade collar of his dress uniform rubbed at his neck. The chafing irritated his skin, made worse with his fear sweat.

'Please, join me,' said Dante.

There was a long banqueting table of white stone supported on fat legs of gold. A dozen candelabras, each with nine arms, stood on the table, bathing the room with gentle light. The scale of the table impressed Danakan, and he was a man well used to Imperial grandeur. Enough seats for fifty transhumans, a hundred mortals could have dined there, but only two places were set, away at the far end, facing each other. An ornate carver chair dominated the head of the table, its back beautifully decorated with the commander's personal heraldry and stylised letter Ds, but Dante had opted for one of the normal seats. The chair opposite had been replaced with one scaled for an unmodified human being, though identically styled to the rest.

Blood thralls came forward from shadowed alcoves to take his gun and sword. Another removed his coat and gloves and bore them away. Danakan was mildly surprised to find a couple of steps by the chair's side so he could mount it. They were necessary, for the table was high. He took his place. His plate and utensils were all made for mortal hands. Dante's were huge, and in the tall chair with his small cutlery, Danakan felt like a child permitted to dine with his father. Dante noticed, and smiled.

'I apologise if your place setting seems undignified. We always have this problem when we entertain those who are not of the Adeptus Astartes.'

'The alternative would be to have you squatting on the floor, and that would be far worse, my lord.'

'I have dined in less favourable circumstances than that,' said Dante. 'I thank you for your understanding. I have been accused by others in the past that I wished to intimidate them.'

'Who would say such a thing?' There was a buzzing in his ears. Polished words came out of his mouth that didn't feel like they were his. Someone else was saying them. Meanwhile, the real him was arrested by the candle flames – in each a melting face danced.

'Those who are easily intimidated,' said Dante. 'You are not easily intimidated.'

'Perhaps, my lord,' said Danakan.

'There is no need for formality here, lord admiral,' said Dante. 'We are both leaders of men.'

'You are regent, my lord, of half the Imperium.'

'This is true, but you have commanded far more men than I for most of your career. I was lord to a mere thousand, and suzerain of a few sparsely inhabited worlds. Millions were yours to command.'

Danakan tried to smile. He was light-headed. The smell of cooked meat made him want to vomit. The screaming wailed. His damn collar itched so much.

'Your career is a dozen times and more the length of mine,' said Danakan.

Dante waved a hand. 'Nevertheless, you are not an insignificant personage. You and I are to work together in the service of the Imperium, so I would prefer us to be friends. Our Chapter is a brotherhood. Friendship and family bind us together far better than formality.'

'Then how should I address you, my... commander?'

'Dante will do. It is the only name I have now. I would prefer it. I grow tired of deference. I need men of strength. Men like us must be able to sit down together and look one another in the eye with respect and a sense of mutual responsibility. I cannot rule for the Primarch Guilliman in the Emperor's name if all men and women of the Imperium cower before me.'

'This is a great honour you do me. I imagine not many are invited to dine with you alone.'

Dante smiled ruefully. 'More from lack of time than sense of majesty on my part. Truthfully, were we on Baal now, you and I would eat with a hundred other men and women of importance. But here we are, waiting to return home. I have the time to speak with you alone. You and your ships are important to my plans.'

'It is difficult to look you in the eye, lord,' said Danakan. Dante's eyes were the colour of raw amber flecked with ancient blood. If one stared into them long enough, the deep history of the Imperium stared back.

'Then grow used to it.'

Danakan looked up. Sweat trickled from his brow.

'Is everything all right, admiral?' Dante asked.

'My given name is Seroen,' he said.

'Seroen.'

Danakan did not enjoy the way Dante looked at him. He knew. Danakan was sure of it.

'I see doubt in you.'

The words thumped into Danakan with the force of boltrounds. Panic grew inside him.

'I have rarely seen the Adeptus Astartes free of their armour,' he said, which was a half-truth at best. 'You are more imposing without it, than when battle clad.'

'Is that so?' said Dante. He beckoned to his servants. They brought two ewers of wine, also fantastically decorated. They were identical in all but scale, the same figures and scenes embossed into the silver, though one was sized for mortal needs, the other for those of a Space Marine.

'Yes,' said Danakan. He dabbed his face with his napkin. The cloth was the softest he had ever felt. The Blood Angels had a reputation for luxury that would have seemed decadent, were it not also widely known they made everything they used themselves. He tried another smile that hurt his face. 'This uniform is warm, I apologise. And I have not had much sleep these last months.' He could not speak of the true cause, the burning faces in the candle fires, and the screams forever on the edge of hearing, so he did not. He gulped at his wine, then, mindful of the commander's gaze, forced himself to slow.

'Forgive me,' said Dante. He called a young, handsome blood thrall to him. 'Colma, adjust the environmental controls for the admiral's comfort.'

Cool air blasted from hidden vents. It didn't help much.

Food was brought to them. There were steaks of meat and vegetables, and a thick gravy filled with fragrant fungi. Dante's plate was piled high by his servants. Danakan held up his hand as soon as he could while remaining polite. He couldn't face eating.

'So, admiral, let us leave the business of war and governance for a short time. Tell me about yourself. I would know as much as I can. You will command the fleets of Imperium Nihilus for me. It is good for men who will fight together to know one another. Let us leave the business at hand for a while.' Dante put a forkful of food into his mouth. His eye teeth were very long. He looked at Danakan expectantly.

Danakan could think of nothing worse. He wished to be left alone with his terrors. At least then he could allow himself to become numb. Then he did not have to speak, or to make any decision.

He forced himself to eat. The larder of the Adeptus Astartes was evidently well stocked, but each morsel tasted like ground bone, and he had to wash every mouthful down with wine. His stomach was tight, its juices painfully acidic. So he drank more. The wine helped numb his fears. The burning faces receded, but nothing could expunge the smell of burning flesh haunting his nostrils.

Nevertheless, he managed to speak, answering Dante's questions about his service and his life. He asked a few questions of his own in return, but Dante was intensely interested in what Danakan had to say, and deflected his own conversational gambits.

Danakan had once been a charming man. He had thought of himself so, and had been told he was by men under his command. It seemed a hollow sham. Now he knew he was a coward, had always been a coward. He had the idea he was a shell, with a lying image of another man projected onto the surface while he wept inside.

He told his life story, complete with well-rehearsed anecdotes and humorous asides. Dante was not given to mirth, but he smiled at Danakan's jests, and not solely from politeness.

As he slipped into his act, Danakan's nerves steadied. He ceased to sweat. His hands stopped trembling. But the terror never went away. He saw the burning faces reflected in the Chapter Master's intense eyes. He smelled their cooking flesh wafting off his dinner. Still he spoke of his youth on Piscea, of its boundless oceans and great sailing vessels. He spoke of his journey to the sector Naval Academia, his first command, his recent actions. It was a story he had told many times.

More courses came and went. For each, Danakan ate enough to be polite. Dante devoured mountains of food, so much that surprise penetrated the fug of terror clouding Danakan's soul; it was, he later thought, the first genuine emotion except fear he had felt in some time.

He glossed over the action at Teleope, where a single mistake had cost four hundred men and women of his command cadre their lives, describing it in the broadest terms only.

'You were becalmed at Teleope for six weeks after the battle?'

'Yes, my lord,' said Danakan. 'We took extensive damage, and hauled over to make repairs to the ships we could. We did not expect to make port for some time, and I deemed it necessary to be as thorough as possible.'

'That was wise,' said Dante.

'Maybe, but it was poorly timed. After that, the Rift opened, and the storms closed in. Our astropathic messages received no response. We entered the warp three times, but each time our Navigators were blind. There was no way through. After deliberation with my captains I ordered a real space course set for Retis, but it would have taken us a century to cross the distance. We are fortunate you heard us.'

'You are. Time is bent out of true by the Rift's opening. A week passed on Baal while years ran on elsewhere. It seems the same is true for you. Intelligence in this environment is hard to gather, and there is no indication it will become easier. Your message was but one of hundreds our astropaths have intercepted, lost fragments with no hope of reaching their destination. I do what I can to answer them all.'

'These are bad times,' said Danakan. The screams agreed. 'I have never encountered so many of these warp xenos, and their ability to take action at a distance has increased. When the xenos on the *Dominance* counter-attacked and slew your psyker, such madness coursed through us all. Terrible rage. We were fortunate your men weathered the psy-blast and finished the creatures.'

'They were daemons,' said Dante flatly.

Danakan hesitated. Knowledge of daemons was dangerous. He knew what they were. In the past it was politic to pretend otherwise. He took a risk.

'I know,' said Danakan. 'The term was proscribed but most of us within sector command were aware of the word, and what it described. There has been a policy of pretending not to know for many centuries. In our part of the Navy,' he added. 'I cannot speak of others.'

'We had best name them for what they are,' said Dante. 'Or else we will not be able to combat them effectively. Where once they assailed single worlds, now they bedevil whole sectors. As leader of Battlefleet Nihilus, you will need deeper briefings on the perils of the warp. I will not have those who serve me make war in ignorance.'

Danakan looked down, away from Dante's penetrating gaze.

'My lord,' he said. 'You offer me a great honour, but I must request that you consider another.'

Dante was silent. Danakan thought he would burst waiting for the commander's rebuke.

Dante was only curious. 'Why?' he said.

'Because I cannot do it,' said Danakan. He had not intended to confess. He washed the error of admission from his mouth with a gulp of wine. 'There. I have said it.'

'How so? You are the highest ranking Naval officer I have encountered since Lord Guilliman charged me with stabilising Imperium Nihilus. This dark half of the Imperium requires a rapid reaction fleet. The old Naval system is no longer suitable, until we establish some sort of order. I cannot think of anyone better for this role.'

'I cannot do it because I am no longer worthy,' said Danakan. He put his fork down. His meagre appetite had completely deserted him.

'Explain yourself to me.'

'I am afraid,' said Danakan. He looked into Dante's eyes again. The commander's expression was stony, yet not judgemental. 'I have not been entirely honest with you, my lord. I have lost my mind. I sit here and make conversation with you, but it is all a play... I...' His throat constricted. Tears prickled the corners of his eyes. 'I made a mistake. A manoeuvring error. The Heretic Astartes we battled at Teleope wounded the *Dominance*. The cruiser *Azimuth* came abeam at my ship while we were engaged with the grand cruiser *Kaimon*. They were so fast, good voidsmen, better than I.'

'They are Space Marines, you are not. The Red Corsairs have one of the largest fleets in the galaxy, and the skills to use it. It concerns me that they hunt north of the Rift, but you acquitted yourself well against them. You drove them away.'

'Most of their fleet was chaff, my lord. Stolen ships crewed by mortal men, but these two... They were something else. They caught me, burned right through the voids, and cut across the command deck. The *Eternal Blade*, my last command vessel, took a direct hit from the *Kaimon*'s ventral plasma casters. It opened the deck to the void and incinerated everyone on the bridge. I escaped only because of the safeguards built into my command station. I can still see them burning. Their skin peeling off, flesh running, and they were alive, screaming as they cooked. It was my fault. Now the screams and sights haunt me day and night. I lost good men and women. They had served me for years, some of them. I called some of them friends.'

Dante was silent. Danakan awaited his response fearfully.

'I understand,' said Dante eventually.

'You understand, my lord, I have seen death. But this, this was something else. This I saw first-hand, not through an oculus. The devastation was complete, and...' He picked up his fork and fiddled with it. 'It was my fault. I hesitated, only for a second, when I saw the *Kaimon* bearing down on us. For the first time in my career, I did not know what to do. I have replayed that moment over and over again, and if I had given the order for our starboard cannons to fire, I could have driven it off and given us enough time to power forward and escape without damage. But I did not. I froze, commander, and four hundred people burned alive.'

Dante stared at him, but Danakan could not stop his confession now he had begun.

'After the battle, I could have made another choice. The fleet could have moved on. But I could not. I compounded my earlier mistake. If we had had entered the warp before the tempest closed in, we might have made Port Harden. More ships lost on my account. More servants of the Emperor dead.'

'Do other men go through life without committing errors?' Dante asked.

'No,' said the admiral. 'But mine was egregious. I am no longer fit to command.'

'Who am I, lord admiral?'

Danakan looked quizzically at Dante. 'Lord Commander Dante, Chapter Master of the Blood Angels Chapter of the Adeptus Astartes, Regent and Warden of Imperium Nihilus.'

'I am. Therefore, I shall be the judge of whether you are fit to command or not. Leave us!' he called to his servants. 'Speak no word of what the lord admiral has said.'

The thralls departed as soundlessly as they had worked. The candles flickered when they opened the doors to go. Dante waited for them to be gone before continuing.

'You are afraid, Seroen.'

'I am,' he laughed bitterly. 'I am terrified.'

'This is good news.'

'In what way?' said Danakan, despair robbing him of courtesy. He took a deep breath. 'My lord,' he said. 'Forgive me. I am sorry. I am not myself.'

'Be at ease,' said Dante. 'I took no offence. We are allies, you and I. I mean to help you. You should not be afraid of your fear. Fear is nothing, admiral, all brave men feel fear.'

'It has unmanned me. What if I make another mistake? I could lose an entire fleet.'

'You will not, of that I have the utmost confidence. Fear is an enemy that can be conquered, Seroen. It is a ship you can break. It need not rule you. Feed it, and it will overcome you, face it, and it shall shrink away, and you shall wonder what these terrors were that made you weep in the night.' Dante lifted up his glass, turning it so it caught the light and sparkled. 'We know no fear, we Space Marines, so it is said.'

'Everyone knows this,' said Danakan. 'They are the words of the Emperor Himself. His promise to you, and the people you were made to defend,' he said, then added quietly, 'I envy you.'

'Envy of what?' said Dante. 'Of power? We have little. Envy of might? It is ours, for a while, before we die, but it is put always in the service of others. Envy of our lives? They are austere, and often short, and if long, no less full of conflict.'

'I envy your fearlessness, Dante,' said Danakan. 'You face all this, and you are not afraid.'

Dante shook his head. 'There are warriors among the Chapters who genuinely do not feel fear, but they are rare. To be genuinely fearless means you lose an essential part of your humanity. A warrior without fear is dulled to risk, and therefore to tactics. He takes no account of the limitations fear places on others. He can become cruel. This is one road to the ranks of the likes of the Red Corsairs,' he explained. 'The sentiments of humanity are complex and tangled with one another. You cannot remove one without affecting the others. We do not fear to die, or fear pain – these things are nothing to the Adeptus Astartes. We do not feel the terror that afflicts normal humans. We fear we will fail. We doubt. I doubt I can fulfil Lord Guilliman's mandate, but I am so commanded by the Emperor's last son, and so I will try. We are trained and changed and so made bold and careless for our own lives, but we know fear. Our advantage is that we have the weapons to slay it.'

'But you make no mistakes! Not like I did.'

Dante laughed. 'No mistakes? Do you know how many times the Blood Angels have come to the edge of extinction in the last thousand years? Do I see these incidences as my fault? Were they my errors? Perhaps. But I cannot dwell on yesterday's mistakes when tomorrow another thousand battles wait, and so I win more often than I lose.'

'How many times?'

'Four,' said Dante. 'Four times.' He filled his goblet again.

'That is sobering,' said Danakan. He took another drink of wine. The screams were quieter now. 'But I still do not think I can do what you ask of me, my lord.'

'You have commanded a fleet for over two decades with exemplary skill. You will again.'

'I wish I could agree.' Now his secret was out, Danakan felt weak, like his bones had been filleted from his body, and all that remained was a sack of fluid clad in a ridiculous uniform. He was covered in rank brocade and medals, but he felt naked, and ashamed. 'My skill is gone. I cannot think. I cannot sleep. I can make no decision, in case it leads to a similar outcome. I am paralysed.'

'Then you shall pretend not to be,' said Dante. 'If you can maintain the facade of conviviality, you can maintain the facade of authority. In every man is terror. This galaxy is full of dreadful things. A man's courage is measured by how he deals with his fear. You can do this,' said Dante. 'And you will, because you must. Men such as we do not have the option to be afraid. We do our duty, or we are nothing.'

'I understand, but–'

'Do you still wish to hide from your purpose?'

'I do not, but I cannot perform it.'

'Do you know how I became Chapter Master?'

'No, my lord.'

'Then I will tell you,' said Dante, 'and when you have heard you shall tell me again why you cannot do your duty.'

CHAPTER TEN

KALLIUS

The air smelled of dust and bodies trapped in the ruins, but Dante was grateful to be free of his helm. Guns had pounded Castrigatum night and day for the last six weeks. Without them the world seemed deathly silent.

A city should teem with life. This one was a corpse. No sound either human or machine broke the morning quiet. Dante's ceramite boots crunched loudly on fragments of rockcrete. Ferrocrete powdered by bombardment tickled his nose with its iron scent. Plascrete chunks glinted like volcanic glass.

Castrigatum was a tangle of debris. His toes clipped metal with plangent tolls. Wooden beams kicked aside sounded ideophonic notes. There was no way a man in power armour could move there stealthily. Streets and buildings had been rendered into a rough landscape. Debris-choked roads were linear valleys, the wreckage of buildings ridges cloaked in scree. In places they gleamed like star fields as shattered glass caught the rising sun. The wind stirred veils of dust up from the ruins. Dante's hair was dry and itchy with it. It ground against his teeth. It rubbed against his gums. His neck was raw with grit trapped under the soft seal, a persistent erosion of the flesh even his Space Marine body could not confound.

All of human life had been pounded into an undifferentiated mess. Very few objects retained a recognisable shape, and those that did leapt out at him, though all were covered in dust. A shoe. A bent spoon. A piece of machinery. An Emperor's Tarot deck. A burned-out groundcar half covered in stone blocks. The abandoned wrack of human lives abounded.

Before a tall mound made of fallen starscrapers, a doll lay atop a broken pillar face up, as if placed there. It was a crude representation of a female soldier, with hair of cina wool and lopsided features badly stitched on a tight cotton face. Dante paused and, after a moment's consideration, picked it up. The doll was a tiny thing in his ceramite gauntlets. He shook dust free, which was carried away on the wind.

He stared at it a moment. A poorly made thing, fragile, like the human body.

The screaming whine of engines in atmospheric mode had him looking to the sky. Into the dusty air, orange with the scattered light of dawn, a blood-red gunship rose, freeing itself by painful effort from planetary gravity. Exhaust shimmered in wavering columns. Dante felt the heat as a warmer breeze on the freshening air. As the engines' rising call ascended into the sky and faded, he became aware of distant shouts, and the sounds of industry on the other side of the collapsed row of buildings.

'Dante!' Lorenz shouted down to him from the hills of broken walls, his bass, Space Marine voice thinned by distance.

He cupped his hands around his mouth to better call. 'Where by the five graces have you been? He's waiting for you!'

Dante shrugged and tapped his ear.

'Turn your vox back on, then!' Lorenz did not care to hide his exasperation.

'Turn it back on, brother-captain,' Dante said to himself. Lorenz had never changed and likely never would. He was as cocky and over-confident as the boy Dante had first met atop the Angel's Leap on Baal Secundus. Although they had disliked each other on sight, war and time had forged a bond between them. Lorenz was his closest friend. Dante forgave him his lapses in protocol.

He set the doll down gently atop the broken pillar, smoothed its hair from its stitched eyes, and made the sign of the aquila over his heart, his head bowed in respect for all the dead of Kallius.

Only after that did he commence climbing the hill of tumbled stone.

As he crested the ridge the noise of men at work increased in volume. On the far side a landing field had been carved out of the wreckage. Hundreds of blood thralls were busy erecting temporary shelters and assembling strongpoints dropped by voidships. The sun climbed behind him, pushing out his shadow over the landing ground. Nearby, company banners snapped in the breeze above an observation post.

Another gunship was cycling up its engines, preparing to accompany a fat cargo shuttle up into orbit. Rhinos with the stencilled helix of the apothecarion rolled across roads between the landing pads, carrying injured brothers to be evacuated.

'Dante!' Lorenz clambered awkwardly over the broken rocks towards his friend. 'I've been looking for you everywhere.

Malafael's waiting for you.' He pointed at the observation post. Lorenz's armour had taken a couple of direct hits from an autocannon three days previously. The first had shattered his plastron and spun him about, the second had dented his reactor casing. His backpack still puttered noisily. 'Why did you turn your vox off?'

'Because.'

'That's no answer for me, and it won't sit well with Malafael either. Come on.'

They set out together along the ridge. The weight of their armour shoved slips of debris down the ridge, slowing them considerably.

'You should have come up on the far side. There's a path there, almost like you're supposed to go that way.'

The wind was rising with the sun. Dante's black hair blew out around his head.

'I needed a little peace. A moment of thought before we are called to fight again.'

'That's you, brother. I don't like these quiet times.'

'Don't worry, we will soon be called upon to fight again,' said Dante. 'One must grab the opportunities one is presented with to reflect upon the graces.'

Lorenz gave him a pained look. 'Honestly. Listen to yourself. You'd be a better Chaplain than a captain.' He winced and worked his shoulder. His armour grumbled. 'Emperor of Terra, I'll be glad to see the back of this place. What a miserable war.'

'We are pledged to protect the citizens of the Imperium. It is a misery when we must destroy them.'

'You know that's not what I meant,' said Lorenz. 'The people of this city were traitors. They received judgement and punishment.'

'Do you never wonder why they might have turned upon the Emperor's rule?'

'No, and nor should you. We do what we must because that is our duty,' said Lorenz. 'Though there's precious little glory in slaughtering terrified conscripts. There's been no challenge to this action since we wiped out the Sundered Blade.' He spat. 'Heretic Astartes. I grant that these common folk might warrant a little sympathy. I'd much rather have been killing more of those treacherous bastards. I hear the action's much better elsewhere in the cluster.'

They climbed upwards and came to the observation post, which was set on the highest point of the ridge, and clambered over a low wall of bricks sintered from the city's debris. They emerged onto a level area paved with huge blocks. The plasteel drop bunker that made the observation post sat beside this main plaza.

Malafael was waiting for them, his back to the busy landing fields, his skull helm in place as tradition demanded. He stared out across the levelled city.

The ruins stretched away for miles in every direction. Lone survivors of the bombardment jutted out like broken bones from the wastes. They were few in number. A range of blue hills rose beyond the city limits. The defensive facilities there had not escaped destruction. Their locations were marked out by blackened craters punched into the crags and fields of heather analogue.

'When I came here, that first day,' said Malafael, 'it was impossible to see the hills through this city. Seven hundred thousand souls dwelled here. Now look at it. When will humanity learn that as cruel as the hand of Imperial governance is, it is too heavy to be cast off.'

'Many people died here,' said Dante neutrally.

Another ship took off, thundering its way to the void.

'Are the ruins clear, captain?' said Malafael.

'They are,' said Dante. 'All the remaining population has been moved to the processing centres. There they must face the judgement of the Adeptus Ministorum and the agencies of the Adeptus Terra. Perhaps some will be spared. The most innocent, maybe. I hope so.'

'I look upon this ruin and it sorrows me,' said Malafael. 'But there is no innocence in mankind any more, Dante, not in the youngest babe or the most naive idealist, if indeed there ever was. The course to destruction was set for them the day they renounced the Emperor. We, as the righteous instruments of His justice, passed judgement. Now their fate is out of our hands. They will at least be fed and watered until they receive their sentences. How many of them have known a roof over their head since the rebellion began? Perhaps now they will see a measure of mercy, and regret what they have done.'

'I pledged to protect these people, not slaughter them,' said Dante.

'This is your first major action against a rebellious populace as a captain. It will get easier,' said Malafael. He looked upwards, where a flock of local aviforms flew towards the horizon, untroubled by war. 'Life has its ways. It will return here. Those who are deemed pure of heart will be permitted to live, though they may no longer be able to call this place home. Penal worlds await most of them. The nobility of this planet will be executed, those that survived the battle.' Malafael lifted up his hand and rested it on Dante's pauldron in a fatherly fashion. He had selected Dante to join the Chapter. They had grown close in the decades since.

'How goes your command of the Eighth Company?'

'They are a fearsome group,' said Dante. 'I miss the balance of the Fifth, but an assault company suits my temperament. When deployed en masse, there are few sights so glorious as their charge.'

'Personally, I'd have taken it as a kick in the gut,' said Lorenz. 'Fifth Captain has more sway on the council than Eighth.'

'You are as you are, Brother Lorenz, and that is why you remain a sergeant, when your brother here commands a hundred angels,' said Malafael. 'The word of the Fifth Captain outweighs that of the Eighth on some matters – yet the Lord of Skyfall is a more important position than Keeper of the Arsenal. So is the balance of power in the Chapter maintained.'

Lorenz shrugged. His armour complained with a series of piercing whines. 'Politics is not something I'm interested in. Just tell me where the enemy is.'

Dante gave his friend a hard look. Lorenz grinned at him.

'Where are we bound next, Chaplain Malafael? Have you any notice?' asked Dante. 'This region of the planet is secure, but the embers of war still glow here on Kallius, and elsewhere in the subsector the war goes on.'

'As it happens, I do have a message for you, lord captain,' said Malafael. 'I received word this morning that four battle-groups are inbound to the subsector. Millions of men under arms and three more Chapters have come to take up our burden and conclude this campaign. We have been relieved. We are to return home to see to our wounded and replenish our numbers. The Kallius war is over for us.'

Lorenz squinted against the rising sun. 'It's about damn time,' he said.

* * *

Shortly after Malafael's announcement, Dante received word from Chapter Master Remael that his company was to prepare for withdrawal. His men were scattered about the city, searching the ruins for hidden survivors, for among such groups the last insurgents concealed themselves. There were precious few. The guns of the Imperium had done their work well.

All through the day Blood Angels trickled into the landing zone. More ships came down from orbit. Dante prioritised the extraction of the Eighth's equipment first. The Bloodblades had numerous attack bikes, Land Speeders and other light craft permanently assigned to them, and a handful of tanks and heavy assault vehicles had been apportioned to them for the campaign. He also desired to get the company's Dreadnoughts off-world quickly. Men were easier to withdraw than machines, and although Dante did not expect a return to violence, the Codex Astartes said that peace was fleeting, and the assets of a Chapter were as valuable as its warriors. So the machinery went first, along with the gene-seed of the fallen.

Among the Bloodblades coming to the landing zone were warriors of other companies. Malafael remained in the role of Chaplain-Recruiter, and oversaw a contingent of scouts in the battle zone. There were half a dozen squads attached to Dante's command from the Seventh and Ninth, to grant the force a little tactical flexibility. All told he had one hundred and twenty warriors in the arena, three-quarters of his initial command. Forty were dead in the grinding campaign.

Groups of men in blood-red armour dusted with grey came into the camp around the temporary port. Dotted about were warriors in darker red. The dust made them look the same, covering over their heraldry. They moved the same way. They appeared part of the same throng, and were treated as brothers, for they were of the Blood, being battle-brothers of the Angels Numinous.

The landing field became busier as more support units of blood thralls arrived from orbit to help their masters. Warriors took the opportunity to see to damaged gear. Techmarines strode through the camp, searching out weapons and armour in need of their attention. Logisters took stock of supplies remaining to the company, down to the final round. Blood Angels laughed off grave wounds. Apothecaries made them take them seriously. After a time, food and wine were brought in and served under tarpaulins shading pale angelic skin from the sun. Men rarely free from war took pleasure in these hours. From some quarters laughter rose over the turbine whines and exhaust roar of voidships and the ringing clatter of men at work.

Dante worked with his thrall staff to catalogue his men and their supplies. In mortal terms, his force was small, nothing compared to the millions-strong armies of the Astra Militarum, but Space Marines had a mighty need for materiel. Everything made for or by them was of great value, and so had to be accounted for.

Safe in an open-sided tent, surrounded by loyal men in the middle of a fortified encampment overlooked by voidships in orbit, still Dante's warrior instincts would not rest. The half-heard purr of active fibre bundles approaching from behind made Dante tense, then smile and speak a name.

'Captain Toranis,' he said.

'There's never any creeping up on you, Dante.'

Dante turned to face his comrade. Toranis grasped Dante's arm, wrist to wrist.

'I am glad I have seen you again,' said Dante. 'It would have been ill-mannered for me to go without bidding farewell to the Angels Numinous.'

'I heard you were leaving,' said Toranis. His armour was a darker red than Dante's, and his skin paler, but Sanguinius' gene-seed had left its mark on both of them. They were beautiful, and physically similar in appearance. They could have been brothers. 'I thought I should say goodbye.'

'Time to prepare for another war,' said Dante.

A magna-transporter came down to land, its engines drowning out all other sounds from the world. Backwash from the engines buffeted the tents and set Dante's documents fluttering. His servants moved forward, putting paperweights in place to stop them flying from the table.

The Space Marines waited until the engine howls had dropped to tolerable levels.

'There is always another war.' Toranis glanced over Dante's work. 'By Terra, getting ready for them is a tedious business. I leave all this to my servants.'

'As is your prerogative. I like to know everything. It helps me formulate my strategies well if I know we're not going run out of ration bars on the third day.'

Toranis smiled. Ten long service studs were embedded into the bone of his forehead. 'And they say you're a dull one, Dante. I'll make sure your reputation as a warrior is properly known once you have departed.'

'You are to remain?'

'My Chapter started this. We are to finish it. Chapter Master Deren wants to see it through. Besides, we have lost a lot of our strength stopping this revolt. We've not the warriors to begin another war. We've barely enough to stamp out the last flames of this one. It will take us a long time to recover. We shall see it through to the bitter end then go back to our monastery to lick our wounds and sing our laments.'

'You did your duty.'

'We did,' said Toranis. 'There's nothing more we Adeptus Astartes can do other than our duty, and die doing it.' He ran a finger down a column of numbers on a leaf of paper on the table. 'A hard life, and thankless.'

'The traitors say the same,' said Dante cautiously.

Toranis looked up from the paper. 'I heard them say it, and then I killed them. Nothing could make me betray my vows or my Emperor. If my death saves even one human life, I will be glad.'

'Then you must be very glad. You have saved this world.'

'I am,' Toranis said. 'And so have you.' He swept his hand over the documents. 'Now, if I can persuade you to leave the counting of belt pouches to your servants, maybe they can have a turn at doing their duty and you can come and have a last cup of wine with me before you go.'

Dante looked at his work, then at his logister. The blood thrall bowed quickly. 'My lord, allow me to serve in my way. You have served in yours.'

'We do not have much time,' said Dante. 'We are due to load the last of our equipment before nightfall.'

'It will be done, my lord, I swear,' said the logister.

'Listen to him. I'm sure he can count perfectly well,' said Toranis. 'Come on. Tell yourself you are building inter-Chapter ties or working on your diplomatic skills or something, then you won't feel guilty about taking a few moments for yourself. I won't take no for an answer.'

'He's going to do it. I told you he would. He's finally worked up the nerve.'

The scout had been glancing at Dante for some time. Lorenz betted with Dante over a private channel about whether or not he would crack.

'Captain,' the scout said. 'May I ask you a question, my lord?' The young Space Marine shouted over the Thunderhawk's engines as it pushed hard for the void. The last stages of ascent always demanded the most from the ships. Were the occupants of the transport hold normal men, accelerative force would have rendered them mute, if not unconscious. Thunderhawks carried little in the way of force dampers.

'I told you,' said Lorenz smugly. 'You're famous already.' Lorenz sat back on the bench, letting the transit cradle take a little more of his armour's weight. Though relaxed, he held his gun on his knees. Most of them did, preferring to carry their weapons rather than put them into the racks.

There were four scouts with the youth, a full demi-squad. They glanced from their spokesman to the captain.

'A novitiate may ask what he wishes of his superiors,' said Dante without looking at the young warrior. 'Whether or not they choose to answer is another matter.'

Lorenz snorted with laughter. 'How very wise.'

The scout looked a little unsure, but spoke up. 'I have heard many tales of your deeds already, captain, though I have also heard you are reckoned young. I would know, is it true you have seen the Sanguinor, Captain Dante?'

'And why would you ask me that?' said Dante, turning his head towards his questioner.

'I have heard talk, my lord,' said the scout. He looked down at his admission. 'I know that rumours are not to be heeded.'

'Then do not heed them,' said Dante.

'Yes, captain, I am sorry.'

'I think you should stop tormenting him,' said Lorenz. His helmet voxmitter clicked as he turned it on. 'Do you know who this is, boy?' he said. 'This is Captain Dante.'

'I know,' said the scout, puzzled.

'Then you already know that he has seen the blessed messenger of Sanguinius more times than any other brother in living memory. Why ask him?'

'They were rumours, sir...'

'What did the captain say about rumours?'

'I meant no offence...'

'Then don't be offensive!' Lorenz said. The other scouts were looking warily at Lorenz. Commendably, they did not seek to distance themselves from the questioner. Already their ties of brotherhood were strong.

'Now you are tormenting him, brother. Leave him be,' said Dante.

'I am trying to teach him something, brother-captain,' said Lorenz. He never could give the title with total seriousness. 'Captain Dante here has seen the Sanguinor on no fewer than five separate occasions. That's impressive, boy, you should look impressed. We have long memories, and longer lives. You'll remember this. You will be less clumsy in future.'

'I will, my lord.'

'Brother-sergeant,' said Lorenz. 'I am no one's lord. We are brothers, you and I, though you are yet young and stupid. Do not forget it.'

'I won't be so insolent in future.'

'You aren't being insolent!' said Lorenz. 'I am not chiding you for your temerity. I am testing you! An angel should be bold, and sure of himself. Respecting ranks and obeying orders are sacrosanct, but if you are to challenge them, even in so small a way as to ask a question of one of your elders out of turn, it must be done with confidence, and with flair, and yet with humility. We are angels, the instruments of the Emperor, not bashful farmhands. Remember it.'

'I shall try.'

Lorenz settled back into his cradle. 'Do not be hard on yourself. Our life is riven with contradictions,' he said. 'You will master them all, eventually. I'm going to sleep. It's been a long war.'

Seconds later, he was snoring softly.

Dante looked at his friend, then back to the scout.

'He could have turned his voxmitter off,' said Dante.

The scout looked back at him, now thoroughly confused by Dante's tone, and unsure of himself because of it.

'What is your name?' asked Dante.

'Amanteus, my lord.'

'I will remember it. It takes courage to ask questions as you did. Better to enquire in an attempt to learn the truth than be a slave to custom. There is no better blade than truth to slay the monsters of rumour.'

The engine noise on the Thunderhawk changed. The rush of air over the hull petered out to nothing. Gravity released its grip. The ship put on a final burst of acceleration, pushing them back hard.

'Perhaps you will serve under me,' said Dante. 'I shall speak to your training sergeant.'

Half an hour later, the Thunderhawk set down on *Bloodcaller*'s embarkation deck.

Dante paused in his tale. Danakan shook the effect of the story off. He was heavy with wine, and pleasingly warm. Dante's voice was rich and powerful, fine for storytelling. Danakan was surprised but did not really know why; the Adeptus Astartes were more than men. They excelled at everything they tried, and the Blood Angels were among the most excellent of all.

Amazingly, he had not thought of the melting faces in all

the time Dante spoke. Instead the hot, dusty air of a ruined city and the roar of gunships taking flight had filled his mind. It was remarkable, but then he glanced at his empty wine cup. In lifting the ewer to fill it again, he found it light, and realised he was more than a little drunk.

'I tell you this, Danakan, so you will know that we are human beings still,' said Dante. 'Within our armoured shells are human hearts and minds. We are changed by the infusion of Sanguinius' spirit, but not entirely.'

'If I may be so bold to ask, my lord, what has this to do with the burden of command?'

'Everything,' said Dante. 'One cannot command men without being a man. What happened next is the more pertinent part of the tale. I shall–'

He frowned. Danakan made to speak but Dante silenced him. Far off on the edge of hearing, Danakan heard a series of tones playing.

A serf came and whispered in Dante's ear. Dante nodded, and the serf withdrew.

'I am sorry, lord admiral. I must cut short our dinner. A matter of importance has arisen that I must attend to personally. Do forgive me.' He stood and placed his napkin on his plate.

'My lord,' said Danakan. He made to rise.

'Please,' said Dante. 'Stay a while. Drink the wine. Sometimes, it is good to indulge. I shall continue this story another time. It is instructive for both of us.'

He left then, leaving Danakan alone with a single thrall.

The admiral finished his wine, then took himself off to bed.

CHAPTER ELEVEN

SERVANTS OF CAWL

Space rippled like a pond disturbed by stones. The stars danced. A wound of wretched light split the cosmos, and a small ship passed from the warp into the stable reaches of reality.

The ship was a Mechanicus cutter, a few hundred yards long and lightly built, yet its narrow hull was covered with equipment blisters and docking ports for attaching more.

It had no name, but bore a simple number repeated on brass plates on many places upon its hull: *0-101-0*.

Bright thrusters flickered around its prow. Jets of gas ejected the domicile blisters of failed Navigators. Three detached, and exploded miles out from the ship. *0-101-0* plunged through the fires. Micro-debris sparkled on void shielding, and then was gone, and the ship speared inwards from the Mandeville point towards a glaring, red sun.

Qvo-87 sat enmeshed in the systems of the craft. Information poured into him from the myriad machine-spirits that made up his vessel's soul. Around his throne a dozen tech-priests stood rooted by mechadendrite connection to their command stations. A hundred servitors operated in specialised-function choirs behind them. The rest of the command deck space was filled with cogitators, servo-skull roosts, and auto-sanctifiers that blessed the greater machines. Qvo didn't have a big crew, and as many of the functions of worship as possible were performed automatically. Nor was *0-101-0* a big ship, but it was fast, and it was strong.

<Three Navigators of Navigator compliment = negative existence,> canted one of his transmechanics. This being had abandoned his human name in favour of a number string. Being somewhat impish in humour, like his creator Cawl, Qvo called the transmechanic Sixer after the first numeral. There was a lot of Cawl in Qvo.

<Life status negatory. Crew [Navigator subgroup] reduced = five. Two > +/- functionality. Sum of functioning Navigators = three.>

'Query – do enough Navigators survive to return us to Lord Cawl when our mission is done?' Qvo asked. He spoke aloud. His was the only human voice heard amid the chittering of machines.

<Unknown. Quantity of Navigators deficient.>

'Then the houses of Terra will have to send us more,' said Qvo. 'The journey to Imperium Nihilus was expectedly hard. They knew what we asked of them. Every success we make gains contributing houses influence.'

Another of the machine-priests spoke. 'We have indeed been successful. The houses should be rewarded for their scions' efforts.'

'I recognise and appreciate you using human speech, Magos

Cartographicus L'mard,' said Qvo. 'I am feeling somewhat verbose today, and binharic doesn't always suit.'

'When the master speaks, the follower should listen and respond in kind. It is no good to have components of the same function group communicating in different code-cant,' said L'mard. His lower jaw had been removed and replaced with an array of metal pipes, but the voxmitter adorning his forehead passably synthesised speech.

'A little obsequious of you, L'mard, but I appreciate the sentiment,' said Qvo.

'I exist only to serve you and the Lord Cawl,' said L'mard.

'Ah, there's the truth then. Pleasing Cawl is what we all desire,' said Qvo. 'There's no need to flatter me.'

Qvo stood from his throne. Input lines detached themselves and snaked back into the guts of the machines around him. Qvo had a human head with a pleasant face. Everything else about him was machine, from his banded metal neck, through a torso sporting multiple extra bionic limbs, to his piston-powered feet.

'Show me our location,' he said.

L'mard likewise detached himself from his station. When his cables reeled themselves in, a nest of mechadendrites upon his back activated and lifted themselves up, dancing like serpents over his hood.

With a gesture of a steel hand, L'mard called a cartolith into being. 'As you can see, Adept Qvo, our Navigator cadre has delivered us directly where requested.'

The map showed the whole system in compressed form: a huge red sun that was meanly furnished with worlds – a large inner rocky planet orbited by two immense moons, and further out another world of thin clouds and dry lands. Labels sprang up around the cartolith, naming all the component parts. They moved with smooth celestial clockwork, as the Machine-God had intended. Seeing star systems spin induced a feeling of calm in Qvo's mechanical being.

'The Baal system,' L'mard said. 'We are at our destination.'

'Excellent,' said Qvo. 'Open the oculus.'

Pulses of light raced around the deck. Machines sighed and clattered as they came online. For all its dangers, moving through the warp was a mechanically simple matter. More numerous machines were required to traverse the void. Servitors sighed and champed redundant teeth. A plasteel iris curled in on itself, opening the window at the front of the deck to space.

'We are receiving hails,' Qvo's alpha lexmechanic informed him.

'From where?' asked Qvo.

'From here.'

A dot of golden light flashed on the oculus. Active crystal displays boxed it in and magnified it, pulling it out and presenting the magnified point as a hololith.

'Well, that's impressive. Quite the statement, don't you think?' said Qvo.

'Indeed,' said L'mard.

<{opinion} Ostentatious,> pulsed Sixer.

They were looking at a station made in the shape of an angel twenty miles tall, with a sword another seven long held aloft. The statue stood upon an orb etched with a star map of the Imperium that was the size of a planetoid. The angel's wings spread widely either side. There were a great many ships docked to thousands of jetties projecting from the orb like the rays of a sun.

'Skyfall. Designated starport and defensive station of Adeptus Astartes Blood Angels Chapter.' Qvo swiped across the air, and a multiplicity of views of the angel bloomed in front of him. 'This is a significant upgrade. I must update my records.' He spoke with enthusiasm. All members of the Cult Mechanicus enjoyed new information.

L'mard stomped away to the cartographic dataloom set into the side of the deck, his mechandendrites already reaching to interface with it.

'Give me some specifications, please,' Qvo said.

'Ultrus-scale starport and fleet facility,' Losoel-Azeriph, his Arch-Belligerus, reported. 'Undergoing extensive refit.' More views sprang up, highlighting areas without plating or in the process of internal reconstruction.

'0-101-0 receiving transmissions from multiple Imperial craft,' said Adept-Dialogus Kurubik. 'Mechanicus, Imperial and Adeptus Astartes, seven Chapters.'

'Quite the hub,' said Qvo. 'Well, with all this activity occurring it appears it is high time the commander received an embassy from Archmagos Dominus Belisarius Cawl.' Qvo-87 peered at the images his underlings called forth, and co-opted the ship's augury and auspex to probe deeper himself. 'Adept-Dialogus Kurubik, better let them know we are here. Prepare a message of appropriate floridity. The Blood Angels can be a fulsome bunch. Arch-Belligerus, disengage stealth shielding, we don't want to frighten them.'

'As you command, Adept Qvo,' the two said simultaneously.

'Put the shields up, just in case. The sons of Sanguinius have their aggressive side.'

'Compliance,' said Losoel-Azeriph.

'I have a communications channel ready. Generating optimally diplomatic overtures. Please provide meaningful message content for insertion,' asked the Adept-Dialogus.

'Tell them Belisarius Cawl sent us, and we come bearing

gifts. I require an urgent audience with Lord Dante. That should do it.'

Kurubik sent the message. Shortly after, the stern face of a Blood Angel in full armour appeared as a hololithic image. He wore no helm, and his long, blonde hair hung freely over his breastplate.

'Greetings, acolytes of Mars,' the captain said. 'I am Matarno, Lord of Skyfall and captain of the Bloodblades, the Eighth Company of our brotherhood. We gratefully receive your embassy.'

'The cordiality of your personal greeting is favourably noted, lord captain,' Kurubik responded. His voice had been designed to be as appealing as possible, and was rich and deep. 'We are honoured by this token of your respect.'

'It is right that the servants of the saviour of the Blood be treated with honour,' said Matarno. 'Docking coordinates and Chapter pass codes will follow a deep scan of your vessel.'

That didn't seem very respectful to Qvo, but he kept that to himself.

'Your caution is commendable,' said Kurubik. 'We submit ourselves openly to your scrutiny.'

'However,' Matarno went on. 'We regretfully inform you that the Lord Dante is not present in-system, and the day of his return is unknown. I can send a message to the Chapter Council and bid them gather the relevant lords together to hear your tidings, if you wish.'

'That will not be necessary,' said Qvo, speaking for himself. 'We bring news of import and aid to your Chapter that Lord Dante himself must hear. We shall wait.'

CHAPTER TWELVE

RHACELUS CONSULTED

Antargo was waiting outside Dante's quarters in full armour. He emanated cold, and had the gunpowder smell of the open void. His face was moist with sweat.

'I am sorry to disturb you, my lord. Lord Rhacelus has woken. I have been at work with my men on the *Dominance*. I came as soon as I was informed.'

'Then we shall go to him,' said Dante. He allowed a thrall to help him into a long coat. The injuries to his chest made the movement difficult to accomplish alone. Once he was garbed, they set off. The Sanguinary Guard standing sentry on the door fell in behind them.

Dante's private quarters were large, designed to impress Imperial and alien potentates alike. They marched from the banqueting room and its antechamber into a long gallery. Ornate windows looked out onto the macrocannon turrets mounted along the length of *Bloodcaller*'s slender neck. The fleet was arrayed around the Blood Angels vessel in battle formation. Being deep in interstellar space, there was no telling what might find them.

The *Dominance* had been brought in close to the *Bloodcaller*. Shuttlecraft from all over the fleet flowed to and from it. A tender sat high over its port side, casting its shadow, weak in the scattered starlight, over the front part of the battle-barge.

'Work progresses. You are on schedule?' asked Dante.

'There is now enough personnel on the *Dominance* to bring it back to Skyfall.'

'Was the task difficult?'

'Beyond the questions of purifying the vessel and transporting new personnel, no. I did not need to invoke your name,' said Antargo. 'There were sufficient volunteers from among the Imperial Navy ships to provide a skeleton crew. They are brave, and honourable. Most of them will remain upon the ship for the rest of their lives. They are giving up their homes.'

'A mortal man may bear his duty as seriously as an angel of Baal, Antargo. This is a good lesson for you. A mortal can understand that it is not for my sake they do this, but for all Imperium Nihilus. Is the *Dominance* free of the influence of the warp?'

'I have had Naval armsmen sweeping the ship for the last two days, and psykers from the astropathic temples where they can be spared. My men are leading the efforts. The astropaths and their divining rituals speed things along, but it will take weeks to check the ship thoroughly. Mephiston's remaining Librarians are a great aid, but more battle-trained psykers would speed up the process.'

'What is the final count on the Librarius' dead?' asked Dante.

'Two, my lord. Brother-Codicier Maelon has joined Peloris in death. Rael is recovering.'

Dante took the news without comment. 'When we return to the Baal system, the ship can be scried again with greater thoroughness,' he said. 'In the meantime, station fifty brothers on the ship, and make sure there is a strong contingent of priests aboard. I do not care for the religion of the Adeptus Ministorum, but it is efficacious in holding back the evils of the warp, especially when the minds of those around them are fired with faith. Who did you place in command?'

'That lieutenant, Juvenel, he seems to know what he's doing. I expect the admiral will want to get aboard soon.'

'Maybe,' said Dante.

They left the gallery, and entered a large hall of exquisite craftsmanship. The lumens were at a low burn. Great statues were shapes in the shadows.

'I have not known you long, my lord, but I know you enough to understand that "maybe" is a bad word coming from your mouth.'

'Am I so transparent?' said Dante.

'Every man has his tells.' Antargo glanced at his lord. 'I remember a little of my life before Cawl took me away. My true father was a gambler – he was good at it too. I have always been able to read people. Danakan is damaged.'

'He is,' said Dante. 'He will require help before he is ready for active service again. I would prefer he remain in his role, so he will get it. There are no officers in our current roster with as much experience as he, and he has an undeniable flair for battle. He is well known and popularly regarded as a hero. He must lead. It will be a significant blow to morale if he is removed. First their flagship is overrun, then their lord is deemed unfit. It cannot happen.'

'What is the problem? Is it exposure to the daemonkin?' Antargo shook his head. 'More and more people are being confronted by these nightmares. The whole galaxy is going mad.'

'What once was secret is now impossible to hide. There was a time in my life when a Chapter exposed to the things of the warp would have been mind-wiped. Worlds have been burned by friendly hands for witnessing less than what we saw aboard the *Dominance*. But it is not that,' said Dante. 'I believe he has the fortitude to survive encountering them. He has a simple case of combat shock.'

'You're saying exposure to daemons did him less harm than fighting?' said Antargo. 'Incredible.'

'He made a costly mistake. It haunts him. An admiral must be confident, to the point of arrogance, and a serious error can shake a man like that.'

'They're so weak,' said Antargo dismissively.

'Tell me, captain, is it a sign of weakness to suffer a grave psychological injury and then recover from it? We are arrogant. We think ourselves immune to human frailties. If that is so, why are there warriors out there, in armour designed by Terran smiths, and with bodies empowered by the Emperor, fighting on the side of the Ruinous Powers? Space Marines are men. Their minds are stronger, but they can break.'

Antargo paused a moment before speaking next. 'My lord, what if Danakan does not recover? How will you deal with that?'

'Then I shall replace him, captain. A pity, but if it must be so, then it will.'

They left Dante's quarters, and went out into the wider ship. All was quiet. They saw no one.

'How are your men?' asked Dante.

'They are fine,' said Antargo. 'Excepting those taken by the Rage.' He became almost angry.

'Have our Chaplains screen the men for diabolical contamination, nevertheless.'

'There's nothing wrong with them,' Antargo insisted. 'They're veterans of Lord Guilliman's crusade. They fought worse creatures than those perfumed wretches when they were Unnumbered Sons.' Antargo was displeased. 'I know we are new to the Chapter and the ways of Baal, but I assure you that my men will do nothing to dishonour the memory of the Great Angel. They are pure of heart and spirit.'

'As were the Legions in the days of Horus, my brother. Monitor them. Have them speak with your company Chaplain daily. The worst enemies come from within. We are exposed to the warp when we travel. We battle creatures of terrible evil. Corruption can take root in the stoutest heart. And now we have this new problem with our bloodline's curse.'

'As you say,' said Antargo. 'I've never seen it in the Mars-born. Four of them fell into madness. They were good warriors, now they are little more than raging beasts.'

'They have been granted a vision of our lord, the Angel,' said Dante. 'In some sense they are blessed. There have been some among the newcomers who feared they could never be true sons of Sanguinius without the Thirst or the Rage. That is no longer the case.'

'Should I be thankful? They lost everything for this moment of revelation,' said Antargo. 'They were good men. A bitter draught to drink.'

'Indeed,' said Dante. 'All hope that your kind was immune has gone. It is a grave development.' Dante thought a moment. 'We must get to the bottom of why it happened here and now. If we are fortunate, then its triggering here was a unique occurrence. However, we must also deal with the issue of Mephiston, whatever the truth of the Primaris brothers' susceptibility to the Rage. Has he become a risk to us all?'

'The daemon said the curse could be cured, Maybe it did this as a display of power.'

'Daemons lie, Captain Antargo. Daemons are lies, and we can credit none of what it said as truth until otherwise verified. For now, we can only rely on what we have seen, and what we know. Firstly, as far as we know, no Primaris Marine has ever succumbed to the Black Rage. Secondly, they did so only in the presence of Mephiston. The triggering of the Rage could have been a trick of the daemon, or it could have been an effect of Mephiston's powers.'

'Rhacelus will tell us.'

'Perhaps he will.'

'You are calm, my lord.'

'Calmness is a great virtue, captain. Despair serves no man. Even now, at this black hour, I must remain aloof from the implications of this circumstance if I am to understand it.'

They spent the rest of the journey to the Sanctum Psykana discussing the lesser matters of supply, morale among the non-Astartes personnel, and journey times. Seemingly insignificant matters dictate the outcome of all endeavours, and they had to address them, as all great men must, if they wish to remain great.

Rhacelus met them at the doors to the Librarius. Not even Dante could enter the Sanctum Psykana without permission. A pair of acolytes stood guard outside. They had been granted their armour, and this was the celestial blue of the Librarius, but otherwise they retained the basic Chapter heraldry, having not yet been initiated into the mysteries of their sub-order. Dante did not know them. He wondered if they would succeed in earning the moulded badges of a battle psyker. Attrition among recruits to the Librarius was high.

Rhacelus stood proudly at the threshold, his horned skull staff set against the floor, but he had yet to recover. His skin was grey, and the warp light of his eyes dim. There was more white in his beard than before.

'Lord Commander Dante requests entry to the Librarius,' Dante said.

'As do I, Captain Antargo of the Third Company,' said Antargo.

'Do you approach free of doubt and mental weakness?' said Rhacelus.

'We do,' the commander and captain said simultaneously.

'Then I bid you enter,' said Rhacelus.

The short ritual over, Rhacelus seemed to lose some of his strength, and leaned on his staff for support when he stepped back to allow the officers entry. Dante and Antargo went inside. The Sanguinary Guard remained without, taking up position next to the acolytes.

Dante stopped inside the entrance. 'How do you fare, Gaius?' he asked.

'I am recovering.'

'Your wounds?'

'They are more mental than physical, my lord,' Rhacelus said. 'My facility with the warp has been reduced, temporarily, I believe, but it pains me yet. I have never been in contact with such power. I was in battle, my mind fully alert, and my gear primed to protect me, and yet – Mephiston's strength...' He looked at Dante worriedly. 'It overwhelmed me.' He smiled. 'I have a terrible headache.'

'You are strong, Gaius. You will recover,' said Dante.

'Given time, aye, I will,' said Rhacelus. 'Mephiston is another matter.'

'Where is the Lord of Death?'

'He is secure. I will show you, come.'

Rhacelus led Dante and Antargo into the centre of the sanctum. The Librarius' territory took up the entirety of a subsidiary tower attached to the command decks. It was a vast space for so few warriors. Even if all of the Chapter's psykers had been present they would have been lonely figures in the Sanctum Psykana. Most of its space was taken up by rooms of neatly stacked data crystals. *Bloodcaller* and the *Blade of Vengeance* had identical facilities, copies of the Chapter's archives on Baal held against the originals' loss. Other chambers were equipped as scriptoria, where the Librarians could record the details of every campaign *Bloodcaller* took part in. Ancient tradition harking back to the time of the IX Legion dictated that the scriptoria have many stations, though there were not sufficient staff in all of the Librarius to fill even one.

'You said there are matters that should be discussed,' Dante said as they walked silent corridors. 'I would hear them now.'

'In the years since his rebirth, Mephiston's power has been growing. Calistarius was powerful, but...' Rhacelus' voice trailed away.

'I am aware of this,' said Dante. 'It has disquieted me for a long time. I am sorrowed that my suspicions have proven correct.'

They came to a great door of brass, covered in esoteric symbols inlaid with silver.

'He is in here,' said Rhacelus.

'Open the door, Epistolary. Let me see him,' said Dante.

Rhacelus bowed his head, and removed a ring of keys from his belt. There were many locks in the door, and he muttered warding cantrips as he unlocked each.

They stepped into a spherical chamber. A sarcophagus hung in the middle, suspended in a contragrav field. Four spinning, nested rings engraved with sigils orbited it. Flexible pipes and wires snaked up from a circular aperture from the floor, feeding Mephiston blood.

'Do not step over the line,' said Rhacelus. He indicated a ring of solid salt that ran around the room, the first of several protective circles of increasing complexity, until the innermost became an illustrated wonder, filled with minor works of art. Machines sang under the golden decking. 'Can you feel his might?'

Dante nodded. 'I can.' There was a pressure radiating from the sarcophagus. It was gentle, a dull push against the mind, but hinted at great power.

'He is warded by every art of the Librarius. This chamber is used to contain the direst of psychic threats. In here, we take that which cannot be destroyed for containment in the Carceri Arcanum.'

'This is making me uneasy,' said Antargo.

'It should, captain,' said Rhacelus. 'Mephiston is the most powerful psychic being I have ever encountered. Power such as his is not meant to be wielded by men.'

'How did this come to pass?' asked Antargo. 'Is the Rift the cause?'

'Mephiston's growth in strength began before the Rift opened. Do you know the story, Captain Antargo?'

'Some details. Only the legend, not the true account,' said the captain.

'It happened at the battle for Hades Hive during the Second War for Armageddon.' Rhacelus stared at the stern ivory face on the casket exterior as he spoke. 'He was Calistarius then, my friend, a fine warrior and worthy psyker. During the battle he went missing, and we thought him lost. He had been caught by a partial collapse of the hive, and buried beneath its rubble. While he was entombed the Black Rage descended on him. For seven days and nights he warred with himself, finally succeeding in overcoming the Black Rage entirely. He is, as far as we know, the only Blood Angel ever to achieve this feat.'

'Chaplain Lemartes also mastered it, did he not?' said Antargo.

'Lemartes still suffers from the Black Rage,' said Rhacelus. 'It is only through sheer act of will that he manages to retain his sanity while experiencing the visions of our lord's end. By any objective measure he is quite mad. Mephiston is different. He has cast out the Rage completely. The changes to him did not stop with this miracle. When he emerged from the wreck of the hive, he was transformed in mind, body and spirit. He was faster, stronger and more deadly than any Librarian before him. But he was also silent where Calistarius was voluble, solitary when Calistarius was gregarious. He does not accept that name any more. Calistarius, he says, is dead. In a sense I believe him to be right. His memory of his earlier life is certainly incomplete. The Sanguinary Priests say his gene-seed was reactivated somehow, rewriting his gene-code into something else, something new. I believe it to be something more profound. A spiritual transformation more than a physical one.'

'Is this something that exists in all of us?'

Rhacelus smiled grimly. 'That is a question Corbulo has asked a great many times. He is ever one to seize on a cure to the flaw, but when Mephiston was examined, whatever qualities his gene-seed has were elusive. Corbulo wanted to experiment further.'

'I denied him,' said Dante. 'Mephiston is dangerous. The Black Rage is a part of who we are. It should not be toyed with. Corbulo has been searching for a cure his entire life, but in this case, where the changes wrought on Calistarius were so extensive, and so clearly connected to the warp, I could not countenance their further exploration. Corbulo was being drawn onto the path of sorcerous genomancy.'

'Then why did you permit Mephiston to live?'

'He is our brother,' said Dante. 'You have seen him fight.'

'We accepted him back, content that Calistarius had returned to us, only it soon became apparent that he was no longer Calistarius,' said Rhacelus. 'He was astonishing. Nobody in the annals of the Chapter is recorded as being able to achieve feats like his. In little time, he had risen to the head of the Librarius, though he was forced to submit to many tests and trials by the Council of Bone and Blood before his appointment was approved. Since then his abilities have been growing year after year. After the attack on Baal, and our deflection of Ka'Bandha from Baal to Baal Primus, these gifts have become greater. In battle he is unstoppable. But there are consequences.'

'The Black Rage,' said Antargo. 'He triggered it in my men.'

'We cannot say that for certain. The Great Rift has opened,' said Dante. 'Many strange things are afoot. Daemons stalk the stars at will. The Astronomican is shrouded. I have received reports of an increased prevalence of psykers in the systems we are in contact with. That is another task to attend to, the finding and the protection of the Black Fleets.' Dante looked thoughtfully at Mephiston's casket. 'Corbulo has notified me of a rising incidence of the Rage among our veterans. The Red Thirst hounds us harder, even those of Cawl's Gift. Can Mephiston be responsible for all of that? The galaxy is a large place. Mephiston has been at my side since the fall of the Arx Angelicum. He showed no sign of influence on the warriors of the Blood then.'

'But we witnessed the Black Rage in the Primaris Space Marines for the first time, right in front of us,' said Antargo. 'It cannot be coincidence that it occurred when Mephiston lost control of his powers. The psychic shock of it killed his own brothers, decks away.'

'I doubt it is, but perhaps it has happened elsewhere,' said Dante. 'The galaxy is large. Communications are disrupted. There are thousands more Space Marines of our heritage.' He frowned. 'I will make no swift judgements, not on any matter. This is a question for the Chapter Council entire – the Red Council of war and the Council of Bone and Blood combined. Let all the great minds of our brotherhood debate what must be done with Mephiston.'

'The Quorum Empyrric will wish to be consulted,' said Rhacelus.

'They shall be included in the council,' said Dante.

'Will you kill him?' asked Rhacelus quietly.

'If that is what is necessary, I will have to,' said Dante.

Rhacelus closed his eyes, shutting off the constant glow emanating from them. 'He spoke to me before he was placed inside the sarcophagus,' he said. 'I saw concern in him for the first time, and perhaps, deep in his eyes, a hint of Calistarius of old.'

'What did he say?' asked Dante.

'He said "I fear what may occur should I let myself free, Gaius. I fear what I am becoming."'

CHAPTER THIRTEEN

A DIFFICULT COAT TO WEAR

Juvenel had to wait a full five minutes before the admiral's guard admitted him to the inner chambers. They were big men, faces hidden behind mirror-visored white sallets and their bulging chests covered with bronze-plated plasteel breastplates. They had better equipment than most officers Juvenel knew, high status. The trouble was, they behaved like they knew it. How easy it would be to bypass them altogether. But he would not sneak like a rat.

'He'll see you now, sir,' said the man as the outer doors opened. His tone was less than deferential. Juvenel glanced sidelong at him as he marched through. Too much brawn, not much brain, he thought. They behaved like lords of the galaxy on a ship of the Adeptus Astartes, warriors who could crush them without a second thought. He thought it hubris, but as he walked down the corridor to the admiral's temporary quarters, he reconsidered. Every human being was the product of its own, self-generated myth. If the guards let themselves be cowed by Space Marines and put aside their pride, they probably would have nothing left.

He stopped outside the door to Danakan's chambers while its machine-spirits scanned him. He frowned.

'How much of human endeavour is dependent on the heroic lies we tell ourselves?' he said to himself.

<NEGATORY RESPONSE PATH,> the door opined. <INPUT CONTENT UNRECOGNISED.>

'Ignore,' Juvenel said. 'Continue scan.'

<COMPLIANCE. JUVENEL, A. FLAG-LIEUTENANT FIRST CLASS, IMPERIAL NAVAL VESSEL *DOMINANCE*. YOU ARE PERMITTED ENTRY.>

The door opened. Juvenel stepped into a large room made fusty by an overabundance of ancient, heavy furniture.

The room was lit by a trio of electro-flambeaux and a single candelabra on a massive dining table. It was therefore unpleasantly dark. A large, oval window looked out over the fleet, but was so heavily scratched the view was poor, and let in little of what light there was to be had from the stars.

Danakan stood next to one of the flambeaux. Juvenel's eye was drawn directly to him. The admiral was in front of a mirror framed by an enormous amount of gilt-work. It was old. Paint had rubbed away from the frame, revealing the wood and plaster beneath. None of the dozens of cherubim worked into the riot of weapons, motifs and acanthus leaves had a full complement of fingers. Several were missing their noses. The silver backing to the glass had tarnished, rendering the reflection dull, and spotting it all over with lead-grey blotches. Danakan was visible in those parts that still reflected, in full dress uniform, fiddling with the fastenings to his greatcoat with obvious frustration.

'My lord,' said Juvenel.

'Ah, Arran, just the man,' said Danakan without looking behind himself. His coat took all his attention. Three attempts were required to do up the lowermost clasp.

'I have the reports on the recrewing efforts here,' said Juvenel. He held out the dossier.

'Put it down over on the table,' said Danakan. 'I'll get around to not reading them later. You may report the highlights to me now. I assume under your able guidance the *Dominance* will soon be void worthy?'

'The ship is fine,' said Juvenel. He dropped the dossier by the candelabra. It slapped loudly on the dark wood. The admiral was making jokes. That was a good sign.

'Good,' said Danakan. 'She's a good old warhawk. I'd hate to see her die.'

'It's the crew that's going to be an issue in the future. We've enough men in the fleet to get her back to Baal, but I wouldn't want to take us into an engagement. After the attack a lot of the ships are dangerously undermanned.'

'A great benefit of our Imperium, Juvenel, is that men are always in ready supply.'

'Are they now, though?' said Juvenel. 'System after system devastated by xenos and worse. All of them cut off from contact. The Astronomican out, the astropaths deaf.'

'It's not a good picture.'

'No,' said Juvenel. He lowered himself into an armchair. Clouds of dust rose from the upholstery, and he coughed. 'Emperor's bones, where have they put you?'

'This is a very large ship, with not that many people on it,' said Danakan. By now, he had reached the middle clasp of his coat. 'I doubt anyone has been in here for generations.'

'It certainly looks like it. This mix of furniture is maddening.'

Danakan looked about. 'Yes. Old. Only half of it sized

for normal men. I tried to sit in that.' He jerked his head in the direction of a huge chair made to Space Marine proportions. 'Extremely uncomfortable. My feet didn't reach the floor. I'd go back to the *Dominance* if Dante hadn't insisted on keeping me here.'

'Why?'

'Strange as it is to say, I think he wants some company,' said Danakan. He had reached his throat. The clasps were becoming increasingly fiddly the higher he went. The fastenings were designed to be hidden within the join of the cloth, and the lack of space to move his fingers hampered Danakan. That they trembled didn't help. Juvenel noted that. Perhaps the admiral was not quite so well as his behaviour suggested.

'I assume he'll let me go back before we depart,' said Danakan.

'You're not a hostage, my lord.'

'You seem to be managing without me, lieutenant.'

'Maybe you should step down then, and let me run the show?' Juvenel joked.

Danakan's response was devoid of humour, and Juvenel knew then that he wasn't getting better at all. 'I do want to step down. I don't think I can do this any more, Juvenel. It's just... I fear I am not going to recover, but Dante insists. These dinners he has with me, he's telling me about his past. Before Teleope, I think I would have been fascinated.' He fiddled with his collar then swore. 'Damn thing. Help me with this, would you?'

Juvenel came forward and struggled with the last few clasps at the high neck of the coat. 'These things are impossible,' he said.

'Whoever designed these uniforms never thought about comfort,' said Danakan. He tilted his neck, exposing his throat to the lieutenant. 'I wonder who did design them?'

'Someone thousands of years dead. That's better,' Juvenel

said, snapping a clasp shut. 'Lord Dante is doing you a great honour.'

'I don't deserve it. Not any more.'

'You are a great commander.'

'It's high time for me to retire.'

'Then convince him to let you stand down.'

'Hungry for command, eh, Arran?' said Danakan. The sharpness of his response reminded Juvenel he was on dangerous ground.

'Yes, of course I am. But not at your expense, sir. I'm thinking about my career. I'm thinking about our men. If you freeze again...' Juvenel tailed off. He had thought often what would happen if Danakan froze again.

'Don't you think I know that? Don't you think I know how many lives depend on me not making another mistake?' Danakan said testily. His beard's untrimmed, ragged ends tickled Juvenel's fingers.

'I'm sorry, sir.' Juvenel's hands dropped from the clasps.

'Don't stop!' Danakan growled. 'I can't do it myself, can't you see that? Like every bloody other thing, I need you. I should retire, but he's not going to let me. He's made that abundantly clear. How can I refuse the regent of Imperium Nihilus. I mean – ow! Emperor's will, man, you're pinching me.'

'Almost got it,' said Juvenel through gritted teeth. 'And there we are.'

The admiral's greatcoat was closed all the way up. Medals gleamed in intimidating abundance on his left breast.

Juvenel stepped back and smoothed down the front of Danakan's uniform, plucking stray hairs from it, and adjusted his belt.

'How do I look?' asked Danakan.

'Fit for a meeting with a man who rules half a galaxy.'

'I don't think I'll ever be fit for that,' said Danakan. 'This is a difficult coat to wear. Damn annoying that I'll be in it only as long as it takes me to walk through those doors. Can't eat in it. Ceremony. Pompous nonsense.'

Juvenel took Danakan's sword from its stand and handed it to his superior.

'What are you going to do, sir, if he really won't let you step aside?'

Danakan gave a tight smile as he took the weapon. It tautened the aged skin around his jaw. Just for a second, his eyes glinted with the ferocious courage he was once known for.

'I better bloody well get better then, hadn't I?'

For a moment Juvenel's heart lifted, but then he glanced up into the admiral's eyes, and saw the fear in them.

Danakan hooked the sword onto his belt. The admiral's face was grey with lack of sleep. Despite his attempt at boldness, he was worn down. Juvenel was looking at a beaten man.

'I need a drink,' said the admiral. 'I shall see you later. Keep up the good work, and keep me informed.' The door slid open to let him out, but Danakan stopped in the opening. He gripped the edge with his hand. 'I understand what you're trying to do for me, Juvenel.' He didn't look back. His voice cracked with emotion. 'I appreciate your efforts.'

'It is my duty, sir,' said Juvenel.

'It's not, you know,' said Danakan. 'It's not at all.' He stood a little taller. 'I will remember.'

Dante was waiting for him in a drawing room. The setting was far less formal than the banqueting hall. Dark wood panelling covered over the plasteel inner skin of the hull. A fire burned in a grate beneath a fluted extraction unit. A table that was low for a Space Marine was surrounded by chairs of differing sizes, although as before they were all made in the same style. On the table were a small number of plates with various delicacies upon them. Dante was standing, reading from a book on a solid wooden lectern. Like the furniture in Danakan's quarters it was old, polished by the touch of so many hands that the carvings had become soft-edged. He looked up when the door opened, and gave Danakan a warm, genuine smile.

'I am glad you accepted my invitation, Danakan.'

'It is my pleasure, my lord,' said the admiral.

One of Dante's servants came forward from the shadows, undid Danakan's weapons belt and took his sword and pistol. Another undid his coat and swiftly slipped it from his shoulders. He bore it away so quietly the medals did not so much as clink.

'Your thralls have defter fingers than either myself or Juvenel. It takes me an age to get that coat done up,' said Danakan.

'You have no servants?' said Dante.

'All dead, I expect. I have a few of my guard with me here on *Bloodcaller*, but they make awful handmaids.'

'I did not think.' Dante shut his book with a soft thump. 'I am sorry. I will assign you some of my thralls.'

'You have a lot on your mind, my lord.'

'Indeed I do. Please, as I said before, do not feel the need for such formality in future.'

'I am a man of the Imperial Navy, sir. I have standards to uphold.'

'Yes, of course.'

Danakan paused. 'That was my attempt at a joke, my lord. I would be grateful to leave the coat behind.'

Dante smiled apologetically. 'I find it hard to tell sometimes,' he said. 'I am not without humour, but we Adeptus Astartes can be overly serious.'

'These are serious times.'

'Sit.' Dante gestured to one of the chairs. 'The dinner seemed to be a little too much last time, so I took the liberty of opting for a lighter meal today. Do not feel obliged to eat, if you do not wish. On the other hand, if this food is not sufficient, then I shall have my servants prepare you something more.'

Danakan was quietly horrified that Dante saw how much he was struggling. He wasn't hungry at all, but forced himself to taste some of the smaller canapés on offer, some sort of seafood on a hard, dark bread. He began to chew mechanically, but slowed, then began again enthusiastically.

'This is delicious,' he said.

Dante took a giant chair opposite him and poured them both some wine, from the same carafe this time. 'My staff includes a number of excellent cooks. I understand that for men in your position, small amounts of flavoursome food are best.'

'My position.' Danakan looked down. A scream from the past rang in his mind, so clear he was half sure Dante would hear it too. 'Yes. A tactful way of putting it.'

'Tact is another thing that the Emperor's gift strips from us,' said Dante. 'Have I offended you?'

'No,' said Danakan.

'Good.' Dante held out a goblet to the admiral. Danakan took it. Dante had such an earnest expression, it reminded Danakan of a child's desire to please.

'To your good health,' said Danakan. He raised his goblet and attempted a smile. It came a little easier than in their previous meeting.

'To yours,' said Dante.

They drank.

'Eat, Seroen. Eat your fill. Listen to me now, and I shall tell you more of what happened at Kallius.'

CHAPTER FOURTEEN

AMBUSH

Metal scraped loudly on Dante's combat knife as Lorenz attempted to lock his quillons onto the blade and wrench the weapon out of his grasp. Dante was ready for the move, twisting hard, binding the weapons together. Lorenz stepped close, his bare forearms pressing into Dante's. They were close. Chests touched. Sweat mingled.

'You're not going to win, not in a contest of strength,' Lorenz panted into Dante's face. He turned his weapon harder, putting pressure on Dante's grip and forcing the grip around in his palm. 'I'm stronger than you. I always have been. Yield.'

The leather binding slipped on Dante's sweat. Lorenz would pull down hard next, yanking the weapon out from his hand, cutting into his thigh, and leaving him open to an upper thrust – though he'd stop short of actually gutting him, he would stab him lightly a few times, just to show he could.

'Yield, or I'll make you bleed, Dante,' said Lorenz.

'You never lost your sadistic streak, did you?' said Dante.

The weapon turned further; in a moment it would be aligned perfectly with the opening in his fist, the weakest part of the human grip.

'Baiting me won't make this easier for–'

Dante interrupted Lorenz with his forehead. Reinforced bone smashed hard together with a loud *tock*. Lorenz's eyes widened in surprise. The scent of genetically enhanced blood from his burst nose flooded the room. He stepped back with a look of outrage on his face so comical Dante almost laughed. Instead he threw his weight forward, kicked out his foot, hooked it around Lorenz's ankle and slammed his shoulder into the taller Space Marine's chest. Lorenz went down hard onto the matting. Dante followed him, elbowing Lorenz's weapon arm aside, and landing across his chest, knees pinning Lorenz's biceps to the ground.

'You yield,' said Dante.

Lorenz growled. Red sparked in the depths of his eyes. Dante was sure he was touched by the Thirst, but then he spat red.

'I yield,' Lorenz said. He sniffed wetly. 'You want to wash your training robes, brother, you smell offensive.'

'Are you some kind of child, employing such insults?' said Dante. He got up and offered his hand. Lorenz wiped off his face before taking it. Already his blood was crusting around his nose, though the orbits of his eyes were dark with bruising that would take at least a day to fade.

'So say you, resorting to smashing my nose in with your head.' He prodded carefully at his injury.

'You did not expect me to do it. I am too honourable, you say. I acted outside my usual behavioural patterns, and therefore I won.'

'All per the Codex. Still very you.'

'You should read it more often.'

'Should I now?' said Lorenz. He hawked up another fat blood clot and spat it on the floor, and his voice cleared. 'You have read it a hundred times, yet it took you a couple of centuries to try something as low as a headbutt.'

'That is incorrect,' said Dante. 'It only took a couple of centuries to use it on you. I do not like hurting you, Lorenz. You are my friend, but I was finding your jibes tiresome.'

Lorenz grimaced and pinched the bridge of his nose hard. With a wrenching crack he forced it back into place. He swore loudly.

'The gutter speak of Baal Secundus, issuing from an angel's mouth,' said Dante.

'Oh, so now you've discovered a sense of humour too,' said Lorenz.

Dante spun his combat knife around. 'There is a lot you do not know about me, brother,' he said. 'I challenge you again.'

'That's the first time you have beaten me for a long time,' said Lorenz, retrieving his knife. 'It'll be just as long until you do it again.'

Lorenz swished the knife through the air. It was huge, with an upturned point and serrated teeth along the blade, part machete, part dagger, as long as a mortal human's sword.

'This time, I will not be going easy on you,' he said.

Dante dropped into a fighter's stance, knees bent, knife held out in front of him.

'Begin,' he said.

They circled each other, neither making any sort of decisive move. Lorenz was usually more aggressive, but he was cautious now. Their eyes were locked, their movements controlled, neither of them willing to give anything away.

The ship dipped suddenly, enough to make them sway. They looked at each other.

'What by the blood...?' said Lorenz.

'Gravity wake,' said Dante.

'From what?' said Lorenz.

The alarms began to sound.

'Incoming ships,' said Dante.

Lorenz sheathed his knife and went to the door of the training cell, snatching his tunic from a hook on the way. He slapped the door release, and stepped out into the wider gymnasium. There were a few dozen other Blood Angels there undergoing various training regimens; fewer than was normal. Most had had their fill of fighting.

The alarms blared on. The ship juddered. Accelerative force pushed at Dante.

'We're turning.' Dante tried his vox-bead. His ears filled with squealing static. 'And we're being jammed.'

The ship's vox-network boomed on. Chapter Master Remael's voice addressed them. He sounded as if he were speaking over the hardlines.

'Brothers, arm yourselves. Enemy fleet inbound, thirty thousand miles and closing. Prepare for immediate combat.'

The vox snapped off. The ship trembled under the first long-range lance strikes a few moments after that.

There were many armouries aboard the *Bloodcaller*; all of them were filled with sudden activity. The one assigned to Eighth Company was no different. The gymnasium was a short run away from the armoury, but by the time Dante and Lorenz arrived it was already teeming with battle-brothers hurrying into their armour while dozens of thralls rushed to and fro.

'By the Angel, it's chaos in here!' said Lorenz disapprovingly.

Dante pushed his way through the mass of men. 'Some

of our warriors are missing armour pieces. Their equipment is in the forge, with no time for replacements. No time to repair, no time to resupply.'

The ship shook. Lumens blinked.

'They've already taken one of the shields down,' said Lorenz. 'They must have broken warp right on top of us.'

'The vox carrier waves are still blocked. I'll get some confirmation as to what's happening,' said Dante. 'Blood of Baal, out of my way!' he shouted, pushing past a sweating thrall carrying a pauldron stripped down to the bare ceramite.

More impacts followed. The ship shook under an intense, close-range barrage. The lumens blinked off completely, leaving the armoury saturated in the blood red of emergency lighting. Dante reached a hardline vox-set, wrenched the housing door open and lifted the speaking horn.

'Dante, captain, Eighth Company, requesting elucidation of current situation,' he barked into the receiver.

A mortal answered him tensely. *'Enemy forces on top of us. Two warp exit points, cutting in at the fleet from both sides. Lead assets are within close engagement range. Predicted void shield failure within thirty seconds. All Chapter warriors to prepare to repel boarders. Chapter vox undergoing restoration to full function now. Armour yourself, captain, and await further direction, so orders Commander Remael.'*

Dante slammed the horn back into its box.

'Prepare my armour!' he roared over the tumult of voices and whining power tools.

'How bad is it?' asked Lorenz.

'As bad as it can be,' said Dante. 'Brothers!' He strode onto the gangway running between the arming cells and shouted as loud as he could. 'Brothers! Hurry! The enemy are coming.'

'Get your wargear on, brother,' said Lorenz. 'We need you.'

'Lorenz, I want a report on our strength and battle readiness as soon as possible. See if you can find Sanguinary Priest Etherael or any of the Chaplains. I want the men checked over for signs of the Rage before we engage.'

Lorenz nodded and ran off towards his own armoury unit. Two of Dante's command squad were already armoured, and they joined Lorenz in his cell to help him.

Dante ran to the far end of the Eighth's armoury where his own equipment was kept. Thankfully, all his gear had been brought there for checking before being sent to the forge for repair. He was missing only a few pieces from his set, for which he had spares.

His equerry and three servitors awaited him. He pushed his way through them and began tugging on his armour's rubbery undersuit while shouting for his thrall to bring the layer of flexible mail that went over that. His servant was commendably calm, obeying Dante's orders with alacrity and anticipating what he would require next. Ordinarily it took time to don battleplate, especially if all the ritual stages of machine purification and blessing were incorporated.

A massive explosion sounded somewhere close. More alarms wailed. Dante worked fast, stepping into his boots, snapping his greaves shut for the servitors to bolt securely, already moving on to his cuisses, groin guard and waist assemblies while they locked him in. He needed help with the torso armour. It was too heavy and too awkward to don alone. He was forced to stand still, his arms out, his blood singing with impatience as the servitors plodded to him with the plates held in their grips. *Bloodcaller* rumbled with cannon fire when it gave another broadside from its primary armaments. Each discharge ran up the ship from the stern as the bombardment cannons discharged in sequence. The temperature rose. Air circulation was dying off. His men were working as fast as he, those on duty and already armoured when the attack came helping those who were not. The Eighth, being an assault company, had a full complement of jump packs, but these were left on their racks, being next to useless in the close confines of shipboard fighting.

Another huge explosion shook the ship. Dante's cowters flew from the tray they rested on and bounced along the floor. His thrall dove for them, risking being trampled by the heavy steel feet of the servitors.

Dante's rerebraces and vambraces went on. The retrieved cowters covered over his elbows. He was reaching for his gauntlets when the atmosphere in the armoury began to change. An electric mist gathered in the middle of the gangway, near the armoury gates.

'Teleport,' Dante breathed. 'Teleport!' he shouted. He turned to his serfs urgently. 'The power plant! Get my power plant on! Get it on now!' Dante stepped back into the arming cradle, his gauntlets clutched under his arm. He stabbed the button to bring his backpack out from its alcove. His thrall came around the back of him, dodging the lumbering servitors to plug power feeds into his armour. Dante pulled on his gauntlets, and locked them closed around his wrists. They were heavy, awkward without the energy from his backpack to power the suit's supplementary musculature.

The mist glowed brighter. Transit lightning arced out from the centre, earthing itself in the deck and blowing out the grav plating beneath. A mortal running to his master with spare magazines of ammunition was speared by a bolt of power and fell down dead, ghostly light glowing in his burnt-out eye sockets.

'Quickly!' Dante shouted. The power plant slammed into

place, magnetically and mechanically clasping itself to his armour. 'My helm! My weapons!'

The light glared so brightly it was impossible to look into. It collapsed inwards with a thunderclap of displaced air. Three immense shapes stood where the glow had been, high cowls over their helms, spiked trophy racks scraping the ceiling with their spear tips. Red eyes glowed balefully over tusked masks.

Dante had time to snatch up his sword before the Terminators opened fire.

Two carried combi-bolters of ancient design. The third bore an archaic heavy flamer. Bolts were already speeding at a high rate of fire from the heretics' guns when the flamer was unleashed, vomiting a rolling cloud of high-temperature flame that consumed everything that it touched.

A blast of heat singed Dante's eyebrows. The servants of the Chapter screamed as they were kissed by fire. Promethium burned hot, and it ignited the fat on their bodies in an instant, turning them into human torches. Disciplined as the servants of the blood were, they could not withstand the pain, and they ran about as they died, adding to the confusion. Servitors burned while they worked, until their circuits melted or brains cooked, whereupon they stopped dead. Only those brothers who had donned their full armour had any amount of protection, and even ceramite was not fully proof against the fires. Those without helms or who were partly armoured were roasted in their battleplate. One died as the ammunition pouches on his belt ignited, the explosion of so many bolts going off together cutting him in half. The rest were beaten back, their ceramite glowing red hot and crumbling, aflame from head to foot.

But the Blood Angels were bolder than any mortal man,

and rallied fast to face their foes, charging with their battle cries roaring from their voxmitters.

'For the Emperor! For Sanguinius!'

The first leapt at the lead Terminator, a monstrous champion whose helm was decorated with dangling human skulls. The Blood Angel came down hard, using his impetus to add power to his chainsword's blow. His screaming blade drew long tails of sparks from the armour. The champion batted him aside, the power field around his fist crashing louder than meeting shield walls as it obliterated the Blood Angel's chest and flung him dead to the ground.

The Terminators set to work in earnest.

They were slower than the sons of Baal in their heavy warplate, but nigh invulnerable to the chainswords and bolt pistols most of the assault company carried.

The three of them waded into the unprepared Blood Angels, fists rising and falling with thunderous death strokes. The heavy flamer gave forth its dragon's roar again, spewing flame down the gangway. The mortals trapped in the room did their best to hide in the armoury cubicles, but most were cut down, blasted to pieces or roasted to ash. Fire suppressant rushed out of nozzles in the ceiling. Those mortals that were not slaughtered outright would soon suffocate. Gas drenched red by the emergency lighting blanketed everything.

Dante's armour chimed out readiness for battle into his vox-bead. He considered charging into the foe helmetless, but against Terminators that was as good as suicide. 'My helm!' Dante shouted. 'Now!'

His servant hurried up with the helm, struggling under the weight. As he lifted it to Dante's waiting hand, a stray bolt took him in the back, and he exploded into a mist of blood and flecks of meat. Bone fragments stung Dante's face. The helm fell into what remained. Dante scooped it up, ignoring the stinking fluids clinging to it as he thrust it onto his head and reached for his scabbarded power sword resting on its stand.

Displays flashed on. He selected an image-enhanced view from his auto-senses to help him penetrate the murk of gas and fire. The three enemy warriors stood out boldly, outlined in blood red. He brought them into sharper focus, and bade his armour systems scan them.

They were champions of their kind, the mightiest of the mighty. Their armour was festooned with chains bearing gory honours: skulls, severed hands and scrips of flayed skin covered in blasphemous prayers.

He took all this in as he charged, drawing his sword from its sheath and igniting the power field with one movement. He roared out his hatred of his foe as he struck hard at the nearest Terminator.

The impact glare was refracted by the fire suppressant mist, flashing like lightning in a storm cloud. Dante's blade cut deep into the Terminator's vambrace, slicing through the outer layers and the fibre bundles, but the armour's adamantium frame stopped it, and it stuck fast. Dante wrenched it free and moved aside just in time to avoid having his head taken from his shoulders by a swing from the traitor's power fist. It hit the walls and punched a deep hole into the metal. Dante ducked down and cut again, slicing into the warrior's greave. Electrical systems sparked as the blade cut through them. A tongue of flame licked its way up the warrior's black armour. The Terminator was slowed, but not stopped, limping on his malfunctioning leg as he turned about and brought up his bolter to fire.

Dante threw himself sideways, bouncing through the mess of burned human meat coating the floor. Bolts vanished into the fire suppressant, exploding on the far wall with diffuse yellow flashes. One of Dante's warriors saw his chance and swept his chainsword at the heretic Terminator, catching the warrior's knee. A second Space Marine moved in with a primed krak grenade, intending to slap it onto the warrior's side and shatter his armour, but the Terminator anticipated the ruse, and was already swinging his fist to meet the real attack. The blow slammed into the warrior's pauldron, breaking it into a hundred pieces and flinging him back, his arm flopping uselessly from his ruined shoulder.

The other two traitors were standing back to back, battling against all the Blood Angels could throw at them. More formid-able weapons were being brought to bear. A meltabeam punched a dripping hole into the side of one, but it was Lorenz who finally tipped the balance.

Dante saw him through the smoke, distinguished by the black sergeant's laurels circling his golden helm. The charging coils of plasma on his pistol glowed brightly in his hand. The moment Dante saw it, Lorenz opened fire.

The plasma stream slammed into the heavy flamer's promethium flasks. The resultant detonation blasted flame all through the armoury. Blood Angels flung up their arms to protect their vulnerable eye lenses. The fire burst pushed back the fire suppressant still gushing from the ceiling.

The enemy were caught full by the explosion. None of them fell – their armour was much too thick to fail against so weak a threat as flame – but the warrior facing Dante staggered, his massive bulk rocked by the force of the explosion.

Dante took his chance. His armour flaming, he drove at the Terminator with his sword held in both hands, point first. The warrior saw him too late, and Dante evaded the swipe of his fist.

The sword punched into the breastplate of the warrior's armour, its power field eating rapidly through plasteel, ceramite and adamantium, then through his body suit and into his primary heart. The warrior grunted with pain. Two of Dante's Space Marines leapt forward, grappling the champion's arms to allow Dante time to withdraw his sword and finish his foe.

Teleportation lightning played around the three. An unholy screech signalled their departure, along with a thunderclap of air rushing into the void they left.

Bits of Dante's warriors fell to the floor smoking corposant, neatly cut by the displacement effect. His sword hilt rattled down next to the scattered limbs.

The flames died. Dante got to his feet. 'Shut off the fire control!' he commanded.

The jets of gas ceased. Atmospheric cyclers sucked it away, revealing a scene of devastation.

'By the blood,' said Lorenz. 'They knew exactly when to hit us.'

Fires burned throughout the armoury. A dozen mortis chimes sang in Dante's helm. There were as many wounded warriors again, and nearly all the armoury serfs were dead. A single servitor stood immobile in the centre of the aisle, its organic components blackened and giving off a greasy smoke.

'Command, this is Captain Dante.' Dante ran through all the vox-channels. The warble of active denial signals replied. 'We're still being jammed,' he said. He glanced at the hardline unit, finding it smashed. 'Send a runner to the apothecarion,' he said to Lorenz. 'We need medical assistance, immediately.'

Danakan watched Dante over the top of his wine goblet. The dancing flames on the scented logs reminded him of his burning crew. Dante's story of promethium slaying his men strengthened the image, so much so that Danakan was sure Dante had chosen that anecdote specifically.

He took a sip of his wine. It was spiced, with a heavy, soporific scent. He was drowsy, but focused, in that way a person can be before they fall into sleep, and he supposed that the wine was drugged and this too must have been deliberate. He bridled a little at being manipulated so, yet Danakan felt more at ease, he couldn't deny it.

Dante continued speaking. He ate little that night. Though he drank a great deal of wine, emptying three ewers, it did not appear to affect him.

'When our runner got to the main apothecarion, he found it devastated,' Dante went on. 'The situation was in confusion, but it was not long before I decided they were after the ship. Heretic Astartes must rely in the main on piracy to replenish their fleets and weapons. The traitors chose their targets as well as they had their timing. Ordinarily, more of us would have been under arms, but our equipment was worn from the fighting and we were weary. There were three companies of my battle-brothers on board the battle-barge. Only one was ready for action, none were at full strength, and all were dispersed.'

'They chose a risky strategy, breaking warp so close to your vessels.'

'They are reckless,' said Dante. 'They abandon the precepts of the Codex Astartes. On many occasions I have seen them act against its teachings purposefully, defying the Emperor by ignoring the words of His son, even if it goes against good sense.'

'They did not pull back and bombard you into submission?'

'They could have,' said the commander. 'If they had, we would have split and fled. I was entirely unaware of the size of force we were fighting. Later, I discovered that it was about the same size as our own: two capital ships – one a battle-barge, the other a grand cruiser – four strike cruisers, a number of lesser craft. Their fleet was in poorer repair, but they had more men, and they were fresh to the fight. The Adeptus Astartes are made not to tire, but we do eventually. Kallius had been a taxing war.'

'Then they boarded you,' said Danakan. 'Teleport strikes on key facilities of the ship, rapid withdrawal, a second round of bombardment to weaken your defences, followed by a full boarding action of boarding torpedoes and gunships, supported by strike craft, with a perimeter of faster craft to chase down anything that tried to get out.'

Dante smiled more than Danakan had expected him to, but although his smiles displayed a warm and generous nature, they were uniformly sad. They were smiles of acceptance, of old grief. 'That is what happened,' he said. 'You live up to your reputation.'

Danakan shrugged. 'It is what I would have done were I in command of a thousand Space Marines and wished to claim a good number of prizes. Boarding actions with unmodified human troops are harder. There have been many occasions when I've wished for a company or two of your kind to swing the balance in my favour. There are a good half a dozen ships of great power I could have captured if I had. Instead, they are clouds of debris, and the Emperor's fleets are poorer.'

'A warship is a precious thing,' said Dante.

'I can drink to that,' said Danakan. He did, perhaps a little too greedily.

'You are correct,' said Dante. 'After the battle I was able to review our combat logs. They attacked at close range, straight out of the warp. Risky, but they surprised us and were able to bring down our shields and send in teams of heavy assault troops, targeting our medicae, armouries, forge, training halls and refectoria. They kept the shields down long enough to retrieve their men after that first strike, no more. By then the damage had been done. My company was at less than half strength after the attack. My warriors were forced to strip their dead brothers to complete their armour before we moved out. We lost a good deal of gene-seed, and many loyal servants.

'As Lorenz and I moved through the ship, we found they had left much of the *Bloodcaller* unharmed, including our weapons,' Dante continued. 'It was us and the crew they struck at. The halls were awash with blood.' He became thoughtful. 'We were divided, leaderless. My company was well equipped for close melee, but as a pure assault company we lacked the variety of armaments necessary to prosecute war successfully against our traitor kin. Our Dreadnoughts were inactive, their sarcophagi removed from most of them so that they might undergo medical checks and their chassis be repaired. All told, it was the worst possible time for the Chapter to be attacked. They took us when we were a day's void sailing from the nearest help, far out in a system thought pacified. How they avoided our patrols, I never discovered.'

'Space is large. The finest net one can cast over the cosmos still has holes large enough to pass a sun through.'

'It is so. We were isolated, alone, unprepared. Soon it became apparent we were in a fight for our lives.'

'You did not despair?'

'Despair is a part of war. You cannot have one without the other. As is fear, and horror. It is how you deal with those things, admiral, that sets men apart.'

'Now you are referring to me directly,' said Danakan.

'I am. I know you can overcome this. I know you will recover your courage.'

Danakan looked away.

Dante sat his goblet down. 'Forgive me. I have spoken at length. You are tired, and must rest.'

'There are few more comforting things in life than a warm fire, a good tale and fine wine,' said the admiral. 'I assure you that your efforts are appreciated, as fruitless as they may prove to be.'

'We shall see about that,' said Dante. 'Tomorrow we shall re-enter the warp. If you wish, you may remain on the *Bloodcaller*.'

Danakan shook his head. 'Thank you, but no. I must return to the *Dominance*.'

Dante looked satisfied. 'That is good, admiral. We shall talk again when we are at Baal.'

'I would like to hear the end of your story.'

'You shall,' said Dante. 'For as our Chapter lore says, no task should be begun that we do not intend to finish.'

CHAPTER FIFTEEN

A NEW IMPERIUM

Exposure to the warp was physical agony. Rhacelus hurt everywhere. Spiritual pain he had expected, but this passed through the soul, and sank its teeth into the marrow of his bones.

How does Mephiston do it? he thought. How can he bear it?

Rhacelus performed a lesser miracle than the Lord of Death. He did not venture from the ship into the empyrean. If Dante had commanded him, he would have done so, but he would have gone certain of death and worse. He saw the things alive in the swirl of colour and noise, the predators that lurked between the hopes and fears of a trillion trillion sentient beings.

The Sanguinor was a solitary candle of pure light set against all the poison of the Sea of Souls. Rhacelus could do no more than lend his strength to the cabal of Navigators guiding the ships. They were faint presences to him, restive as sufferers of fevers. From time to time one would steady, and bring greater fortitude to the others; just as often a soul would flare, then almost go out, and thin screams would drift over roaring infinities.

Hopes that the tempest might have diminished went unrealised. The warp was as deadly as ever when the fleet translated again, and only grew more agitated the further they went into their voyage. Things came at Rhacelus, excited by the beacon of his psyker's soul. He fought them off with his mind, slicing them apart into coloured smoke. It was exhausting. There were too many to slay himself, and he was forced to scan an endless array of nightmares and pick out those that might conceivably breach the Geller fields. When one was torn to pieces, a thousand more emerged from the psychedelic chop of the warp to take its place.

'Insanity,' muttered Rhacelus. He forced himself to focus. To display weakness in the warp was to invite disaster. He had to be strong. Millions of lives hung on his fortitude. A personal doom waited for every man, woman and child within the fleet if he failed. Only the flicker-thin skins of the Geller fields kept the nightmares out. Only Rhacelus could deliver them to Baal before the fields began to fail. If the ships were lost, billions more Imperial subjects would be slain for their lack. Rhacelus hoped he never had to do this again.

And then, a sea change. The warp altered, though subtly at first. Rhacelus had little experience as a navigator of ships. Had he been born to the role he might have noticed sooner, like ancient mariners tasted the shift from salt to sweet in the waters of Terra's lost oceans. But soon it became apparent to him that the tempest was calming. The shrieking ideoforms and psychopomps struggled to take shape.

Those that manifested were sucked back to nothing among the energies that birthed them. Colours bled away. Currents stilled. A black wall was growing ahead, as impenetrable as the densest fog bank and infinitely more forbidding. The task force sped towards it. The armoured angel glinted in front of the darkness, and vanished within completely.

Against all the laws that governed it, the empyrean lost its mutability. Blackness seeped from the rolling wall of shadow. The visions and images weakened, and then stopped altogether. There was a brief passage through warp space of a primordial calmness, smooth and bright as a moonlit pond, and then the flotilla plunged into the darkness.

A new terror assailed Rhacelus. A vast, godlike mind turned its attention upon the ships, so puissant it quelled the fury of the warp.

The hive mind was the truth of the tyranids. The Blood Angels believed the war beasts that plagued the universe were merely the material extrusion of something far greater, and that thing dwelt in the warp.

The pressure of the hive mind's regard was immense, crushing Rhacelus' soul until it felt infinitely small. At great remove he felt blood trickle from the corners of his mortal eyes.

Gold flashed ahead. Rhacelus fought to support the failing Navigators. With strength he could ill afford to share, he held them up, and directed their attention to the distant angel. The ships turned. Though the shadow in the warp blinded all eyes, its quelling of the tempest eased passage, if one only knew which way to go.

Rhacelus saw the angel clearly, the Sanguinor, exemplar of their kind, a warrior out of myth, yet he was real, ever with them, the guardian of the blood. From across the unmeasurable distances of a dimension that obeyed no law but its own, the Sanguinor's golden eyes looked into Rhacelus' soul. He beckoned, then turned with a flash of brilliant wings.

The hive mind's awful presence waned. The fleet punched through the shadow, out into garish spirit shoals, then back into the black. They raced through the edge of the darkness, where it was shredded on swift currents. It was but a fragment of the power it had attained when Leviathan assailed Baal itself, but though this shadow seemed isolated and diminished, Rhacelus could sense its connections to further, greater parts, and felt the brooding presence of the alien god all around – withdrawn from its prize, wounded, yet still alive with dangerous malevolence.

The end was near. The mass of planets and of stars bent space-time, and the indentations pushed also into the warp. Rhacelus hoped they had reached Baal, and not been drawn off course to unknown worlds. He had no strength left to him. He could not do this again.

Matter had no voice in the warp, but souls did. They pressed heavily into the spirit sea. Millennia of suffering on the Blood Angels' home worlds showed as a gallery of horrors, a heaven cast down into a living hell. A realm of angels who harvested the strong and ignored the weak for the sake of a corpse on a distant throne. The Sanguinor flew around the images, inconceivably huge. A darkness grew beside him, and before Rhacelus could understand what was happening, the Sanguinor was locked in battle with an angel completely garbed in black.

Aeons were compressed into moments. He saw triumph and sorrow in Baal's warp shadow. He saw blood. He saw all the sins of his kind displayed.

'Baal,' he said through gritted teeth, as the ships raced through immaterial currents. His words were collected by the mute servants of the Librarius, and passed on by machine. 'We are at Baal.'

Words became news. The news became orders. Klaxons blared all over the ship, then on other ships. A rapid countdown commenced. After the Great Rift opened, there was never time to properly prepare for translation. Opportunity had to be grabbed. Without decisive action, they risked falling into the gravity wells of celestial bodies, where safe translation was nigh impossible, or overshooting their goal entirely.

To the screaming of awakening void engines and the reedy cries of the dead, *Bloodcaller* speared into real space, Dante's prizes racing behind it.

Within a dark room that stank of blood, watched by tongueless serfs, Rhacelus fell to the floor, blood weeping from every orifice.

Outside the ship, in the void, the red sun Balor glared at the newcomers, defiant even at the return of its master.

The fleet made all haste to Skyfall. Word was sent ahead, and Dante commanded that the Red Council and the Council of Bone and Blood be convened in time for his arrival on Baal itself.

Bloodcaller put in to the main docking pier of Skyfall. Dozens of berths were taken up by the tattered flotilla the Blood Angels had gathered from across the stars. Clouds of service craft descended on the ships within the hour of their coming to port. Repairs were begun immediately. A small army of logisters marched aboard to take stock of supplies, condition and crews. Resupplying a fleet was the work of weeks, much more where overhaul was required. Every second counted.

Within Skyfall Dante saw to his own tasks. Hundreds of reports awaited his attention, along with scores of dignitaries who had made the perilous voyage to the system to beg for aid. They all had to wait. Before Dante's arrival had been officially announced, Qvo-87 contrived to send him a direct message, against all protocol and despite the Chapter's noospheric security, to demand an audience.

Dante immediately agreed.

Dante met Qvo in an observation gallery overlooking the station's largest dry dock. A beautifully wrought metal structure bridging a gap in the station, sealed in by polished armourglass, the gallery was a walkway cleverly supported so that it appeared to float in space. Every ten yards a statue of a tall, hooded angel stood sentry, all different, ten in all, each bearing devices which, to the initiated, were rich with symbolism. Every rivet was a masterpiece of the jeweller's craft. Sullen scarlet suns provided a backdrop of rubies on the red velvet void of the Scar.

Qvo wasn't interested in any of that. He looked at the dry dock and the ship clasped tightly in its cradle. Pinprick lights glinted all over the ship's half-plated hull where thousands of Cult Mechanicus personnel were at work.

Being who he was, Qvo had little trouble securing entry to that part of the station where so many of his kind laboured. He had chosen the meeting place deliberately.

In doing so, Dante supposed Qvo was making a point about how much the Adeptus Mechanicus had done for the Chapter. Doubtless this prefigured some demand or other. In return, Dante made his own point. He arrived in his full battle regalia, accompanied by Daeanatos and three more of his Sanguinary Guard. They had burnished their armour specially for the occasion, and they approached facing the sun, so that Balor's ruddy glow caught them full and made them shine like red gold. A true heavenly host, their appearance was a display of martial glory.

Qvo-87 was not an impressive creature. But Dante was far too wise to judge on first appearances. Dante had little direct experience of Belisarius Cawl, and not much more by the way of intelligence on him, but he knew the archmagos was dangerous. Not only was Cawl's skill beyond the ability of most tech-magi, but his ambitions outreached those of all others too. That meant Cawl was very dangerous indeed.

Dante's guard halted with perfect synchronicity, crashed their weapons on their shining armour and turned to face each other either side of the walkway.

'You are the servant of Belisarius Cawl?' said Dante. He wore a power pack festooned with art. A pair of golden wings inlaid with rubies curled around the sides of his head. A rich red cloak covered over one of his pauldrons, contrasting handsomely with the solar glare of his armour. If Qvo was daunted, there was no sign of it in his amiable expression.

'I am Qvo-87, the servant of the Archmagos Belisarius Cawl, Prime Conduit of the Omnissiah, yes,' said the adept. He spoke pleasantly, but his use of Cawl's full title was an obvious rebuke.

'Then know that name of the man you call master is the only reason I agreed to see you,' said Dante. 'I have many pressing matters to attend to. A thousand voices clamour for my attention.'

'I see,' said Qvo-87.

'First, I extend to you my gratitude. We owe the archmagos much. Without his reinforcements, our Chapter would have taken centuries to rebuild, if it would have survived at all.

These new weapons he brings us will aid us in executing the Emperor's will.'

'Like this ship,' said Qvo, extending an arm in the direction of the incomplete battle-barge.

'Like that ship,' said Dante. *'Baal's Fury*, it will be called. My Keeper of the Heavengate informs me it excels our current vessels in every way. Your master is talented.'

This seemed to please Qvo. 'Archmagos Dominus Belisarius Cawl is a marvellous polymath,' he said. 'Although he is modest enough to acknowledge the aid of two hundred and thirty-eight other magi of high rank in its creation, he was responsible for the majority of its design. See, its engines are of a completely new mark, created for the specific stresses of void–'

'Do you have a point to make for me in enunciating each of its advantages? I have little time.'

Qvo blinked slowly and smiled. 'Not really, I thought that it might be of interest to you.'

'I am Commander Dante, lord of the Blood Angels. I have perused the plans for this ship thoroughly, and the very little I did not understand was adequately explained to me by my forge master. Why did you wish to meet me, magos?'

Qvo looked out over the ship. Dante wondered what he thought when he regarded it. Was he possessive of it? Did he see it as a lever to his influence?

'Commander, if I may ask, if you are so grateful to my master, why are you behaving with this aggression towards his servant? I understood you to be a master of diplomacy,' said Qvo.

Dante gripped the guard rail and looked over *Baal's Fury*. 'I speak my mind, and I speak truthfully. Lord Guilliman told me to be wary of any offers Cawl might make. There are many voices that warn with their concern at the activities of your archmagos.'

'I do not see why that should be so. We are all on the same side.'

'Are we? Is that true of anyone in this Imperium? Even the noblest man has his own agenda. Factionalism dogs humanity's efforts to survive. Cawl forces his own path. That makes many people, including the lord regent, uncomfortable.'

'Only because the lord regent chooses not to listen. I understand he made you a regent too.'

'Regent and warden of Imperium Nihilus.'

'And in whose name do you rule, I wonder, Lord Guilliman's, or the Emperor's?'

'The Emperor's name,' said Dante firmly.

'Well, you see, there are many in this Imperium of ours who say similar things about Lord Guilliman that are said about the Prime Conduit. Does the Lord Guilliman rule in the Emperor's name only, while in truth seeking power for himself? Did you hear, for example, what he did to the High Lords when he returned to Terra?'

'I did,' admitted Dante. 'One could argue that his actions were proportionate.'

'You were told these things by whom?'

'By a historitor the primarch left to advise me,' said Dante.

'Hardly an unbiased source of information,' said Qvo. He shrugged. Mechanisms clicked inside his body. 'The Lord Regent Guilliman does not pay close enough attention to the archmagos. You are master of half the galaxy. What will this regent choose to do, I wonder? Listen, or not?'

Dante stared at Qvo, then reached up and unclasped the front of his helm. He removed Sanguinius' howling death mask, exposing his true, aged visage to the tech-priest. After the booming delivery the mask had leant him, his own voice sounded soft. Qvo peered at him interestedly. Lights flashed at the back of his eyes.

'I will listen,' said Dante. 'But I have been warned. The Adeptus Mechanicus grows arrogant.'

'There is nothing to be warned against. You speak of arrogance?' said Qvo. 'In this facility I see the badges of Ryza, and Cypra Mundi, Mars itself, and others. All of the forge worlds, from the most famed to the most obscure, seek power of their own. They are arrogant, because they believe they are right. They believe this, because they, unlike my master, have abandoned the true spirit of enquiry which knowledge depends upon. They are dogmatic. Their religion is self-aggrandising. They profess a unitary scripture but in truth they each preach from their own books, and in those individual holy tomes, their own creed is naturally pre-eminent. By contrast, Lord Cawl seeks no power for himself. He wants only humanity's survival, and subsequently its prosperity, for the greater glory of the Machine-God. He has far more humility than these fellows you have working here, despite what you might think.'

'The Lord Guilliman told me he would say that.'

'That is only because it is true. Why do you doubt his good intentions?'

'Secrets have cursed the Imperium since its founding. We are in need of honesty. Cawl keeps too many secrets.'

'And does this desire for honesty apply to you and your kind also?' Qvo-87's neck extended a little. His head leaned in towards Dante's face. 'My master has looked into the very soul of your beings. He knows what horrors you hide beneath your shining exteriors. You are paragons with troubled hearts. The thirst for blood, the draw of madness, neither are very far from your thoughts.'

'Your first threat,' said Dante. 'The revelation of our secret.'

'There is no threat.'

'I disagree. Revelation of knowledge is an implicit threat, for it displays the holder of the knowledge is unafraid to say the secret out loud. The keeper of the secret fears who else they might tell.'

'No one!' scoffed Qvo. 'Why would I?'

'For influence, for power. Because you say all of you tech-priests crave power. You are arrogant as all the rest.'

'Not I,' said Qvo. 'I am as the archmagos made me to be.'

'Why are you here?'

'You have many heroes among your kind, do you not?'

'Indubitably,' said Dante. 'All of the warriors of the blood are heroes.'

'Some are the greatest heroes in the galaxy.' Qvo looked at Dante sympathetically. 'Some of them are growing old. My master has delivered unto the Chapters of the Adeptus Astartes the salvation of mankind. The Primaris Marines are bigger, stronger, superior in every way to the Principia.'

'Principia?'

'My master's term for the original kind of Space Marine. Personally, I would have used the term Tertium for your sort. There were two others before your kind was made – the Thunder Warriors of old Terra, and the Adeptus Custodes. I would have labelled these Principia and Seconda.' A dozen tiny limbs spread on Qvo's torso in an insectile shrug. 'In his greater wisdom, Belisarius Cawl opines that the Thunder Warriors were prototypes to both the Space Marines and the Guardians of the Throne. Furthermore, he told me that the Adeptus Custodes are of another line of research altogether, related but distinct. Bespoke pieces to your masterful, mass-produced gene-forging.'

'I know nothing of this. I know nothing of these "Thunder Warriors". I am Adeptus Astartes. Our new brothers are Adeptus Astartes. That is all I need to know.'

'You speak from a position of ignorance,' said Qvo gently. 'So much knowledge has been lost. So much that what I am going to say now, you must take on trust, because I have this knowledge and you do not.' Qvo paused a moment to watch an enormous cannon be guided into its place on the battle-barge's spine by a hundred tiny ships. The vibration when it locked home shook the walkway. 'Cawl respects the experience and wisdom of the older sort of Space Marine. He has therefore devised a way to elevate your kind to the status of the new.'

Dante frowned at Qvo.

'Turn my kind into Primaris Marines.'

'Exactly.'

'I take it this procedure has been undertaken before.'

'Many times now. Marneus Calgar of the Ultramarines was the first, along with members of his honour guard. I understand some have taken to calling it the Calgar Procedure. Misleading. If it must be named for a person, then surely it should be named for Archmagos Dominus Belisarius Cawl, Prime Conduit of–'

'Was it successful?' Dante interrupted. 'I would have heard of Calgar's death, I think, even with the current difficulties.'

'Lord Calgar survived. Only two of his guard made it through the process.'

'Then it is not a guaranteed success.'

'No, my lord, though we have improved the procedure greatly since then, so much that I suspect in time it will become a matter of course. We are confident that our understanding of how to upgrade existing stock Space Marines into

Primaris Marines is advanced enough that we can pass the knowledge on to the apothecarions of each Chapter. They have the relevant skills and training to make it a success. That is why I am here.'

'What of before?'

'Either I or one of Archmagos Cawl's other servants travelled to the Chapter in question to perform the surgery. To be frank with you, I am glad that we are ready to pass this knowledge on. I am ready for a new challenge.'

'Then you have done it before.'

'Many times, but I do not wish for you to be complacent. There are certain idiosyncrasies in each of the gene-lines of the Space Marines. The rootstock of the line of the Primarch Sanguinius is more divergent than most. In fact, it is the most divergent of all the remaining loyal gene-lines except that of the Space Wolves, but they're another matter altogether. There are more extreme variations, but those are mutations, not intended. Your gene-seed is the way it is because it was designed to be so.' He smiled. 'The procedure is especially difficult with your type. Of course you are as hardy of body and mind as the rest, but there are delicate matters that complicate the issue, and bring the margins for success uncomfortably low–'

'You mean the curse of my line,' said Dante abruptly. 'There is a further matter I would raise. It has been suggested Cawl had attempted to repair the damage done to our gene-seed by the passing ages. Let me tell you he has singularly failed.'

'I am aware of this,' said Qvo softly.

'Then why should I put any faith in what you say?'

'The archmagos' attempts to repair the damage to your gene-seed could not be successful,' said Qvo.

'Because we were made this way?'

'Your propensity for savagery was engineered into your original Legion,' said Qvo. 'All the flaw does is exacerbate what is already there. Cawl suspects the affliction is spiritual rather than physical, but he did think he could ameliorate the condition. This is why the Rubicon Primaris is dangerous for you to cross.'

'You refer to this Calgar Procedure?'

'Archmagos Dominus Belisarius Cawl calls it the Rubicon Primaris.'

'I am not familiar with the word "rubicon" either,' said Dante. 'You shame me for my ignorance again.'

'I expect few but Cawl himself know this word. It is the name of a river, a reference to an event from the most ancient of times. The dawn of human history, he told me. The Emperor reconstructed much of Terra's ancient past during the period of the Great Crusade. These histories were lost, as so much else was after the Great Heresy War, but Cawl remembers, somehow.' Qvo smiled to himself. 'Somewhere in those great memory banks of his, it is all there.' Qvo shrugged. 'If he had but the time to remember.'

'You digress. The Rubicon.'

'Yes, yes. I apologise. Cawl made me with the habit of meandering. It gives more of an illusion of personality, I suppose. There was, on ancient Terra, before even the first millennium had run its course, an empire. This was the great realm of the Rumani, which ruled all the lands about the middle sea, the blue heart of the ancient world. The Rumani had an emperor, as we have an emperor – Julus Kaiseri, the most powerful man in the world. There was a river, it is said, that Kaiseri had to cross to win the empire. Crossing the river was a gamble, because once crossed he would be committed to rebellion. He would either win or he would lose – what he could not do was go back. The name of that river was the Rubicon. It became a byword for irreversible decisions for many ages, though it is forgotten by all but Belisarius Cawl.'

'And you.'

'I remember it now but I will no longer remember it when it is of no use to me. I am a limited creature, Lord Dante. Not truly alive. I know this information at this moment because I must in order to convince you to do what is right. The memory storage required for this anecdote will be repurposed when it has served its purpose.'

'Then you are not a man?' Dante reappraised his guest.

Qvo smiled apologetically. 'Strictly speaking, I am not. Part of me was a man once, a very long time ago. Cawl tried to save that man. He could not. I am a facsimile of that man. A servitor, of sorts. I can never be regarded as human. I am an echo of something lost, like this Imperium of ours.' He chuckled. 'All human endeavour becomes an echo of itself, in the end. Palaces to piles of ruin, impressions in the sand to be swept away by the next strong wind.'

'You think. You speak. You have agency. You are no servitor.'

'The term does not fit me truly,' agreed Qvo. 'I am more than a servitor, less than a man.' He sighed contentedly. 'Enough of one to appreciate the beauty of this view, and the artifice on display, not enough to really understand it. I have no soul.'

'There are laws in the Cult Mechanicus against such things as you, are there not?'

Qvo laughed. It was a pleasant, musical sound of amusement, and Dante felt a chill at its perfection, knowing all of it – the mirth it stemmed from, the sound, the smile that accompanied it – to be wholly artificial.

'Of course there are, but I fall just close enough to the

rules to give Archmagos Dominus Belisarius Cawl room to manoeuvre around the lore, if the need ever arises. My Lord Cawl has never played by the rules, Lord Dante, and if that gives you misgivings, I ask that you abandon them. The archmagos has saved your Chapter, and he might yet save all humanity.'

'If I decline this knowledge?'

'Then I shall depart,' said Qvo. 'I would not hold it against you. The reason Cawl calls this procedure the Rubicon Primaris is because of the risk. As with our ancient emperor, there is no return from the other side once you start across. Success brings rejuvenation, elevation to a new level of ability, and the benefits of Cawl's improvements to the Emperor's design. Failure results in death, always.'

'What is the success rate?' said Dante.

'Sixty per cent, give or take. For your Chapter, the number is lower.'

Qvo patted Dante's arm with a metal hand.

'I sympathise with you, as much as I am able.' He scrutinised the lines of Dante's face carefully. 'The first Space Marines were superior beings to those of the current era. Genetic deterioration has corrupted the Emperor's work. The warriors of the Legions were functionally immortal, you know. They did not age in the same way you have. You have my pity.'

'I require no man's pity,' said Dante coldly.

Qvo withdrew his hand. 'There is more than age that troubles you.' His eyes strayed down to Dante's chest, as if he could see the wounds he bore. Dante took a half step back.

'I shall leave you to consider this information. It could bring many benefits to you.'

'It must be discussed before the Chapter Council.'

'Ah, the fabled conjoining of the Red, the Bone and the Blood. I understand only the Chapters sharing your heritage allow their Chaplains and Apothecaries so much influence.'

'It is a system that works well for us,' said Dante.

'We all do what we think right,' said Qvo. 'We all make the best of what we are given, blessings and curses both. I will remain for a period of two weeks, after which I will depart. There are others to whom this technology must be delivered.'

'You came to me first?'

Qvo bowed. 'Not quite first, but you are Commander Dante. You are one of the greatest heroes alive in this terrible time.' He smiled again. The expression made Dante's skin crawl. 'Now, if I may be permitted, I wish to examine *Baal's Fury* more closely.' He paused. 'You will become powerful. Three is a large number of battle-barges for any one Chapter.'

'Too many for the regent of Imperium Nihilus?'

'Perhaps I misspoke,' said Qvo.

'You are correct,' said Dante. 'I do not have enough warriors to fill two to capacity. The *Blade of Vengeance* is undergoing refit after crashing on Baal during the invasion,' said Dante. 'Once it and *Baal's Fury* are out of their docks, I will donate *Bloodcaller* to our brother Chapter in the Blood, the Angels Numinous.'

'That is...' said Qvo in surprise. He glanced up at the Chapter Master. 'That is a gift beyond measure.'

'More than you can calculate. *Bloodcaller* has been with our Chapter for thousands of years, but I will give it away if it is right to do so. The Angels Numinous lost most of their fleet acting in our defence. It is not the first time they have come to our aid. I owe them a great debt that has been too long in the settling.'

'That is no small thing, commander, to grant another

Chapter such a ship. The stories I heard about you were true.' He gave Dante a long, careful look.

'What stories were those, magos?'

'I am simply Qvo.' Qvo smiled, and bowed. 'I am no magos, commander. By your leave? There are many of my people here who wish to see me, and my time is as limited as yours.'

Dante nodded. Qvo bowed again, then walked away, humming to himself.

Dante let him go.

CHAPTER SIXTEEN

GHOST SHIP

Teus stood up from the body. It was broken into several pieces and scattered across the corridor. A tangle of intestines joined parts of the torso to the separated pelvis. The legs spread back at an extreme angle, disarticulated at the hips. One of the feet was a yard away from the ankle. So it went on. His stablight picked out all the little frosted mounds of meat stuck to the floor, the walls and the ceiling.

'Another body,' he voxed to Arael.

'How many is that now?'

'One hundred and six, at my last count. Not many, even for a ship of this size. It looks like a skeleton crew. Whoever these people were and wherever they came from, they left in a hurry.'

'The forge will be able to tell us both of those things. As soon as we have notice to them they will send a Techmarine out here to commune with the ship's central spirit convocation.'

'I am curious to know.'

'Do not expect them to share what they find, unless it is deemed necessary.'

'That does not seem fair somehow,' said Teus. 'We found this ship.'

'You do as you are ordered, brother. Service is its own reward.'

Arael was Teus' brother-mentor, assigned to guide him through his first years as a battle-brother, although in some ways Arael was as much of a stranger to the Blood Angels as Teus was. Teus might have been newly elevated, fast-tracked through apotheosis and the Tenth Company to help refill the Chapter's depleted ranks after the invasion, but he was Baalian. Arael was not. Arael was one of Cawl's Mars-born, from Terra itself if Teus had correctly read the hints he dropped, born a galaxy away and eight thousand years ago. The thought of such vast distances in time and space awed Teus. He was surprised at the emotion. He had thought angels were beyond such mortal feelings. He still had much to learn.

'Do you have any contact with the command deck?' Teus swept his bolt carbine across the corridor. The stablight attached to the side of the gun cast a brilliant circle of white on the frosty walls.

'None. Nothing but blood and scraps of flesh. Sound off your sensor readings, and boost power to your data array.' Arael's vox-signal was choppy. The walls of the ship presented serious obstacles to short-range communications.

'Negative on life signs. Negative on power emissions. I am proceeding to the enginarium.'

'Go carefully, brother. Watch your back. Keep half your attention on your auto-senses and make sure they are tuned to the optimum input feeds. Your battleplate sees a lot better than you do.'

Teus grunted at the warning. Arael was an overly cautious warrior.

Thin air moved sluggishly as he passed down the corridor. Heat spill from his reactor curled in smoking eddies from his venting ports. There was a major breach on the tenth level, but otherwise the ship was undamaged, and its atmosphere had been retained for the most part. The ship's power must have been down for some time. Void cold had seeped into the bones of the craft. A lot of the air had frozen out onto the surfaces, making the interior unsafe to traverse without void-sealed armour. It was also beautiful. Frost sparkled under his stablight beam, as rich as a galaxy of stars.

The ship was small, a noble's cutter, Arael said, as not many craft of that size were warp capable. He was probably right. All of it was luxuriously appointed. Even down in the bowels of the ship where only menials would go, the surfaces were decorated with scrollwork, and the lumens were finely cast, branching affairs that arched out of the walls in miniature facsimiles of tree boughs. There were glimpses of gold and red paint, while Teus' sensorium reported a concentration of semi-precious metals on the fitments. By eye it was hard to tell. Everything had been turned the same eerie white-grey by the frost, making it look like the ship had been coated with ground silver and diamond dust. The combination of luxury and natural glory was beyond his experiences. There had been precious little beauty in his life on Baal Secundus. Even now, after months in the fortress-monastery, beauty daunted him more than violence.

Teus had yet to decide which of the arts the Blood Angels practised suited him the most. As his light snapped across the dark ways, illuminating possible points of ambush, he idly contemplated how best he could capture the play of light. He considered painting, sculpture, tapestry and silverwork. None seemed right. Perhaps it was not possible, and any attempt to recreate the display would look trite. He would ask the senior brothers when he returned.

None of this distracted him from his mission. His officers taught him to see beauty where he could, to preserve his hope so he could pass it on to others, and to distract himself from the road to the Thirst. None of it could be allowed to interfere with his first duty as a warrior.

His boots thumped onto the deck, their maglocks holding him fast with every step. The corridor opened up and the ceiling climbed, sprouting a fan of pipes that turned inwards to run parallel with each other. The way split in three, two smaller corridors curving towards the outer hull, out around the massive block of the reactor housing.

'Enginarium ahead,' he voxed.

'Go carefully. I am returning to the shuttle to begin our report. Meet me there as soon as you have swept the area.'

A large gate sealed the way. Depressing the button had no effect, so Teus set his bolt carbine aside and took out a power driver from his belt to unscrew the door panel. When its innards were exposed he pulled out an input jack from his armour. Phobos plate was replete with useful functions. He was only into his eighth week of training in the Vanguard, but he was already beginning to appreciate the lighter armour configuration, even if he did feel a little more vulnerable in the open void.

He plugged in the jack. His reactor pack shuddered as it spooled up to provide the energy necessary to open the door. The enginarium gates were huge, and their motivators power-hungry. Teus felt the suit grow a little heavier on him as his battleplate diverted power to feed the door.

Dim lights came on in the wall interior. Tech-priest things, blinking for no one to see. Teus had no idea what they were for, but his armour sang him a fanfare of readiness, and a row of icons in his retinal display went from red to green.

'Open,' he said. He had no need to speak. He could have thought it. His armour would have done the rest. Old habits were hard to shake.

Frost cracked along the door's dividing line. Ice snowed from the top. A light spun around at the side of the entrance, and the doors parted.

They rolled back into their housing with the solid noise of plasteel meeting plasteel.

'I have entry.' Teus picked up his gun.

'Do you see anything?'

'Not yet.' The enginarium was a large space of several levels. He passed his light over the interior.

'Remember, check your auto-senses. When there are just the two of us like this, we cannot rely on our squad brothers. We must be our own guardians.'

'Yes, brother,' said Teus.

'Take this seriously, Teus. You are bold but you are also impetuous. Be wary.'

'I meant what I said.'

'I am at the ship now. Keep reporting.'

Teus went inside the enginarium.

He'd been on the reactor decks of other ships. They were usually ferociously hot, and alive with energies of such potency they could be tasted on the air. This one was dead. The reactor core was cold, all the consoles were inactive.

He idly flicked a few switches. 'Whoever shut this down did a thorough job, there is no residual energy at all. All the batteries are drained, secondary power supplies are offline. This is definitely sabotage.'

'It could be a scuttling,' said Arael.

'I do not think it is.'

'Explain your reasoning,' Arael said. He never missed an opportunity to teach. It annoyed Teus, even though he was wise enough to see how invaluable Arael's experience was.

'If you were going to scuttle your ship, then it would be best to blow the reactor, to harm your enemies and to prevent the ship falling into their hands,' said Teus.

'The same could be said of sabotage,' said Arael. *'So why is it sabotage?'*

'The nature of the opponent. There has been a battle here,' Teus said. He stepped over the body of a tech-priest. Transmechanic specialisation badges showed through the coating of frost. The man had been torn apart. Afterwards, something had taken the time to sort his mechanical components and his organic parts into two distinct piles. 'Very quick. They were taken by surprise. No projectile weapons loosed in here, melee only.'

'What did it? Think it out, Teus.'

He went further around a corner. Piles of stripped bones were scattered over the deck.

'The dead have been devoured.'

Alien bio-markers blinked on in his retinal displays.

He brought up his gun, raising the barrel until it pointed to the ceiling.

'Genestealers,' he said. 'That is why the ship is intact.'

He recognised them as soon as he saw them. Two legs, four arms, a pair of hands that were horribly human, a human face on a bloated alien skull. He had fought them upon the Arx Murus before his apotheosis. His memories of the days before he was dragged from the sarcophagus were a jumbled mess, but he remembered these things, and he hated them.

They were hibernating out their transit across the stars,

waiting for the moment some blundering salvager or incautious pirate woke them up to start the whole insidious cycle again.

One of them stirred. Yellow eyes opened in a corpse-white face. Clawed feet opened. Powerful legs bunched, and it pushed off from its perch. It turned as it came down at him, four arms outstretched for a deadly embrace.

Teus blasted it to pieces, then turned his gun on the others.

Chunks of xenos flesh ricocheted off the walls. Bright alien blood froze upon his armour. The genestealers died before they woke, their bodies floating in pieces around the enginarium. The detonations of bolts reduced them to chunks that spun and bounced as chaotically as the rocks in an asteroid field.

Teus didn't stop firing until his magazine was empty.

Fyceline smoke floated across the enginarium, making strange patterns in the microgravity that showed as hot oranges in Teus' heat sight.

'Teus? Teus? Respond!'

'I live,' he said. He looked over his kills. 'Four dead xenos. Ironic that they chose to come to Baal.'

'There will be more,' voxed Arael. *'We cannot take on an infested ship on our own. Return to me immediately. We shall leave and call in a cruiser to obliterate it.'*

A faint signification note sang in Teus' helm. He brought up the details on his helm display.

'Wait,' said Teus. 'I have a life signal, dormant, but human.'

'Ignore it and return.'

A dozen more bio-signs were flashing into life, further out, all xenos. He calculated the distance between himself and the survivor.

'I can make it.'

'Negative, brother. Return.'

'It is close by. I will investigate. It is our duty to save those we can.'

'Teus!'

Teus ignored his mentor. The signal was faint, coming from outside the enginarium. He was forced to double back through the entrance, losing the signal in the process. He kept his guard up, his senses straining for any immediate sign of the xenos, but he found none. The alien markers in his bio-scanner remained far away. He took the starboard corridor, and soon regained a sensor return on the survivor, breaking into an awkward, maglocked run.

He went outwards, towards the edge of the ship, and stumbled upon the site of a massacre. There were bodies in the corridor – man, alien and twisted mixes of the both. Human soldiery in unfamiliar uniforms were iced together with the creatures that had killed them.

'Soldiers,' he voxed. 'Looks like some sort of guard unit, ornate uniforms. Lots of dead xenos too. There was a big fight here.'

'Teus…' Arael replied. *'I have multiple indications of hostile activity on the ship's augur. Return!'*

Life signs sang in Teus' helm.

'I see them. They have not spotted me yet. They're still waking. I'm nearly there. The human bio-sign is at the end of this corridor.'

'It could be a trap.'

'I'm aware of that.'

The bodies were so tightly packed he was forced to disengage his maglocks and haul himself along the wall, his bolt carbine held one-handed before him. The bodies mounded up, forcing him to bend double. Thereafter they sloped suddenly away, half burying a makeshift barricade. There were fewer dead on the far side, and his way became easier.

The corridor terminated in a large airlock, the kind ships of that size used to dock with larger craft or void stations; big enough for cargo pallets, small enough to take passenger umbilicals.

It was closed, its orange paint covered with arcs of arterial spray. A lone soldier sat with his back to it, his legs stretched out in front of him. They were ruined by claw strokes. Pooled blood frozen black as tar glued him in place.

The man had his gun clasped to his chest. His head lolled forward, and his shako had fallen over sideways. A feathered cloak iced with blood clung to his flesh.

He wore a nameplate upon his hat. Teus read it.

'Sergeant Ebasso.'

Teus nudged the dead man gently with his boot. He was solid with ice.

The signal was coming from inside the airlock. He peered through the small window set into the door. Inside was a pristine salvator pod wired up to some sort of equipment.

'I've found the source of the signal,' he said. Once more he was forced to hook himself up to the ship's dormant systems. The door creaked loudly as he opened it. The dead man would not come loose and broke in half at the waist. Then the door slid open fully and his upper body was knocked free. It floated into the gap between the doors before bumping into them.

The noise was heard. Threat alerts flashed in Teus' retinal display. Stealthy footsteps, automatically enhanced by his auto-senses, played loud in his ears.

It wasn't much of a warning, but it was all that he needed. He pushed through the door, shoved the dead man aside, and pushed his hands hard against the metal.

According to his armour senses there were a dozen genestealers running at him, far too many for him to stop. He didn't try. He'd kill a few and then they would swamp him. He had seen what their claws could do to Adeptus Astartes battleplate.

The unpowered doors ground closed slowly. The genestealers were luminous patches in the dark, moving swiftly. He looked up and his suit light glanced off a snarling face, quickly gone. Then the first of them was close by, scuttling along the wall. It leapt for him. With a final heave he slammed the door shut. The genestealer crashed into it, its hideous hissing deadened by the thick metal. It smashed its arms against the glass a few times, before a change came over it. Its face smoothed, and it dropped out of sight.

A sound of claws rasping at metal began.

'Teus, report,' demanded Arael.

'I'm in the airlock. I have a dozen enemy. They are attempting to dig through.'

'You should have obeyed me.'

'It's too late for that.'

'Keep your head.'

'I will not lose my head, brother,' said Teus. He felt cold inside, dispassionate. He still expected fear. He felt none.

'I can't get a solid data link to your auto-senses. Describe what you can see.'

Teus turned around to examine the object he'd risked himself for. 'There's a salvator pod, an advanced unit with full animation arrest. The man inside is in suspension.' He peered through the frosted glass. 'Must be highborn. He looks young, richly dressed. There's a battery hooked up to the pod, still live.' Teus looked at the outer door of the airlock. 'I have an idea. Get to the ship, bring it around.'

Arael made a sound of exasperation. *'What number airlock are you in?'*

'Four,' said Teus. 'Fifteenth deck, aft section. It's a big one.'

The noise of the genestealers hammering at the door was getting louder. Teus heard them screeching at each other, fighting for places at the metal facing so they could be first at the prey. Arael heard them too.

'Be quick, or you'll die.'

Teus yanked out the power feed from the salvator pod. Lights on its front flickered from green to amber. The pod's power supply was exhausted, he didn't have long before the emergency revival system kicked in. It didn't matter. Either this would work, or they'd both be dead.

There was a socket in the door for power input and output. He twisted the battery feed into place, waited for the door console ready lights to activate. He pulled out a length of rappelling wire from his utility kit and looped it around the pod's retrieval handles, tying it fast. He'd have to catch the pod if they were vented into space, or it stood a good chance of smashing into him and breaking open his armour.

The airlock system showed ready indicators. He pressed the release button. An error signifier showed on the small screen. An ugly noise accompanied it.

Teus looked behind him. The metal was being pushed inwards. Raised lines appeared on the door where claws scraped at it. A loud slam sounded. Three raised points appeared where a claw had nearly punched through.

'They are almost in. The outer door is malfunctioning. I am going to have to crank it open.'

He searched for the manual release. He wasn't familiar with the model of airlock and it took valuable seconds to find, during which time the pounding on the interior door increased. The metal deformed.

He opened the manual release by the simple expedient of crumpling the metal door in his fist and wrenching it off the wall. Inside, a small crank handle was held in place by a pair of brackets. A socketed wheel took the end. It was sized for human hands, and his mild wonder at his own strength was replaced with frustration as he tried to manipulate the fiddly object. It clicked home. He forced himself to wind it slowly in case he broke it in half.

The door cracked open. The small pocket of air contained within the airlock was sucked out instantly. Sound changed. The banging on the inner door receded to muffled thumps conveyed through the metal. He was confined in a silent world defined by his battleplate's hum.

The door opened mercifully quickly. Within seconds it was wide enough for him to squeeze out, if he shed his power plant. But the pod would not fit. He had to get the doors open completely.

His auto-senses picked up a high-pitched whistling. Teus continued to crank the handle as he looked behind him. A claw tip had punched through the door and a white plume of gas geysered through the hole, hitting the far wall with some force. Teus cranked faster. A claw jammed into the hole, working at it dextrously, slicing it open like a knife would a ration tin.

Another breach in the door. A three-clawed hand punched clean through behind Teus. A blast of howling air buffeted him, knocking his hand off the delicate crank.

The holes widened. A bulbous alien head thrust through into the airlock, snapping its teeth, ovipositor sliding in and out of its jaws. Its face was covered with frost, but the vacuum and the cold had no effect on it. Genestealers could live for hours in hard vacuum, and would fight until they died from exposure if they had to.

The door ratcheted open. Teus grabbed the drag handles on the salvator pod. It was ten feet long, four wide, and massed at least a ton. He maglocked his boots to the floor and heaved. Air continued to howl out of the holes in the airlock, and would until the ship was voided. There were no functioning machine-spirits and no power to close up the ship's bulkheads.

A genestealer forced its way half through the gap, tearing open its pallid flesh on the jagged edges. It screeched plumes of hot breath into the frigid void. Teus lifted his gun one-handed and put a bolt through its head. Its fellows immediately began to tear it apart so they could get at their prey.

The salvator pod refused to move. Teus yanked back hard, stressing his limbs and his war suit. He wished then for the greater strength boost Intercessor armour provided. Muscles tore. His armour whined loudly in his ears. He disengaged its safety parameters. Alarms peeped as fibre bundles overtaxed themselves and broke.

The salvator pod shifted on the metal. Teus leaned back from the movement, hauling for all he was worth, building up the momentum of the pod so that it finally came free. Getting it moving was the hard part. He grunted as he swung about and slung the pod into space.

He disengaged his maglocks before the line tethering him to the pod snapped taut, yanking him out into the open void. Billows of frozen atmosphere whirled him around. He fired off his bolt carbine on full automatic, the resulting force accelerating him away from the ship, but the line snapped tight again, and he and the pod began to orbit each other in a rapid spin.

The genestealers burst through the inner door, launching themselves straight out into space. It was said that genestealers were as intelligent as men, but they were slaves of the hive mind, and the needs of the tyranid whole compelled them to sacrifice themselves without a second thought.

A heavy body banged into him, jarring his gun from his fist and sending his orbit around the pod into wild swings. A moment of desperate fighting ensued. The xenos beast tried to wrap its lower arms around him while the upper, wickedly sharp claws smashed into his battleplate. Only their spinning saved him. The genestealer struggled to hit him accurately. The tips of its plate-breaking claws skidded off his armour.

Teus punched the thing in the midriff, cracking its chitinous exoskeleton with the force of his fist alone. Somehow, he got his combat knife out of its sheath and rammed it up through the creature's chin, skewering the brain.

The pod continued spinning. The ship blurred past his vision, each revolution granting him the sight of genestealers floating out of the ship, arms waving like those of insects trapped in oil, and gas spewing from the side of the vessel, the force of it sending the ship into a slow spin also. He sent out bursts from the stabilisation jets mounted on the top of his backpack, but their force was too feeble to counteract the mass of the wheeling pod. Every reduction in speed was minute, and followed by the line snapping taut and hurling him out again.

He was racing away from the craft, into the depths of interplanetary space. He lost sight of the vessel. The bright dots of the Baalian trio and distant Kheru blurred by.

'Arael, Arael!' he voxed. 'I am outside the ship with the survivor. Arael! I am drifting.' He felt no fear of death. The Sanguinary Priests had promised him he would not feel fear of any kind. They were right, but he was ashamed that he should die in so ignominious a way.

Something bright flared at the edge of his vision. A proximity alarm wailed in his helm. A mag grapple clanged onto his armour, bringing him to a rapid, painful stop. The rappel line yanked hard and snapped, sending the pod racing away on its own course like a bullet released from a sling.

'I told you to come back to the ship,' said Arael. *'I'm winding you in. Then let's get after this survivor you almost died saving. I cannot abide a wasted effort.'*

CHAPTER SEVENTEEN

THE CHAPTER COUNCIL

As the master of ceremonies read through the names of all present in the Chamber of the Great Red Council, Dante let his mind wander. A hundred concerns troubled him, problems of the mind that accompanied the hundred aches and pains of his injured body.

Most of the faces on the Chapter Council were new. It had been several months since Cawl's Gift had brought the Chapter from the brink of extinction to full strength, and although Dante was learning the foibles and talents of each of his new captains quickly, as yet he felt he did not have the measure of them. What was true for the Blood Angels was equally true for their successors. Ranking officers in the system were invited to the council meeting. Most of the Chapter Masters and captains among the Blood were replacements, either Primaris Marines arrived with the crusade, or veteran brothers promoted out of the ranks, and in both cases Dante knew them little. Members of the reinforced Flesh Tearers,

Angels Encarmine and the Angels Sanguine predominated, with representatives from several other Chapters besides.

Dante had commissioned the Chamber of the Great Red Council for the gathering of the Blood before Leviathan struck. It had been despoiled along with the rest of the Arx Angelicum. Little was contained within its huge hall that would have been of interest to a predator, but the tyranids had treated the Chapter spitefully. No piece of art or commemoration was left untouched. Everywhere they had torn down the monuments and destroyed the art. Large sections of the chamber were screened off. There was centuries worth of work in the Arx Angelicum to repair the damage.

Those who believed the tyranids to be beasts put the destruction down to animal savagery. More enlightened souls suggested the hive fleet saw, without understanding, ways to break their prey's morale. These sages maintained emergent behaviour drove everything the hive fleets did, produced by interactions between uncountable components: intelligent, but unthinking.

Dante knew differently. He had seen into the hive mind. He knew it was sentient. He knew what had happened to the Blood Angels was vendetta, and that the invasion had been launched for reasons of vengeance as much as strategy.

The council stood at the hollow, circular Table of Communion while the names were read. There was space for five hundred warriors around its circuit. Fewer than half the seats were occupied. Of those, fewer than half again played host to captains or Masters. Many of the reinforced Chapters had departed for their own fiefdoms. Dante had not required that they stay, and in some cases had ordered them to leave. How could the Chapters of the Blood hope to fulfil Guilliman's orders if they could not even obey their most basic oaths, to secure their own regions? They had worlds to protect, sectors to patrol, and pledges of alliance and support almost as old as their loyalty to the father Chapter. Dante was skilled enough in statecraft to know he could not rescue Imperium Nihilus from destruction if his first act was to demand the breaking of ancient promises. He was born into the years of darkness. He understood this age better than the primarch. He did not have Guilliman's reforming zeal.

Although all twenty-five officers of the Blood Angels' own council attended, half the gathering were lesser warriors: veteran sergeants, Librarians, Chaplains and, in several cases, trusted mortal servants of the Chapters. The inclusion of baseline humans would only happen more frequently, Dante thought.

He sought out Corbulo. The Sanguinary High Priest looked troubled. Dante had had little time to speak with anyone, but he had passed on the news of the Rage among the Primaris Marines. It had affected Corbulo deeply. He had hoped the new breed to be immune. They knew now for sure that was not the case. Astorath's place was next to Corbulo's. He was present, for once, and had returned with similar tidings concerning the new Space Marines. The occurrence of the Rage on the *Dominance* was not the only instance.

The reading of names dragged on. It was a tedious affair, but necessary. There were prideful men among those present. There were those who might not take the word of a mortal man as equal to that of a Space Marine. They needed reminding the opinions of everyone in the chamber were equal.

The master of ceremonies was new, and young. Nearly all the Chapter thralls had been slain by the tyranids. What the Chapter had gained in youthful vigour it had lost in wisdom. The master did his best with the titles and the names, but he faltered more than once, and he struggled to identify all the warriors correctly.

Dante's eyes strayed to the crack in the pure white marble of the tabletop. When his fist had made that mark there had been five hundred heroes in the hall. Most were dead. However he looked at their survival, the Chapters of the Blood were a diminished brotherhood. New technology and fresh warriors by the thousand could not make up for the loss of so much experience.

The master of ceremonies was coming to the end of his litany. He concluded with Dante's list of titles. 'Commander Dante, Commander of Baal, Master of the Blood Angels, Keeper of the Blood, Lord of the Angelic Host. Regent and Warden of Imperium Nihilus, by the grace of the Emperor, lord of Terra and of the Imperium of Man...'

A flock of cyber cherubim flew in, carrying Dante's personal banner in chubby fists and mechanical pincers. They stopped and hovered directly over his throne.

'Dante, Lord of Angels! Dante, Lord of Baal! Dante, Lord of the first-born sons!' they sang.

'Dante!' the others said. Those blessed with the Emperor's gifts slammed their right gauntlets into their chestplates. The mortal humans placed their hands over their hearts in the sign of the aquila, and bowed respectfully.

'All be seated for the lord regent of Imperium Nihilus,' said the master of ceremonies.

A hundred armoured bodies lowered themselves into stone chairs.

Dante remained standing. The downdraught of clumsy mechanical wings stirred the air.

'I thank you for your attendance, brothers of my Chapter, and brothers of the Blood. To our honoured friends who are not of the Adeptus Astartes yet loyally serve the Imperium, I bid you welcome.'

Dante was masked. Rarely did he appear in public without his face covered. He did not like to show his age, and he recognised the effect the visage of the Great Angel had on others.

He leant on the table, and let his fingers trace the crack before him. Golden armour bumped over fractured marble. 'I made this mark when I proclaimed my intention that Baal would not fall. I confess to you, my brethren, that when I said those words, I did not know our survival was possible. Yet here we are.'

Dante stood upright. His armour sighed, nearly silent, a suit of the finest quality.

'Months have passed since the battle. Much work has been done. Much more remains. The Arx Angelicum is refortified. Skyfall is almost ready to play host to the fleets of Imperium Nihilus. Our scouts return. Our plans are ready.'

A hololith ignited in the hollow centre of the table, its projection depicting the northern portion of the Red Scar and the systems to the north beyond.

'The attack on Baal blunted the talons of Leviathan, but it is far from dead,' said Dante. An overlay imposed itself on the cartolith, showing the spreading limbs of the hive fleet, split like the branches of a coral, each limb heading for a different life-bearing system. All systems that had life in the Scar were human worlds, colonies maintained by technology in the face of the Red Scar's dangerous radiation.

The largest tendril of the fleet engulfed Baal itself, but it stopped there and was covered with marks of extinction. A dozen others passed through systems Dante had enacted Exterminatus upon. Where they departed these patches of scorched earth, the tendrils were smaller. 'After our destruction of the major tendril here, the fleets have split, and spread among the remaining inhabited systems of the Red Scar. The number of tyranids is diminished, but they are feeding, and will replenish their numbers quickly if not contained.'

'My lord, if I may speak.'

'Captain Raphaen, Fourth Captain, the Lord Adjudicator, Blood Angels Chapter, the Knights of Baal,' announced the master of ceremonies.

'Do so,' said Dante.

'Have we not delayed too long?'

Raphaen was a belligerent man. His impatience tested Dante. One of Guilliman's reinforcements, he had plenty of experience fighting in the Indomitus Crusade, but had yet to shape himself to fit the Chapter.

'I assume we are not to hear a question, but a criticism of the plan,' said Dante.

'I only wish to understand your reasoning of the delay in our retaliation,' said Raphaen. 'I see you wished to rebuild the Chapter and the others of the Blood, and gain true understanding of the situation around Baal, but why has Kheru not been purged of the tyranids still infesting it? Why have we not attacked the tyranids at these other systems nearby? We know they are there.'

'Reasonable questions, captain,' said Dante. He kept his annoyance hidden. Raphaen had been a vocal critic of the scheme since the beginning. He was using the opportunity of the council to make his objections known publicly. Given his indiscreet nature, most were aware already, but his speaking then marked an escalation of his defiance. 'The tyranids must be attacked simultaneously, across a broad front. That requires organisation, and in the current circumstances, with the warp being as disrupted as it is, that organisation takes time. Attacking one tendril gives the hive mind time to reorganise and react. It is at its weakest when given no time to adapt. Kheru remains infested because it must be purged utterly. To do that we must deploy our full strength. The turmoil in the warp affects the mind of the tyranids as much as it does our own psykers, but I will not risk the knowledge of our new capabilities being made known to the greater hive fleet. If we attack, it will realise it failed here. The creatures on Kheru are isolated for now. They must be slaughtered, and they will be, but the attack on Kheru must take place as close as possible to our other assaults. If we attack in isolation there is a risk that the tyranids will become aware of our new assets, and work to counter them, either through evolutionary shift, strategic response, or both. We will retain the element of surprise. That is why we do not fight yet.'

'You already know our lord's reasoning,' added Antargo. The master of ceremonies began to announce his titles, but Antargo silenced him with a glare. 'The details of the Angel's Halo are finalised. That is why we are here. We will attack soon. You know this too.'

Raphaen pulled a dissatisfied expression and sat back.

'All your questions are about to be answered,' said Dante. He wondered how many of the new members of the Chapter felt like Raphaen. They were not in awe of Dante's legend. They had fought at the side of a primarch. 'I understand your experiences in the Imperial Regent's service have bred a little impatience into you. Roboute Guilliman moved fast, his gains were great. We must be more cautious, but only in the planning. The time for caution is almost over. The execution of our strategy will be swift and devastating. I have chosen these systems as the primary staging posts in our war of extermination.'

Three bright stars lit up in the cartolith, each bearing a bright data-tag: Ashallon, Gamma IV and Bhelik Alphus. Together, they made a rough arc to the south of Baal, between the Chapter world and the Cryptus system. A red arrow moved out from Baal and split, giving the appearance of a trident.

'The Points of Grace,' said Dante. 'All of them likely nexuses from significant tyrannic activity. Once taken, each of these systems will serve as forward bases for multiple attacks on smaller tyranid tendrils, and from those, smaller divisions of the hive fleet, until we have plucked out every root and vine of the xenos threat. Each also has strategic importance in its own right.

'Ashallon is an industrial world whose forges will equip the rebuilt armies of Imperium Nihilus,' Dante continued. 'Gamma IV offers further industrial capability, and a good anchorage for fleet operations deeper into the Scar. The fortress world of Bhelik Alphus contains a great supply of hellfire acid, which we should secure to use against the enemy.' An expanding sphere painted itself onto the image, crawling outwards from Baal. 'I dub this the Angel's Halo,' he said. 'A growing area of control and reconquest that will emanate in all directions from Baal while the Points of Grace are being secured. Once they are, the tyranids will be isolated within the Scar and can be dealt with.'

Numerous other star systems along the edges of the Red Scar blinked.

'Most of the systems to the immediate north of the Red Scar are relatively safe, or suffering minor attacks. Communications remain poor, however. Where our scouts have not yet been, we shall go as reconnaissance in force.'

'And what if the tyranids turn away from the Scar, my

lord?' said Raphaen. 'If they break for the north, they will cut past our main forces. By the time we are in a position to respond, they will be among the richer systems beyond the Scar, where they will feast and grow in number again.'

'As yet, there is no indication that this is the case,' said Dante. 'The few arms of the hive fleet heading into these sectors are small and have been engaged successfully by various Imperial forces. Nevertheless, I have anticipated the arrival of greater numbers of them, for it is inevitable. To counter this, the Charnel Guard are to be placed in reserve at Toth. The Angels Vermillion are already at Kandar. Both Chapters will be in a position to provide rapid response groups to support local forces and the armies advancing from Baal, should the tyranids make a mass attempt on the north.'

'Then there is something I should bring to your attention,' said Raphaen. He was grimly satisfied. Dante anticipated new knowledge the captain had deliberately kept back. 'There is a matter that requires attention, and may deflect us from our chosen path if not dealt with.'

Several of the others looked to Dante.

'Speak, brother-captain,' said the commander.

'Brother Teus, bring in the governor of Ronenti,' Raphaen voxed. Then to Dante he said, 'My company has been on patrol in-system. They discovered a drifting vessel, only one survivor aboard. Your strategy appears sound, my lord, but I inform the council now, the tyranids are already out of the Red Scar.'

Dante watched Governor Jemmeni closely as Teus brought him in.

He was young, with the dark skin of a people raised under strong sun, still with a youth's slightness that was accentuated by the huge figures of the Adeptus Astartes sat at the table. He was daunted by the assemblage of heroes, but the prince held himself well, and his eyes did not dart like a nervous man's would. There was more to his bearing than the arrogance of an Imperial Commander's brat. He was frightened, but he withstood the scrutiny of a hundred powerful lords calmly.

Astorath stood from his black throne and stared hard at the boy. The boy shivered a little, but kept his composure.

'You are Governor Jemmeni of the Imperial world of Ronenti?' asked Astorath.

The boy nodded. 'I am, and of its domains of Antrigus and Roosen that are situated within the same system. Although I have had no coronation, and have yet to receive my grant of fiat from the High Lords of Terra, I am of the line of Sigaari, first governor. My father was Imperial Commander. I am his only heir.'

'You come here to speak for the world of Ronenti and its attendant domains?'

'I do.' Still the boy held his composure, impressing Dante.

'You stand before the assembled Chapter Council of the Blood Angels Chapter of the Adeptus Astartes – that is the Red Council of war, the Council of Bone and Blood who are our spiritual guides, and our allies and our brothers in the Blood. To speak falsehoods before us is a grave crime, and a greater error. Do you swear by the Emperor, the Master of Mankind who sits upon the throne of Terra, that you will tell only the truth?'

Dante watched Astorath. Too often the throne of the High Chaplain was empty. It was good to have him present. If only the news he had brought with him from Dulcis were not so grim.

'I swear I shall not bear false witness,' said Jemmeni. 'I shall speak only the truth, and only in the interest of my subjects.'

Astorath looked to Dante. 'Will you hear his petition, my lord?'

'I will,' said Dante. 'He may proceed.'

Raphaen sat back. With a look of triumph on his face, he stared at the boy commander, unnerving him.

The prince showed his first sign of hesitation, looking from the Chaplain to the commander uncertainly.

'The Lord Dante said you should begin,' said Astorath, more softly. 'Speak.'

'My world is divided in two by the Encircling Desert. To the north and the south are habitable lands, in our tropics and further away. The rebellion started in the south,' the prince began. 'We don't know why. When I was a young boy, a political movement began in the Djesseli Combine agitated against my father's rule. We are a planet of many nations, but we have had peace for generations. Our parliament was adept at resolving disputes between our peoples. We have enjoyed centuries of calm. They said they wanted greater freedoms. These were granted, but more were demanded, and they became more extreme. Eventually, my father said no.'

'The ultimate decision remained with your family?' asked Dante.

'We are the ruling Imperial House,' said Jemmeni. 'But my father and his fathers have always sought approval from the Chamber of Representatives. It was instilled in me from a young age that involvement in governmental process makes the populace easier to govern, and it forces the governors to treat the governed more fairly.' He drew in a deep breath. 'Ours was a good world, a fair world, but the complaints the Djesseli brought against the rest were provocative. They wanted war. Every attempt to address their issues was turned down, or if resolved, another complaint would be brought. My father saw this too late. We had faith in our political system. By the time we realised they were determined to fight, they were ready, and we were not. The Djesseli took two other nations into their rebellion with them. Half our planetary defence force committed to their cause, though our system fleet remained loyal.'

'What was the cause?' said Astorath.

'Xenos influence, my lord,' said Jemmeni. 'There was a change in appearance of the Djesseli. Long before their rebellion, their rulers began to shun our way of life. Our world is warm and the climate good, but they locked themselves away indoors. Rumours came to us that they were physically changed, becoming paler in complexion, and intolerant of the heat. We suspected genetic deterioration. Medicae purity monitors were sent by the local Administratum offices to test the populace, but they never returned, and shortly after that the war began. Towards the end, monsters fought alongside the men, hideous things with skin the colour of corpses and armoured plates of a bloody red bonded to their bodies. They had many limbs. They were not human, yet the rebels venerated them.'

'Genestealers,' said Corbulo.

'A full-scale insurrection,' added Raphaen. 'Given the travel time, cult infestation there will already be expressing a psychic call to the tyranids, and more systems will be falling.'

'Please, my lord, help us,' said Jemmeni. 'My men died to bring me here. We have had little contact with your Chapter, we have borne our difficulties alone, knowing that the terrors faced by others were more severe. We have never petitioned you before. We come to you for the first time.'

'We have many requests for aid,' said Dante.

Jemmeni failed to hide his disappointment. 'My lord, I accept your judgement, as I must, but please tell me to who else I should turn? There is no help to be had elsewhere, you are our only hope.' The prince's eyes shone with tears. 'My people died to save me. They died to bring me here.'

'The whole galaxy is in turmoil,' said Dante. 'You are not likely to receive your grant of fiat from the High Lords, nor any other news from Terra. I, Lord Dante, rule this portion of the Imperium in the Emperor's name, as I was so commanded to do by the Imperial Regent Roboute Guilliman himself. It is to me you must submit, in the name of the Emperor.'

'I shall, my lord.'

'Do you swear fealty to the Imperium, as embodied by my person and rulership?'

'I do!'

'Then you may submit your notification of succession to me when we retake your domain.'

'You will do it? You will save my world?' Jemmeni's face turned from despair to joy.

'You have saved your world,' said Dante, 'by risking all to come here when you could have fled, as many other aristocrats would have. If Ronenti is saved, it is your doing. My captains, my fellow Chapter Masters,' Dante said to his assembled brethren. 'We are honour pledged to defend all the domains of mankind. Kheru can wait a little while longer.' He looked back to the prince. 'You are going to go home, my lord.' Dante turned Sanguinius' howling face fully onto Raphaen, and was gratified to see the captain's confidence slip. 'Raphaen is correct. If the tyranids receive notification of a ready prey source from the cult, they will turn north.'

Raphaen bowed his head. 'By your command.'

Dante rested his fingertips upon the Table of Communion. 'You of the new breed, Captain Raphaen... I am aware some among you believe me to be too old to lead adequately. You are not daunted by my legend, and I see this as a good thing. But I am Master of this Chapter, and you will not question my orders again.'

A murmur of voices set up. Raphaen had allies among the new captains, but more of them, like Antargo, were offended by his manner towards Dante, and all the veterans were.

'And yet, once more I find myself in agreement with our argumentative captain!' said Dante loudly, silencing the crowd. 'I am old! I am in need of renewal. An answer to my quandary presents itself. An emissary of Belisarius Cawl has come to us, bringing with him new technologies that will allow existing Space Marines to be transformed into the Primaris strain. This process is dangerous, and I cannot in good conscience ask that any take this risk if I myself will not. Therefore, I have decided that I shall undergo the procedure first, tomorrow, and when I have recovered, we shall begin our reconquest of Imperium Nihilus.'

The chamber was already primed with tension by Raphaen's challenge. Dante's pronouncement was met with absolute uproar. Warriors old and new got to their feet. Many questions were put forward, and many arguments made against Dante's choice. Astorath left his throne and came to his lord's side.

'You should not do this,' he whispered.

Calls to order fell on deaf ears. The old Space Marines would not allow their lord to take such a risk. The new were split. All argued loudly, and the clamour increased, until Rhacelus stood from his place at the table, slammed his staff hard onto the floor and sent out a pulse of psychic power that dazzled all eyes and quieted every voice.

'Be silent! Your commander orders it,' said Rhacelus. A nimbus of red light burned around his head. His eyes glared ferociously with warp shine as he turned to the Chapter Master's throne. 'My lord, you are too valuable to risk as an experimental subject.'

Murmurs of assent went up.

'But if you would permit me,' Rhacelus said. 'I have a better idea.'

CHAPTER EIGHTEEN

DEATH IMPRISONED

The black-robed guardians of the Chemic Spheres stood sentry with their heads bowed, only the faintest glimmer of gold visible of the horrific masks they wore. Rhacelus ignored them as he worked the minor rituals needed to open the door. They were always there. There were only ever two. What exactly they were, who they had been, where they came from, what oaths they had taken, Rhacelus did not know. Mephiston might not even know. To learn their identities he would have to interrogate the spirits of past Librarians clinging to existence in the Sepulcrum Maleficus, or rouse the most ancient of the Chapter's Librarian-Dreadnoughts. Rhacelus would rather not do either of those things, and so let the matter remain a mystery. It was safer that way.

The door opened, and he stepped within. A pearlescent dome lit red by the sluggish light of Idalia rose before him. This was the Chemic Spheres, one of the Blood Angels' most secure psychic prisons. Never had it been more needed.

Rhacelus leaned his staff upon the wall and went close to the dome. He did not open it. He did not need to. Incredibly, he could feel the Lord of Death's presence behind the wall.

'It should not be possible,' he said to himself. The barriers woven into the dome were inviolable, yet they were violated.

Fierce energies crawled down the walls from the star captive in the vaults above. If he could feel Mephiston's soul even through the barrier of the spheres, would Idalia be enough to restrain the Lord of Death if he finally lost control? The thought worried Rhacelus greatly.

He sat himself upon the engraved steel of the floor surrounding the dome. The hall of the spheres was large, but the dome took up most of the space, leaving a circular strip around its perimeter only a few yards wide. His robes rustled as he settled.

Rhacelus closed his warp-touched eyes, and reached out with his mind.

Mephiston, he thought. The wards were prominent to his witch-sight as runes burning with cold, awful fire, each one as big as a man, floating immovably around the dome. The dome showed itself as a bloody hemisphere alive with crawling script. Nothing of the spirit should be able to penetrate those defences, but as soon as Rhacelus reached out, the sense of Mephiston's presence grew enormously, and a black shape rushed out from the depths of the warded space. The runes blazed with an intensity great enough to scorch his soul, and he flinched from them, before the approaching blackness swallowed them and blotted out everything. It loomed over him, emanating a terrifying power. For a moment, he had the impression of a great, black angel, as terrible as the end of time. The sense dissipated. The darkness faded. The runes contained most of the furious power within the spheres, allowing only a sickening trace out to touch Rhacelus' being.

A ghostly image of Mephiston manifested before him.

+You should not have come, Gaius,+ said the phantom. Mephiston was a shadow shot through with threads of red and gold. +This place is dangerous to you. I am dangerous to you.+

Rhacelus believed it. Mephiston's spirit voice was strained. The dangerous energy behind the wards waxed strong. Again he saw the black angel, standing where his friend should be. When it receded, Mephiston had changed, becoming Calistarius, though his voice and psychic imprint were those of the Lord of Death.

+I cannot contain this power that is in me any longer,+ said Mephiston. +Soon the Chemic Spheres will be insufficient to hold me.+

'What is happening to you?'

Mephiston laughed bitterly. +I do not know. Not since Calistarius died under the rubble of Hades Hive and I clawed my way out. I have known nothing of what I truly am.+ The image wavered, taking on the semblance of Mephiston clad for war, potent and terrible, his armour glistening like blood. +All through our adventures, my friend, you have watched my becoming. Now I feel the final transformation is on me, and I do not know what is on the other side. I fear you must slay me soon, before I cease to be, as Calistarius ceased to be before me, lest I become something evil.+ He looked behind him, where his body was caged. +A great darkness is coming for me.+

He closed his eyes in pain.

'The Black Rage?'

+Something else. I do not know how to describe it. It is

eating away at me, body and soul. Soon there will be nothing left but the darkness. I called the Rage down on us, Gaius. I almost killed you. You must destroy me.+

The sight moved Rhacelus. He had called Mephiston friend since before his change. The Lord of Death had tried to push him away, like he had all his former colleagues. Only he and the Sanguinary Priest Albinus remained close to him. It was a one-sided affection. Mephiston was confident, and decisive, but rarely warm.

'I see a great black angel here. I have seen it before, at war with a golden angel in the warp,' said Rhacelus.

+When did you see this?+

'I took upon your burden of guiding the ships home to Baal.'

+I am sorry, my brother.+

'We all live to serve, Mephiston.'

+Your next service will also be onerous,+ said Mephiston. +You must kill me.+

'That will not be necessary,' said Rhacelus. 'Firstly, you are not responsible for the emergence of the Rage within the Primaris brothers, as we first feared. Lord Astorath has returned from the world of Dulcis, where he too saw the warriors of the new blood fall to the old curse. Brother Corbulo believes now they always were susceptible. Its manifestation on the *Dominance* and on Dulcis is an effect of the warp, or so it has been theorised, not you.'

+That is good to hear,+ said Mephiston. The ghosts of blood-red wings spread and furled around him. +But I still cannot control the power growing in me. I remain a threat.+

'There is something else,' said Rhacelus. 'A servant of Belisarius Cawl has come to Baal. He has brought the means to transform a Space Marine, giving him all the strength our new brothers possess, but there are risks.'

+You have proposed me as the test subject,+ said Mephiston.

'Dante volunteered. The council would have vetoed his decision. I proposed you in his stead.'

+What did the others say?+

'Some objected, as is to be expected,' said Rhacelus. 'They do not wish to risk you, but I believe it offers the only hope we have to contain your gifts. You have seen the new Librarians that came with the primarch. They are stronger in mind as well as in body. Your rebirth could help you control your power.'

+And Antros? What does he say?+

'He is yet to return from his mission, brother. It is for the best.'

Mephiston did not agree. +What is the price, I ask, of this transformation?+

'If the procedure fails, you will die,' said Rhacelus simply.

+How much can we truly trust Cawl?+

'It is a question we have all wrestled with. Perhaps we should not examine his gifts overly closely in these times of crisis. Without Cawl, our Chapter would be extinct.'

+A wise man examines everything, especially those things of great value that are given freely.+

'This is true, my brother, but what choice do we have? Dante will surely give the order to kill you if you remain here. You are growing stronger with every day that passes.'

+A choice between two deaths,+ Mephiston said. +Somewhat fitting.+ He looked at the dome again. +This conversation should not be possible,+ he said. He looked back at Rhacelus. +I agree to the procedure. But promise me, if I seem to be losing myself, you will finish me. Only you have the might to oppose me, my brother, and even then you must be swift.+

'Very well. I shall inform Commander Dante,' said Rhacelus.

+Quickly,+ said Mephiston. +Death approaches us all on swift wings.+

CHAPTER NINETEEN

RUBICON PRIMARIS

A procession of men climbed their way up the Tribunalis Victorum, the long, broad stair that wound its way up the Walk of Angels. Dante went at their head. Sanguinary High Priest Corbulo marched a few paces behind him, Sanguinary Priest Albinus at his side. Dante wore his armour, but the priests had delicate work to perform, and wore plastek coats over surgical robes. A pair of cruel-faced cyber cherubim flew overhead, dragging a large banner through the air marked with the sigils of the Sanguis Corpusculum. Behind Corbulo and Albinus came Astorath, grim-faced, his axe held sideways across his body. Behind him was Cawl's servant, Qvo-87, and a gaggle of specialised medical servitors. After them came a dozen blood thralls, dressed in the high-necked, pure white surgical coats of the apothecarion's servants. Then a squad of veterans, their golden helms and crimson armour freshly polished. Bringing up the rear marched a full ten of the Sanguinary Guard, led by Daeanatos.

The brothers sang a funeral song as they marched, one saved to mark the passing of the Chapter's greatest heroes. Whatever occurred, Mephiston was going to die. Qvo assured Dante of that.

They passed through the Arcus Elim onto the Walk of Angels. During the battle for the Arx Angelicum, the Walk had seen ferocious fighting, and had been all but destroyed. The Arcus Elim had been reproduced perfectly, only the sharpness of the carvings and the freshness of the stone giving away the fact that it was only a few months old. Scaffolding still covered over the rest of the Walk.

Art was the heart of the Blood Angels' order. Utilitarian work deadened their souls. Dante looked on the scaffolds, the artisans and brothers standing quietly, tools in hand, waiting for the procession to pass. He recalled the names of the hundreds of brothers who had died during the invasion, and the thousands of those of the Blood. So many had bled on those steps.

They passed on out of the Walk and through gates of solid adamantium into the Heavenward Redoubt. From there the procession made its way through the keep up to the walls.

A hot wind was blowing off the desert. All work had ceased on the marshalling yards out beyond the fortress-monastery. A host of men of all kinds laboured to rebuild the outer curtain wall. The new wall was bigger, stronger, fitted with its own banks of void shield generators. Between the extinct volcano and the outer perimeter, the land was crowded with new facilities, some fully constructed, others as yet but outlines in the sand. Accommodation for bureaucrats and officials alongside barracks for human soldiery and storage plants, defence batteries, temples and more. A city was rising where sand had ruled for millennia. The Arx Angelicum was changing from desert monastery to the hub of half a galactic empire. Lining the new road leading out from the Maxilliary Gate were a dozen giant statues, all of heroic aspect, the Chapter Masters of the Blood who had given their lives. Dante's gaze lingered on the stern visage of Castellan Zargo of the Angels Encarmine. Beside him stood Sentor Jool, last Master of the Knights of Blood, his Chapter's honour redeemed through sacrifice. Five Masters alone had fallen within the walls of the fortress-monastery. Many of them had died along with the entirety of their Chapters. The names and colours of the Chapters lived on, but knowledge, experience and tradition had been lost, devoured as surely as their flesh. Their memories would be honoured. Upon the plinths of the statues, Dante had ordered the same legend be inscribed: 'One Blood, One Brotherhood.'

Before the invasion, ruins from the time of the Great Crusade had been uncovered. Now, all traces of the past were buried beneath millions of tons of 'crete, stone and metal. Dante wondered what Sanguinius would do in his position. Would he countenance this vainglorious recreation of the Imperial Palace in miniature? Would he have refused Roboute Guilliman's demand that he should rule in the Emperor's place, as Dante now effectively was?

In truth, Dante could not guess. He was not sure of his own motives. They were matters that needed meditating upon, if he ever got the time.

The procession continued along the murus to the uppermost precincts of the Librarius, and there descended an outer stair down several levels of the fortress-monastery to the Orbicular Tower. It stood proud of the wall, its top not quite reaching the ramparts. The bulk of the Librarius Sagrestia was buried within the rock beneath it.

A gate of blue and gold opened into the volcano's side. Beyond, Rhacelus waited with all the members of the Librarius on Baal.

'My Lord Dante,' Rhacelus said. 'These constructs must remain outside.' He pointed with the head of his staff at the flock of skulls, cherubs and other cybernetic familiars hanging over the procession. Dante heard Qvo tutting as he dismissed his devices.

'The rest of you, I permit entrance to the Librarius of the Blood Angels,' intoned Rhacelus with great formality.

'As lord and Master of the Blood Angels Chapter, I accept your permission, and your right to give it,' said Dante.

Rhacelus bowed and came to stand beside Dante, and remained at his side as the procession moved off into the depths.

Qvo-87 greedily recorded all he could of the Librarius. Space Marine Chapters rarely allowed outsiders insight into their cults, and the sub-orders were even more secretive.

Rhacelus led them down through a labyrinth of passageways. Qvo's internal locators placed them far beneath the surface and more than a mile out from the fortress-monastery by the time Rhacelus led them onto a more level path, and yet the rock remained the same, glossy volcanic stone as the Arx Murus.

They reached a huge gateway guarded by thralls in polished blue armour, armed with long energy pikes. Psi-monitors in Qvo's chest showed these thralls all to be psykers of a minor sort.

The mortal guards parted and slammed their pikes into the ground in salute. Rhacelus stopped by the gates and turned to face the procession.

'Behold, the Diurnal Vault,' he said. 'The living heart of our order. Be honoured. Few who are not of the Psykana Librarius ever see it.'

He pushed his right hand against the air. A pulse of psychic force flung the doors wide. Unbearable light flooded the corridor, along with a stifling heat.

Qvo held up a metal hand to shield his eyes, unconsciously reverting to baseline human behaviour.

The Diurnal Vault must have been constructed according to trans-dimensional principles, for it was far larger a space than could have been contained by its supposed location. The source of the light was a blazing orb, forty feet across, set into the chest of a gargantuan statue of an angel carved from black stone and lit strongly red by the orb. The angel's right hand rested upon the pommel of an immense sword. The left hand was held palm upwards, three enormous crystalline menhirs floating above it in a haze of crimson light.

Qvo stepped inside the room. Banks of machines were arrayed around the room's periphery. Fat power conduits passed through into them, splitting inside the machines and emerging as a dazzling web of glowing strands that led from the room.

'Behold Idalia, the Emperor's boon,' said Rhacelus, 'given to us by His hand. It is she who powers our Librarius.'

The sight was too much for Qvo to process. The shrivelled stub of a human brain that served as his central neural architecture struggled to stay active. The mechanical structures that surrounded it frantically reordered themselves to keep Qvo conscious.

'I have seen many things,' said Qvo. 'This is a sight of true grandeur. What technology creates the fusion ball?'

'None that you shall have,' said Rhacelus. 'Idalia is no

common reactor, but a star, plucked from the heavens and crushed by the Emperor's will. It provides power to the Librarius, keeps our defences and preserves our knowledge. Not even in the direst hours of the Devastation of Baal were the wards of the Librarius broken. No single tyranid made its way within our walls. It proved the match of the hive mind. You will not take our secrets.'

'I'm sorry?'

'You are recording everything you see.' Rhacelus slammed his staff down, and his eyes flared. 'It does not matter. If you were to attempt the labyrinth again, you would never find this place. Your presence here is a singular indulgence, and you will take no knowledge with you, Belisarius Cawl.'

'I am Qvo-87,' said Qvo.

'I see what and who you are,' said Rhacelus.

A buzz of cognitive dissonance disrupted the integration of Qvo's systems.

The Epistolary turned away. 'Be mindful of your step. Idalia brooks no gravity but her own.' He walked forward, and as he did so he rose into the air. 'Stay behind me. I and my brother-Librarians shall guide you onwards.'

The star pulled at the procession as they followed, but they were gently shepherded by the Librarians' witch powers towards a door hidden within the angel's robes. Crowds of cyber cherubs and servo-skulls dipped down from on high to examine them. Qvo attempted to sound the heights of the room lost in the blazing light, but most of his sensing equipment was foiled by the tumult of energies. For a few moments they were swimming in a sea of light, then the door opened, and a telekinetic push guided them into a small stone chamber where they were set gently on the ground.

'My lords, this way,' said Rhacelus, and led them on.

They passed through to a stair, then downwards into another maze, this one of crumbling brick. Though Baal was arid, the air here was moist, and grew moister, until soon the walls were oozing water, and moss clung to the mortar. Again Qvo attempted to gauge his position. Once more he failed. They were far off the edge of every map, and so he contented himself with scanning the bricks' mineralogical composition.

'These tunnels are ancient,' said Qvo. 'I hypothesise they were not made by human hand. They do not exist within the confines of normal space-time. Do you know their provenance, Lord Dante?'

'This is the Carceri Arcanum,' said Dante. 'No one knows who built these tunnels or when. Only Rhacelus, Mephiston and the most learned of their servants know their full extent.'

'It is a mystery even to you?'

Dante nodded. His voice emanated hollowly from behind Sanguinius' shouting face. 'Even to me.'

The tunnels wandered seemingly without aim, branching in every direction. Rhacelus led them on a long and illogical route. Many stone doorways barred the way, each psychically locked. Rhacelus paused before each one and drew a sign in the air, causing their lock runes to glow for a second before the doors rumbled open. There was no one but the procession in the Carceri Arcanum.

Eventually Rhacelus reached a worn marble door so old and pitted with erosion that the figures on it had softened to meaningless shapes. Only a numeral IX, very faint in the stone, was discernible. Two Adeptus Astartes stood sentry either side of the doorway, unarmoured, clad in black robes and armed with two-handed swords as big as a man. They rested their hands on the pommels, the tips buried in the damp sand that floored the tunnels.

Rhacelus pushed open the doors onto a large, circular vault awash with the crimson starlight of Idalia funnelled down glowing cables embedded in the walls. Most of its area was taken up by a large dome. To human sight it appeared to be fashioned from seamless ivory. Qvo saw it was something far more sophisticated: a psychically resonant, semi-organic poly-plastek, a little like wraithbone.

'Interesting,' he said. He flitted through multiple sensor feeds, measuring the dome's energy emissions, and attempted to read the millions of tiny words playing over its surface that were revealed by certain ocular modes.

'This is the Chemic Spheres, the most heavily warded place for hundreds of light years,' said Rhacelus. 'It is the Lord Mephiston's self-imposed prison, and at this current time, the only thing keeping him from destroying us all.'

The Librarians filed into the chamber, circling the dome to take up station at regular points. Qvo examined the floor. What appeared at first to be featureless steel was etched with fine ritual lines, including warded circles within which the Librarians went to stand. Once they were in place, the pyskers commenced chanting, and the atmosphere became heavy with emanations from the warp.

'Where is my machinery?' Qvo enquired.

'It is being held not far from here. Once we are ready, it will be brought within,' Rhacelus said. He approached the dome, and unhooked a small syringe full of blood from his belt. 'My lord Dante, I will be forced to bring the entire dome down so the procedure can be undertaken. The brothers of the Librarius will contain Mephiston's powers, but should anything go wrong, without the dome you will be in grave danger. Perhaps you should withdraw until all is finished.'

'I will stay and observe,' said Dante. 'The future of many of us could be forged here.'

'As you wish,' said Rhacelus.

'Brother Daeanatos, deploy your men,' said Dante.

The Sanguinary Guard went around the dome, taking up station between the Librarians. Qvo did not need to ask why. They were executioners.

'We are ready to begin, then.' Rhacelus lifted up the syringe and uncapped its needle, and then plunged it into the dome. The surface yielded like skin. Injected blood billowed out in scarlet threads, before racing outwards, and forming a rectangular outline. The lines pulsed, and filled with Idalia's sacred light, becoming an open doorway as red as a wound. The atmosphere became heavier. A great presence was trapped within.

Rhacelus went around the dome, taking more syringes from his belt. The dome split into segments, and with each administration of the blood, more of the segments disappeared until the dome had gone completely.

The Librarians chanted louder.

At the centre of the vault was a single, heavy sarcophagus.

'Mephiston's resting place. I had it brought here from the Sepulcrum Maleficus,' said Rhacelus. 'When we remove Mephiston from its confines will be the moment of greatest risk.' At his words the black-clad sentries came into the vault, and stood either side of the sarcophagus. Astorath joined them, set his axe head upon the steel floor and fixed his gaze on the carved representation of Mephiston's face.

'Magos Cawl, do you wish to bring your machinery within now?' said Rhacelus.

'Qvo,' said Qvo. 'And indeed I do.'

'Then it is done,' said Rhacelus.

A few minutes later Qvo's medical servitors entered, all of them freshly cleaned and with counterseptic garments hiding their organic components.

Others came with them, pushing large metal crates containing the equipment necessary to transform Mephiston.

'This is far from ideal,' Qvo said to Rhacelus as he unpacked and assembled his devices.

'It is what we have,' said Rhacelus. 'Doing this anywhere else would invite disaster. It is by necessity we work in the Carceri Arcanum, not by choice.'

'Well,' said Qvo. 'At moments where delicate machinery has to be assembled quickly, a number of subroutines are activated within my hardware that equate to stress. I can only assume my original model was an anxious character. It is rather bothersome, though.'

'You are a strange creature,' said Rhacelus.

'I am,' said Qvo-87. His gaze wandered past Rhacelus to where three servitors struggled to erect a chirurgeon unit. 'Oh, do watch that!' Qvo-87 snapped. 'We have only one of that grade with us, and it is vital to the procedure.'

The servitors looked at Qvo dumbly while he berated them.

An hour and a half sped by as the machinery was assembled. Albinus, Corbulo and their mortal servants went to the sarcophagus and began checking over its machinery. Qvo had a number of machines that puzzled the Sanguinary Priests. Part of Qvo's mission was to begin teaching the Blood Angels the art of the Rubicon, but he held his silence for the time being. They didn't want to share their secrets, so he wouldn't share his until he felt like it.

A huge operating table was assembled close to the sarcophagus. The chirurgeon was installed over it. Once the machines' network was established, Qvo checked it thoroughly, losing himself in the intricacies of the work. He wondered if this was how actual human beings felt when they concentrated.

The last display ran its readiness message. The last notification of good function chimed from the chirurgeon. It twitched its spindly limbs all at once, then fell still.

'The machines are ready to be blessed,' said Qvo.

Dante looked at Rhacelus.

'Be quick,' said the Epistolary. 'The Lord of Death is stirring.'

'Yes, yes,' said Qvo. 'I am a creature of Cawl. Both he and I are true believers in the Machine-God, but neither of us is blind to the actual science we do, unlike most of the Archmagos Dominus' colleagues.'

Qvo rapidly blessed each machine, switching to binharic to speed the process. He refrained from bringing out his aspergillum. Scented oil all over everything would not help, but he did extrude an incense trumpet from his left shoulder and jet out noisy blasts of smoke over his machines, surgical instruments and tools. He could feel the Space Marines' disapproval, and yet they had adepts of Mars among their number. He seethed at their impatience.

He let out one long, last blast of thick lavender smoke. The smell of holy oil permeated everything.

'I am done,' he said. 'Bring out the subject.'

'Show respect. He is a lord of humanity, and our brother,' said Dante.

'Bring out Lord Mephiston,' Qvo corrected himself emotionlessly.

Albinus depressed a panel on the sarcophagus. The guardians of the spheres and High Chaplain Astorath hefted their weapons.

The lower part of the sarcophagus opened up with a loud hiss. A torrent of blood poured from the base into a drain around it. A low, steady alarm pulsed through the spheres. The mechanisms of the sarcophagus clunked and whirred. The lid rose up and forward. A pair of curved arms popped out of the side, lifting it up and clear of the casing.

Mephiston lay unconscious inside. Black flames burned all over him, seemingly on the verge of guttering out, but never doing so. Qvo peered at him curiously.

'Peculiar. Is this a manifestation of his power?'

'It is,' said Rhacelus.

Qvo looked at him expectantly. Rhacelus looked stonily ahead.

'Be assured that he is dormant,' said Rhacelus.

A little tension left the room.

'Good,' said Qvo. 'Then let us begin. Quickly.'

CHAPTER TWENTY

SINS OF THE FATHER

Mephiston looked down on his body from above as Qvo's machines sliced him apart. They flayed his skin, they scraped off his flesh down to the bone. His black carapace was peeled away. His neural ports were cored from the organic plastek. The nerves grown into them during his first transformation were carefully looped and placed in bowls of counterseptic on stands around the operating table.

Mephiston had spirit-walked uncountable times, but this time his actions were not his to command. Something was pulling his soul out with a sensation akin to the sticky feel of skin peeling free of muscle. Above him, a shaft composed of writhing red and black shadow came into being. As it twisted into life, the upward pressure grew.

He turned back to watch the circles of men, of machines, and the designs in the floor, contained by the greater circle of the warriors of the Librarius. All faced towards the operating table, eyes fixed on the horrors being performed in the name of saving his soul. He tarried there, resisting whatever it was that sought to pull him away.

The Librarians' chants drew power from the empyrean. Mephiston saw it clearly as winding ropes of energy curling out of warped portions of space. Dark energies curdled reality, but the efforts of the Space Marine Librarians teased pure light from the dark. By the time it entered their bodies it shone clean reds and blues, and yet the faintest taint lingered. There was no usage of the warp without corruption.

The machines were skinning his face. Tubes sucked away the blood welling up from his hideless body. His exposed muscles glistened. With each cord of sinew and muscle fibre on display, his body resembled his gory armour. His face came free, carried up and away from his body in delicate metal claws by an armature composed of sliding rods. Teeth pink with blood grinned death's grin. Lidless eyes stared up, directly into the eyes of his spirit form. He had the sudden thought that there were two Mephistons regarding one another, and for one terrifying moment he did not know which was real: Mephiston the spirit, or Mephiston the corpse.

But the eyes were sightless. They saw nothing. The light had gone from them, and ascended.

The force tugged hard at his soul, causing him pain in every part of his being. His soul was black as pitch, a silhouette of a man. He was an absence. Where his being should shine bright with pure psychic energy there was only darkness.

The force pulled him harder, dragging him towards the throat of the vortex. He looked up and saw fleeting shapes in the shadows of red and black: men, monsters, and the things in between, the awful truth of what lurked beneath the Blood Angels' noble facade.

He should not have been able to leave the Spheres. The

Carceri Arcanum existed beyond the normal laws of space and time, and the Chemic Spheres was its strongest vault. His spirit should have been trapped, it should have been seen, but he passed before the witch-sight of master psykers without notice, rising up and up, the scene becoming smaller beneath his shadowy feet. The chanting droned without losing volume, as if it carried him, an ember on a rising column of fire, until a dazzling light opened above him, and he flew towards it with incredible speed. The shadows of black and red spun faster, and faster, losing their forms to become a marbled whirl.

The light engulfed him, and then he was in some other place.

Mephiston came awake with a gasp. Cold air rushed into his lungs. He opened his eyes upon a pale sky where clouds raced with unnatural speed.

He sat. He was upon a bed of springy dwarf shrubs on a promontory overlooking a desert. Oddly shaped peaks stretched to the left and right of his position. They mounted up behind him through a twisted forest to fields of dirty snow and ice.

'Baal Primus,' he said.

He was on the moon of his birth.

He was seeing it as it had been before the Devastation turned it from toxic wilderness to lifeless rock. The plains, streaked by garish salts, were unmistakable. As the desert drew near to the mountains, it rumpled up like cloth into ridges that grew into stunted foothills. Yet the geography was wrong. The mountains were not mountains at all, but the remains of orbital facilities downed before the dawning of the Imperium, and the foothills were pressure ridges slammed into the surface.

This was the Necklace, the sole mountain range on Baal Primus. Long ago it had been his home.

The landscape was of the past, but his body was that of a Space Marine, tall and strong.

He looked down at himself. He was dressed in ragged clothes.

I once wore clothes like these, he thought, though he had no memory of them. He frowned, fingering the pattern of steel nuts and deep-cave snail shells stitched around the neckline. Images floated just beneath the surface of recollection. A flash of a woman's face, prematurely aged, handing the clothes to him. They had been new then, and though they were primitively tailored she'd given them over with pride, the tunic and the trousers neatly folded, moccasins on top. He remembered these garments. He hadn't worn clothes *like* them, he had worn those exact clothes, for years, until they were patched and torn and worn away to nothing. His hand went to his side. Here at his belt was his knife, there beneath his shirt the simple necklace he had made with a twine of human hair, upon which he had threaded a pretty piece of ancient glass. He lifted it up and looked into it. The way the glass caught the light caused a small avalanche of memories. Caves, fires, stinking machines, snows on the mountaintop and blood in the desert. Laughter, tears and death unlooked for, though always expected.

All these items had been smaller then, to fit a mortal frame not fully grown.

'Illusion,' he said, letting the necklace drop. 'These garments are dust. Baal Primus is a dead world.' All traces of poisoned life had been scoured away. It was airless, and uninhabited.

But not there, in that warp-memory. There the clouds

continued to race, mottling the land with their shadows as they passed, the darkness slithering over features in the landscape like hurried, living things. They ran before an unnatural wind. A hurricane would make clouds rush so, perhaps, but on Mephiston's face was only the gentlest breeze redolent of snow, dust and promethium fumes that tingled his nose.

He closed his eyes, delved deep within himself to where his dark power resided, focusing, reaching past the imminent now into a more profound, timeless state. He called upon his Librarian's art and searched for the truth. Though he was psychically powerful, his gifts were not the sole source of his ability. Discipline, experience and training were as much his allies. They made him strong in the face of the warp's madness.

He reached outside himself, seeking a way to escape the illusion. Mephiston had traversed many lands in many times beyond the material realm. The warp offered an infinity of vistas, for those who knew how to see them. They could trap a man.

'None of them are real,' he said. 'This is not real.'

He concentrated. He pushed at the limits of his mind, but met nothing but the bony walls of his skull. He could not return from whence he came.

'There is no way out, Kali,' said a rough voice. 'You are here for the duration. You have to ride this one out.'

Mephiston opened his eyes. A man stood on the slope above him. He was small and malnourished as all the peoples of Baal's moons were, but especially ratty in appearance; a man of spare, strong muscles and crooked bones. He stood awkwardly. His pelvis tilted to the left. The lords of Baal were beautiful, all of them. Their subjects invariably were not. This one had a huge nose, bent out of shape by a poorly fixed break. His ears were lopsided from either mutation or injury. His filed teeth were blue with decay, and what little hair he had stuck out in tufts all over this head. Even so, he was no fool. He had eyes that glinted like knapped flint, sharp and dangerous.

'Do you remember me, Kali?'

He wore clothes similar to Mephiston's, though filthy to the point of stiffness. A sour reek came off him. In one hand he held a staff of curled wood.

'I am Mephiston–'

'Lord of Death,' the man mocked in a whining voice, as if Mephiston were a sulky child. 'You were a pompous little arse when you were a person. Power's only made you worse.' He shook his staff.

'You are not real.'

The man pinched his own cheek with a filthy fingernail. 'I feel real.' He sniffed his armpit. 'I smell real.'

'You are a figure from my past given the semblance of life by whatever entity has trapped me in this psychosphere.'

The man shook his head in disbelief, hawked and spat a fat gobbet of phlegm onto the ground. 'By all the ancient gods, listen to you. If you'd spoken like that when you were with me, I'd have tanned your hide. I don't think there's any saving you now.'

'I know I am damned.'

'I'm not talking about damnation, boy, I'm talking about pomposity.'

'Who are you supposed to be?' said Mephiston. 'Are you my father?'

The man blinked in surprise, then laughed uproariously. 'Father, your father?' He laughed so hard tears ran from his eyes, and he began to cough. 'Don't you remember your father? Big man, prone to outbursts of murderous violence?'

Mephiston shook his head.

'I remember nothing at all from before the time of my apotheosis. Perhaps I did when I was Calistarius, but since I became Mephiston, I do not even recall if I ever remembered.'

'You are beginning to remember now, though, aren't you?' said the man, leaning on his staff and leering. 'Kali, Calistarius, Mephiston... Are you going to take another name if you go back? You're going to die, you know, back there, on that bloody table. Doesn't matter how many names you have or how many fancy words you know.'

'All men die.'

'Not one of them wants to, not really, so don't play brave with me,' said the man. 'How many names do you need, Kali? How many are you going to take?' The man trudged down the hillside until he stood in front of Mephiston. He was forced to crane his neck to look up into his face, but he kept his eyes on Mephiston's the whole time. He was not afraid. 'It doesn't matter if you bury yourself in names. You'll never hide what you are.' He poked Mephiston in the chest. The man's finger was filthy and hard. 'You're a dirty little witch, like me.' He turned about and walked further down the mountain. 'Come on, you'll be wanting to get this all over and done with, I'm sure. You never did have any bloody patience.'

Mephiston followed after. The man moved surprisingly quickly, hopping down the uneven path with great agility.

'Who are you?'

'It doesn't matter. It never really did, not from the moment I spotted the psy-shine in you. I knew they'd take you eventually. Looking at what you've become, I wish I hadn't bothered hiding you in the first place. I should have let your father kill you.'

'Then you must be long dead.'

'Am I?' the man said resentfully. 'Nothing ever dies, not really. I mean yes, obviously, I am dead, but time means nothing. Physicality isn't the be all and end all.' He turned round again and shook his staff angrily. 'I tell you, it's shit being dead. If you avoid fading away or being ripped apart by warp predators or swallowed by a god, there's just places like this, and that's if you're lucky. Nowhere. Nothing. Rubbish.'

He resumed his bouncing hobble down the slope.

'I have an inkling it's not supposed to be this way, or else why would we be bothering with all this?' He stopped by a cave mouth in the mountainside. 'In there,' the man said.

The cave was dark, and noisome, and at first glance looked to be an irregular crack, but when Mephiston held aside the swags of moss around it and brushed dirt and corrosion from the opening, he saw that once, a long time ago, it had been a metal doorway in a metal surface.

'But this is the way things are.' The man looked up and sniffed. 'Though it might not be for much longer. Warp's changing. Big things are happening. Bad things.' The man peered at Mephiston. 'If you're not careful, you'll be one of them.'

He tapped Mephiston on the rump with the butt of his staff. The gentlest of blows, but it hit Mephiston like a power-fist strike. The door rushed at him, and he was flung into darkness.

He fell a while in total darkness, so long he lost the sensation of falling. His senses were starved. Within moments time ceased to exist. He found himself in a limbo that could have lasted forever. By the time light came to him again, he was motionless, kneeling upon a hard floor, with no clue as to how he had got there.

A ruby glow spread through the darkness, lighting upon him so gradually he did not realise he was starting to see, until suddenly he could.

He got to his feet. He was still wearing the tribesman's garb, but he was no longer on Baal Primus. There was no sign of the door or of the man. Instead, he was deep under the ground. Red crystal surrounded him on the walls, floor and ceiling. A cave of another sort. It appeared natural. It could equally have been crafted.

He looked around. The light continued to grow, until it was light as dawn on Baal, and flames danced deep within the walls of the cavern. The cave could have been a twin for the Ruberica in the Cruor Mountains. But that was a natural wonder. A sense of the supernatural clung to Ruberica even when it was inactive. This place was dead from the heart out, for all its seeming similarity.

There was a wall behind him and a tunnel ahead of him. Having no other choice, the Lord of Death went forward.

For some time he walked, his way lit dimly by the crystals' weak inner light. The tunnel kinked about, presenting hundreds of reflections of Mephison in its faceted walls. They were all different, showing the Lord of Death as he had been at every stage of his life. In some, he was a boy with a face Mephiston did not remember. In others, Calistarius, as neophyte and initiate, as psy-acolytum and as Librarian. He saw his trials, he saw his triumphs. Calistarius fought well and laughed often. He was of a different character to the Lord of Death, and like the images of the boy walking along beside him, Mephiston did not recognise the man as himself. Fascinated, he turned to stare into a facet that showed Calistarius as if he stood in front of him.

Calistarius had Mephiston's face, but only in a nominal

way, so that if by some impossible twist of time the two of them were to stand side by side, then an observer would have taken them to be blood brothers rather than twins; certainly not the same man. A face with a knowing smile looked out from the ruby crystal, mirthful eyes above it. Calistarius was beautiful whereas Mephiston was fearsome. On Mephiston's face, Calistarius' straight nose was hard and angular rather than noble. His pale skin was corpselike and waxy rather than fine. There was power in both of them, but it shone from Mephiston's eyes with a baleful intensity that Calistarius lacked.

Around Calistarius, other reflections faded into being. Each showed Mephiston rather than Calistarius. Each one was crueller looking than the last. A hundred iterations of Mephiston's face glowered, surrounding Calistarius' friendly mien in a hateful halo.

Mephiston examined every one. In each, he was a monster. Before his eyes, the images wavered again, and they changed. He saw in them his gene-father Sanguinius, and he marvelled at the vision. For him the Great Angel was little better than a legend, yet there he was, living and acting. He saw Sanguinius fight. He saw him speak with his brothers. He saw him perform acts of selflessness. He saw him commit atrocities in the name of the young Imperium.

'I am not without darkness,' Mephiston whispered, quoting the scrolls of Sanguinius. 'No man is truly good. No man is truly evil.' He saw planets burn. He saw entire races expunged. The parade of war went on and on, each scene darker than the one before.

'Forget not the sins of the father,' Mephiston said to himself.

The images vanished, leaving Mephiston reflected from a hundred angles. Only Calistarius' unmoving image remained.

'Forget not thy own sins,' Mephiston said, and Calistarius' lips moved with his own.

Calistarius lifted his left arm. It passed out of the false bloodstone.

The Lord of Death stared into the eyes of the man he used to be and grasped his proffered hand. Dead-white flesh gripped flawless blue armour.

There was a flash of heat, and the cave was gone.

CHAPTER TWENTY-ONE

QVO'S GAMBLE

Five hours of the droning of the Librarians' chant made Dante's teeth ache. Even through the psychic protection afforded him by Sanguinius' mask, he suffered from the power in that place. Lines of sigils ran bright down the inner surface of the chamber. They swayed and pulsed, oddly alive. Red light ran in the circles cut into the floor.

At the centre of it Mephiston was carved up, a flayed sacrifice to himself. His skin floated in a nutrient tank, the plates of his black carapace in another.

'First the old must die before the new can be reborn,' Qvo said, as his machines removed the last of Mephiston's skin.

Dante thought that Qvo did not understand the import of that. This was Mephiston's second rebirth. Calistarius of old had been lost when Mephiston crawled out of the rubble of Hades Hive. Dante feared what might emerge from the other side of death this time. He checked again that his Sanguinary

Guard were in place, a circle outside the ring of Librarians. They had to be ready to strike.

'He is prepared,' said Qvo. 'We shall now begin the second part of the procedure, the insertion of the Belisarian Furnace. This will help the Lord Mephiston survive the process of elevation.'

Qvo bowed his head to Corbulo. The Sanguinary Priests stepped forward. A pair of blood thrall personnel came with them, helping Corbulo to cut through Mephiston's chest muscles and pull them back from the bone. Albinus checked a number of machines, satisfied at the readings they displayed, then spoke.

'Proceed.'

A buzzing saw descended from the chirurgeon crouched over the table. It whined loudly over the Librarians' chants, the pitch increasing as it bit into the Lord of Death's sternum. The sharp smell of hot bone cut through the air, the whining became wetter, then abruptly ceased. The bone saw withdrew, and at Qvo's command a rib spreader slotted itself into the gap carved through the muscle. Cogs spun along a toothed track, forcing the spreader open.

For some time the bone refused to give. The crack Mephiston's rib box made as the machine broke it open was as loud and sharp as a bolt-round explosion. The spreader clicked loudly. On the screens mounted away from the table, Dante saw Mephiston's hearts exposed, red and glistening, naked to the hot air. A nozzle rotated down from the chirurgeon and squirted out a mist of counterseptic. A servitor wheeled forward. In soft grabbers it held a lidded, glassite bowl. Within was a new organ.

'This furnace has been force-grown to maturity,' explained Qvo to the assembled witnesses, more for the pleasure of the knowledge he possessed rather than a need to educate. 'This is the key to the transformation from Principia to Primaris Space Marine. Once it is implanted, it will rapidly bond with the Lord Mephiston's hearts and immediately begin to excrete specialised hormones into his body. These will soften his bones, and reactivate the ossmodula, facilitating further skeletal growth. The trick to all this is modulating its activity. It is remarkable. I would say it is Cawl's finest achievement.' He undid the lid and very carefully scooped out the organ with a secondary pair of hands. 'We do not wish to be working against its formidable healing abilities while we cut, but we do need to harness them when the time comes.'

Medical servitors extended the soft paddle scoops they had for hands and gently pulled Mephiston's hearts aside. The organs quivered unsurely but continued to beat. Into the space made between them, Qvo carefully placed the furnace.

'Master Corbulo, if you please.'

With a signal to his aides, Corbulo directed that an electric pulse be passed through Mephiston's body. The hearts' activity ceased. A machine played a small clarion, and the pump within spun up to full power, forcing blood through soft tubes and then through arterial shunts into Mephiston's system.

Corbulo looked to Qvo.

'Begin. I shall watch. It is important you learn the steps of this procedure yourself. You have six minutes remaining to attach the organ to the blood supply, before it begins to die.'

Corbulo nodded, and bent over the Lord of Death's open chest. With deft movements, he cut into Mephiston's arteries, and stitched the mouths of the Belisarian Furnace's tubes onto them. He worked fast, and Qvo intervened only once, pointing out with a fine probe the exact location of attachment for one of the furnace's nerve clusters.

'I am done,' Corbulo said.

Qvo checked his work. 'You are. A surpassingly excellent job, Master Corbulo. Stop the pump. Restart his hearts.'

A blood thrall worked a console. Mephiston's flayed body jerked as power surged through it.

Machines keened. Lines ran flat on grey screens.

'Again,' commanded Corbulo.

Once more a pulse of electricity speared through Mephiston's body.

'We should cease the procedure,' said Albinus. 'If he is replaced within his sarcophagus, then he may recover.'

'Negative,' said Qvo. 'We must continue whether he is alive or not. His bodily systems will restart, and all will be well, or they will not. In either eventuality, the enhancements must be in place and the procedure finished, or he will die for certain.'

Albinus looked to Dante for guidance. Above his surgical mask his eyes were angry. 'We should never have started this.'

'Albinus, calm yourself,' said Corbulo.

'Proceed,' said Dante.

'I will hold you personally responsible if Mephiston dies, Qvo,' said Albinus.

'The risk was calculated before it was taken. I shall do all I can. The furnace and hearts must be stimulated manually to release its healing cells. Do so now,' said Qvo.

'Albinus, aid me,' Corbulo called. Albinus left the machines and joined him.

Together, the two Sanguinary Priests leant over the open chest cavity and began massaging Mephiston's hearts with their gloved hands. The machines ceased their maddening chiming, settling into a rhythm that matched the priests' efforts. An artificial pulse set, Corbulo turned his attention to the furnace.

'Continue,' said Qvo-87. 'We shall proceed with the implantation of the sinew coils.'

A bundle of metal cables was raised up out of a tank by a small crane. Suspended in the air, they resembled a network of veins, roughly in the shape of the human body.

'The sinew coils are different from other Space Marine implants,' Qvo continued. 'In effect, they are a cybernetic implantation where the others are purely organic enhancement. Even so, ordinarily, the coils can be grown within the body from multiple seed locations. Durasteel powder is added to the neophyte's nutrient feeds, and the machinery of the coils is built up within his musculature. But in the case of the Rubicon we need to be quicker. Let the machines move his blood once more!' Qvo commanded. 'The chirurgeon needs space to work.'

Spinning pumps took over the job of circulation from the Sanguinary Priests again. Albinus and Corbulo stepped back. Mephiston's hearts lay still.

Qvo went to an instrument bank and activated a number of servo-skulls festooned with small contragrav projectors. The skulls floated up out of the machine and into position. Through the interplay of the fields, the network of cables was lifted gently up, until it lay horizontal in the air, and filled out. Now it resembled an abstract sculpture of a man, of the sort Dante had seen in more decadent societies, where the truth of forms was abhorred.

Qvo directed the grav-skulls to lower the coils towards the Lord of Death's body. Numerous supplementary limbs emerged from within his robes, moving about with hypnotic rhythm as if he were conducting a piece of music. When the floating steel sculpture was fractions of an inch away from Mephiston's body, one of Qvo's main arms snapped upright. A machine responded with a rapid pattern of blinking lights, and the coils came to sudden, writhing life, squirming around each other like a knot of serpents, losing their semblance to the human form. They speared down, slipping noisily into the spaces in Mephiston's flesh. For a moment Mephiston's body jiggled with the coils' activity as they infiltrated every part of his body.

Servitors gripped the Lord of Death's limbs, and activity subsided. There was a brief writhing in his flesh, then bands of metal, slick with blood, peeked out from between his exposed muscles.

Qvo checked it over, first by eye, then with a succession of sensors.

'The sinew coil net is in place. He will be sore for a few weeks while it bonds with his body, but it should function. Now we begin the implantation of the magnificat. This is the most perilous part of the operation.'

The table tilted upwards. The section beneath Mephiston's neck pushed forward, raising the Lord of Death's head. The chirurgeon extended another device that clamped around Mephiston's temples. A hidden bonesaw shrieked and the device withdrew, taking the top of Mephiston's skull with it and exposing his brain.

'Bring forth the magnificat,' Qvo proclaimed.

A machine began to chime urgently. Then another.

'My lords,' a blood thrall called to the two Sanguinary Priests. 'There has been a sudden and total cessation of brain activity.'

'Magos Qvo-87, what is happening?' said Albinus.

Qvo looked unsure.

'What is happening?'

Qvo tilted his head, examining streams of data on his internal systems. 'The Lord of Death is dead,' he said. 'We must be swifter still.'

CHAPTER TWENTY-TWO

THE BLOODY ANGEL

Light shone through Mephiston's closed eyelids, though he did not recall closing them. Warm wind blew upon his skin. Dry air tightened the skin in his nostrils.

Mephiston opened his eyes. The rough clothes of the Baal Primus tribes were gone. He was clad in the pure white robes aspirants to the Chapter wore.

The wind pressed the rough fabric into his body, outlining his muscles through the weave. Bone-pale hair flew out behind him. Grains of sand stung his lips and gritted his eyes. Fine dust caked his face.

A desiccated plain stretched in all directions, reaching for low hills that bounded it on every side. The sky was orange, overcast. Soft wind blew serpents of dust across the ground.

'Baal,' he said.

He found the sole element of the landscape that broke the desert's monotony. A set of pillars in the distance, so far away they were upright threads on the horizon, that drew pencil lines of shadow on the sand.

He set off towards them.

Ancient, crusted sand broke under Mephiston's feet, leaving a trail of shallow craters behind him on the featureless land. The wind blew constantly. The air was oxygen-poor. It was as perfect a facsimile of Baal's deep desert as could be. Once more he attempted to break out of the vision. Once more he failed. His environs were too real. They held him tightly.

He walked. Days sped by in seconds. The sky cleared. The complicated dance of Baal's daughters cast brief shadows over the land with each accelerated eclipse. Darkness came and went. Stars shone in the short-lived dark, the Red Scar glowering across a different portion of the sky as the weeks raced past, but always there, always attempting to exert its malign influence upon the worlds of the Baal system, always failing.

Mephiston approached the pillars and saw that there were nine arranged in a circle. Each looked like it had been thrust up from the ground by a subterranean force. Each was topped with a pile of age-greyed, xenos skulls.

Within the circle were ten more pillars, these only as tall as a man, arranged in two lines of five facing one another. Whereas the outer pillars were rough-hewn and ancient, these were finely carved. Those to the left were of ivory, and topped with golden statues representing the Angelic Graces. Those to the right were of black marble, and topped with statues of carnelian representing the Warrior's Virtues. They made a short avenue, at the end of which, in the centre of the circle, stood an empty throne carved from a single block of sandstone stained brown with old blood.

When Mephiston passed though the stones a tremendous

peal of thunder roared over the land. He looked upwards and saw the titanic angels from the warp warring in the sky.

They were insubstantial enough that the procession of the moons was visible through their bodies, but the clang of their weapons upon one another was real enough, each strike clashing with sufficient force to shake the earth. One was clad in the gold armour of the Sanguinor, the other was hooded, entirely black from the tip of his sword to the feathers of his outstretched wings. The Sanguinor's sculpted mask was impassive in comparison, yet his movements were strained, and his wings were flecked with blood from a dozen minor cuts.

Instinct drew Mephiston's attention down to the empty throne. As soon as his gaze alighted upon it blood poured, liquid and hot, from some unseen place. The figure of a Space Marine in armour filled from the boots upwards, as if the blood flowed into a glass vessel. Blood frothed and bubbled up his torso. Hollow hands filled with red. Liquid sloshed around an empty space in the shape of a chestplate, filling it with red threaded with black. Then the head filled, the blood curling around it in a rushing vortex.

When complete, the figure stood. Mephiston expected to feel something from this apparition, yet it had no psychic imprint.

'Lord of Death,' it said. Its voice boomed out across the desert, where it mingled with the clash of the angels' weapons.

'Who are you?' Mephiston replied. 'You know me, I would know you.'

'You know me well enough,' said the red figure, 'as well as you know them.' It pointed to the sky. The blood was still liquid, and it swirled within the being's volume as he moved. Threads of black came and went.

'Then tell me what you want of me, and release me from this place.'

'Make no demand of me,' said the bloody angel, 'and I shall make none of you. You will be released soon enough.'

'At least tell me why I am here.'

The bloody angel nodded. 'What do you see in the sky?'

'I see two angels at war, one of gold, and one of darkness.'

'They have been at war forever,' said the figure. 'Even before your kind came to Baal. Those who dwelled here in distant epochs, they knew the angels of gold and black, though they did not see them as you see them.'

He gestured at a space between two of the outer pillars. An image appeared there, presenting Mephiston with a vision of spindly xenos, heavily robed and bedecked in bloodstone, labouring to raise monuments long since ground to dust.

'And there, where millions of years later men lived in brief paradise upon Baal Indicus and Baal Fortunata. The first men here knew the angels too, but refused to believe they existed, until times changed and they let the black angel in.'

Mephiston looked through the phantasmal angels. Both moons were present in the sky. Both were living. Baal Secundus sparkled with blue-green oceans. Baal Primus was drier, mottled with biomes of soft greens and greys. Around Primus was a complex of orbital stations so extensive and radiant it resembled a necklace.

'The moons no longer bear those names,' said Mephiston.

'Names come and go. Those names became corrupted in form. In time, they will be forgotten completely, as will your species. Another race, then another, then another, will come and uncover the things left behind in days long dead, and wonder what manner of hand shaped them.' The bloody angel turned its attention back to Mephiston. 'Or the universe will fall to Chaos, and yours will be the last of creation's children, and no more beings will choose their path twixt grace and rage, but all will be madness, and pandemonium will reign.'

'This is the warp. All things of the warp are lies. Return me to my mortal form.'

'Truth is subjective,' said the angel of blood. 'Lies are subjective.'

'Then judgement is meaningless,' said Mephiston, 'and we are prisoners of circumstance.'

'No, judgement is all,' said the being.

It walked down from its throne. Where it trod, it left footprints of blood upon the stone.

'The warp is a mirror to the material realm,' said the bloody angel. 'The shape of the warp is the shape of the mortal soul. If it harms us, we only have ourselves to blame. You are strong with the warp. You live.' It walked past Mephiston to stand between two of the great sandstone pillars, and looked up at the battling angels. 'These creatures are the reflections of your bloodline. The golden angel is your purity, the black angel is your flaw.' The bloody angel turned back to Mephiston. 'You are, all of you, of the blood of your father. In the least of you is a residue of his power. Thousands of years of sacrifice, denial and endless war. Every time one of your brothers creates a work of beauty, or lays down his life for those weaker than he, it strengthens the angel in gold. Each time one succumbs to the flaw and in his madness slays his brothers, the black is made more powerful.'

The black angel swung at the gold angel's head. Silver blade intercepted black. The heavens rang.

'The black is winning,' said Mephiston.

'The Black Rage will one day destroy all those of the Blood. It is inevitable,' said the bloody angel. 'The question is, how those of the Blood choose to spend their days before that happens. As paragons, or as monsters?' He stared at Mephiston with eye lenses of living blood set in a helmet of the same. 'The Great Rift has split the sky. The Emperor stirs. The minds of men are opening. Your madness calls all the louder because of it. Your priests and your tech-magi search fruitlessly for a cure. The Black Rage is not a malady of the body. It is a flaw in your souls.'

'Why am I here? Why are you telling me this?'

'You are who you are. You must make a choice,' said the bloody angel. 'The daemon you faced. Kyriss. It offered a choice given to the Lord Sanguinius many centuries ago.'

'I refused,' said Mephiston.

'You are wise.'

The Lord of Death watched the battling angels. The angel of gold seemed to have regained a little strength, and was pushing hard at the black.

'There was another choice your father had, and he took it.'

Mephiston looked at him sharply. 'He would never accept a daemon's bargain, not even to save us.'

'How can you be so sure?' said the bloody angel. 'All you know of him you learned from dusty books written long after he was dead. Traditions change. Legends grow in the telling. Even the meanings of his own words are lost beneath a hundred centuries of reinterpretation. Your primarch speaks to you, but you cannot hear. You rely on supposition at best, superstition at worst.'

'Do you seek to provoke me? I know Sanguinius was pure.'

The bloody angel rested a hand upon Mephiston's shoulder. Blood soaked the white robe red. The smell of it teased Mephiston's nostrils, tempting him to feed.

'I do not speak of daemons' tricks,' it said. 'You know the golden angel?'

Mephiston nodded. 'He is the Sanguinor.'

'He was once a man, like you. Into him has poured all the nobility of your kin for one hundred centuries. See how powerful he is.'

'Then...' Mephiston frowned. 'Then who was the black angel?'

'No one. The Rage roams free throughout the warp,' said the bloody angel. 'It has no anchor. As time has passed and your bloodline degenerated, it has grown stronger and stronger, until now, with the Great Rift open, it becomes the mightiest it has ever been, and the Sanguinor is no longer enough to balance it. It cannot be stopped by any but you.'

'Am I...' Mephiston looked swiftly to the bloody angel. 'Am I it?'

The bloody angel stared at him.

'I should never have survived Armageddon. What if I were to die? Would that stop it?'

'No. You and it are joined, but you are not one.'

'Then what is this choice?'

'The black angel needs an avatar to match the angel in gold. Take the essence of the Rage into yourself. Ground it in reality. Become its prison. If you accept a second rebirth, you will become the living manifestation of the Chapter's darkness. All will fear you. All will hate you. The role will consume you, and your soul will be damned, but your bloodline will be safe, for a time.'

'And my other choice?'

'You can choose to die. You have a powerful soul. Perhaps you may retain your self. Perhaps you will become a monster, or perhaps you will succumb to greater powers. Release yourself. You need not go back to this. That is the other choice.'

Between two of the pillars a vision appeared. They looked together into the operating theatre where men worked frantically to revive Mephiston.

'I am dying,' Mephiston said.

'You are already dead.'

'What if I take the choice that serves me? What if I choose not to go back?'

'This,' said the bloody angel.

In the gap next to the image of the Carceri Arcanum, another scene came into being. Warriors in battered red armour ran howling across a battlefield. They leapt frenzied into a huddle of human soldiers, and there committed a great slaughter. They used their guns as bludgeons. They opened throats with their teeth.

'And this,' the bloody angel said.

A third vision appeared, another world, more brutality, this meted out to screaming civilians.

'And this.'

In each of the gaps a similar scene opened. Warriors of Sanguinius' bloodline smeared in filth and gore, slaughtering people no matter who or what they were, and feasting on their blood and flesh.

'If you choose to die, the Chapter and its successors will quickly descend into madness.' As he spoke, anguished screams of pain and terror rang from the battlefields displayed to them. 'Thus I present you the true choice of Sanguinius – self, or selflessness. A choice given to you all, over and over again. What will you do now, Lord Of Death?'

'They already hate me,' said Mephiston softly. He looked deep into a burning city. The things he saw running amok there could barely be called human, but they were his brothers. 'They that know no fear, fear me. Even Commander

Dante cannot mask his disquiet at my approach. Astorath despises me. My existence brings peril to them all.'

'They will hate you all the more,' said the bloody angel. 'They will not know why. They will never know the burden you carry. They will never know you had a choice.'

'I will become that?' He looked up to the giant black angel fighting in the sky.

'One day. It exists now, so it has always existed, and always will. But you may hold it back.'

'So I have already made my choice.'

'Fate is strong. The choice needs making all the same.'

'How will I prevail over it? How can I keep it in check?'

'No man is free of sin,' said the bloody angel. 'All he is is the sum total of his choices, good and bad. If you can restrain it, you will.'

In the Chemic Spheres, activity was reaching a frenetic pace. Mephiston watched it. He could not feel the pain of his body, but he imagined it. That world was pain. He was weary of it.

'No,' Mephiston said at last. 'I cannot do it. I cannot. I have given so much already. I have given nearly everything there is, and far more than I thought there was to give.'

'Then see this, before you decide.'

The bloody angel pointed at one of the panes of vision, away from the operating room where men and machines battled to keep Mephiston alive. It was a scene composed only of fire. In it the most bloody acts were being performed, the wanton torture of innocents. The perspective shifted, moving away from the wailing crowds to a figure hanging in the sky over all of them. He resembled the Sanguinor, but where that warrior's armour was purest gold, this one's was blackest sable. Its helm mask was haughty and cruel. Blood ran freely from its hands and the mouth of the screaming visor.

'Is this what I become?'

The warrior lifted a hand shaking with rage to its visor, and swung the mask up. The face in the helm was wild with bloodlust, fangs out and digging into pallid skin.

The warrior was as different to Mephiston as Calistarius was, but it was still, undeniably, him. This Mephiston screamed inhumanly. Black flames blazed around its eyes, obscuring most of his features but the wild mouth. The image zoomed in, making his face huge in the space between the pillars. Mephiston watched as it raised a bloody fist to its mouth. Clasped in armoured fingers was a small human arm. The Lord of Death turned away as the warrior bit down and fed upon the flesh.

'The Rage seeks an outlet,' said the bloody angel. 'It needs an avatar. It will find its way into you whether you choose to live or choose to die. If your soul remains here, your body will play host to all the fury of the flaw, and it will strike down all you care for. Rhacelus, Antros, Dante – all the rest will go to their deaths knowing that you betrayed them, and that the darkness was always in you. You will become the agent of the Rage. You will destroy the bloodline of Sanguinius.'

Mephiston was soaring over the battlefield, if such a slaughterhouse could be named so, casting bolts of red light from his unsheathed sword.

Mephiston lowered his head. 'Then I have no choice. You torment me.'

'There is always choice. There never is. Fate demands we choose. Fate gives us no choices.'

'You reveal the worst in me!' Mephiston snarled. 'Your choice is a lie! You know what I will choose, and you will know my concern for my honour is what made me take it. You know I care more about that than about the fate of the Blood.'

'That is your lie. Think again.'

'My friends...' Mephiston said. His face hardened. 'No. I have none.'

'Not Gaius Rhacelus? Not Albinus? Then why do you care? Let your soul be free.'

'I make my choice.' Mephiston looked up defiantly at the bloody angel. 'Who are you?' he asked again.

'I am what I am,' said the figure.

'You are the red angel I saw in the realm of the lord of blood. You are the harbinger of our doom,' he said.

'I am that and much more.'

The bloody angel swelled to enormous size, so that it dwarfed Mephiston, yet still retained the shape of a man. The helm receded, revealing a face of unsurpassed beauty. Gold crept over the red. Blond hair, much like Mephiston's own, blew out in the wind. A titan was revealed, a lord of men, and yet he was human. All the sorrows of the world were expressed by his eyes. With a sharp snap, great white wings opened behind him, washing scented air over the Lord of Death.

A terrible understanding smote Mephiston's hearts. He knew then he had failed an important test.

'Sanguinius! My father, I did not know. I did not know.'
He fell to his knees.

'Failure is not an option for any of us,' said the Angel.

'How? It is not possible,' said Mephiston. He started to weep. Emotions he had not felt since before he was Calistarius swamped him. 'This is not real. You cannot be him.'

'It is not real,' agreed the figure. 'The warp is in turmoil. Things that were not possible before the Rift are possible now. The Warmaster Abaddon played a desperate gambit. He has unleashed forces that he can never control. The warp itself is not evil, always remember that, Mephiston. It is corrupted, but it contains everything, and that includes good as well as evil. It includes you.'

Behind the white wings the figures in the sky shrank. Still fighting, they descended from the heavens, in the process becoming no bigger than children, then smaller. As they diminished, so the image of Sanguinius grew, becoming a true giant, and a fearful halo blazed around his head, until the angels came to a halt either side of the vision, gold to the right and black to the left. Only then did the titanic angel cease to grow, and the angels let their swords hang by their sides. They looked blankly down on Mephiston.

'My lord Sanguinius… I am sorry.'

The vision of the primarch smiled sadly down upon him. The angels blurred. They faded, and the last spectres of them were drawn within the primarch's being.

'I am not Sanguinius. Sanguinius is dead,' said the thing that wore the primarch's face. It smiled sorrowfully at the Lord of Death, then collapsed suddenly into a tsunami of blood that crashed down with the force of a falling mountain, drowning Mephiston in rich vitae. Upon its hot wave, he was carried thence out of the warp, and back into the realm of the living.

CHAPTER TWENTY-THREE

MEPHISTON PRIMARIS

Rhacelus watched as the cap of Mephiston's skull was set back in place. Bone welders worked quickly to seal his braincase. The smell of hot meat filled the hall. He could feel nothing from his friend. His soul had fled.

'The last implant is in place. Restart his hearts,' said Qvo. 'We must return circulation to his body. Begin reattaching his skin. Once it is in place and his hearts beat anew, the Belisarian Furnace will activate and finish our job for us.'

'There is still no sign of brain activity, magos,' said Corbulo.

'We must work on, regardless,' said Qvo.

Servitors replaced the Lord of Death's black carapace, unwinding his nerves and replacing his neural ports with hands far steadier than a living man's. Nozzles squirted adhesives to hold the pieces in place. When it was all attached, Mephiston's flayed skin was retrieved from the nutrient vats and draped, dripping, over his exposed muscles.

The chirurgeon descended, legs cycling like a spider spinning out silk as it unwound yards of suturing thread. Needle-tipped legs darted at Mephiston's flesh, pulling his hide together with near-invisible joins, as if the pieces of bloody skin were a pattern of cloth to be made into a suit. While the machine worked, his chest remained open to the air, his hearts still exposed.

'He has been inactive too long, bring him back!' Albinus demanded.

'Not yet,' said Qvo. 'Begin his hearts.'

Rhacelus took an involuntary step forward. 'His spirit is gone.' His glowing eyes flashed. 'It is too late.'

'Can your chanting psykers reach him?' asked Qvo.

'Maybe,' said Rhacelus.

'Then call to him!' said Qvo.

Rhacelus gave orders. The chant changed. The fatigued Librarians sang with cracked voices through bloody lips.

Medicae thralls brought cormeum stimulant paddles to the table. A generator wheezed into life. They positioned the paddles around the Lord of Death's hearts and looked to the magos.

'Now!' Qvo shouted.

The generator buzzed and cracked. A jolt of power ran through Mephiston's body. His body arched as his muscles fired, threatening to rip the seams of the reattached skin.

'It is not working,' Albinus said. 'Qvo, do something!'

'No, no, no!' said Qvo-87. Machines blinked in alarm. Vital signs on screens ran flat. Piercing tones started up from one, then the others. Corbulo looked at him.

'He is dead!'

'Again!' cried Qvo. His robes parted. Dozens of manipulators emerged, plugging into machines, turning dials, jabbing at buttons. 'Now!'

Qvo watched a screen intently as another surge of energy raced through Mephiston's body. Again, his body arched. His still skinless face grimaced blindly.

'No, stop, it is done. He is dead, he is dead!' said Albinus.

'I will not!' said Qvo. 'They said Marneus Calgar would die, and he did not. Mephiston will live! You have a star in these vaults. I require a little of its power.'

'Idalia will incinerate him,' said Rhacelus.

'Do it,' said Dante.

'My lord,' said Rhacelus unsurely.

'Do as I command,' said Dante. 'Give Qvo what he wants.'

Qvo's servants quickly unrolled ribbed cabling and attached it to the glowing conduits running down the walls of the hall. They worked efficiently, completing their work before a minute was done.

'Ready, magos,' one said.

'You had better do this, Corbulo,' said Qvo. 'A human body will not survive the motive force overspill from the cormeum shock. You might.'

'I will do it,' said Albinus. 'He is my friend.' He took the paddle handles from Qvo's servant. 'Ready.'

'Release the star's energy!' Qvo commanded.

A tech-priest threw an enormous switch. It gave out a shower of sparks. Loops of charged gas writhed around it. The runs of light pouring down the walls flickered and dimmed. The machines shrieked. Several of them exploded. The hall of the Chemic Spheres was plunged into a ruddy gloom.

'I cannot hear him, I cannot see him,' Rhacelus said. 'His soul is too deep into the warp.'

'Now,' said Qvo.

Albinus depressed the shock buttons.

A roaring flood of energy poured into the Lord of Death.

His body danced on the table, ripping open his sutures. Yellow sparks rushed all over Albinus, who stood as long as he was able, his jaw locked, until with a cry he was thrown backwards, crashing into one of his human orderlies. The man fell down, his bones shattered, crushed by the Priest. The last of the machines blew out, spraying glass and plastek all over the floor. Fire sprang up on the cables siphoning power from the star.

The light dimmed further. Mephiston's open chest steamed.

Corbulo went to the smoking corpse and pressed his gloved fingers against Mephiston's neck. 'His hearts are still not beating.'

'The connections to the star are burned out. Our machines are destroyed,' reported one of Qvo's lesser priests.

'That was our last chance to save him,' said Albinus. He picked himself up from the dead man's corpse. 'You killed him.'

'Magos?' said Dante.

'It should have worked,' said Qvo. 'It should have–'

A cry went up from one of the Librarians. A glow kindled in his open mouth and his eyes, then burst out in hot daggers of light. He fell dead. The chanting faltered. Another Librarian fell to his knees, clutching his head. The others continued to chant, but they were faltering.

'By the Great Angel,' said Rhacelus. 'I feel him, he is coming back!' But his face changed from joy to horror. 'He is changed! By the Angel, what have we done?' He looked at Dante. 'We have failed in every way.'

The sound of immense wings beating filled the chamber. Once, twice, thrice.

Silence.

With a great bang, the conduits on the walls of the spheres

burst. Fat trails of energy poured into the Chief Librarian. The Space Marines threw up their hands to their eyes as a ball of light as bright as the sun encased the body of Mephiston.

The orb lifted. Mephiston was a shadow in the fire.

The orb exploded.

A burst of energy washed over the room, knocking all present off their feet and sending the remains of the machinery slamming into the walls. The unmodified humans among them were lofted high into the air. Space Marines crashed into the walls. More of the Librarians fell, some unconscious, others dead.

The Sanguinary Guard struggled to keep themselves upright. They levelled their weapons at the entity before them, but few could shoot. A howling storm of witchfire raced around the chamber, ripping up everything and sending it whirling into the air. The conduits leading down from Idalia pulsed and flared.

Rhacelus leaned into the storm, keeping himself upright only by dint of his own formidable psychic talents. Others were not so fortunate. He felt the stirrings of the Black Rage in all of them, even in Dante, as the thing that had been Mephiston hovered over them.

At the eye of the storm he created, Mephiston flew, an angel of destruction. Through the searing light, Rhacelus saw his ribcage snap shut, and skin flow back over the parts of him not yet recovered. His hair grew out from his scalp even as it crawled back over his exposed skull. The black fires ignited and rushed upwards from his skin, filling the chamber and beating back the light of Idalia. Black lightning arced down from his hands, earthing itself in the ground.

Rhacelus had rarely felt such power. Mephiston's being was a furnace of psychic and material energies mixed. As he watched, Mephiston's silhouette darkened, and black wings opened behind him. Rhacelus had to kill Mephiston, but it was too late.

For a moment, Rhacelus saw the dreadful black angel manifest before him, and felt the screaming insanity of the warp wax strong in all the Blood Angels in the room. He heard the clatter of guns in ancient wars. He felt the wounds of fraternal hatred. He saw the leering face of a treacherous brother.

Then it stopped. The energies of the room expanded, then rushed in towards Mephiston in a screaming implosion. The crash it gave was a physical blow that crackled the walls of the hall of the Chemic Spheres, and knocked the Space Marines back again.

The angel of shadows was gone. The black fire went out. Mephiston floated down to the floor, naked and pristine, all his wounds from the procedure gone. Ever since Calistarius had died and Mephiston had taken his place, Rhacelus had found his friend sinister, with a harsh physical perfection that could never be called beauty, but this Mephiston was beautiful. Light shone from his alabaster skin. For a moment he looked like the images of Sanguinius found all over the fortress-monastery, only purer, more vital, than any statue could be.

Mephiston's feet touched the floor. He stood amid the ruin, staring down at his hands. He was taller, stronger, perfect in form.

'He lives. He is Primaris,' whispered Albinus.

Quiet of a more natural sort fell. The moans of the injured and dying filled the space. The smell of blood tormented Rhacelus. He felt his fangs slide out of his gums. The images of the past danced at the edge of his vision. He wasn't the only one. They all struggled.

Mephiston knelt and closed his eyes. As if he had shut off

a valve, the visions ceased. The beginnings of the Rage vanished as quickly as they had come.

The people in the room recovered. Those medicae personnel still capable of movement went to the sides of their fallen comrades. Corbulo was hauled to his feet by Albinus. Qvo-87 limped forward, nursing broken mechanical arms against his chest.

'We did it! Another marvellous success!'

He was shoved out of the way by Dante's Sanguinary Guard, who formed around the Lord of Death, their Angelus boltguns aimed at his head, their swords presented to strike. The snap of activating power fields ran around their circle. Storms in miniature raged over the metal of their blades.

'We should kill him,' said Astorath, clambering to his feet. 'We should be done with all this. He has always been a danger. Look at this!'

'Wait,' said Dante.

Mephiston knelt with his head bowed. The light of his rebirth had faded, but he still glowed a pure white in the red light of the hall. He was the image of a fallen angel.

Dante approached. His guard moved aside.

'Mephiston,' Dante said.

The Lord of Death did not respond.

'Calistarius,' Dante tried.

Mephiston looked up. 'Not Calistarius. Not Mephiston. I am something else.'

'You recognise me?' said Dante.

'I do. You are my lord and my brother. You are Dante.'

'Whom do you serve?' said Dante.

'I serve the Librarius. I serve the Chapter. I serve the Emperor.' He got to his feet. 'I serve mankind.'

'Rhacelus?' Dante asked.

Rhacelus tentatively reached out with his mind. Mephiston's psychic might was greater than ever, but something in his new body held it in check.

'It is him, but is also not him,' said Rhacelus.

'Kill him,' said Astorath. 'Kill him while he is weak.'

'Is he in control of his abilities?' asked Dante.

'At the moment, yes,' said Rhacelus. He relaxed a little. 'Welcome back, brother.'

'I serve you, my lord,' said Mephiston. 'If you decree that I must die, then so be it.'

'A remarkable success,' said Qvo, coming to the fore. 'Remarkable.' He laughed uneasily. 'The process works on your gene-line after all, Lord Dante.'

'Look at the cost of your success, tech-priest,' said Astorath, waving his hand around at the corpses lying in the wreckage of the room. 'What is your command, lord?' The High Chaplain hefted his axe.

Dante's true expression was hidden behind Sanguinius' howling visage. 'Fetch Lord Mephiston his robes. Clear this space. Tend to the wounded. Rhacelus, reinstate the containment dome.'

Dante looked at Astorath.

'Mephiston lives, for now.'

CHAPTER TWENTY-FOUR

HONESTY AMONG FRIENDS

The Sepulcrum Maleficus was not somewhere that Dante went often. He had been to the resting place of the Chief Librarians perhaps a dozen times in the long centuries he had commanded the Chapter, but for all the Librarius' autonomy within the Blood Angels, when their Chapter Master requested entrance, the Librarians obeyed.

Dante went unarmoured to show his respect for Mephiston's suffering, with his long white hair bound up in a supplicant's knot.

A silent blood thrall with ink-stained fingers hurried Dante through the vast warren of the Librarius. Thousands of years of history was kept there, most of it written on painstakingly illuminated scrolls, and much of the thralls' time in the Librarius was taken up with copying them before they decayed into dust. When not at war, the Librarians helped. There were more sophisticated methods of data capture, and the information was preserved in multiple ways, but doing things the hard way sharpened the mind and kept the Thirst at bay.

The thrall took Dante down a gloomy, vaulted corridor. It ended at a blood-drip-shaped alcove containing a candle-lit shrine, the chief feature of which was a beautiful golden death mask upon a marble plinth. When they reached the shrine the thrall bowed, waited for Dante to give his leave, then hurried away without a word.

Dante stared into the closed eyes of the mask. Its expression displayed such a sense of serenity it never failed to move him.

He took it from the plinth and placed it on his face. He jolted a little as hundreds of needles on the inside pierced his skin. The mask warmed, and Dante removed it, replacing it on its stand, leaving his age-thinned skin streaked with lines of blood.

The mask's expression changed. The metal did not move. One instant it was one mask, the next, another. In its new iteration the eyes were open, and the serene expression accentuated by a knowing smile. A click emanated from behind the mask. It rattled on its stand then sank a little, displaying white stone in its eyes.

The shrine dropped noiselessly and swung back, opening up on a pitch-black corridor. Moist air blew over Dante's face, carrying the sound of rasping metal upon it. Dante stepped forward onto a metal stair that led steeply down. Stars shone high overhead, although it was full day outside the monastery walls.

There was insufficient light for Dante to see, so he proceeded by touch and memory. The stairs were moving slowly, sweeping around in long, lazy arcs. As he descended a faint glow became apparent, enough to light other sets of stairs turning about each other in the vastness of the pit. Many terminated in platforms bearing ivory sarcophagi. These passed by Dante as pale smudges, but as he drew nearer to the source of light their details sharpened, revealing the great artistry that had gone into their creation. Each contained the mortal remains of one of the Chapter's Chief Librarians. Scores of them, dating back to the dawn of the Imperium and the sundering of the IX Legion.

Metal hissed against metal as the stairs moved, passing through each other by cunning mechanical contrivance. Dante paused as they intersected; passing over the scissoring steps as they opened and snapped closed would have killed him.

Presently, he arrived at the source of light: a small number of platforms attended by glowing lumen orbs. The largest platform was furnished, containing a table and chairs and a large bookcase made of the same ivory as the caskets. Another supported Mephiston's sarcophagus, attached to the usual machineries of blood purification required by living Blood Angels. A third bore Mephiston's dread sword, Vitarus, suspended in a contragrav field. The last supported an armoury, where a blinded serf worked quietly upon a huge suit of armour.

Mephiston was sat upon a carved chair at the head of the table, leafing through a huge, mouldy tome. A wide salver covered in scratched symbols sat in front of him.

'Commander Dante,' he said. He sat back and tugged a black silk cloth over the bowl, hiding it. Dante descended the last few steps into Mephiston's living quarters. The other lit platforms orbited the main like a model of a planetary system.

'Chief Librarian.' Dante took a chair at the opposite end of the table. 'You have returned from the Chemic Spheres.'

'My brother-Librarians deemed me safe to be let free,' said Mephiston. 'I concurred.'

'Tell me how you fare.' Dante examined him carefully. Mephiston's appearance had changed again and was now much as it had been before. His skin was still ghostly pale, his eyes piercing, his face too sharp and intent to express the beauty inherent to its features. He was a little bigger. A little taller. But the same grave-cold emanated from him. The same deep sense of unease. The same immense power.

'As you see. I am calm. The sense of power outstripping my control is gone.' He held up his arm. The robe he was wearing fell back from milk-white skin. The black carapace appeared like a series of massive bruises beneath. 'Physically there is not a mark upon me.'

'There is not,' said Dante.

'Does this trouble you?' asked Mephiston.

'Should it, brother?'

Mephiston looked down at his book, and traced ancient words with his fingers. 'You have never truly trusted me since I ceased to be Calistarius, and became what I am.'

'It is not lack of trust. You are a noble warrior, and my brother,' said Dante.

'Then you fear me.'

'I fear nothing,' said Dante.

Mephiston looked up and smiled. His teeth were perfect, white as snow. 'You fear what I might become, and what it could mean for the Chapter. I do, too. But I am in control of myself. The incident aboard the *Dominance* will not be repeated.'

'Are you sure?'

'I am sure,' said Mephiston. He spread his hand palm up and looked at it. 'I am made anew.'

'Physical strength is commendable, but what of your soul, brother?' Dante asked. 'Is that, too, fortified? If not, then your enhanced physiology only makes you a greater threat.'

'There is more to this body than the added strength Cawl's servant gave me.' Mephiston frowned thoughtfully, choosing his words with care. 'I do not think my self-control comes from the change.'

'From where, then?' asked Dante.

'I saw him. Or something that could be regarded as him.'

'Who?'

'Our father,' said Mephiston simply. 'I sense something in you. You too have changed since Leviathan fell upon us. You saw our father too.'

'Sanguinius,' said Dante. 'I did have a vision.' Dante stared into Mephiston's eyes. 'I was on the verge of death. I think I would have died, if he had not sent me back.'

'I saw something similar. A choice was given to me.'

'Then you are more fortunate. No such offer was made to me.' Dante spoke neutrally, but he could not hide his rancour from Mephiston.

'You are ready to rest,' said Mephiston.

'I have seen more war than any being should have to,' said Dante. 'There is little in my life but despair.'

'What we saw, both of us, it could not be Sanguinius. He is dead. He has been dead for nine thousand years,' said Mephiston.

'What, then? Is it more likely our sense of duty brought us back?'

'Possibly.'

'Duty is my undoing.' Dante paused. 'Could it have been him? Could he persist somehow, in the warp?'

Mephiston shrugged. 'Sanguinius is recorded as being one

of the Emperor's most psychic sons. Would that have been enough? As far as it is understood to us, a powerful soul might persist in the warp for a time, but they are never whole, never what they were in life. Aeldari lore is rich with horrible tales about what occurs to the dead.' Mephiston stood. 'If we take a radical step, and assume that what we saw could possibly be our lord and father, then we must ask ourselves why he has not shown himself to us before.'

'You do not think it was him,' said Dante.

'I could not be certain,' said Mephiston.

'Then you do not believe?'

'The warp is a strange place, beyond the understanding of mortals.' He closed his book and took it to the bookcase. 'When we begin to think we understand it, that is the first step on the path of damnation. It is an illusion. Everything the warp gives us is a lie of one kind or another. It cannot be trusted in any way.' Mephiston gave one of his rare smiles. 'Even trusting that it cannot be trusted–'

'Cannot be trusted,' said Dante.

'I was going to say "is folly",' said Mephiston, 'but you are correct.'

'Mine is not the most poetic of phrases,' said Dante.

'It is possible to try too hard for beauty in everything,' said Mephiston. He slid the book back into position with a soft thump. 'What will you do with me, my lord? I do not want to be left behind when we attack Kheru.'

'It is time for a little honesty among friends,' said Dante. 'You may yet be a risk to the Chapter.'

'I do not feel I am, brother.'

'Even so, I will not deploy you on Kheru, not yet. Although you appear completely in control of yourself, we must test you in battle. If your abilities still outmatch your discipline, and you manifest the same devastating effect on the warriors of our Chapter, I would rather it were somewhere far from Baal itself. Kheru can wait a few weeks more.'

'What do you propose?'

'Shortly before we decided to test Cawl's procedure on you, a ship arrived in the system with a sole survivor upon it – the son of the deceased governor of Ronenti.'

'I have never heard of it,' said Mephiston.

'They have not requested the aid of our Chapter for over four thousand years. Peaceful, until now. It is not far, one of the hundreds of systems to the north of the Scar. The world has been overwhelmed by a genestealer uprising. If we do not cut off their psychic call, the tyranids will fall upon Ronenti and devour it, and if the hive fleet in this subsector turn towards Ronenti, they will bypass the trap we have laid for them.'

'Then I will go there, my lord, and end them.'

'We will go there together,' said Dante. 'I wish to see you fight with my own eyes.'

'If there is an effect on the warriors of our blood, my lord, you will be in danger.'

'I have lived too long as it is, Mephiston. I have never shied from duty. If you do lose control, if you show signs of turning into a threat, then I will end you myself.'

'I understand.'

Dante stood. 'We will depart tomorrow for Skyfall. There will be a small contingent. You, me, and a handful of men. For the rest we shall rely on the Imperial Fleet. See that you are ready.' Dante looked to the armourer on the platform.

'New armour, a gift from Incarael of the Blade,' said Mephiston. 'My old battleplate no longer fits.'

'Until tomorrow, then.'

'As you command.' Mephiston spoke louder. 'Dante?'

'Yes?'

'Will you cross the Rubicon? You spoke of honesty, so I will speak honestly. You are hiding your wounds. I feel your pain.'

Dante paused before he nodded. 'My injuries from the Devastation are not healing properly. I must take the crossing, if the council allows me to. I am weary. This body of mine has lived too long. As the transformation brought you control, perhaps it can bring me vigour. I have much to do. Without the transformation I may die.'

'You might if you try.'

'Change offers the greatest rewards,' said Dante.

'You have more to accomplish than any other man. You should wait.'

'That is why I want to be able to trust you, Mephiston,' said Dante. 'I need you. The Imperium needs you. I want this matter of the threat you supposedly pose laid to rest for good. It is time we moved on. Too many foes demand our attention. When you arrive on the battlefield, I want our enemies to take fear and our allies to rejoice. I want no doubt about you. I want no doubt in you. You are to be an emblem of Imperial might, not a symbol for our excesses or our failures. You have one opportunity to prove yourself.'

'I will not fail you,' said the Lord of Death.

'I am counting on that,' said Dante. 'Until tomorrow.'

He left.

CHAPTER TWENTY-FIVE

DESERVING MEN

Shortly after Dante returned to Skyfall, Admiral Danakan received a summons. He welcomed the distraction, and he wished to hear the end of Dante's story.

'I am glad you could attend me,' Dante said, when he arrived. 'I find our conversations a pleasant diversion.'

'I am glad you invited me here,' said Danakan.

'How do your duties go?' asked Dante.

'As well as they can. Resupplying the *Dominance* is proving difficult. There is a paucity of materiel here.'

'We are in the early stages of establishing Baal as a fleet centre,' said Dante. 'And as a governmental centre. You must forgive us.'

'I did not mean to criticise,' said Danakan hurriedly.

'No criticism was heard,' said Dante. 'I require men like you to overcome these problems for me. I cannot do everything myself. Baal has to change. We have much to do.' He stopped, and looked Danakan up and down. 'I see you insisted on wearing your dress uniform again,' said Dante. He waved a thrall forward out of the shadows.

Danakan handed his coat to the thrall. 'I would say that I do it to show you respect, or to maintain standards. The real reason is less noble. It is a form of armour, my lord. While I wear this ridiculous brocade and all these medals I didn't earn, I feel almost worthy of other people's admiration.'

'I understand,' said Dante. 'Please, sit down. You are well?'

'I am better, my lord. The work helps. I do not suffer the visions now, but I have yet to recover my confidence.' Danakan sat with a tired sigh. 'When I was a younger man, I was arrogant. I was so sure of myself, I would have stood in front of you and you would have despised me for my lack of humility. As I got older, and rose in the ranks, I realised that I did not know everything. In fact, I knew very little. But my confidence remained. I was bloody-minded, sure I could learn what I needed to learn.'

'You became admiral. You must have been right about your ability.'

Danakan shook his head. 'I don't think I was. If I were, then why did I lose my certainty? I made only one mistake, but it was a mistake so profound that the scales fell from my eyes. I am a man of middling ability. I got where I am because of my family, because of my background, because I shouted loudest, and insisted longest. How many others of better quality faded into the background?'

'So you ask yourself how many of those men would have made the same mistake, if they would at all.'

'I do.'

'It is a pointless question,' said Dante. 'Wine,' he called. Silent thralls hurried forward to do his bidding. 'You are where you are, whether you believe you deserve to be or not.

You must make the best of what ability you have in order to better serve those who depend on you. I have felt doubt. I feel it now. It was argued when I was appointed that I was not ready for the task of leading the Chapter. They were right, but there was no one else.'

'What happened?' asked Danakan, gratefully accepting a goblet of wine.

'You recall the Chapter fleet was ambushed while withdrawing from Kallius?'

'I do.'

'Then I shall continue,' said Dante. 'During the fighting, it became apparent the servants of the enemy did not only want to take our ships, they wanted to destroy our Chapter...'

Bolts flared as their rocket motors kicked in, speeding them down the approach way on streaks of orange light. Each slash of fire ended in a white explosion, and the curses of the wounded. Adeptus Astartes rarely screamed.

Dante and Lorenz took shelter behind a smashed supply train lying across the spinal way. The enemy had chosen a good place for their ambush. The area had little cover. The rest of Dante's company were spread out, lying behind their own dead or clinging to what little protection the ship's architecture provided.

'We are missing heavier fire support!' Lorenz voxed over the throaty chugging of an autocannon. White-hot bullets screamed down the passageway.

'We have what we have,' said Dante.

'What we have,' said Lorenz, putting a bolt-round into the vulnerable throat armour of a Heretic Astartes, 'are pistols and melee weapons. They're not going to come to us, it will be suicide to charge up there into this, and they know it.'

'But we must,' said Dante. 'We have to join the Chapter Master, or the *Bloodcaller* is lost.' He stood up from his cover.

'Dante, for the love of the Great Angel! They'll kill you! They'll kill us all.'

The traitors zeroed in on Dante the moment he emerged. Tracer rounds belted down the corridor, searing the air with magnesium trails. A shell hit Dante square in the chest, screaming off his aquila and rocking him sideways. His stabilising jets gave out a burst of gas and his armour whined as he righted himself.

'We don't know if Remael is still alive. Dante! Get down!'

'Stay there if you like, sergeant,' Dante said. He broke into a jog, dodging aside as a burst of autocannon rounds sped through the air he had occupied.

'You are too eager for death,' Lorenz said. He stood too and signalled the men. 'Blood Angels of the Eighth Company!' he shouted. His voxmitter turned his voice into a bellowing roar loud enough to be heard over the racket of the battle. 'Stand!'

They emerged in ones, pairs, and by squad. One immediately went down in a burst of sparks. A blizzard of return fire from bolt pistols drove the enemy back long enough for the rest to come out and follow after Dante.

'Forward,' said Dante, accelerating into a thumping run. 'Into them. Leave not one alive.'

'For the Great Angel!' Lorenz said, holding aloft his chainsword. 'For Sanguinius! For the Emperor!'

The roar of dozens of chainblades outcompeted the bang of bolt-rounds.

Dante picked out a helmetless warrior whose face was covered by a breathing grille framed by a silver maw. The elaborate chasing of his battleplate marked him out as a champion of the traitors. Skulls hung from knotted cords in a fringe around his pauldrons. Dante fired at him as he ran, his plasma pistol carving gouges into the warrior's shoulder, yet his enemy stood ready, firing at Dante with a daemon-faced boltgun that spat a stream of rounds from a drum-magazine. The champion's aim was good, his shots slamming in clusters around Dante's hearts, but his armour held, and he drew near the hated enemy unharmed.

The charge was costly. Dante's company released a wall of bolts and plasma streams to keep the enemy back, disrupting their fire, but there were a great many of the foe, and they managed to bring down several of the Blood Angels before the lines of black and red clashed together.

Space Marines at full sprint hit with the force of a cavalry charge of old. Some of the traitor warriors were bowled over by the force of the impact, knocked from their feet and sent skidding down the polished metal of the deck, where they were easy prey for quick bolt and plasma blasts. Dante's opponent had time to set his feet, engage his maglocks and brace, causing Dante to rebound from the impact. The warrior dropped his bolter, and drew a mismatched pair of ancient blades from scabbards at his belt, both looted from warriors loyal to the Emperor. One bore the ultima of the Ultramarines, another a snarling wolf's head. They came blazing towards Dante in a haze of disruption lightning.

The champion was fast. Dante barely got his axe up in time to deflect the swords. The blades came in quick succession, the first a feint that could be turned to deadly purpose, the second a strike that could serve as a secondary feint. Dante twisted his hand slightly, flicking his axe head enough to deflect one blade then the next. His opponent responded with a double-handed drive forward that slammed Dante's axe haft into his chest, staggering him. He let off a blast from his plasma pistol, ignoring the squealing of its machine-spirit as the gun's coils overheated. The champion shoulder-barged him, and the stream went wild, scoring a molten channel into the ceiling that spattered the combatants with droplets of metal.

In seconds the lines of Space Marines were thoroughly mixed, a maelstrom of blood red and midnight black. Warriors who shared a common origin vented millennia of hatred. No quarter was expected on either side. They were tightly packed, banging into each other. Guns went off at close range, the flash of their discharge illuminating faces twisted with unreasoning rage.

Dante ducked a blow from the Chaos champion. A falling traitor smashed into him as he fell, multiple bolt-craters bright red in his black battleplate. Dante staggered. The champion pressed his advantage, using his fallen comrade as a step to launch himself, bearing down on the staggering Dante. Again Dante deflected the champion's strikes, though only just, for he came in from high left then low right, spinning his blades around in dazzling patterns. He never stopped moving, twirling his weapons in his hands so that they flared and buzzed. Dante kept his axe ready to strike, husbanding his strength for a decisive blow. The axe was slow but powerful, the swords fast. Lightning stabbed out in all directions as Dante smashed back the warrior's attacks. The champion stared constantly at Dante's face, his eyes furious and bloodshot, yellowed whites glowering beneath a brow twisted by ritual scarification. He did not boast, as many followers of the Dark Gods did, he did not taunt, but fought with a silent, furious efficiency that drove the young captain back.

The Red Thirst stirred in Dante, a tickling in his throat that became a nagging urge as the champion's blows rang from his axe again. Right blocked by the head, left by the haft. He raised his plasma pistol swiftly, intending to fire it without allowing it to charge fully and take his foe by surprise, but the champion anticipated the move, driving at Dante with his blades, and forcing Dante to deflect a deadly strike with the gun itself. The charging coils on the gun's top caught a blade's edge and cracked. Superheated gas spewed from the side. Dante struggled with the rising Thirst. His senses sharpened. He could smell the traitor's sweat as a powerful reek. His eyes were constantly drawn to the pulsing veins at his temple and the tainted blood within.

With a shout Dante dropped his pistol, disconnecting its power feed with a pulse through his suit's neural links. He cast it down, and crushed it underfoot, sending out a brief, actinic glare that dazzled his opponent. The effect was fleeting, but Dante was wearing his helm and his lenses reacted to shield his eyes. His enemy lacked this protection.

Dante struck, swinging his axe up left-handed, catching the haft with his right hand at the apex of the swing, and using all his strength to send it powering down at the champion. Now it was the warrior's turn to parry. He raised the stolen Ultramarines blade to take the blow of the power axe. Caught by the full force of the attack, the ancient sword broke with the cataclysmic bang of a shattered power field generator.

The warrior rolled with the blow, thrusting hard with his left-hand sword, coming up from below with a strike intended to penetrate the weaker joints between plastron and belly armour. It was a heart-killer, a finishing blow that would blast Dante's internal organs to pieces. Dante turned, bringing his arms down and smashing the haft of his axe across the inside of his opponent's elbow, catching the weapon and diverting it away from the centre of the vulnerable area. The sword was stayed before it could pierce his flesh; nevertheless the point hit the edge of the armour join, obliterating a large chunk of the outer shell with a crack of atomic dissolution, and began eating its way within.

A hammer-blow shockwave hit his hearts, causing him to cry out. Desperately he clung on to the traitor's arm, pinning the sword to his chest with his own weapon. Blood filled his mouth, further exciting the Thirst. He felt his control slipping. His vision dimmed and became tinged with ruby.

The traitor slammed his free fist into Dante's helm. The blow snapped his head back. A second came before he could recover, crazing his left eye lens. His helm display failed in a flurry of junk input. The third hit stunned him, and he sank downwards, still with the traitor's arm clamped to his chest, the sword point crackling and banging as its power field ate through the ceramite. The acrid chemical stink of cooking sealant foams choked him. Where the plating had failed, his under-armour and his bodysuit were suffering. His war-plate spirit chirruped warnings. Soon his flesh would begin to suffer.

'Pathetic,' the champion growled. He aimed another punch at Dante's face.

Dante released his grip from the top of the axe haft to catch his foe's fist. His opponent pushed into him, wiggling the point of his sword further into the breach in Dante's armour. The pair of them were down on their knees, surrounded by the mad dance of close combat. They were alone in the chaos, clasped in an embrace of hate. Their armours whined in competition as muscle fibre and servo motors vied with each other, Dante's to push away the descending fist, the champion's to break his grip. The sword point burrowed further in. Dante felt his flesh begin to cook.

There was a searing flash, and the hot punch of thermal shock. The champion's head was replaced by a puff of smoke. The tall arm of his backpack stabiliser clattered to the floor, cut clean through. The dead warrior fell onto Dante, trapping him in an awkward kneeling position.

Lorenz stood behind, a baroque meltagun in his hand. He threw it aside and grabbed the champion's corpse under its pauldron and shoved it off.

'You were taking far too long killing him,' said Lorenz. He was panting from the exertions of the fight. He offered his hand to Dante.

Dante stared at Lorenz, his thinking dulled by the Thirst. The enemy were dying all around him. The survivors were falling back, firing as they retreated, the infernal glow of their helm lenses receding back down the way the Blood Angels had come, until they vanished into the gloom of the unlit corridor.

Several of his men were gripped by fury, and started after the traitors. This shook him out of his own blood fugue.

'Hold!' he shouted, his voice a hard croak. He grabbed Lorenz's arm to pull himself upright. 'Cease pursuit.'

A few bolt-rounds cracked hard as his men executed the enemy wounded. The taking of prisoners could never be countenanced in a struggle of that sort.

A tense silence fell. The deck shook to the rhythm of heavy guns. The *Bloodcaller* was still shooting.

'Are you all right, brother?' Lorenz said, peering at the mix of blood and sealant weeping from the hole in Dante's breastplate.

'We have to move on. They will return,' Dante said. He shook off Lorenz's hand.

'The command deck?'

Dante nodded. He shut the flickering remains of his helmplate off. He had no direct information as to how many had died, but he counted at least a dozen red-armoured dead among the fallen traitors.

'Two to one loss-kill ratio.' Lorenz shook his head. He passed Dante a bolt pistol and ammunition to replace his plasma gun. 'Never assault a prepared foe head on.'

'We had no choice,' Dante said, trying his best to calm his ragged breathing. A chime rang in his ear. The sealant hardened uncomfortably against his wounded flesh, but at least his armour was void-proof again. 'We shall continue to our objective,' he said. 'Move out.'

They left the great spinal way, taking instead a smaller route above the port batteries. The traitors had boarded in force there in order to silence the barge's guns, and the corridor was breached in several places by the blunt snouts of boarding torpedoes. The hideous carvings of daemonic faces and men in torment adorning their petal doors were blackened by the melta arrays used to burn through the hull. The sites of these landings increased in frequency, until Dante counted several breaching points at least, and after that there were signs of slaughter everywhere. Compared to most Imperial ships, a Space Marine battle-barge carried a modest human crew, but they still numbered in the thousands, and wherever the unmodified servants of the Chapter had been found, they had been killed. At strategic chokepoints, teams of blood thrall armsmen lay dead, their sundered limbs and spilled organs tangled together so that it was impossible to tell where one man ended and the next began. For every ten killed, there were one or two black-clad Space Marine corpses. The bodies of the Chapter servants were further mutilated by the crushing weight of fully armoured Heretic Astartes walking over them to head down towards the guns.

In the places Dante's brothers had found the traitors, more even-sided battles had raged. There armoured bodies in black and red lay in equal numbers.

The sounds of gunfire echoed from far off on a few occasions, but Dante, wary of further ambush, headed resolutely for the command deck.

'We are taking a toll on them,' said Lorenz, as they jogged past a fallen squad of traitors. All had been cut down by bolter fire close to their attack craft.

'We do not know how many they are,' said Dante. 'These are members of the Black Legion, Abaddon's slaves. His forces are of unknown size, and we are depleted from the campaign.'

'They are a long way from the Eye of Terror,' said Lorenz. 'Perhaps it's only a raiding party.'

'This war brings traitors from every quarter,' said Dante. 'If they have reason enough to come here, they will have come in force.'

They were not able to check. Their vox was jammed. They were alone.

Eighth Company jogged on past the sites of the fiercest battles, their footfalls the loudest noise in the quiet.

'The guns have stopped firing,' said Lorenz.

'Then the foe have half their work done. They will turn their attention to wiping us out,' said Dante. 'The hard fighting will begin soon.'

A sudden movement had the company preparing for combat.

'Hold!' Dante shouted.

A figure in the red of the Chapter emerged from the dark. Dante felt an uncharacteristic surge of relief.

'Veteran Sergeant Aminus,' the man announced. 'Third Company.' His insignia were concealed by blood and battle damage.

'We could have killed you,' Lorenz said.

'You did not, brother,' said Aminus. 'Thanks be to the Angel.'

'You are not broadcasting your signum codes,' said Dante.

'The enemy do not appear to be hindered by their jamming of our communications. They have locked on to our friend-or-foe signifiers,' said Aminus. 'They are using them to hunt us down.'

'Where is Captain Theus?'

'Dead,' said Aminus. 'I am the highest ranking member of my company remaining. I have taken command.'

'How many are you?' asked Lorenz.

'Twenty, another fourteen back in hangar ten. The enemy attempted a gunship landing there.'

'Their status?' Dante asked.

'The enemy failed,' said Aminus bluntly. 'But we suffered. We are all that is left of the Third Company.'

'Have you lost any to the Rage?'

'Three men. They sold themselves with honour, holding back a party of reinforcements. They, too, are dead now.'

'We lost no one to the Rage,' said Lorenz.

'The attack was presaged by no omens. No warning, mystical or mundane,' said Dante. 'This attack has been meticulously planned.'

'How many of you are there, brother-captain?'

'Fewer than fifty,' said Dante. 'You will accompany us,' he ordered. 'We are on our way to the command deck to link up with Master Remael. Our only chance to withstand this attack is by gathering our strength in one place.'

'As you command, brother-captain.'

'Lorenz, Aminus, rearrange the squads. We are suffering from a lack of heavier weaponry. Assign short-range fire-teams to bolster the efficacy of our assault units. Break the rest down into full demi-squads. Make sure they have all deactivated their identifiers, and consult the other sergeants. Check them all for signs of the Rage. We can use the Thirst, but only when it suits us. A badly timed charge in this environment will be the end of us.'

A loud explosion rumbled a few hundred yards away. From which deck, they could not say. A few seconds after the detonation a warm wind gusted up the corridor, carrying with it the smell of hot metal and the acrid tang of burning plastek.

'That was from within,' said Aminus.

'Probably the shield generatoria,' said Lorenz. 'It's got very quiet.'

'The ship is under minimal bombardment,' said Aminus. 'They intend to take *Bloodcaller*.'

'It is their most likely strategy,' said Dante. 'For the time being, it is all that is keeping us alive.'

They approached the command deck from one of the small, anterior access points. Like all the ways into the nerve centre of the ship, the door was heavily armoured, protected by emplaced servitor-controlled weaponry and at the end of a corridor deliberately built to provide no cover. Before stepping onto the dimly lit way, Dante spoke.

'I will activate my locator signum, but only I.'

'The enemy will lock onto it quickly,' said Sergeant Aminus.

'Not as quickly as if we all reactivate our identifiers. The enemy will not waste time on one lone brother. Not yet. If I do not, the deck approach weaponry will open fire on us. Take your men to the rear, Aminus. Guard our advance.'

'As you command, then by the Blood I obey,' said Aminus, and turned about to gather his men.

Dante selected the appropriate rune in his helm display and re-engaged his signum beacon.

'How long until they find us, do you think?' said Dante.

'Minutes, if we have fortune on our side,' said Lorenz.

'Fortune favours those of the Blood,' said Dante.

'Until the Rage takes us, and we are blessed to see sacred Sanguinius ourselves.'

They began the walk up the corridor. A party of fifteen Space Marines came with them, hanging back from their leaders. The rest stayed at the corridor junction. Aminus' men were busy taking position further away, covering the approaches to the command deck access corridor from both directions.

The corridor was long. Dull blue biolumes glowed in sconces recessed into the wall, their light shining off their armour in fluorescent stripes. The main access to the command deck was a vast tunnel. This minor way was much smaller, wide enough for only four to march abreast, the ceiling low enough to touch with an upraised hand.

Heavy bolter turrets either side of the portal locked on to Dante. Single sighting lenses were mounted in line with their gaping barrels, which blinked red as target acquisition protocols pulsed through the machine's limited cogitators.

'I am Dante, captain of the Eighth Company. Deactivate.'

Servos purred as the bolters tracked back and forth over the other Space Marines.

'Confirm identity,' Dante said.

'Dante, captain, Eighth Company,' said a dull machine voice.

'Then obey,' said Dante.

'Compliance,' the machine voice said.

The glow in the sighting lenses dwindled to a single point of light, then winked out.

'Open the door,' said Dante.

The door remained closed.

Lorenz went forward, locking his bolter to his thigh as he approached. He peered at the cast-steel skull over the door's embedded data-slate. Its eyes were the steady, blank red of non-functionality. He punched up a simple diagnostic screen.

'The servitor module inside is malfunctioning. The brain is almost dead,' said Lorenz.

'Can you discern any detail of what awaits us on the far side?' asked Dante.

'None,' said Lorenz. 'Only the gun protocols are running. The door is inactive.'

'Can you open it?' said Dante.

'I am not a servant of the forge, but I shall try.' He peered at the access panel. 'An armoury kit would be helpful here, but I have the tool I need.' He clenched his fist, and punched the door mechanism's access panel until it caved in and fell to the floor.

'It appears you have some talent for machinery,' said Dante drily.

'When you start making jokes, Dante, I know we are in trouble.'

Lorenz pushed his hand into the opening. Pale green light shone inside.

'This is no good, I can't feel anything.' He withdrew his hand and twisted the locking ring around his gauntlet, taking it off.

With his hand now bare, Lorenz reached deeper into the cavity up to his elbow, until his poleyns scraped on the aperture. He grunted in frustration. 'The wires are broken. A stray hit, perhaps. Just need to get this cable, and then...'

The light in the skull's eyes switched to green.

'You have it,' Dante said. 'Company, stand ready.'

'There's something in here that shouldn't be,' said Lorenz. 'I nearly have it. Wait until–'

The doors opened with a smoothness that concealed the peril behind. The squeal of venting air became a deadly roar so quickly it was almost impossible to react.

'There's nothing there!' Dante shouted.

Where the vast, cathedral space of the *Bloodcaller*'s command deck should be, there was only the void. The deck continued beyond the door for a few feet before stopping abruptly on the edge of darkness. Jagged girders scraped at nothing. Broken cabling twinkled with electrical shorts along the edge. Past that was the deceptively stately dance of gargantuan ships at war, turning, firing, burning and dying.

The heavy punch of the decompression hurricane struck Dante hard as millions of cubic feet of air tried to vent into the void at once. He ducked one of his company as the man bounced from the wall, and went spinning out into space. Dante activated his maglocks instinctively, sticking his feet firmly to the deck while the roar of liberated air attempted to tear his body free at the ankles.

Lorenz's gauntlet whirled out. The force of the wind lifted his feet, leaving him hanging awkwardly by his arm jammed into the door's innards. The pressure it applied was considerable, and he gripped at the edge of the access hatch with his free hand to alleviate the pain, armoured fingers scraping red-edged silver streaks across the metal.

'Shut the door!' Dante voxed. The howl of escaping atmosphere made it hard to hear, to think – his helmet shook with its fury. The pressure at his back was immense. His armour's motors screeched, trying to hold him upright. The smell of overtaxed fibre muscle bundles filled the suit. His stance was poor, feet next to each other, and he was being pushed forward. A crate careened from his pauldron with such force it wrenched his back around painfully, tearing the muscles around his shoulder and jolting the wound the champion had given him. Blood ran again from under the scabbing.

'Shut the door!' he yelled again.

White rapids of freezing air streamed outwards, coating everything in frost. Beyond that, war played out against the stars.

Death wrapped icy fingers about Dante's chest, and attempted to pull him loose.

'Lorenz!'

Lorenz gave out a great cry of anger, and pulled himself until he was squatting again on the floor. His feet clamped to the deck. Now secured, he reached back into the gap.

The doors slid shut, cutting off the roar of escaping air to a moan, then a squeak, then silence.

'Remael is dead,' said Dante.

'They wanted us to come here,' said Lorenz. He yanked out an ugly, jury-rigged module. 'This is a trap.'

From down the corridor, gunfire sounded. Runes flashed in Dante's faceplate as Aminus' warriors came under attack.

'They've come for us,' said Lorenz. 'We cannot get out.'

Dante looked back at the door.

'There is a way,' he said.

CHAPTER TWENTY-SIX

BURDENS OF COMMAND

Dante set down his goblet.

'The Black Legion did not only want to take our ships, they wanted to destroy our Chapter. What had brought them there at that time, I could not say. In hindsight, I can only suppose it was part of the Warmaster Abaddon's great and subtle plan to topple the Imperium, a plan that has almost succeeded.'

As if provoked by the name of the Archenemy, *Bloodcaller* rocked. Danakan started.

'An area of turbulence in the warp,' said Dante.

'We can no longer claim that the warp is an ocean, and nothing else,' said Danakan. 'It is alive. It watches us.'

'It does, as do many other perils in this galaxy. This is the price of power, Seroen. The human race is in danger because it is worth something. These predators and daemonkin attack us because they covet our strength. There is a comfort in that.'

'How can you say so, my lord?' said Danakan.

'We are a threat. That means we have the strength to beat

our foes. If we were so weak they could safely ignore us, then we would have no hope of victory.' Dante stared solemnly at Danakan. Such a weight of wisdom was in his regard, Danakan found it suffocating. 'I have visited civilisations that thought they could hide. I have seen the remains of hundreds more who felt similarly. They are all dust now. To be a great power is to be a great threat. It is humanity's destiny to rule this galaxy, I believe that with all my heart. The Emperor's plan has surely gone awry, but it can be born anew. The return of Roboute Guilliman to us is only one proof of that. We do not fight only to stave off extinction for a little longer, we fight to win. I will not rest until mankind is safe, and master of his own fate, untroubled by xenos fiend or otherworldly horror. I took many oaths to that effect. I aim to uphold them.

'If I have one virtue, it is that I am dogged,' Dante went on. 'I never give up.' He sat forward. 'We escaped the Black Legion by retreating into the void. I did not give up then, and I will not give up now.'

Dante's salvaged bolt pistol kicked hard. He braced himself on maglocked feet, clinging to the giant, ragged cliffs of plasteel like an insect. His shot scored yellow rocket burn across the void. The shot was a little wild, but caught the Heretic Space Marine following him up the crags square on the shoulder. His shoulder blew apart. His arm sped away, chased by globules of blood. The shrapnel must have got into his innards, for the warrior stopped dead, his body locked to the hull by his magnetic boots.

The gun was empty. Dante lifted it and slapped another magazine in place. It was his last. He walked clumsily up, his boots thumping onto the skin of the battle-barge. The ship shuddered from a thousand small explosions, but Dante heard none of it. Only his breath, loud in his ears, and the rattle of the enemy's comms-denial broadcast, punctuated by electronic squeals and rare voices that managed to break through. What was left of his company was spread all across the broken command superstructure. He was alone.

He came across a statue and began walking up it. It was perpendicular to his feet, a great golden angel armed with shield and sword, its blank eyes staring out at the battle in the void. Dante followed its unseeing gaze, and saw the fleet of his Chapter attacked from all sides. Most of the craft had been boarded. Both the Chapter's battle-barges were present, and both were under threat. The *Blade of Vengeance* floated without power, harried by a flock of ancient ships in black and silver. Some of the smaller vessels still fought hard, looping and turning in the crowded battlesphere, but all were mobbed by swarms of enemy attack craft. As he watched he saw a light frigate come to pieces, bombed into nothing by flight after flight of traitor assault ships. Its reactor broke, and it burst in a distended balloon of fire. The thruster array went one way, the prow the other. All in between was reduced to particles that added to the debris clouding space. Chunks of metal, some hundreds of tons in weight, hurtled across the black, weakening the protection of vessels on both sides as they slammed into void shields. Each craft still active sparkled with a hundred thousand debris impacts and displays of sickly lightning. Those that lacked shields blossomed fields of yellow across their skins with each significant hit. One heavy cruiser was heeling over, dropping out of the battlezone after being hit by a substantial section of a dead ship. Craft of that size and class were not supposed to fight so closely. They were elegant duellists disarmed, grappling desperately in the mud, their swords lost. Coming in so close and committing themselves to a boarding action was a bold plan for the traitors, one that could have gone against them, but despite their heavy losses it appeared they were prevailing.

Bloodcaller bled air from a thousand wounds. Fierce fires raged in oxygen-rich winds, sending curling banners of flame into the void that were snuffed out and endlessly replenished in a pattern that would last until every breath of air was gone.

For the first time since his apotheosis, Dante saw defeat.

He stood and looked across the blocky plains of the cliff. The wound in his chest throbbed. Air hissed slowly from the imperfect seal the gel foams made. A small counter blinked in the upper left of his malfunctioning helmplate, counting down his life in millibars of air. His armour was doing its best to make up the shortfall. The power plant split his water rations for additional oxygen, but it would not last. He had lost sight of his men. Lorenz was nowhere to be seen.

There was a choice at hand. To continue to fight and die, or to allow his body to submit to his sus-an membrane, let the mucranoid coat his body in a protective chrysalis and wait to be rescued.

It was no kind of choice at all.

Dante brought up the comms subsystem and through a rapid combination of blink clicking and neural impulse commands, he reconfigured his power feed to boost the vox. Sliders jagged with broken imaging cells moved up into the red zones. He had a minute, maybe less, of vox capability before the additional power burned out the system.

'I, Captain Dante, speak,' he said. 'Loyal brothers, converge.' He sent a data squirt of coded instructions, giving his position, and turned his signum on. 'While one of us draws breath, we are not yet beaten. Join me. Let us end them.'

Hollow words that met with no response. If anyone heard, the enemy would. They would come for him, and he would die.

He shifted his grip on his power axe. He would make sure many of the foe would perish before he did.

Sure enough, he saw movement coming at him, not on the ship, but out in the void. A trio of Lightning fighters split away from their squadron in a long loop, and came heading directly for his position.

'How disappointing,' he said to himself. They would not even give him the opportunity of a glorious death.

He raised his pistol.

The fighters came at him, holding fire until the last second. They were attempting to impress their diabolical masters. He wondered what favour the death of a loyal Space Marine captain would bring a mortal enslaved in the warmaster's armies.

They came at him recklessly fast.

His pistol spat a trio of bolts at the approaching attack craft. They were close enough for him to see the canopies glinting in the battle light. Lascannon beams slashed back at him in response. He was a small target, difficult to hit, and the beams hit the ship's battered hide with soundless flashes. His own shots passed harmlessly over the lead ship's wing.

He waited before firing again. The Lightnings were a handful of miles away. They were burning their reverse thrusters, but they would be on him in under a second.

This was it, the moment of his death. Luis Dante, raised on the saltpan of a dead sea, a stunted boy doomed to a short life, elevated to serve the Emperor as one of his angels of death, was finally going to die.

'Ave Imperator,' he said, and squeezed the trigger.

The lead ship exploded. The other two immediately split.

Dante's shot punched through the flame burst that briefly marked the craft's demise. He looked upwards.

A pair of interdiction fighters in the dark blood colours of the Angels Numinous sped over Dante's head. One leapt ahead of another, drum magazines spraying out a brass cloud of spent shells, speared past Dante, and annihilated a second Lightning. The third swept around, engines pushing it into an acceleration that would have been nearly fatal for its mortal pilot. The Angels Numinous ships sped after it, and were lost in the maelstrom of battle.

Bloodcaller shook with the gravity wake of an immense ship coming close. A shadow passed over him, and he saw sailing over the stricken battle-barge the Angels Numinous ship *Crimson Tear*, fully shielded, and with guns blazing. Around it flew the entire Chapter fleet. Depleted by the war, yet still strong, it raced towards the heart of the traitor armada.

Dante's vox crackled into life. The enemy jamming signal abated, and a voice spoke clearly into his helm.

'Captain Dante, I am your brother,' said Captain Toranis, *'and I have come to stand beside you.'*

'Then you were saved by the Angels Numinous. You did not escape yourself?' said Danakan.

'We were saved. We would have died without them.'

'The point of this tale you are telling me, commander, is that your heroism was not a deciding factor.'

'You know what I am telling you,' said Dante. 'You are not a foolish man, admiral. I made mistakes. I almost died. I lost good men. I nearly lost my brother Lorenz. There were no noble last words, no touching sentiments exchanged. He was with me, then he was not. The last I saw of him, he was being driven apart from me by the enemy, his hand black from void exposure. It was only days later, and by chance, that he was recovered from deep in space, so far into suspended animation he was almost dead. I was convinced he was gone, and that hurt me greatly.'

He fell quiet. Danakan watched him closely.

'You are surprised,' Dante said eventually. 'After all I have said, do you still not think us capable of emotion? Brotherhood is the foundation of the Chapter. We feel the loss of our comrades deeply. Lorenz was with me from the beginning. He was the last from my intake. He was my friend, and my insistence on making for the command deck led us into a trap that nearly cost him his life.' Dante sighed. 'And yet, despite my stupidity, shortly after the Angels Numinous came to our aid, I was made commander. The decision was far from unanimous. Sometimes, we find ourselves where we are not because of what we do, but because of circumstance. I did no great deeds to be elevated to commander of the Blood Angels. I simply survived. All my achievements come hand in hand with tragedy. All of them come with errors.'

'I have made mistakes.'

'You have.'

'But you can recover from yours, you are a Space Marine.'

Dante's voice rose a little. He had a beautiful voice, like strong music in soft mountain airs. 'What does that mean? Nothing. We are both men, you and I. Courage runs in every human's veins. I, too, was not worthy. Others believed I was. Subsequent events seemed to bear out their opinion. I fought because I had to. I served because I must. I made errors. I learned much from them, and still the Chapter nearly perished while I was its Master. Eventually, I became worthy, because I had to be so. Because it was expected of me.'

'I am not you,' said Danakan. Defiance crept into his voice.

'I am not me either. Look at me, admiral.'

Danakan could not. He dropped his eyes.

'I said look at me.' A feral growl entered the back of Dante's voice.

The admiral raised his eyes painfully slowly, until he looked into Dante's own.

'What am I, really?' said Dante. 'Who is Dante? Is he the boy from the tribe in the sand? Is he the Emperor's unthinking servant, His executioner and His vengeance? Is he instead a being with thoughts and choices of his own – not a tyrant, but a just and noble protector of humanity? Is Dante a hero, is he a monster? Does it in fact even matter, to those who call out for my aid, who is truly beneath Sanguinius' golden mask? The people of the Imperium do not see me when I come to their worlds to free them or to slay their oppressors. They see our gene-father. They see Sanguinius. Dante is a construct. The stories about me are fabrication. The tally of the foes I have slain grows with every retelling. If you were to read all the histories accounting my actions, you would realise quickly that, even with my life being as long as it is, I could not possibly have been to all the places they say, or fought in all the battles I am supposed to have won. Look more closely at the stories, and you will see that I am in several places at once. Impossible – but to whom is the truth of interest, apart from the lord regent's historitors? To whom, indeed, is it useful? It is useful to the Imperium that I am feted as I am. It is useful that my name is known, and spoken of as a mark of hope. This Dante they tell stories about, he is not me. I can never be him. But I can do my best to live up to what people need, and where I cannot be, I can allow the stories to bring comfort.'

His eyes blazed. 'I have read that to some cultures the truth was a principle, something to be strived for and protected as sacrosanct. If that sounds attractive to you, you must ask yourself, whom does the truth serve? Now, in these times, the truth is terrible. It serves only our enemies. So, lord admiral, allow me to tell you something. Your role is to play the part the people give you. It is to be what they think you are, until you die. As long as your given role is positive and has use to the Imperium, it is your duty to perform it, no matter what your feelings are. It is not to find some inner truth!'

Dante stood. 'There is no truth. Your role is to serve. Lie to yourself if you have to. The Imperium sees you as a competent, heroic officer. You are competent. You were once heroic. I do not much care that is not how you feel. You should not care that is not how you feel. Lie to yourself. Play the part, even if you are screaming inside. That is what I need from you, and that is what you will do. Are we clear?'

Dante's tawny eyes regarded Danakan with utter seriousness. The weight of his years and his wisdom pushed out from him in waves.

'Is that an order?' Danakan managed to say.

'It is my command.'

Danakan nodded numbly. 'Is it also a rebuke?'

'If it has to be,' said Dante. 'We do not have the luxury of allowing you regret, admiral. Be who you were meant to be again.'

Dante moved a step closer. Danakan did his best not to shrink into the chair.

'You will return to the *Dominance*, which you will command with a proud heart and with the elan you are known for. You will be leaving with us, to Ronenti. There you will protect us while we make war on the surface.'

The admiral finished his wine. Carefully, he stood. The

screams of his burning crew shrieked at him from the candles and lumens and every other place there was light. But he ignored them, and he bowed.

'If that is what you command, lord regent, then so be it.'

CHAPTER TWENTY-SEVEN

FIELD OF THE DEAD

The *Dominance* and its escort pushed through the spinning wreckage of Ronenti's system monitors. A squadron of Sword-class frigates ran ahead, their laser cannons flickering out in a coordinated pattern of strikes, vaporising the biggest pieces of debris before they could impact the fleet's shields. Void-ship death created a billion fragments of metal, paint, ice and pulverised flesh. Particulate debris passed through the shields in shifting displays. Larger chunks vanished in shimmering waves of void shield displacement.

Upon the dimly illuminated command deck, purple and blue light played in submarine ripples over the crew, swamping the weak red of the combat lumens.

'Beautiful,' said Juvenel. He stood on the admiral's dais beside Danakan's throne. Danakan looked ahead, out of the oculus, his attention switching every few seconds to the hololithic tactical displays dotted around his command platform, and the grand strategic display set centrally on the deck.

'Destruction is alluring,' said Danakan, 'but it should never be celebrated. Those were Imperial craft, they will not easily be replaced.'

'That is true, my lord,' said Juvenel, 'but they had to die. There is nothing that could have saved them. I prefer not to regret, but to appreciate that which is set in front of me. Ergo, I see beauty.'

'Very philosophical,' growled Danakan. 'Just remember there were men and women on those ships who died because they were enslaved to an alien will, or because they had no choice. Loyal Imperial subjects subverted by xenos evil. I will not celebrate it.'

The ships passed out of the far side of the debris cloud. Ronenti grew ahead, the crescent of its dayside growing fuller as the fleet sailed closer.

'You have changed, my lord.'

'For the better,' said Danakan. 'You will change too, and come to value regret.'

'So long as it does not compromise my ability to lead,' said Juvenel.

'I know you're keeping an eye on me, Juvenel, and I thank you for it, and for saving my life too, but don't question me, not where others can hear.'

They were isolated upon the dais, but Danakan was right. Juvenel's eyes flicked sideways. A watch officer overseeing gunnery command met his eyes and quickly dropped his gaze.

'My apologies, lord admiral. It is good to see you on the bridge again.' Juvenel almost asked what Dante had done to his commander. He refrained. He was sure he would find out in due course. Danakan liked to talk when in his cups.

Captain Arturo was taking a scrip from the vox-master.

Important, if old Culin had got out of the vox-pit himself. The captain read it, then he too left his command platform at the feet of the dais' stairs, climbed them, and gave Danakan a short bow.

'My lord admiral, Commander Dante signals that he is ready to begin his orbital insertion.'

'Very good,' Danakan said. 'Take up position in high orbit. Begin denial of signal broadcasts. Give word to ventral gunnery to prepare for bombardment.'

Captain Arturo bowed and returned to his own throne. Danakan watched as the taskforce spread out. It was a small fleet: the *Dominance*, a cruiser, two frigate squadrons and a handful of destroyers. Hidden amid the foremost units was Dante's planetary assault cruiser, the *Angelic Blade*.

'Denial broadcasts are in full effect,' said the officer of the vox.

'We have been targeted. Energy spikes detected. Incoming ground fire in three, two, one,' a junior officer of defence announced.

Sheet lightning blinked throughout Ronenti's atmosphere. Short-lived beams flicked across space. They targeted the smaller ships first. Void shield flare washed over the group of destroyers leading the flotilla.

'They're not stupid, are they?' said Juvenel. 'That's the work of a gunnery officer who knows he can't scratch the *Dominance*.'

'Hold formation,' Danakan commanded. 'Prepare to return fire. *Justified Malice*, switch priority to the defensive arrays away from the principal target.'

The *Dominance* moved implacably towards the equator. Ronenti was a pretty world of bright deserts and small, green seas. Minimal ice caps covered the north, surrounded by a line of green forests like a monk's tonsure. The grey spread of cities covered only a small part of its surface north and south of the tropics. The equatorial belt was a sea of sand mottled with dull brown mountains. A war raged down there, but from orbit it appeared peaceful. Ground conflicts between limited forces were nothing compared to the destruction the *Dominance* could unleash. They were beneath Juvenel's notice.

The *Dominance* rolled. Its prow lifted. The planetscape dropped from view. The escorts moved in perfect formation with the capital ship.

'Close-range target view,' Danakan commanded. The tactical hololiths blinked, and showed a real time tri-d vid-feed of a small city in the south. Targeting reticules zeroed in on defensive installations dotted around it. Three defence laser silos, a missile installation, a military airfield. Moderate protection, but more than enough in that part of space, where the worst threats for centuries had been limited xenos and pirate raids.

The hololith shuddered with interference as the batteries below the fleet opened fire. Laser streaks were followed by the bright flash of missiles bursting from their underground launch tubes. They pushed voidwards on slow feet of fire. They were sluggish, and easy prey for the fleet's point defence batteries. Atomic fire ignited in the atmosphere as they were shot down.

'Return fire,' said Danakan.

The ship shivered as its mass drivers launched solid slugs of metal at the surface.

Dominance was under fire now as the desperate defenders split their counter-barrage.

'They weaken their hand,' said Juvenel. 'They are panicking.'

'They are only men,' said Danakan. 'Pity them.'

The first of the mass shots hit the ground. The vid-feed gave an impression of earth wrinkling under immense force, and buildings crushed by overpressure, before the release of energy whited out the augur views.

'Maintain bombardment while Lord Dante's troops descend. Prepare broadcast demanding surrender.'

'We should obliterate them,' said Juvenel.

'Lord Dante wants this world saved with minimal damage,' said Danakan. 'We must play stupid and pretend we think this a simple revolt to allow him time to complete his mission.'

'Lord Dante's drop force is away,' a report came.

Danakan had a hololith zero in on the *Angelic Blade*. Its drop ports flashed as craft were ejected towards the surface, conveying the Blood Angels to their landing zone under the cover of the shells and bombs of the *Dominance*.

'Start the mission clock.' A large, floating chronograph activated over one of the tactical displays. 'Wait until the commander is down, then move the fleet over the southern capital. We'll deliver our ultimatum once there. Who knows, maybe they'll surrender and save us all an awful lot of bother.'

The crew laughed at Danakan's humour. They were relieved their admiral had recovered his spirit, but Juvenel was closest to him. He could see the haunted look in Danakan's eyes. He saw the sweat trickling down his neck.

Danakan could not fool Juvenel. The admiral was still afraid.

'Nine hours,' said Danakan to Juvenel, 'then we level everything from orbit. Good fortune, Commander Dante. The population of a planet depends upon you.'

* * *

'The Lying Emperor shows his true face,' Hassij said. His feet crunched over the rubble of Edoni. 'As the Prophet of Claws says, give him anything other than servitude, and he will rain down his displeasure.'

'Never truer words said. There is nothing left of the city, only broken brick and bones,' said his corporal, Enchay.

The squad advanced over a pile of shifting debris. They left their transport behind them, shrouded in spirals of dust and smoke whipped up by the heat radiating from the broken ground. That far out from the primary strike zone the buildings had been merely levelled. Further in, they had been vaporised. Hassij's rad counter clicked ominously. He ignored it. His will to do his duty was strong. He would die for it.

'There is nothing here,' said Enchay.

'The prophet commands we look, so we look. We must go further in. Too much smoke out here. Pick up the pace.'

The small squad jogged forward, skirting a vast fire still burning in a crater.

'The Lying Emperor would never send his false angels here. He would not dare. He will see the majesty of the Four-Armed Emperor and he will cower.'

'Have you ever seen a false angel?' Hassij asked. 'I have. Three of them came to Djesseli when I was a boy. They are huge, and deadly. Do not underestimate them simply because they are our enemies. One could kill us all. If they are here, the prophet must know.' The memory provoked feelings of hatred in him, but also an uncertainty. A feeling of momentary disorientation troubled him.

The clatter of rock distracted him from his misgivings.

He held up a fist. His squad came to a halt, lasrifles at the ready.

Three shambling figures loped out of the smoke. They were a blend of human and alien. Their altered physiology meant they held their defence force issue rifles awkwardly, but guns were not their main weapons. Their extra limbs sported deadly triple claws, while their broad, human-like hands were tipped with diamond-hard nails.

They halted close by Hassij's squad. The lead jutted his broad head forward. Knobbled vertebrae pushed at his skin as he sniffed suspiciously at the air.

Hassij had never seen such beauty. Every time he saw the Blessed Ones they stopped the breath in his mouth.

Its dark flesh was mottled ivory white with the marks of the prophet. It wore the same uniforms as Hassij's squad, adapted to its Emperor-given body so that its third arm was on full display. It was possessed of a holy asymmetry that was glorious to see.

His squad knelt. The Blessed Ones shifted.

'That way.' Their leader croaked imperfectly formed words. Drool ran between sharp teeth when the Blessed Ones tried to speak, which they did infrequently, and always in short sentences. 'Enemy,' it said.

They turned and loped off into the smoke. The heat oppressed Hassij, and he could hardly breathe, but he followed, determined not to appear weak before the blessed of the Four-Armed Emperor.

The last of the Blessed Ones vanished through a wall of dust streaming down from the corpse of a shattered building. The sight of the fallen building angered him. Thousands had lived in Edoni. All of them had died.

A crackling gunshot came out of the murk, followed by a wet bang and an alien shriek.

'The Blessed Ones!' one of his squad shouted. All of them

were urged forward by a powerful need to protect the children of their god, without thought, without fear.

A loud thrumming noise preceded a blocky transport that punched through the smoke at great speed. Hassij had time to see blood-red livery, and the buckling of the air under contragrav before it swept by. Then another came, and another.

'Open fire!' he yelled.

Lasbeams scored the smoke, vitrifying the eddying dust into showers of glass spheres that pattered onto the rubble.

Their beams inflicted no damage on the speeding transports. Domes of energy shone over their open transport beds, deflecting all incoming fire. Hassij kept firing.

A third transport growled past. A giant in red stared down at him from the deck. Hassij's eyes locked with the green eye lenses of the giant's helm.

For a split second he remembered how he had felt when he had seen the Space Marines as a boy: excited, awed, protected. He had felt special.

That was before the prophet came.

He didn't see the Space Marine raise his bolter. There was a yellow flash and an impact in his chest, then nothing after that.

Dante rode in the open bay on the back of the Impulsor. The Lord of Death stood beside him. The grav-transport swept rapidly over the ruined city, its repulsor array keeping it high over the upheaved terrain. Smoke billowed around it. Fires were beaten flat by its anti-gravity field. Two of Antargo's veterans sat on the back of the transport, guarding their lords.

'They were quick to respond,' Dante said to Mephiston.

'The cult mind is strong, even out here,' said Mephiston. He looked to the sky. 'They already call out to their so-called saviour. This rot must be stopped, or the tyranids will divert course and come here.'

'You are contesting the scream?'

'I am,' said Mephiston. 'I cannot blot it out completely. You were right to set the mission clock. We have limited time. Every passing hour the risk of the hive mind hearing increases.'

'We will conduct a purge of the surrounding systems,' said Dante. 'The infection will have spread by now. The xenos here reveal their hybrids openly. Their infestation is complete.'

He changed vox-channel to speak to the Impulsor's driver. 'Make sure the enemy's local communications are jammed. Conduct augur sweeps for any further signs of life.'

'I sense none,' said Mephiston.

'There should be some survivors.'

'I feel no living thing within a hundred miles of this place,' said the Lord of Death.

The Impulsor dropped suddenly as it crested the wall of an outlying crater. The last remains of Edoni sped by; burning residential districts and shanty towns. They passed the city limits, and went out over agrifields of squat palmate trees arrayed in neat rows between the high pipes of an irrigation system. The whole area showed signs of neglect. Many of the trees were dead.

Over the trees the Impulsor arrays found a level. The force fanned out into a broad arrowhead, running parallel to a wide, dusty highway. It should have been crowded with ground vehicles, but it was empty, barred every few miles by deserted military checkpoints.

Dante surveyed the parched, empty landscape. 'Did they know we were coming?'

'I think not,' said Mephiston. He closed his eyes. 'There is something to the north-west.'

'Is it worthy of investigation?'

'There is pain. A great amount of pain. Old now, but the echoes persist.' He looked at Dante. 'We should investigate.'

Dante gave the order. Antargo's demi-company obeyed, and the Impulsors swept around, heading obliquely towards the horizon.

They arrived as the sun was setting, staining the world with glorious orange light the colour of autumn fires. The dry grasses, the squat trees – all were painted a vibrant red-gold.

Through the last rays of day, Mephiston and Dante walked a field of bones.

An area many square miles in size had been flattened. Piles of earth and grass were heaped between bulldozed trees lying in untidy stacks around the periphery.

The lack of care taken in clearing the site was in awful contrast to the obscene diligence with which the bodies had been arranged, each laid with their heads to the north, their feet pointing south, each given the same amount of space for their repose.

The massacre had taken place some time ago, long enough that the sun had reduced the bodies to black skins shrunken onto white bones. The clothes they wore in life were discoloured by the leakage of corpse juices. Bright silks and dull utilitarian coveralls alike had been stained an ugly brown, but the diversity of people present was readily apparent. People of all ages, all occupations. Soldiers lay next to manufactorum workers, high bureaucrats beside lowly agricolae serfs.

A faint scent of decay, like aged spices, hung over the field. It stretched on for miles. The piles of debris scraped from the surface on the far side were distant blue marks against the dead orchards.

'Their purity links them,' said Dante. 'These were the people not in thrall to the xenos.'

'It is so,' said Mephiston. 'Slaughtered. The same will be happening in the north.'

Dante stopped by a small corpse. The vibrant green of its headscarf was a shocking contrast to the decay of the flesh. He stared at it for a long moment. Insects chirred in the dried-out landscape.

'I hate them all, Mephiston,' said Dante. 'These fiends and aliens we must fight. When will it ever end?'

'When the last of them stops breathing, or we do,' said Mephiston.

Dante stood, fixated on the dead. 'Life is struggle. How I wish it were not so.'

'So has spoken every wise man in every species ever to think,' said the Lord of Death. He looked skywards. His pale skin glowed in the evening light. 'Night is coming. We are an hour's transit from Djesseli. The centre of this infection is there. I can feel it, even now, a blackness in the warp screaming out for attention. When I touch the warp, I feel the shadow cast by the hive mind, far away on the edge of perception. It is blinded, as we are, by the energies pouring from the Rift. Abaddon's atrocity has bought us a little time. If we slay their leader, and the beasts that brought this disease to Ronenti, then this world may yet have a chance.'

'Then we shall purge it.'

'We might be best laying Ronenti to waste.'

In the dying day Dante's golden death mask looked as if it were aflame.

'If I can save one human life here, I will. I have called too often on Exterminatus this past year.'

'It is not your fault, Dante.'

'No,' said the Chapter Master, 'but it was my choice. It was I who gave the order, I who condemned billions to die.'

'Only so that trillions might live.'

'That makes it no easier to bear,' said Dante. 'I swore to protect the Imperium, Mephiston. The Imperium is not a collection of stars, or flags planted in far-off soils. This is the Imperium.' He gestured at the bones cooling in the gathering blue of evening.

He turned back to the line of Impulsors waiting at the edge of the massacre ground. 'Burn them, Lord of Death. Let your power shine bright in the warp. Commit these bodies to purifying fire. Let the enemy know we are coming, and let them fear.'

'As you wish, my lord,' said Mephiston. He observed the spectacle of the bones a moment more. Something in the arrangement was appealing to him. Then he reached into the warp with his mind and brought out fire.

The whole slaughter ground, end to end, erupted in sheets of roaring flame thirty feet tall.

Heat wafted Mephiston's cloak as he left the field.

Chekeen paced the high walls of Djesseli's Havamor Palace. Night brought relief from the heat of the day. Cool winds blowing off the agri-steppe around the city dried his sweat away. The banners of the Prophet of Claws snapped in the wind. The flag was a purple field bearing a tightly curled ouroboros, signifying the prophet's great message, that in all people the truth of things waited to be awoken.

Chekeen's footsteps crunched dust on the paving. The city was quiet. Not so long ago, night-time Djesseli had rung to immoral revelry. Drink ran freely. The wicked preyed on the weak. Not after the purge. After the purge, a perfect silence fell at every sunset.

He breathed in air scented by the baked lands of the plains. With no unbelievers, the city smelled better. There was less smog. Less effluent to pour into the great river Djess.

He continued on his patrol. As he rounded the Outgate turrets, he met another of the guards. Like Chekeen, he wore the uniform of Ronenti's planetary defence force, and the ridged tattoo of the Blessed Prophet around his right eye.

'Ascension awaits us,' Chekeen said.

'May the day come soon,' the other said.

With a nod they passed each other.

A scrape from behind made Chekeen stop and turn around.

The other guard had vanished. He could have turned the corner, Chekeen supposed, but not at the speed he'd been walking. A sense of foreboding took hold of him.

He walked back to where the parapet turned to the south. Sure enough, the other guard was nowhere to be seen. He unhitched his bulky vox-set from his belt. As he did, he looked down, and saw blood on the rough sandstone of the parapet.

Suddenly afraid, he bent forward and touched the liquid. It was still warm.

He raised the vox to his mouth, opened it to speak, but no sound came out. A sharp agony cut into him from behind. A heavy, ugly sword punched through his ribs, its serrations carrying the remains of his lungs out through his ruptured chest.

A hard hand shoved him off the blade. He fell onto his knees, his mouth gulping for air he could no longer breathe.

A skull-faced giant in red stalked past him, a grapnel line reeling itself silently back into a huge pistol. The giant spared him no backward glance, but whispered menacingly as he moved round the corner.

'Brother Fain reporting. Sector two secured,' were the last words Chekeen ever heard.

An explosive round tore a chunk out of the wall by Ghinac's head, hurting his ears and scourging his face with a storm of shrapnel.

He heard another of the palace guard behind him give a shout that was abruptly cut off.

'Intruders!' he shouted into his vox-set. 'Intruders on the eastern wall!' He cursed the vox-set. When he released the send button it made a weirdly modulated hum, and would neither send nor receive. It was huge and heavy so he dropped it, letting the poor-quality plastek of its casing break to pieces on the stone. He was grateful to be free of the weight. His feet pushed off the paving hard, twisting painfully against the leather of his boots. He ran faster than he ever had before, fear driving him on more effectively than any whip.

He did not look behind. Even the minor effort to turn his head would cost him valuable time. He had no wish to see the ogrish things coming for him, the men-machines with lifeless skulls for faces and killing hands of metal. They seemed too big to move quickly, too massive to be as silent as they were, but the crawling skin on his neck told him they were right behind him. All he heard of his pursuers were stealthy footfalls, much further apart than a normal man's and far quieter than he thought possible, the soft noise of rubber grips on stone coming closer and closer.

He pelted through into the palace and slammed the door, dropping the lock bar into the brackets. He prayed to the True Emperor that three inches of steel would stop his pursuers.

He was mistaken. He was barely thirty yards down the corridor when the door boomed to two heavy kicks and burst inwards. 'Intruders!' he shouted, struggling through his ragged breath to get out the words. 'Soldiers of the Lying Emperor!'

Silenced guns coughed, just as he threw himself sideways into one of the palace's staterooms. At that hour it was deserted, and his footsteps slapped loudly on the wooden floor. He hurtled on, diving down a side passage at the last moment. His pursuers ran past, pale red light cast from lamps set around their eyes, their skull masks ghostly in the gloom of the hall.

He stilled his breathing and jogged forward slowly. The lumens were out in the palace. He heard muffled gunshots and terrified voices cut off mid-shriek.

He was getting closer to the central precincts of the palace. The alarm still had not been raised.

'Intruders!' he shouted. 'False angels! Intruders!' His breath was ragged. He wished now he had never taken up smoking bhaccan tubes.

Finally, an alarm began to sound somewhere far off.

He slowed. The sounds of fighting grew in intensity, but distance dulled them. He heard inhuman roars and the reports of overpowered weaponry, now all far behind.

He came to another grand space. The palace was large. In the darkness and his haste to escape, he had lost his way. He took a tentative step forward.

'Hello?' he whispered. He expected an echo, but the shadows swallowed his voice whole. He hesitated. Darkness was heavy behind him, and growing thicker, with a sense of weight and mass that pushed him on.

The darkness welcomed him. He could see nothing. He had the awful sense that the darkness was alive, close to his face, looking at him with invisible eyes.

Shaking set into his limbs. The tap-tap-tap of his lasgun butt on his uniform buttons was terrifyingly loud. There was something in there with him. He could feel it deep in the animal parts of his brain, those ancient limbic circuits buried deep that gave warning of predators. He turned around and took a few faltering steps forward. He had no idea which was the way out.

'I'm not afraid,' he lied.

The darkness parted. A figure appeared before him suddenly, wreathed in red light. It was not the light that revealed him but rather the darkness that relinquished him, and Ghinac knew in his soul that the being was darkness. Tall he was, and terrible to see, a ghost-white face surrounded by long pale hair, with burning red eyes and the fangs of a killing animal. The monster's masters had seen fit to clad it in armour fashioned to look like flayed flesh: a design that glinted the liquid gloss of fresh gore, with wet muscle ridges newly peeled artfully sculpted on every inch. He held a sword bigger than Ghinac that fluttered soft red flames.

Such terror smote at Ghinac's failing courage that it collapsed entirely. Warm liquid ran down his uniform leg.

He sank to his knees, moaning softly. The prophet said he would be protected. The prophet said he would be saved. Where was the prophet now?

'I pity you,' the giant said, before raising his hand and, with invisible force, crushed the life from Ghinac's body.

Dante waited outside the city. The units he commanded directly were hidden in giant grain silos. They were otherwise empty, and by the look of them had been for some time. A number of bodies were stacked in the corner – unfortunate civilians who had come across the Blood Angels while gleaning for scraps. They were malnourished to the point of starvation.

Dante steadfastly ignored the dead men, but he could not shut their presence from his mind entirely. Blood leaked under them, running in bright sheets to make pools in the pitted ferrocrete of the silo floor. He yearned to take off his helm and lap at it, to take their strength for his own.

A couple of his warriors worked to fit Dante with his jump pack. The Sanguinary Guard accompanying him had already been equipped. Squads of Intercessors and Hellblasters waited to move out. A portable hololith displayed the view from the sergeant of the squad of Infiltrators watching the city's main barracks.

Mephiston's voice spoke to him directly, his psychic might bypassing the need for vox.

+Lord Dante, the outer palace buildings are taken. Reivers are in the process of eliminating the last of the palace guard. I am moving in to eliminate the prime target.+

'Then I shall begin my assault,' said Dante. 'Antargo, give your Infiltrators the signal. They are to engage as soon as the enemy respond to Mephiston's attacks.'

'Signal given, my lord.'

Dante waited for the armoured gates of the barracks to open. He cut off the feed from the hololith as the first shots were fired.

'We go for the palace.'

An explosion from the city barracks rumbled across the sleeping city.

From all quarters, the dirge of alarms struck up.

CHAPTER TWENTY-EIGHT

THE PERSON WE PERCEIVE

Danakan stared at the chronograph. Just over an hour remained before he would have to open fire on the planet below. He imagined the people looking skywards, seeing the fleet come to save them flash and flare with weapons fire, then scream as they realised the shots were meant for them.

They would all burn: men, women and children. The planet itself would be devastated, a living world, killed. The scar of the city he'd flattened still gave off smoke. Hours later, it stretched hundreds of miles across Ronenti's deserts.

What if Dante and the rest were alive when he fired? He would be responsible for the death of the Imperium's greatest hero. The future of the whole of Imperium Nihilus depended on his choice.

Their message to the rulers of the south droned on and on, set to repeat without pause.

'*...in order to ensure your survival. The Emperor is merciful,* *the Emperor is just. Surrender and enjoy pain-free execution. This is your final...'*

His head swam. The chronograph ticked down, second by second.

'My lord!' whispered Juvenel.

Danakan shook off his sense of growing dread. He had to wet his lips before he could speak.

'Is there any word?' he asked. He had tried to keep his requests for information to a minimum, but he had asked the same question a hundred times. Juvenel winced. His vox liaison looked at him uncertainly.

'None, my lord admiral,' said the man. 'The enemy have co-opted the entire planetary communication network to jam our signals. The master of astropaths has attempted communication, but the xenos below are preventing contact by telepathy also.'

'Augurs?' asked Danakan.

'The same situation, my lord,' reported the mistress of sight. 'Some augurs are giving readings, but only those in the low-definition range. Visual scans are unclear.' She called up a grainy image of the capital. 'There are indications Lord Dante's troops are fighting in this part of the city, around the palace here. We believe they have been ambushed.'

'Then the Blood Angels live,' said Danakan.

'They do not yet appear to have broken into the palace, my lord,' said the mistress of sight. 'They are running behind schedule.'

'Then the invasion is stalling,' said Juvenel.

'We do not know that yet!' said Danakan. His officers shared glances at his tone. It was expected that an admiral might shout at his command, but Danakan realised just how anxious he sounded. He took a deep breath. 'I am going to my quarters to rest a while. I will return when the countdown nears completion.'

Danakan deactivated his control implants and stepped down from the dais.

'Juvenel, take a rest as well. Thirty minutes. We have hard choices ahead of us. Captain Arturo, you have fleet command.'

'If it is all the same to you, my lord,' said Juvenel, 'I would rather remain here.'

Danakan struggled to keep his voice level. 'You will rest,' said Danakan. He didn't trust what Juvenel would do in his absence.

'I will rest then,' said Juvenel tersely. 'Prepare gunnery sections for action.'

'Belay that,' said Danakan.

'My lord!' said Juvenel.

'Gunnery command to remain on third level alert, no higher,' said Danakan. He walked past Juvenel. 'You overstep your authority, sir,' he whispered to his flag-lieutenant.

Juvenel gave him a cold look. Before he could respond, Danakan strode briskly towards the private lifter that would take him to his quarters. He passed pits full of crew who were, he was sure, deliberately avoiding his eyes.

The rattle of bolt rifles firing together drowned out the engine noise of the enemy tanks. Three Leman Russ variants were pushing through the broken gate into the palace's outer grounds. The lead machine rocked back on its suspension as its main armament fired. The shell fell among a demi-squad of Dante's Intercessors, blasting them off their feet. They were strong, and four of them got back to their feet, shook off the effects of the cannon blast and recommenced firing from the shelter of the crater. The fifth lay still.

Bolt-rounds detonated across the tanks' dozer blades and thick frontal armour. Divots of metal were chipped from the glacis amid bright flashes and showers of spall, leaving bare plasteel craters in their livery. The tanks finally made it through the central archway of the gate, jerking as their treads reversed to turn them quickly on the spot, the first heading right, the second left, opening up a gap for the third to drive through. Fyceline smoke drifted thickly across the courtyard as their heavy bolters opened up, their steady, bass chugging and the explosions of their large rounds adding to the roar of battle.

The Blood Angels' intelligence was lacking. The enemy had brought their own denial widecast into range, and although it was too unsophisticated to break the Blood Angels' hardened squad-to-squad vox systems, communications with the fleet were severely hampered. They were at risk of being bogged down.

There was a squad of Incursors hunting for the source of the transmission, but the city was large, and time was running short.

'Squad Etruscus, take down the tank,' Dante commanded, painting the target with his unit auto-senses and broadcasting the data to the Hellblasters. Immediately they opened up, coming in from the side to enfilade the leftmost Leman Russ. Blinding plasma streams hit the vehicle, cutting molten gashes into its thick armour. Its sponson blew spectacularly, sending out corkscrewing trails as the rounds in the side cooked off. But the tank was otherwise unharmed, and its turret swung around on whining motors, battle cannon depressing to take aim.

The Hellblasters fired again, melting the links of its left track together. The engine roared as the machine tried to free itself, but succeeded only in breaking its track, which slithered free of its drive wheels to lie flat on the ground, stranding the vehicle.

The battle cannon barked. The shell hit a Hellblaster square in the chest. He flew backwards into the ground, his armour carving up the gravel of the courtyard and digging into the earth. The shell blew while the Hellblaster was on the floor, blasting him to pieces.

Dante resisted the urge to charge into combat with the tanks. Antargo was already among them, gun flashing. His Phobos armour made him nimble, but he was missing the armour-killing strength of a power fist.

'Hold the gate!' Dante said. 'Do not allow them within to reinforce the troops inside the palace.'

Smaller battles raged all over the complex. Blood Angels infiltrators tied up most of the palace guard, allowing Mephiston the chance to penetrate the deeper defences, but the tanks and the mechanised infantry coming in behind could tip the balance.

An alien shriek rose behind them. A heavy iron door clanked up into the inner walls, and through it poured a horde of misshapen hybrids. They ran headlong, almost falling over their feet in their rush to engage with the Space Marines. There were dozens of them. Antargo's force, some twenty strong, were occupied with the tanks. Already, infantry were moving up outside in the cover of the Leman Russ to make an attempt to retake the courtyard. The hybrids were a dangerous distraction.

Dante flicked the activation stud on the Axe Mortalis. Its head flared with a burst of false lightning.

'Squad Quercus, fall back and engage new threat at range. Brother Sulea, Brother Tengrael,' he said to his guard. 'On me.'

He activated his jump pack, arcing high over the racing crowd of tainted humanity. At the apex of his flight, he had a moment of weightlessness when his jets cut out, and saw Squad Quercus turn and fell the first rank of the xenos monsters with a concentrated burst of gunfire. Then he fell down on the enemy like the wrath of the Emperor Himself, crushing a swollen head beneath his boots, incinerating another with the Perdition Pistol. His axe obliterated the chest of a third hybrid with a thunderous bang.

His wounds twinged. He felt weak.

Then claws and teeth were snapping all around him, and he lost sight of the rest of his force.

The psychic scream of the cult was a constant presence, akin to the shadow in the warp in the same way that the shrill cries of young avians bear resemblance to the calls of the adults. It keened in Mephiston's mind, the wail of an infant shrieking for its mother's attention.

Undaunted, Mephiston moved on towards the source. By psychic art he trapped the shriek as surely as if it were encased in a soundproof bubble. No fleet of bio-ships would come in answer to strip the planet bare of life, and reveal to the cultists the truth of what they worshipped – not while he lived. At this close range to the source he could blot it out completely.

He took grim satisfaction in his new powers. They no longer threatened to overwhelm him. The black angel was inside him now. He felt it beneath the layers of his mind: Kali, Calistarius, Mephiston. Blood Angel and man. Buried under all the constructs of his consciousness, the constraints of his training, was a force far greater than any he had ever known before. Like the Rage, but not wild; his alone.

He could reach down inside himself and open the doors to the black angel. It might mean the end of him, but the thought of such power being his to wield tempted him gravely.

This was part of his burden now. Not one of his brothers showed signs of the Rage. If he were to unleash what dwelled within him, all would plummet into unreasoning madness, and the Rage would spread, and spread, until none of Sanguinius' scions remained sane.

This was the truth of what he was. He could never tell a soul.

He turned away from temptation. He walked halls so dark no standard human being could possibly see inside, but to him they were lit as clearly as if both moons of Baal shone full. There was no life down there. The palace was immense, and surely must have been busy with servants before the cult came. He saw no one but the soldiers he slaughtered so casually. It was like the fields, and the starving people. The cult had no need for anything other than the call. They raised up false idols and the people danced while their world died around them.

The call could be trapped within a psychic construct. He could do little about the mental web linking the cult together. He attempted to suppress the threads spreading from the palace's rotten heart that subverted human will into unthinking servitude. Part of a cult's control over the populace was physical, induced by chemical and genetic changes made by direct contamination, but much of it was psychic slavery. Cut off the head, and the body would wither.

The cult leaders were waiting for him. He could feel that. There were several minds tangled together, a partial hive of human slaves, backed by the monstrous intellect of a genestealer patriarch.

They were close. He pushed a greater part of his mind into Vitarus, the Sanguinary Sword. Its red flames danced higher.

'I am death,' he whispered, 'and I am coming for you.'

* * *

Danakan let water into his small basin. As admiral, he was entitled to use as much as he wanted, but he felt that to be wrong when his crews' supply was so strictly rationed, so ran only enough that he could scoop his hands into it and dash it onto his face. He blinked his eyes clear and dabbed the rest away with a towel.

There was a noise behind him.

He straightened and put the towel down.

'It's always disappointing,' he said. 'It's never as refreshing as you want it to be. Always tepid. Stinks of chemicals. I would be glad of a glass of cold, pure water.'

There was no reply.

'I know it's you, Juvenel.'

Another small noise, that of a man shifting position. There was silence a moment, then Juvenel spoke.

'Turn around, admiral.'

Danakan anticipated the gun Juvenel had and lifted his hands.

Juvenel was half hidden behind a wooden dressing screen near the admiral's bed. He came out fully now he was detected. In one hand he held a bronzed laspistol chased with fine inlay. In the other he gripped a glass of spirits so hard his knuckles strained white beneath his skin.

'I gave you that gun you're pointing at me,' said Danakan. He raised his eyebrows. 'And that's my amasec.'

'I'm sorry,' said Juvenel, meaning it. 'I need a drink.'

'Murder is a difficult business,' said Danakan.

'Don't be glib now, admiral, it's beneath you.'

'How did you get in here before me?'

'Through the salvator passages. I think I'm going to post an extra guard at the other end.'

Danakan looked down at the gun again. 'Do you desire command so much you would kill me for it?'

'It's not about command,' said Juvenel softly. 'I mean, I want command, but I'd rather earn it. It's about doing what's right. I'd gladly have served you for the rest of my days. I have respected you for my entire career. I was patient after Teleope. I waited for you to come back, for so long, covering for you, helping you, waiting for the man I followed to show himself again.'

Juvenel's pain moved Danakan. 'I'm recovering, Juvenel.'

'You're not. You put on a good act, but I can see the fear in you.' Juvenel drained his glass, keeping his gun pointed at Danakan. 'You're afraid of making decisions. That's not good. I've been lying awake wondering, what happens if Dante does not come back? Will you do your duty?'

'We both know our orders,' said Danakan.

'We do. But only one of us will carry those orders out.' He put down his glass. His hand was shaking. 'This is harder than I thought it would be.'

'You don't have to do this. Dante has put me right. I know what I have to do. I am doing my best.'

'Damn it, Seroen,' Juvenel said. 'Your best is not enough any more. If the Blood Angels come back this time, there will be another occasion, then another, then another, a string of hard choices that you will ultimately fail to take. Fortune can only save you for so long. Dante puts too much trust in you. If he fails today, I know you will not fire, the xenos cult will triumph, the tyranids will fall on these worlds and billions of people will die, because you can no longer take the long view. Death is too close to you.'

'Very close.'

'Please, admiral, don't make this harder for me.'

'Dante will succeed. There will be no need to condemn so many people to death.'

'If the clock runs down? The lord commander has already given his judgement! It is not our place to decide, it is to follow orders. You have become weak. The hangman does not determine who gets to live or die, he only delivers the sentence.'

'This hangman has developed a conscience.'

'The galaxy is on fire. There's no space for that any more. You are out of your time.'

'Whereas you are the very picture of ruthlessness, convinced you are doing your duty yet shaking like a leaf on a tree stem. Next you will tell me Dante is old, and he is weak also.'

'Of course not.' Juvenel looked aside in torment, then back with fierce resolve. 'But he has not been heard from since he went into the city. Augur captures show fiercer fighting than expected around the palace. Dante and the Lord Mephiston cannot be seen. And you won't do anything. You won't even send down a flight of fighters to help them.'

'You can't peel an apple with a hammer, Juvenel. The Space Marines are made for this kind of war. If Dante had wanted the city bombed into submission, that is what we would have done from the outset. His plan is to preserve life. So we must wait.'

'I am going to have to kill you.'

'You don't, but you have already made up your mind.'

'I don't want to.'

'Nevertheless, you will do it,' said Danakan. 'I don't care, you know.'

'Weakness.'

'It's tiredness, Juvenel. I have had enough. I've seen too many people die. Dante wants me to watch many more, in the name of duty. I can't. You're a capable commander. I can't think of anyone better to take over. You'll do all right, until one day what happened to me will happen to you, if you are not killed first.' Danakan straightened his uniform. 'You will say it was suicide, I assume.' He glanced upwards to the carvings decorating the ceiling. 'And being clever, you will have disabled the surveillance in my quarters.'

'I figured you'd want privacy for your death.'

'What about Fresne?'

'He's a sneaky one,' said Juvenel. 'Got through the invasion of the ship, didn't he? I'm sure he'll understand.'

'You sent him away?'

'I didn't. Somebody else had an important errand for him, though.'

'Very wise. It's not going to be easy for anyone to prove you killed me, but I warn you, you'll always be under suspicion. Dante is not a fool.'

'Then why don't we make this simpler? End it yourself.' Juvenel turned the gun round, grasping it by the barrel and holding out the grip to Danakan.

Danakan laughed. 'I have no desire to see you caught, Juvenel, because you are right. I am no longer suitable for command. But I don't want to die very much, and I'll be damned if I'll make it easy for you. For every bold action, there must be a price.'

Juvenel's face hardened. He turned the gun back round and rested his finger on the trigger, and returned his aim to Danakan.

'This is it then,' said Danakan.

'I am afraid so.'

'Listen to me one last time,' said Danakan. 'If you do not hear from Dante immediately, do not be too hasty to open fire. The death of a city cannot be undone. If you are wrong, it will haunt you.'

'I am not weak like you. I will do my duty.'

'You are human. None of us are as strong as we wish we were. I can still hear them screaming. Soon you will too.'

Juvenel stared into Danakan's eyes.

'Oh for the Emperor's sake, Juvenel, just do it.'

Juvenel's finger convulsed on the trigger, squeezing it harshly. Even having intended to fire, the shot still surprised him. A flicker of ruby las-light left a smoking hole above Danakan's heart.

The admiral smiled.

'Thank you,' he said.

He fell down, still smiling. Juvenel walked over to him and nudged him with his foot, immediately regretting his lack of respect. He bent down and shut Danakan's eyes, and felt for the non-existent pulse, doing it all gently, but it was too late. Juvenel felt worse about that nudge than the shot itself. He was not the man he had thought he was.

He wiped the gun down and put it into Danakan's hand, turned away from the corpse of his friend and marched towards the bridge.

Mephiston went lower into the palace. Everywhere the windows were shuttered and the lights, where active, were dim. The cult had cemented their position of power on Ronenti, for the psychic spoor of his prey led him not into the obscure places under the city, but towards the throne room itself.

The doors were open to him when he came. Utter blackness reigned until he stepped within and the crimson flames wreathing Vitarus flickeringly lit the hall. The throne room was small. In his life Mephiston had fought battles on the shoulders of statues made from mountains. He had saved and condemned cities that covered worlds. He had taken bridges as tall as the sky. He had liberated manufactories that swallowed continents. But as a monument to a single human ego, the hall was sufficient. Large statues of polished metal lined the walls. Artworks hung between them. A complicated, unlovely mosaic covered the floor wall to wall. The ceiling was too high to see clearly, but Mephiston's superior eyesight discerned a similarly vulgar painting.

The subject of these artworks was all the same man. Mephiston knew him from the intelligence reports on Ronenti: Olim Djell, the founder of the south's ruling dynasty. His attempts at immortality were feeble. His house was dust. His memory was fading. A man could not build himself an eternal future.

'Only service endures,' said Mephiston. 'We do what we must for the Imperium.'

He walked into the centre of the room. Scarlet firelight glanced off pale, nearly human faces. Dozens of hybrids watched him. They could have passed as humans of genetic minor deviation, but compared to the dark-skinned Ronenti, their sickly hue stood out. They were hairless. All had the same furious frown, and noses that appeared wrinkled on first glance, but closer attention revealed to be oddly bumped. Only the most generous genetor would have regarded them as pure. Mephiston's Space Marine senses could smell the alien on them. His psychic power laid the truth of their souls bare.

Their robes rustled as they closed ranks behind Mephiston. Rarely had the Lord of Death seen so many late-generation hybrids in one place. That the aliens had been able to conceal themselves so long suggested divisions on Ronenti deeper than Jemmeni thought.

The pool of uncertain light crawled up a set of steps leading to the throne. Here were the leaders. Upon the throne sat a monstrously fat genestealer. Scaling on its exoskeleton and a cloudiness to its eyes showed its great age. Its claws were flaky and lustreless. Mephiston regarded it as low threat, despite its huge size. Its intellect was sharp, and it peered at him with senses other than sight. In the mind of this being the cry of the cult was gathered and projected into the warp. Physically, it was past its best.

Another of the crossbreeds stepped forward as Mephiston advanced, and interposed itself between him and the patriarch. It carried a tall staff topped with a stylised depiction of the Emperor, carved with four arms. A tall cowl rose from its collar, the shape mimicking the alien's ribbed flesh.

'Stop,' the being said. Its voice was cold as the void. 'Kneel before the avatar of the Four-Armed Emperor and we shall let you live.'

'You know with whom you speak?'

'You are an angel of the false Emperor. You are a weapon of hatred.'

'Then you know I will not kneel, magos,' said Mephiston.

The creature's eyes widened at the speaking of its title. Mephiston experienced an echo of surprise.

'You are all called the same thing, on every world your corrupt seeds take root. You are the product of a template. Your enlightenment is engineered. I will not be able to convince you of this, because you are a slave. I know, because I have tried.'

'If you kneel, we will save you,' said the magos. 'We welcome all. Salvation is for everyone. All you must do is accept the truth, and you will know it.'

The genestealer leered at Mephiston. Its hollow-tipped tongue poked from its lipless mouth. A flare of interest washed from it.

'I also know what form your salvation takes,' said Mephiston. 'I should not pity you, for your kind is wicked to the soul, but you have no choice. I feel the blind devotion in you. I taste the rankness of corruption. Know this before I kill you – it is not your fault, and if such a thing is possible, then I commend your stolen spirit to the protection of the Emperor.'

'I have no interest in your god,' said the magos. The static prickle of gathering warp power fogged the air between him and Mephiston.

'The Emperor is not a god,' said Mephiston. 'All gods are lies.'

Light burned around the magos' staff, throwing out a stark illumination onto the beings crowding the room. From around the throne four genestealers slunk, so-called purestrains, their features stamped with humanity's genetic imprint. The nearly human creatures behind him were tensing to attack. They were late in the process of planetary subjugation. What individuality they had was disappearing. Their behaviour was becoming more tyranid than human.

'Witness the power of a god, then, and see you are wrong before you die,' said the magos.

The magos vomited a roaring fountain of power from its eyes and mouth. Brilliant light splashed onto the crowd behind Mephiston, casting a forest of shadows from reaching limbs and outstretched knives. They screwed up their eyes against the light and shrieked at its brilliance, but advanced nevertheless.

The light engulfed Mephiston completely. Every muscle in the magos' body strained with the power coursing through it. The light cut out.

Mephiston was gone.

A satisfied mumbling went up from the crowd of hybrids. The purestrains hissed.

'A worthy effort,' Mephiston said. His voice echoed around the hall. The crowd looked about for him.

He appeared in a blaze of red over their heads, held aloft by a spreading pair of wings made of crimson light. Power coursed through him and out of him, ruby lightning spearing into the crowd from his hands and feet. In his right hand a red lambency grew into a flaring brightness. A spear took shape, and he cast it from him at the bloated genestealer. The magos screamed a wordless challenge, and threw out a shield of light with a motion of his staff. The spear blazed through it, showering sparks, and slammed into the genestealer's head, pinning it with crackling energies to the back of the throne. The spear stayed manifest for a few seconds, boiling the monster's brains and reducing its eyes to hissing tears of jelly, before vanishing with a crackle of ozone-heavy air.

The crowd wailed and screamed.

Mephiston raised his hand. An expanding sphere of power blasted from him, flattening the genestealers. Darkness swelled around him, stealing away every photon of light, until even the xenos could not see.

Mephiston's voice filled the space.

'I am the Lord of Death,' he said. 'No enemy of mankind can prevail against me. Nothing can.'

The killing began.

Juvenel returned to the bridge by a circuitous route, arriving as the counter was ticking down to four minutes. As soon as he entered, the senior crew officers stood.

'Passing command to Flag-Lieutenant Juvenel.'

'I apologise for my delay. Has the admiral not returned?'

'No, sir,' said Captain Arturo.

'Then I will oversee the conclusion of the operation, until

he comes back. Send orders to your gunnery captains, gunnery command, to make ready for immediate bombardment. Pass orders that the fleet break apart and take anchor over their targets. Each craft is to begin attack as soon as it is within optimal weapons range.'

If there was any hesitation on the part of the crew in counteracting the admiral's order, they kept it to themselves. Whole sections of the command deck went into a controlled busyness as orders were passed down to all gunnery decks, then further on, deep into the layered chain of command from the most high to the lowest rating sweating in the magazine. 'Two minutes, forty-eight seconds remaining,' said the master of the hours.

'Begin target acquisition,' said Juvenel. 'Bombardment shall commence on the outer city districts. Give the Blood Angels extra time to extract themselves, if they have survived. Keep attempting to contact them.'

The chronograph counted down. Juvenel had his vox-operators try again and again to reach Dante's command, with no result.

His fingers drummed on the armrests of Danakan's throne. At the last moment, he was beginning to doubt himself. Dante could still be alive on the surface. But the signs of fighting around the palace were much heavier than anticipated. The Space Marines had the best equipment of any Imperial armed force; if there was a way to contact the fleet, they would have.

'Contact the Blood Angels ships,' said Juvenel. 'Tell them to ready their weapons for release on my command.'

A few seconds passed. 'Blood Angels vessels acknowledge request and stand ready.'

Their readiness to open fire made Juvenel sit easier.

'Gunnery decks ready,' announced one gunnery officer.

'Ventral turrets ready,' said another.

'Dorsal turrets ready.'

'One minute remaining, sir,' said the master of bombardment.

'Roll the ship ninety-five degrees to port, prepare port batteries. Prepare turret arrays,' said Juvenel.

'The admiral requested ventral guns only.'

'I am in command,' said Juvenel.

'Thirty seconds,' said the master of the hours.

'Any sign?' He sat forward in the command throne. His hands tensed into fists.

'Ten.'

'Comb all frequencies again. Ask the Blood Angels ships if they have any notice of their surface force.'

'Aye sir.'

'Nine.'

'Primary cannon arrays primed and ready to fire,' called gunnery command.

'Eight.'

'Dorsal turrets ready.'

'Seven.'

'Ventral weapons ready.'

'Five.'

'Begin firing sequences, all weapons,' said Juvenel.

'Three. Two. One.'

The chronograph flashed amber and let out a short, shrill whistle.

The full silence of three hundred people waiting for an order smothered Juvenel.

What if Danakan was right? What if Dante's orders should be ignored, for the good of all?

He looked at the close-in view of Djesseli's central districts. Gunfire seemed to have ceased in the streets.

Dante could have won.

Dante could have lost.

Orders were orders.

The chronograph was at plus three seconds, an unforgivable span of time.

He opened his mouth to speak.

A wave of nausea swept over the crew. Mephiston's voice rang in every mind on the command deck. The touch of Mephiston's soul against his made Juvenel want to tear off his skin.

+The xenos are vanquished. The mission is a success. Stand down immediately.+

The nausea ceased with the voice. Juvenel swallowed bitter saliva, and stood on shaky legs.

'Deactivate all weapons. Fleet stand down immediately.'

A different kind of tension passed into the room as men and women worked fast to power down weaponry sufficient to render Ronenti uninhabitable for generations.

As they worked a vox call came through on a minor hardline. The operative stood abruptly and addressed Juvenel directly.

Juvenel's gut clenched. He already knew what was coming.

'Sir, tragic news,' the officer said. He was white with shock. He couldn't believe what he was saying. 'It's Steward Fresne. The admiral is dead.'

CHAPTER TWENTY-NINE

AN ANGEL'S SORROW

The appointment of a Chapter Master was a sombre affair, following inevitably on from death as they did, but Dante's was remarkably grim.

There was little ceremony at the investiture. The Blood Angels gathered in the grand basilica of *Bloodcaller*, still clad in their battered armour, far too few to fill it even a quarter full. They watched as their last remaining officers did what was required of them, waited on by whatever thralls could be found. There were no choirs, for the thrall choristers were dead, no cyber-constructs to herald him, no music. The dust of near defeat still hung on the air. The silence of two hundred transhumans who had come so close to death filled the basilica with unbearable tension.

The rituals undertaken were similar to those Dante had undergone when he was first made a captain. He was presented without armour. Pledges to uphold the graces and virtues were painted with blood upon his skin. The carriers of Sanguinius' holy vitae were bled, and their fluids mingled in the sacred Red Grail, then Dante was bled of nine drops of blood from his neck in honour of the old Legion's number. As Gallion, now acting Sanguinary High Priest, went to each man in turn with the cup, his armoured boots crushed fallen jewels to dust.

As the assembled brethren watched on, the Chapter officers drank the blood, and one by one they called their agreement with the decision. The number of the council was much reduced, and their saying of the accord was short.

They spoke their assent sincerely and wholeheartedly, even Keshiel, though when he spoke the words there was a plea in his voice that Dante not fail them, or so the new Chapter Master thought.

Dante drained the grail, and Raldoron, the name of the first Chapter Master, was incised into his flesh.

'As Commander Raldoron, he who was the first, did not fail our father, nor shall you,' said Bephael.

'Nor shall I,' said Dante. 'This I do swear.'

Then Dante was bade kneel by the High Chaplain Bephael, and asked to bow his head. Dante stared at angels depicted by a mosaic of semi-precious stones. They were so perfect, they looked real, and appeared as if they were flying upwards from a bottomless sky, and would burst into the basilica. Tesserae smashed out of the mosaics lay scattered like broken teeth, but so fine was the art that the illusion was barely troubled by the gaps. An archangel of surpassing beauty led the host in the floor, looking upwards, arm outreached towards its destination. Dante stared into its calm eyes as Bephael spoke over his head. Blood dried upon his body, chilling his skin.

'This is a grave time for our Chapter,' Bephael said. 'There are fewer than two hundred of us in the fleet left alive, a little more than that in the galaxy entire. Our Chapter has been brought to its knees. It will take us centuries to recover our strength.'

Dante stared at the archangel's face. In its heroic features he saw a resemblance to his brothers, and he remembered Chaplain Malafael, his mentor, slain at the hands of a traitor Dreadnought, and dozens of others he had known, fought with, grown with, bled with: all dead. His head throbbed with the effects of the Thirst. The shared blood he had consumed made him crave more. He yearned for Sanguinius' might so that he could smite his enemies.

Give me strength to resist instead, he thought. Do not let me fall into darkness, not yet, not now.

'Do not allow your hearts to grow heavy, my brothers,' said Bephael. 'We survive. The legacy of the Blood Angels will continue. The enemies of the Imperium desire to see us destroyed, because we are a threat to them. We remain so, and shall it ever remain, unto the end of time. Rise now, Dante, commander of the Blood Angels, Chapter Master of Sanguinius' first-born sons.'

Dante got to his feet.

'Do you take this burden?'

'I do,' said Dante, 'with all my heart.'

'Then I proclaim you Commander Dante, Chapter Master of the Blood Angels!'

Dante had meant what he said, but even as his brothers called out his name, and burst into song, the great statue of Sanguinius on the sternward wall stared down, and Dante felt the primarch's burden settle heavily upon him.

Over a millennium later, Dante stared at the same image of his father. It had not changed in the intervening years, having been lovingly maintained by the brothers of the Chapter. The beauty of the work his kind produced uplifted Dante.

He sat in the Chapter Master's throne upon the central dais of the cathedral. He was alone, facing the great doors of the basilica, so he saw the port gate open and Mephiston come through.

'You have finished your meditations,' Dante said to him. In the perfect acoustics of the basilica, his voice travelled far.

'I have,' said Mephiston. He strode towards the dais and stopped in front of Dante. 'The hive mind did not hear the cry of the Ronenti cult. I felt it move a little in the warp, then the cry ceased, and it turned away. We were in time.'

'Only just,' said Dante.

'Only just is good enough, my lord. We won a victory. Let victory be remembered, and not the nearness of it.'

Dante inclined his head in agreement.

'Have you reached a decision on the other matter?' asked Mephiston.

'I am not going to demand you fall on your sword, my brother,' said Dante.

'You still deem me a threat.'

'I always will,' said Dante. 'You are a threat, Mephiston.'

'We have tried to hide it, but the warp is in us all,' said Mephiston. 'It runs in our blood. We are the sons of the Great Angel.'

'For those reasons,' said Dante, 'for now, I am inclined to see your second rebirth as a good omen. You are faithful, Mephiston. You are my brother. But we will never know the truth of what you are.'

'As the primarch said, the greatest enemies come from within. I could swear to you I shall always remain loyal.'

'If you were going to, then you would do so without my

asking,' said Dante. 'You do not because although you would be sincere, you cannot see what the future will bring. It is of no matter. You are a potent asset. You are a son of the Great Angel and a true servant of the Emperor.'

'For the present,' said Mephiston. 'I trust you or Rhacelus to kill me should that change.'

'We have nothing but the present, Mephiston. All we can do is make it count, so that we might have another present, and another, and by effort build them into a future.'

Mephiston bowed. His armour purred as it accommodated the movement.

'May I speak with you honestly, brother-commander?'

'Always.'

'I hear your thoughts. You are considering undergoing the crossing of the Rubicon. I advise you against it.'

'I am old. I am tired. My wounds from the invasion of Baal are not healing. I need renewal. We have fallen far. Look at me. I am ancient.'

'You were still strong, until recently.'

Light glanced from the death mask of Sanguinius. 'Until recently. No more. Something is not right within me.' He took a troubled breath. 'I may be dying. Corbulo will not be honest with me, but I see it in his manner.'

'One does not need to be a psyker to know Corbulo's thoughts,' said Mephiston.

'No.'

'We all die. Even you.'

'I cannot die now.' Dante held up a gauntleted hand and looked at it. 'My body fails me as the greatest task of all is thrust upon me.'

'You have taken blood.'

'More than I would wish. Since I broke my long fast, I

have needed to drink more, so I have.' He became quieter. 'But I have also wanted to. The taste. The energy. To see the memories of another man...' His hand clenched, stilling the tremor. 'It disgusts me, what I am reduced to.'

'Nevertheless, you must not undergo the procedure. It will kill you.'

'That is my choice,' said Dante. There was more of an edge to his voice than he would have liked. He unclenched his fist and let his hand fall again to rest upon the throne's arm. 'Fear not, brother,' he said calmly. 'I have not yet decided. Maybe I will cross the Rubicon Primaris. Maybe I will not. There are a few battles left in this body yet, before time runs out and my hand is forced.'

'Time is running out for all of us,' said Mephiston.

'That is why I must fight.' Dante quelled the tiredness in his voice. 'We return to Baal. Kheru has suffered the tread of xenos for too long. It is time to let the tyranids know their banquet is over. Let our fury rain down upon this last infested outpost. Let the evil thing that rules them see that it failed to beat us. Let it know our intention is to destroy it. Let it fear, and when we are done with the tyranids, let that fear spread to others. The Angel's Halo shall shine in the heavens, and by its light, let all beasts, traitors and xenos be illuminated with certain knowledge.'

He gripped the arms of his throne.

'Let them understand that Imperium Nihilus belongs to the Emperor.'

ABOUT THE AUTHOR

Guy Haley is the author of the Siege of Terra novel *The Lost and the Damned*, as well as the Horus Heresy novels *Titandeath*, *Wolfsbane* and *Pharos*, and the Primarchs novels *Konrad Curze: The Night Haunter*, *Corax: Lord of Shadows* and *Perturabo: The Hammer of Olympia*. He has also written many Warhammer 40,000 novels, including *Dawn of Fire: Avenging Son*, *Belisarius Cawl: The Great Work*, *Dark Imperium*, *Dark Imperium: Plague War*, *The Devastation of Baal*, *Dante*, *Baneblade* and *Shadowsword*. His enthusiasm for all things greenskin has also led him to pen the eponymous Warhammer novel *Skarsnik*, as well as the End Times novel *The Rise of the Horned Rat*. He has also written stories set in the Age of Sigmar, included in *War Storm*, *Ghal Maraz* and *Call of Archaon*. He lives in Yorkshire with his wife and son.

YOUR NEXT READ

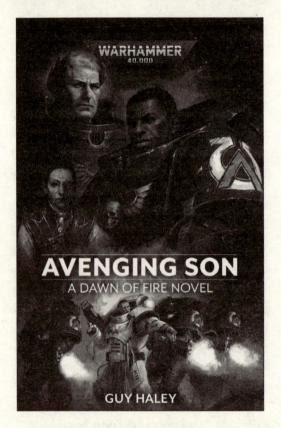

AVENGING SON
by Guy Haley

As the Indomitus Crusade spreads out across the galaxy, one battlefleet must face a dread Slaughter Host of Chaos. Their success or failure may define the very future of the crusade – and the Imperium.

For these stories and more, go to blacklibrary.com, games-workshop.com, Games Workshop and Warhammer stores, all good book stores or visit one of the thousands of independent retailers worldwide, which can be found at games-workshop.com/storefinder

An extract from
Avenging Son
by Guy Haley

'I was there at the Siege of Terra,' Vitrian Messinius would say in his later years.

'I was there...' he would add to himself, his words never meant for ears but his own. 'I was there the day the Imperium died.'

But that was yet to come.

'To the walls! To the walls! The enemy is coming!' Captain Messinius, as he was then, led his Space Marines across the Penitent's Square high up on the Lion's Gate. 'Another attack! Repel them! Send them back to the warp!'

Thousands of red-skinned monsters born of fear and sin scaled the outer ramparts, fury and murder incarnate. The mortals they faced quailed. It took the heart of a Space Marine to stand against them without fear, and the Angels of Death were in short supply.

'Another attack, move, move! To the walls!'

They came in the days after the Avenging Son returned,

emerging from nothing, eight legions strong, bringing the bulk of their numbers to bear against the chief entrance to the Imperial Palace. A decapitation strike like no other, and it came perilously close to success.

Messinius' Space Marines ran to the parapet edging the Penitent's Square. On many worlds, the square would have been a plaza fit to adorn the centre of any great city. Not on Terra. On the immensity of the Lion's Gate, it was nothing, one of hundreds of similarly huge spaces. The word 'gate' did not suit the scale of the cityscape. The Lion's Gate's bulk marched up into the sky, step by titanic step, until it rose far higher than the mountains it had supplanted. The gate had been built by the Emperor Himself, they said. Myths detailed the improbable supernatural feats required to raise it. They were lies, all of them, and belittled the true effort needed to build such an edifice. Though the Lion's Gate was made to His design and by His command, the soaring monument had been constructed by mortals, with mortal hands and mortal tools. Messinius wished that had been remembered. For men to build this was far more impressive than any godly act of creation. If men could remember that, he believed, then perhaps they would remember their own strength.

The uncanny may not have built the gate, but it threatened to bring it down. Messinius looked over the rampart lip, down to the lower levels thousands of feet below and the spread of the Anterior Barbican.

Upon the stepped fortifications of the Lion's Gate was armour of every colour and the blood of every loyal primarch. Dozens of regiments stood alongside them. Aircraft filled the sky. Guns boomed from every quarter. In the churning redness on the great roads, processional ways so huge they were akin to prairies cast in rockcrete, were flashes of gold where the Emperor's Custodian Guard battled. The might of the Imperium was gathered there, in the palace where He dwelt.

There seemed moments on that day when it might not be enough.

The outer ramparts were carpeted in red bodies that writhed and heaved, obscuring the great statues adorning the defences and covering over the guns, an invasive cancer consuming reality. The enemy were legion. There were too many foes to defeat by plan and ruse. Only guns, and will, would see the day won, but the defenders were so pitifully few.

Messinius called a wordless halt, clenched fist raised, seeking the best place to deploy his mixed company, veterans all of the Terran Crusade. Gunships and fighters sped overhead, unleashing deadly light and streams of bombs into the packed daemonic masses. There were innumerable cannons crammed onto the gate, and they all fired, rippling the structure with false earthquakes. Soon the many ships and orbital defences of Terra would add their guns, targeting the very world they were meant to guard, but the attack had come so suddenly; as yet they had had no time to react.

The noise was horrendous. Messinius' audio dampers were at maximum and still the roar of ordnance stung his ears. Those humans that survived today would be rendered deaf. But he would have welcomed more guns, and louder still, for all the defensive fury of the assailed palace could not drown out the hideous noise of the daemons – their sighing hisses, a billion serpents strong, and chittering, screaming wails. It was not only heard but sensed within the soul, the realms of spirit and of matter were so intertwined. Messinius' being would be forever stained by it.

Tactical information scrolled down his helmplate, near environs only. He had little strategic overview of the situation. The vox-channels were choked with a hellish screaming that made communication impossible. The noosphere was disrupted by etheric backwash spilling from the immaterial rifts the daemons poured through. Messinius was used to operating on his own. Small-scale, surgical actions were the way of the Adeptus Astartes, but in a battle of this scale, a lack of central coordination would lead inevitably to defeat. This was not like the first Siege, where his kind had fought in Legions.

He called up a company-wide vox-cast and spoke to his warriors. They were not his Chapter-kin, but they would listen. The primarch himself had commanded that they do so.

'Reinforce the mortals,' he said. 'Their morale is wavering. Position yourselves every fifty yards. Cover the whole of the south-facing front. Let them see you.' He directed his warriors by chopping at the air with his left hand. His right, bearing an inactive power fist, hung heavily at his side. 'Assault Squad Antiocles, back forty yards, single firing line. Prepare to engage enemy breakthroughs only on my mark. Devastators, split to demi-squads and take up high ground, sergeant and sub-squad prime's discretion as to positioning and target. Remember our objective, heavy infliction of casualties. We kill as many as we can, we retreat, then hold at the Penitent's Arch until further notice. Command squad, with me.'

Command squad was too grand a title for the mismatched crew Messinius had gathered around himself. His own officers were light years away, if they still lived.